BREEDER

BREEDER

The Ephemeral (Book 1)

ORPHIC
PUBLISHING

E. GALLEGOS

Published by: Orphic Publishing

ISBN: 979-8-9987239-1-9 (paperback)

Cover design by E. Gallegos

It's finally here—over a decade later.

At 17 years old, I outlined this entire series, start to finish. I completed Breeder *before my high school graduation, and I proceeded to write, revise, and edit the trilogy throughout college, my environmental career, a global pandemic, two inguinal hernias, and my first home purchase. Ten years later, this passion project has attracted readers around the world— and received far more attention than I ever anticipated.*

Despite feeling like this trilogy doesn't reflect my current writing potential, nor my ever-evolving preferences, I couldn't bear the thought of shelving these precious characters.

So, I dedicate this series to the thousands of readers who gave this story its wings—and the community that gazes upon my creative journey with much kinder eyes.

RHEA

THE RIM

NORTHERN PASS RTE

Primm

THE GORGE

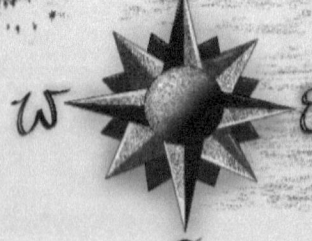

ARK

COLSTON

DILL

HAVENBROOKE

BRECKSHIRE

LAWRENCE

HOLLY

CAMP PTARMIGAN

AVERLY

BELGATE

THE RANGE

ELLS

THE SOUTHERN RIDGE

If woman is not given to man for help in bearing children, for what help could she be?

—St. Augustine, *De genesi ad litteram, 9.5-9*

PART 1: Skyfall

1

My fingers danced across leather spines as if they had little minds of their own, little eyes that widened and crinkled when they recognized old friends and weathered faces.

"It's after closing."

The short man stuck his head around the corner, irritable and impatient. His droopy ears, nose, and eyelids formed a face of melting candle wax. A face that, upon our first encounter, had earned him the everlasting nickname Mr. Wick.

"Really?" I flashed him my best apologetic smile—the same one I used to feign contrition when I overslept on a school day. "I must've lost track of time."

He was not amused. His lips flattened with dissatisfaction, squinching up his features like a rotten Jack-o'-lantern caving in on itself.

"Just another minute?"

He refused to dignify my plea with a response. Instead, he just slowly retreated from view, his face still contorted in that awful, droopy grimace.

Trading escapism for investigative history, I traipsed down the nonfiction aisle, passing faded titles, soiled cloth, and broken spines in my pursuit of crisper bindings. I sailed past the engineering textbooks, the autobiographies, and the childbirth resources, then perused a column of Ellsian military feats and innovations.

Deciding it was high-time I revisited the Patrons' Era, I snatched the fattest book off the shelf, and my arm dropped to my side like an anchor at sea.

Brain food, my mother had called these. They were brain *fiber*, really—practically indigestible. But my options were limited.

Most records were lost to the Crash or abandoned to the elements, confining our history selection to the High Court's squeaky-clean manuscripts: epic chronicles that glamorized the rebirth of human civilization; parables that immortalized the Patrons who united us; collections stitched with secondhand knowledge and ancestral oral lore; and biographies sweet enough to rot the brain.

The Court maintained that we'd failed to preserve reliable accounts of life before the Crash. They claimed our textbooks documented everything we knew of the Ancients, that our libraries harbored nothing more than molding, anecdotal fiction. But the chronicles of the Holocene didn't erase themselves. The scribes didn't snap their quills and flush their ink. The *victors* did.

And everyone else was, conveniently, moondust.

I joined Mr. Wick at his desk and set the book down between us. His eyes flicked over the cover and back at me, entirely unenthused. "All that deliberation over a book you've read a dozen times?"

I huffed at his criticism. "I'd spend less time *deliberating* if there were something new to read."

"Every new arrival takes you a week to consume, at most. Then you're right back where you started, venting about monotony." In the logbook that lay open before him, he added my name beneath the other hastily scribbled *Alex Kingsleys* on the page.

"You know, I heard Havenbrooke has three whole floors' worth of novels in their library," I shared, chasing eye contact while he purposely avoided my gaze. "It's a shame we can't make some sort of exchange. I could probably spend a whole month or two absorbed in fresh literature. At home, in my own space … not bothering anyone."

He handed me my due-date slip with an exasperated sigh. "I'll see what I can do."

"You're a gem among gangue, sir."

"*Goodnight*, Miss Kingsley," he pressed, and he pushed the history book so forcefully in my direction that it nearly toppled over the edge of his desk.

Saluting the candlestick of a man, I slipped through the library's creaky doors into the relentless autumn wind, wincing at the assault on my senses. I spat a few hairs out of my mouth and adjusted my wool cardigan around my shoulders, then glared at the missing sphere of gold in the sky.

The sun should have barely kissed the Range at this time of day. But, like every afternoon for the past ten years, I could only detect its faint radiance behind the ashy canvas above—the emanation of a wraith who'd killed the sky.

The upper atmosphere sure looked like a corpse, anyway. Gray, dreary, perhaps a bit rotten and foul. Some folks blamed the everlasting firestorm to our west. Others postulated that a volcano had erupted down south, plaguing humanity with airborne carcinogens.

Still, the smoke never cleared, and the ash didn't fall. The soot remained in the sky like a thunderstorm that never bled rain. Like a giant veil shielding us from colorful horizons, blocking the warmth of the sun and smothering the stars.

The stars …

I'd been so young when the lights vanished into the pit of nothingness that yawned above us now. It had felt like the end times back then, as if we'd said goodbye to the only constant across human history. The last witness of our timeline.

But part of me always wondered if the stars hadn't disappeared at all.

If instead, they'd examined life here on Earth and turned their backs on us in shame.

***

Lucky's Liquors welcomed me with dim auburn lighting and pipe smoke strong enough to pinken the eyes. I weaved through the after-work crowd and approached Leith's favorite corner booth, digging through my belt bag for change.

"Come on, Frankie. You know there's something wrong about all this,"

Leith murmured, swishing the contents of his pint around as he spoke. "No one even retires from the military anymore. No grunt ever lives that long!"

"Just 'cause the Court won't admit we're losin' to a dictator like Godric Sterling does *not* mean we're dealin' with the supernatural, you welt."

The subject didn't surprise me in the slightest. Only three topics seemed to waltz upon civilian tongues these days—gossip of marriage, anticipation for the annual Tournament, and whispers of war.

Over the past decade, we'd watched soldiers perish at an unprecedented rate, and the rising death toll had hatched rumors of a new enemy encroaching on our border. Civs suspected an ally of Rhea, our malicious neighboring kingdom. But according to authorities, no other societies still *existed* in the Northern Hemisphere.

So, what kind of threat, exactly, were we losing whole battalions to?

"Not dealin' with the supernatural? Then explain the sun! Where's the sun gone, Frankie?"

"It's still up in the sky, ya numbskull!"

A harsh laugh. "Tell that to the farmers who can't grow our barley."

I cleared my throat, and both men swiveled to address me.

"Leith," I greeted.

He sighed and held out his hand. At forty, the man spent his workdays tending to his music shop, stone-faced and miserable. The only time his soul awoke was here at Lucky's, where he could shed his formalwear and discuss conspiracy theories with his drunken peers.

I dropped the skits into his palm. "To keep quiet should the old man come asking."

"Yeah, yeah, I know the routine," he muttered, slipping the change into his trouser pockets. He leaned back in his chair. "Say, Kingsley. You're always thinking more than a girl ought to. How do you feel about the military keeping its activities on the Rim so hush-hush? You suppose they're hiding something?"

I jiggled the history book at my side—a transcript of inconsistencies. "They're always hiding something, Leith. It's how they keep us on our knees." I paid a furtive glance in either direction before bending closer to their ruddy faces. "The real question is what they plan to do with those secrets, and how far they'll go to ensure we never find out."

He pointed at me, then his skeptical companion. "What did I say?"

"Not that!" Frankie exclaimed.

With a quiet laugh, I left them to their speculation, trading the dark, hazy bar for the suffocating crowds of Belgate.

Around me, midday masses hovered in thick clusters, loitering about the stalls and *gritz*, walking so slowly. Women shopped with male escorts at their side, never to be trusted among a brood of hens. Small boys weaved around them, picking pockets or stuffing them with Tournament flyers.

The little girls were nowhere to be found.

Swerving through bodies, I felt as though the buildings were closing in on me from all sides, cracking the cobblestone beneath my boots, pushing the residents even closer to one another—as if this town weren't incommodious enough.

Established on the western outskirts of Ells, Belgate had become a hybrid city of entrepreneurs and hardy country folk. Like most conurbations, it penned its citizens within giant stone walls to secure its water treatment technology and fertile farmland. To our east, forested, rippled terrain isolated us from the Interior. And to our west, the Rim served as the mountainous borderline between Ells and Rhea.

It was a city of rules and snitches, smiles and curtsies. No one really said what they meant, and no one really meant what they said. Granted, those who did were sentenced to a multitude of behavioral write-ups and remedial counseling courses—a punishment I'd grown quite familiar with upon entering academia.

I'd almost escaped the marketplace when a woman shouted my name, halting me in place, much to a nearby vendor's delight. I was tempted to dismiss her beckoning entirely, not particularly eager to receive another lecture before nightfall, but something about her timbre gave me pause.

"Alex, love!" she called again, and this time, I recognized the cottony rasp of her voice.

Nova.

I pivoted, grinning at the shrunken, wrinkled woman sporting ugly jewelry and a few million shawls. Gray hair tickled her shoulders, and she'd pinned her face-framing layers back with the decorative beads and wires she'd collected on her voyages.

"Don't you eat?" the merchant grumbled as I made my way over to her wooden traveling stall. Her maternal gaze swept over my knotted, windblown hair, my skinny legs, and my scuffed and battered boots. "You look thinner than yesterday!"

"I *do* eat."

"Mm."

She handed me a heavy sack, distributing the weight evenly between the history book and her favorite gift. "More beans?"

"They warm your heart." She poked my arm. "And fill your bones."

I smiled at her mischievous brown eye, partner to an empty left socket. *It's good for business*, she'd said when I asked her why she didn't cover the orbit. She also claimed to have sold the organ in exchange for the Eye of Sight, and I was inclined to believe her.

I perched myself on the edge of her counter, setting my items aside and admiring the array of trinkets lining her shelves. "Any new fortunes for today?"

Nova could predict anything from weather patterns to the juiciest scandal in town, but most city dwellers treated her like a stray dog—or worse. To the elites, she was either a loon who believed in magical abilities or a quack who preyed upon those who did. To the rest of us, she was simply the widowed, childless merchant on the corner of Market Square.

She grinned, removing the old drawstring pouch from her belt and emptying the contents into her dark, age-speckled hand. Closing her eye, she mumbled a few incantations before dropping the collection of bones, nuts, shells, and pebbles onto the circle of painted wood.

I examined their orientation, wondering what the wishbone landing next to the crow's foot could mean, or if the die landing blank-side up had any significance. Then I watched the woman's interpretation unfold.

It was my favorite part, seeing her piece it all together.

Her eye latched onto the contents, and her breath hitched, bony fingers twitching away from the circle. For a heartbeat, her features flared with something akin to terror, then pain. But the moment passed as quickly as it came, and then she shook her head, dismissing whatever she'd seen.

"What was *that*?" I demanded. Considering her spotless track record, her reaction was nothing short of disconcerting. "What did you see?"

She swept the bones back into her pouch, seemingly unalarmed. "A day full of troublemaking and dire consequences, love."

I sensed there was more to it than that, but I wouldn't push her to tell.

When Nova chose not to disclose something, it was typically for good reason.

"So nothing out of the ordinary, then?"

She chuckled, shaking her head again, and I slid off the counter, deciding I'd rather not know the details of my inevitable grounding anyway.

"Ah—Alex? Won't you do me a favor before you go?"

I pursed my lips, eyeing her suspiciously. "What kind of favor?"

She seized a ceramic vase from her shelf and placed it between us, looking up at me with that *face*.

My bones frosted over. "Nova, you—"

"I want to know how much it's worth so I can price it appropriately, that's all. Just think of it as practice!"

I rolled my eyes. *Practice* was the last thing anyone needed, but I slipped off my glove anyway; it was only fair after she'd gifted me a pantry's worth of beans this year. Checking my surroundings to make sure no one was paying us any special attention, I pressed my hand against the smooth, convex surface of the vase.

Instantly, white fire assaulted my vision, burning the center of my palm, searing my flesh. It felt like I'd grasped the rungs of a grill, and I fought the impulse to jerk away.

"*An exotic antique,*" said a hollow voice, a faint whisper bouncing off the dark corners of my mind. A pale, manicured hand slid a pile of coins over a wooden table, and I lived a thousand static memories along a crumbling road. Then I was falling, crashing, drowning in a whirl of blues and blacks and greens...

I gasped, wrenching my hand back and balling my fist.

The memories vanished, leaving only a spell of dizziness in their wake, and by the time I unclenched my fingers, the crescent-shaped mark on my palm had faded to a begonia pink.

Nova stared at me expectantly, completely unperturbed.

"About six skits . . . give or take. That's how much it sold for." I wiped the beads of sweat from my temple, and the delighted woman clasped her hands together like I'd made her day. "Where did you even get that? The bottom of the river?"

"Many valuable things find the riverbanks, Alex," she said, addressing the disapproval in my tone. "Lost items want to be found. Almost as much as keepsakes yearn to be lost."

I snorted. "Right."

I'd always envied Nova for her career path. Although her income barely sustained her lifestyle, she was free to roam the country, permitted to visit the other gated cities in Ells. Of course, she acted as if there was nothing to see between mountain peaks, but I knew she harbored extensive knowledge about the world—and a thousand precious secrets.

I slid my glove back on, sighing at the comfort of concealment. They were typical fighting gloves, fingerless and black. Not unusual to see on a sentry or a postman. But covering my hands all day every day never ceased to weird everyone out.

"Chin up, Raven," she whispered, and I grinned at the old nickname. "Someday you'll realize that different is better, and better is progress." She shooed me along. "Now go on, before you miss your lesson!"

As I hustled away, I could feel her gaze lingering on my hands—and the two organic weapons at my sides.

2

At the top of the hill sat a large, circular stadium capable of seating the entire population of Belgate. Most days of the year, it served as a training ground for soldiers, but today, the Council would be working hard to prepare the grounds for tomorrow's festivities.

I hurried toward the flat-roofed building adjacent to the stadium and slipped through creaky double doors.

Inside, swords and shields and other training equipment bejeweled the mortared stone walls. The room had that old gymnasium smell—almost like the blood, sweat, and overtly male musk had seeped into the floor and festered in the building's deepest crevices.

Using the mounted shields and helmets as grips, I climbed up the wall to my left and pushed myself through the hatch in the wooden ceiling. Closing the access door behind me, I wriggled through the narrow attic space on my hands and knees, avoiding boxes and miscellaneous training gear. The air reeked familiarly of rat droppings and mildew, and I wondered if any new vermin had claimed my territory since last winter.

In the dark, I located the loose ceiling plank and moved it aside, peering through the lath-shaped hole as trainees pooled into the room below.

"My father bought it in Holly. The 'smith said it was one of a kind, first-class! Paid two whole decks for it," Mason revealed, thriving off the startled gasps of his companions. The boy's pale eyes were permanently fixed in the shape of disdain, and his golden hair ran in tangled rivulets toward the back of his head. He sort of looked like a deranged eagle that way. "Worth it, though. I can already tell the difference."

He swung his new rapier around like a doofus, the others admiring the object in awe or sinking with envy.

I tutted quietly. Typical Mason, parading around with his new toy, flashing his family's wallet in our faces. Like all weeds, he descended from the families who'd monopolized essential resources while the world was burning. They thought their inheritance bought them the right to become a public nuisance.

Easy to pick out. Even easier to offend.

He leered at the boy in the corner—the only trainee who'd yet to acknowledge his existence. "Jealous, Tooms?"

Will blinked back at him, entirely listless. He wore his usual black pants and a gray, threadbare shirt, and his boots were even more decrepit than mine. Which, of course, made his lack of interest in Mason's affluence all the more enjoyable.

Naturally, his silence failed to deter the blond. "See, my father recognized my skills. Thought I deserved the best equipment in Ells—top of the line for a proper soldier." He arched a golden eyebrow. "I guess your fire iron speaks for itself."

"I guess it does."

Mason bristled at Will's docility. He didn't want the outcast to indulge him; he wanted to pick a fight, as usual. "Is that all you have to say, welt?"

Will dragged his tired gaze to Mason once more, lips parting to deliver a witty insult, but then his eyes flicked to the boy's wrist, and he frowned. "You're holding it wrong."

"What?"

"Your sword. Hook your finger around the ring. It'll keep you from overextending. Won't mess up your hand if you ever manage to kill a Rhean."

Titters spilled throughout the room, and Mason flushed, dropping his provocation.

Will drew his eyes away in a lazy, unimpressed motion.

William Tooms, much like his speech pattern, was built of sharp edges and jagged corners. Messy black hair fell over his forehead, and he wore the rest of it back in a short, scraggly ponytail. His eyes were dark as well— darker than brown, but not quite black—and in the four years I'd known him, he'd only worn two distinct facial expressions: exhausted disinterest and what I could only describe as "back off, I bite."

The others included those I'd nicknamed over the years. Potato and Potahto, the twins. Chinger. Rex, Breath, and Boy, among others.

Despite our single-sex educational system, I'd grown up with these idiots. Across hundreds of training sessions and sporting events, I'd watched them develop their skills, break bones, make and lose friends. I'd seen Mason pick a thousand fights and lose twice as many. And in many ways, it felt as if I were part of their cohort, part of their team.

Even if I couldn't identify as such.

The room quieted as Frost strode through the door, his hands folded at the base of his rigid spine. His pointed face contained several distinct wrinkles, so it was difficult to decipher his actual age. He could have been sixty or forty, though he acted about eighty-five.

"Attention," he commanded, and the boys formed a long, crooked line across the room.

Every night, the retired army officer provided close-combat training to help prepare our youth for the Tournament—a series of contests that determined enlistment qualifiers. With humanity skirting the edge of extinction, the Court thought it unwise to send just anyone to war, so they'd designed a national tournament to rule out the individuals who didn't stand a chance on the battlefield. A game to pinpoint the strongest, the fiercest, and the most strategic of an entire generation. Like a military colander.

I'd always questioned their decision to send the most skilled and able-bodied men to their deaths, especially if they cared so much about preserving humanity. But above all ludicrous customs was the exclusion of women from the system.

As detailed in our shiny history books, there came a time when humans had consumed and depleted their limited resources, and a warming climate had brewed a starving, desperate people. A rebellion formed in the aftermath—and with it, an international war over water.

In the rampage that followed, entire cities were leveled, poisoned, and abandoned. Epidemics swept through towns to kill off survivors. Forests burned to ashes, and hurricanes swept away the remains.

We called this chain reaction the Crash, and it had left our species on the threshold of oblivion.

Due to the population bottleneck, fertile women became as scarce as drinking water, and like any limited resource, we'd appreciated in value. In response, the infant nation of Ells passed the Propagation Decree, which mandated that every woman bear at least one boy and one girl within a lifetime, or three children of any sex, in order to "repopulate" our species. Primarily, to build an army.

If a woman refused, she was hunted down and persuaded, and if she wasn't capable of childbirth, she was ostracized. Like Nova.

I hated the decree as much as its brother: a law that prohibited women from joining the very army we so desperately needed.

We were banned from the war. Stuck as an inferior class falsely portrayed as something fragile, a demographic too valuable to have value. Princesses locked in their towers for their own protection, then forced to breed.

And because women weren't allowed to fight or train or even breathe violence, I received my lessons here. Covertly.

Illegally, if we're being technical about it.

Frost cleared his throat the way old people do—like you weren't quite sure if they were choking or not. "Class, the Tournament is upon us. Tomorrow is the day you've been waiting for since your class of disruptive, ungainly schoolchildren stepped through my door." He looked them over critically, as if nothing had truly changed on that front. "Tomorrow, you'll be competing against every boy in your cohort—each of whom believes he has what it takes to defend this nation. Each of whom has dedicated years of his life to building muscle, honing skills, and nurturing battle instincts. Should you place within the top rankings, you'll join your comrades in boot camp early next year."

"And we'll send those Rhean rats back to the gutters," Mason concluded, a few trainees murmuring their agreement.

"Did I ask for your charming insight, Price?" Frost hissed, and Mason's expression soured. "You'll learn to hold your tongue if you hope to serve your country one day."

Mason appeared to do just that, his face twitching with restraint and self-discipline, and Fudge, the smallest student in class, offered him a sympathetic pat on the back.

Of all the boys in his cohort, Fudge was the sweetest—and by far, the least aggressive—which made his name a perfect fit. Granted, Fudge was technically his surname, but his classmates had decided early on they liked it better than Nicholas, and somewhere along the way, he'd given up correcting them.

Frost walked the stretch of their line formation with his head held high—an admirable feat considering the massive ego it contained. "For your last session, I wish to review the values you will uphold as Ellsian federates. The principles you must embody, should you prevail tomorrow."

As one, the group deflated. Frost always stressed the severity of war, the struggle, the *sacrifice*, finding any and every opportunity to remind us of the leg he'd lost in battle, as if the 90-skit prosthetic didn't get the point across. And at least once a week, he discussed Ellsian core principles, transforming the army's mission statement into saccharine poetry.

Basically, he liked to hear himself talk.

"Tell me, why are we fighting Rhea?"

Mason opened his mouth to respond, but he caught himself and lazily flicked his wrist in lieu of raising his hand. He didn't wait for Frost to call on him. "Godric Sterling plans to conquer the continent's arable land and water resources. We resisted, and now the king has pledged to annihilate and enslave any Ellsians who get in his way."

He seemed rather proud of his textbook answer, but the officer wasn't impressed. "You're merely scratching the surface, Price."

Fudge raised his hand, and the officer gestured for him to take the floor. "It's not just the threat of invasion that has us taking up arms. Or the loss of natural resources. It's the threat of Rhean ideology," he said, pausing to polish his explanation. "After the Crash, Rheans rejected democracy for autocracy. Now the king is a tyrant, and his people have no voice, no personal freedom. So not only are we defending our borders from violent dictators … but we're also attempting to contain an authoritarian regime."

"Indeed," Frost replied, granting Fudge a satisfactory nod. "As federates, we become the stewards of our nation. We become enforcers of the Three Pillars."

He turned to his students expectantly, and they exchanged harassed looks as they mumbled, "Liberty, Unity, and Personal Responsibility."

"Correct. Liberty, unity, and personal responsibility. Ideals born from the Crash. Ideals that planted deep, durable roots in our soil and provided us with the nutrients to prosper." He halted in front of Will and studied his pupils. "These are the values I want you to remember when you're sent to the Rim and deposits of fear and uncertainty begin to weigh on your brittle bones."

He drew curious gazes now. Open, impressionable gazes.

"The day you cross the Gorge, remember that you're not fighting for your own survival," he warned, "but humanity's."

***

While the boys donned their armor, I blindly searched for my pencil and notebook in the dusty space beside me. But when my hand found my abandoned school supplies, it also found something soft and hairy, and I released a startled squeak into my elbow as the creature shuffled away.

Gross.

I'd forgotten how much I loathed this spot.

Weather permitting, Frost usually held his sessions in the outdoor stadium, where I could observe his class from the bleachers. But with the Tournament tomorrow, I'd had no choice but to impose upon my disease-ridden hosts.

The sound of steel and footsteps reverberated beneath me, and I peered down at the class of sparring boys, grinning at the most predictable pairing of all.

"Is that the best you can do, Tooms?" Mason taunted.

The blond hastily swiped at Will, who sidestepped casually and lifted his hand in earnest. "You're being too loud with your movements, Mason."

"Don't lecture me."

I rolled my eyes.

Mason was always competing with Will, mocking him for his poor upbringing, his father's vocation, and their life in the slums. He'd realized early on the legitimate threat Will posed to his triumph in the Tournament, and he'd hated him ever since.

Will usually ignored him, which only fueled the weed's wrath. But I had to give Mason credit for pestering the least approachable boy in Belgate.

My eyes roamed the classroom, critiquing Breath's rigidity, assessing Chinger's feint, and admiring Fudge's personal mission to dent, puncture, and scratch every inch of armor he'd ever worn, much to his instructor's chagrin.

Blades had emerged as the military's primary choice of weaponry after the Crash eradicated aboveground armories and arsenals, oil reserves, gunmetal mining operations, and any manufacturing facilities capable of sustaining the warfront. Unfortunately, shooting drills offered faster skill acquisition than swordplay, so most soldiers started training around nine years old to ingrain the body movements in their prefrontal cortex—or in my case, began observing said training from a reasonable distance, absorbing anything remotely useful. And, as annoying as Frost could be, he did have a firm grasp on technique; I'd made a habit of jotting down any helpful advice he spouted.

Propping myself on my elbow, I tried to move crosswise to the next loose ceiling board, but the Fates decided my day was going too well, and the foundation splintered below me like ice on a riverbed.

My hand fell through the rotting wood faster than I could react, and I sank into the ceiling laths up to my shoulder. I cursed myself, and Mason echoed my sentiments loudly from below.

The room fell silent as everyone stared at my arm dangling overhead, and I quickly removed my appendage, sitting still in the dark for a few seconds, wondering if maybe I could pretend nothing had happened.

"Kingsley!"

Gritz.

I crawled back to the attic hatch and pulled it aside, sighing at my cursed existence. With my back to the group, I descended the wall and hopped to the floor, landing on my feet with my beans and book in tow.

Head up, Al. Breaking asinine rules doesn't warrant shame or embarrassment.

Schooling my features, I spun to greet my perturbed audience.

"Alex?" Fudge marveled, his blue eyes bugging out of his head. The other boys gaped at me as I brushed the cobwebs from my hair, the dust from my clothes. "You were hiding up there this whole time?"

I didn't respond. I just stood there at the edge of the room, glaring back at the limelight.

"Aren't there rats up there?" someone muttered.

For a split second, I thought Frost was having a stroke, but then I realized it was just *fury* that caused his face to spasm like that. "For Patron's sake, Kingsley," he growled, marching forward. "Must you pester a veteran to no end? How many times have I caught you in here now?"

"This would be eight, sir."

His wide, livid eyes told me it had been a rhetorical question. "Do laws mean nothing to you?" He didn't wait for me to answer. With a disgusted sound, he seized my elbow and dragged me toward the exit. "This is unacceptable behavior."

"I was just watching."

"*Just watching* is not permitted." He halted, facing the others. "The rest of you run through the drill set one more time. You can leave once you best Tooms."

There were groans all around, and Will looked like he'd rather sacrifice himself to the attic rats. In other words, no one was going anywhere. Not until Will was too tired to put up a good fight or stopped trying altogether.

My feet slipped at Frost's urgent tugging. "Captain—"

"Not a word out of you. I'm taking you home."

I wrenched my arm away. "I don't need an escort!" I rolled back on my heels, biting my cheek as I met his frigid gaze. "Please just ... let me stay."

"Stay?" Mason sneered, astounded by my gall. He propped his rapier on his shoulder and jutted his chin forward—a raptor establishing his place in the food chain. "This is *military* training, breeder. You don't belong here."

My glower faltered. The words cut deeper than they should have.

I glanced around the room at the passive faces, the smirks, the glares. No one willing to argue on my behalf. No one even willing to try.

"You're right," I decided, pivoting for the door. "I don't."

3

We reached the old two-story house at the end of Bellevue Road, all wooden planks and peeling white paint. Warm light illuminated the front porch and the rusted swing my mother used to frequent. Two pairs of work boots sat in the corner, crusted with mud.

Frost banged on the door with my grandpa's favorite lionhead knocker, and one agonizing minute later, my father appeared at the threshold. The collared shirt and black dress pants indicated that he was hosting a gathering of some kind, and I could barely contain my surprise. We rarely had company, and if we did, we never dressed to impress. Honestly, the man wore his ranch clothes so often I sometimes forgot he owned professional attire.

His distracted gaze flitted between Frost and me, and his smile dwindled. "Captain?"

Frost bowed his head in greeting. "Evening, Max. I caught this one at the training grounds again. She was hiding up in the attic this time, disrupting my class."

I opened my mouth to protest, but I thought better of it.

The last thing I needed was another demerit—I already had two this year, and a third strike required a city internship and additional volunteer hours. The Council always pushed community service on our youth, eager to wring out any societal contributions before shipping us off to war or drafting us for motherhood.

Conveniently, it also prevented teens like me from securing apprenticeships and building occupational skills.

My father's eyes fell on me, narrowing. "Is this true, Alex?"

"Of course it's true!" Frost cut in. "She's absurd. Thinking she can fight alongside men. It's not a place for a young lady. Not an honorable—"

"Forgive me, sir, but I was speaking to my daughter."

My lips twitched at my father's assertive tone, but the feeling died when I remembered I, too, was the recipient of his anger. I studied the porch paneling beneath me, fiddling with the straps of Nova's bean sack. "...Pretty much."

"I see. Thank you for escorting Alexandria home, Captain. I'll see to it she does not interfere with your teachings again."

I sauntered inside. *Proper name—not good.*

He closed the door with the grace of a man who could masterfully repress his fury. I hardly recognized him with his clean-shaven chin and groomed hairline, but the disappointment on his face was an expression I knew all too well. "I thought you were at your music lesson," he said calmly. "Did you cancel?"

I stared up at him, wincing at the depth of the grave I'd dug.

A beat of silence passed, and then he sighed, the realization pulling his features into an unsurprised grimace. "You've never once gone to your lessons, have you?"

I didn't dig myself any deeper; he already knew the answer. What he didn't know was that I'd bribed Leith into going along with my ruse for several weeks now. But that was a detail I was happy to keep to myself.

He placed his hand on my back and physically redirected me. "We'll discuss this later. We have company, and you're in dire need of a bath."

I faced the guests sitting at our dining room table. Plastic smiles. Plastic eyes. They sat as stiff as hay bales, their chins too high, their clothes too ironed, and they carried an air of superiority much like their son.

"The Prices?" I murmured. What in the world were Mason's parents doing here? Were they *lost*?

My father didn't meet my eyes. "We were just discussing finances."

I frowned at the two weeds across the table. *Finances*? What could the city treasurer want with our ranch? As far as I knew, we had no investments at this time, no reason to apply for a loan. But a dinner as formal as this one hinted at a serious business matter.

Or . . . perhaps a personal one, I realized, and it finally clicked.

"You've got to be kidding me." I whirled on him. "Not again, Dad."

"Alex," he warned, but it was too late. Any remorse had dissipated in a matter of seconds, replaced by hot-blooded betrayal.

"A marriage interview? Really?" I demanded. "And to Mason of all people. Does he know about this?"

He looked at me like I'd burned the world down.

No, in other words. *He doesn't know.*

"I didn't think so. He'd have a heart attack at the ripe old age of *seventeen*." Not that I'd mourn the evil piss-brain.

"Ah, well, I think we should be going now. It's getting late," the treasurer said, setting his half-empty drink back on the table and shooting us a strained, apologetic smile. He and his wife collected their belongings and swiftly made their way to the door. "Thanks for dinner, Max. We'll be in touch."

My father glared at me before waving them off. "Always a pleasure. Tell your son I wish him the best of luck tomorrow."

The door shut with the force of a hasty getaway, and I threw my hands in the air. "I can't believe you! I told you I'm not ready for marriage. I'm not even a legal adult." It was a fact he liked to remind me of often, particularly when I protested his arbitrary rules and conditions. And yet here he was, trying to pair me off with a lifelong partner. Apparently, I was mature enough for *that*.

He rubbed the bridge of his nose, his elite façade replaced with the presentation of an honest working man. "Please don't raise your voice. If anyone has a right to yell, it's me."

I gaped at him. It was like he wasn't even listening, like he didn't want to listen and had built some kind of impenetrable wall in his ear canals. "I am not getting married right now. Not to Mason. I *hate* Mason."

"First of all, you were very disrespectful to the Prices. They were here for your benefit, and you made a terrible impression. Secondly, these interviews are preliminary. They revolve around financial planning—aligned interests, co-investment opportunities. No one's getting married today." He shook his head. "Honestly, Al, this topic doesn't really concern you right now."

Indignation sparked to life in my chest. "It *concerns* me a lot."

He dropped his hand back to his side. "Just … go to your room and we'll talk tomorrow, when you're ready to be reasonable."

"You're the one—"

"Alex!" he challenged irritably, a fire burning through hazel irises. "You promised me you'd try. You said you'd try to be a polite young woman, sociable. You said you'd attend your classes, attend your music lessons. Remember?" He pushed on before I could get a word in. "We both know that on her own, a woman has limited prospects here in Belgate. Without a husband who can support you, support your family, this ranch—"

"It's *my* life! I don't care about prospects." *Prospects* was just another word for chains. "I want to fight. Like Tom."

The name hit him like a poisoned dart—sapping his strength, just as I'd known it would. Mentioning my brother was a way of wounding him, so I only reserved it for serious arguments. It wasn't like I wanted to hurt him. I just wanted him to understand.

"We've talked about this, Al. Your obsession with the military needs to stop. It's federal law. It's life. Life's not fair." He grabbed a dirty plate off the table, and I worried it might shatter in his grip. He had strong hands, worn hands, yet they trembled. "So start thinking before you act on your impulses. *Please*. And really think about what you're saying. War is a terrible, vicious thing. If what happened to Tom doesn't prove that, I don't know what could."

I walked away, itching to slam a door and scream like a child. But I wouldn't give him the satisfaction.

I gracefully shut the garden door behind me and marched for the barn, hushing my stubborn, howling soul.

4

I threw all my weight into the blow.

Again and again, I struck the barn's wooden pillar, my knife leaving small yellow nicks on the surface. Down and diagonal, across the breast, around the belly—tip never leaving my imaginary aggressor.

My life felt like, in many ways, an Ancient's ball game. I was a possession constantly passed between players, blocked from my goals. And if I happened to fly out of bounds, someone launched me back into the game, refusing to heed my protests.

All I wanted was to stretch my legs and run far, far away from here and this suffocating fog, but I was stuck in a game with rules I couldn't change. Ensnared by weeds and obstacles.

Adults always said life wasn't fair.

But if life isn't fair, shouldn't we change *it?* Why wasn't it that easy?

Exhausted and sweaty, I sank to the floor. Richard ambled up to me and dropped his chin on my thigh, his graying ears folded back against his head. He dug his wet nose into my leg, and with a quiet snicker, I shoved the tickling device away.

My entire friend group was composed of an elderly psychic and an ill-behaved mutt, which I supposed summed up my social skills pretty well. But they were good friends—*true* friends—and if Nova and Richard were all I had in this world, then that was perfectly fine with me.

Besides. The more people I welcomed into my life, the more I'd lose. And I couldn't afford to lose anyone else.

My gaze dropped to the weathered knife in my hand, perhaps my oldest friend of all. It bore a steel, stout blade; a bronze guard and pommel; and a wooden belly eaten away by years of practice and exposure to the elements.

Chipped by carelessness and stained with the blood of inexperience.

I slipped off my glove to stroke the spine, and a young Tom appeared behind my eyelids, haloed in sepia light. He was focused, working intently to craft and forge the blade, his tongue sticking out of the corner of his mouth, his dark curls dangling over his forehead. In the next memory, he passed the weapon over to me, and my young, hazel eyes widened as I observed his workmanship. We sparred playfully at first, and then as competitively as a seven-year age gap would allow.

His voice reached out of the soundless frames to pat me on the shoulder.

"Don't give your lunge away. Surprise me. Be quick."

"That's it. Good job."

"Easy! I'd like to walk away in one piece here."

I lingered on the last time we sat on the barn roof together, watching the smoky sky. "Tomorrow's the big day."

He was only seventeen then, and the resemblance between us now was uncanny. He too had inherited our mother's dark hair, tanned olive skin, and high cheekbones. Even her deep-set honey eyes, always lit with mirth. But he'd also acquired our father's jawline, nose, and crooked smile, and the combined traits gave him a kind of natural charisma that was easy to envy— a genetic gravity that granted him a fruitful social circle.

"What am I supposed to do when you're gone?" My voice was brittle. I was holding the knife in my hands, so the perspective was a worm's viewpoint, warped and awkward.

"You're gonna work hard at school and question everything they tell you. You'll help Dad with the ranch, even when he pisses you off. And most importantly, you're gonna keep practicing with that knife of yours, playing pranks on the Council, and beating up all the boys in town." I giggled, and he knocked his head against mine. "You be good for me, Al. I'll write when I can."

"Promise," I said. "Promise you'll write me. On the stars."

His eyes softened.

Before bed every night, Tom always spoke of life before the darkness, back when the sun shone brightly on our faces and brilliant orbs of fire floated in the night sky. He spoke of travelers who used the stars as guiding lights. He told me fables of men breaching the smoke to the world above, men who kissed the surface of the moon. I drank every word, captivated by a world I couldn't remember.

Swearing on the existence of such things was sacred to a child.

Still, he gazed at me and promised.

The scene eroded into the many nights I'd cried with crumpled letters in my fist, longing for a miracle. Dreaming of a world where men in uniform never found our porch. But there was no denying our reality: my brother had left when I was ten, and while his badge of honor had made it home, Tom hadn't.

I'd lost him. Just like I'd lost Mom.

I dropped the knife, shaking out my hand and the sting of recollection.

Apart from my mother, Tom was the only person who truly understood me, and like everything I allowed myself to approach, to love, they'd both disappeared into the unknown and unreachable. They'd withered to nothing more than dying memories and fading imprints.

Even my father had died back then, in a sense.

The door to the barn creaked open, and the rancher cautiously slid inside—the way someone might approach a rabid dog.

"Hey, kiddo."

I turned away from him, anger overwhelming my capacity to resist a juvenile response. He'd yet to grasp that a teenage girl needed space, and it made it difficult to like him sometimes. I loved him, ineffably, but liking someone was hard enough for me as it was, even without the other person ordering me around.

He sat on the hay bale beside me, waiting for my iciness to thaw. When it didn't, he released a long, heavy sigh. "Listen, Al. I only want what's best for you. I want you to be well-off—comfortable and *happy*—so you don't have to worry about supporting your family for the rest of your life."

Like I do, was left unsaid.

"Ever since your mother died ... it's been hard. We used to talk about your future in the event that you lost one of us, and I promised her I'd provide you with everything you needed to succeed in this world." He swallowed his pain. "To live a better life than we did."

I stared at the wall, refusing him eye contact.

My mother never would have backed him on this. As the only child of a widowed law professor, she'd sharpened her mind and trained her tongue before she'd ever stepped foot in a classroom. Her intelligence had intimidated her elders, and her sociability had attracted every young man in Belgate, resulting in the rejection of a dozen marriage contracts before my father finally won her over.

Top of the nation's Institute, she could have done anything, been anyone, but she married a rancher instead, determined to escape the claws of the city. She'd even fought the procreation laws, insistent on raising an only child, choosing to never raise a girl in a world as cruel as this one.

But seven years after my brother's birth, the Council came knocking, and they threatened to take away the ranch if she didn't comply with the statute.

She'd had no choice but to give them what they wanted.

My father cleared his throat, treading water. "The way women are treated…you know I disagree with it, Al. You know I want more for you. *Patrons*, if it were up to me, you'd be the chairman of the High Court! But this is the way it is—the way it's always been. Sometimes we have to accept things we don't like for our own good."

Lose the blossoms, strengthen the stem, he used to say when my ideals led to discourse. Until I asked him why he wanted me to look like all the other ugly stems.

"But I *can't* accept it," I groaned, closing my eyes. "That's not who I am. Washing dishes and folding some weed's laundry isn't me. It never will be."

"You know very well that's not what I expect of you. You are your mother's daughter, after all." He shifted in place, trying to get me to turn around. "You can take over the ranch when I'm gone. Or graduate from the Institute and become a midwife. You can start a family."

He just didn't get it. I didn't want to be a housewife. A caretaker. A mother. That future—it was like a script the world had given me, telling me when to speak and how to behave. I could look at any married woman in this world and know exactly how my story ended.

"I realize it's not what you want right now. Settling down, starting a career. But you don't have a lot of options, sweetheart. Not with your illness." I felt his gaze on my bare hand. "It's dangerous to seize the world's attention."

"I do have options. You just don't like them."

He let my comment simmer for a beat, deciding to forfeit a battle he'd never win. "Do you still want to go to the Tournament tomorrow? I was thinking we could get there early, snag a good seat. Then we could go to the festival after. It'll be a day off."

I spun to face him. His eyes were pleading and hopeful, and it hurt to see him like that. To know I would never make him happy. Never make him proud.

"Dad," I began, gentler than before. "I don't want to watch the contestants. I want to *be* one. And that's never going to change."

The edge of his mouth lifted in a sad, defeated sort of way. Then he squeezed my knee and walked out of the barn, leaving me there with Richard and the echo of my own confession.

"I didn't ask to feel this way, you know," I told my hairy companion, and those curious round eyes blinked up at me. "To want what I want."

I'd always dreamed of following in Tom's footsteps and finishing the work he'd died for. Growing closer to him by experiencing his journey firsthand—and ending the war that tore so many families apart.

I also knew the military would grant me freedom from Belgate and my societal obligations as a woman. It would open the doors to this dungeon and the mysteries beyond, launching me into a world so chaotic, gender would mean nothing.

But there was more to this path than familial love and forbidden fruit.

Inside me was an inexplicable passion to fight, to prompt change. To do something *more* in spite of the written laws of our Patrons. And soon after my mother had died, those feelings burned through me like root fires.

Now, ten years later, I was clawing at the back of a lock, choking on smoke, and despite the absurdity and futility of my efforts, I just couldn't help myself. I had one shot to live this sliver of a life, and I wasn't about to waste it in shackles.

5

I glared at the old watch hanging on my bedpost, three hours off. Someone had welded the edges shut, so it was perpetually out of sync—destined to operate abnormally, determined to stray from all possible utility.

My father's bedside note informed me that he'd left early to reserve good seats. He must have felt guilty for yesterday; he rarely let me sleep in past daybreak. Not with mouths to feed and weeds to pull.

I flung the covers off and scavenged my drawers for any unstained clothes. After a comfort debate, I decided on my only pair of holeless pants, a long-sleeved shirt, and Tom's hand-me-down army boots.

Much to my professors' horror, I refused to wear "female apparel," though my preference stemmed from a practical mindset most of the time. Ranching, fighting, climbing fences—a dress hindered all of that. But even on formal occasions, I still chose pants and boots over anything with ruffles. Not because delicate colors and fabrics repulsed me, but because these staples of femininity promised rapacious interest, unwanted compliments, and conditional chivalry.

I'd learned early on that men were threatened by women who dressed like them. They found our defiance unsettling, our nonconformity treasonous.

And because I wasn't keen on the idea of involuntary commitment, I had to rebel in the small ways I knew how.

Kicking against the current was the only way to keep from sliding under.

My dad complained. He said skirts were cheaper than pants, and I wore out my pants faster than socks. I told him I'd be happy to roam around naked if our budget demanded so, and he let it go.

I ran downstairs, snatched the monkey's fist knot from the back porch, and chucked the rope into the open field. Richard shot after it at the speed of lightning, launching himself off the deck and sending the chickens scrambling in all directions.

I leaned against the door frame, my gaze sweeping over our ranch at the onset of harvest season. Beets. Cabbage. Carrots. Greens. Only a few thriving fruit trees left. Guinevere and Ophelia, our dairy cows. It wasn't much, but we helped provide food to the poorer districts of Belgate, and with the growing population, we were never short of consumers.

Just sunlight.

Even after switching to shade-tolerant plants and equipping the gardens with grow lights, we still struggled to produce enough to support ourselves. Which was why my father was so adamant about marrying me off. With an agricultural crisis on our hands, we'd both need a new source of income and a proper safety net.

I grabbed the pail of feed from the porch and moved for the coop.

Now that it was just the two of us running things, my duties had tripled, and when I wasn't pulling weeds or filling the trough, I was at school, wishing I was pulling weeds or filling the trough. It was easy to envy the boys' after-school sporting events and part-time apprenticeships.

But I had to admit, tending to this ranch was far from a bad life. I enjoyed living a few miles east of the city, our property surrounded by aspens, our crops fringed by a snaking river.

When I closed my eyes at the far end of the field, sometimes it even felt like I'd escaped this place.

***

Colorful streamers, ribbons, and garlands festooned our dull town—a splattering of bright hues on a bleary, repetitive backdrop. Vendors and craftsmen prepared their stalls along the main streets, and in the distance, children laughed and screamed in startled delight.

It all felt like a slap in the face.

How was I supposed to feel remotely festive today? My father had almost sentenced me to a fate worse than prison, and now every boy my age had a fair shot at the career path their fathers denied me. I wasn't about to pretend everything was okay just so they'd feel better.

Nothing about growing up in this twisted place was okay, but it had become increasingly intolerable over the past few years.

Now that I'd aged out of girlhood, every conversation circled back to marriage—or more precisely, *security contracts*, which paired individuals from specific trades or family lines in order to maintain a healthy, thriving society. The Council didn't force people to tie the knot, exactly, but if you envisioned a partner in your future, you had to make reservations early. Otherwise, your most attractive prospects—across financial, social, and aesthetic categories—would be snatched away by other women. Or *war*.

And frankly, competition made people behave like wild animals.

Each time I crossed paths with desperate parents or eligible bachelors, I was skewered by appraising gazes, then questioned relentlessly about my engagement status. Classroom gossip orbited prospects, courting, and marriage interviews—every tale exaggerated or underplayed to gauge a rival's reaction. And when it came to weddings, it was hard to tell if I was attending as a guest or an auction prize.

Their efforts were as tireless as they were degrading. But they'd soon realize they'd have to chop my hands off before I signed a contract with Mason *Cretin* Price.

As I made my way up the hill, the autumn wind delivered the scent of honey apple crisps, potato skins, and pretzel cups straight to my cerebral cortex. It was nostalgic—the smells, the sounds, the enthusiasm. My father used to apportion pocket money for such treats, warning Tom and me not to spend everything on licorice, only to speak it into existence every time.

I could almost taste the sugar on my tongue.

Outside the arena, crowds swarmed the food stands, trading coins in exchange for treats and Tournament paraphernalia before entering the stadium with their families. Meanwhile, the contestants lined up at the training gym for check-in, chatting with their peers or wrestling their anxiety independently.

They each wore the same leather armor around their torsos, forearms, shoulders, and thighs—all recycled military materials donated to the city—and upon registration, they received metal helmets, each painted a different color and assigned a unique number. The headgear covered their faces, preventing biased judging. It only worked to a certain degree; body type and skill usually gave people away, but it leveled out the playing field, if but a little.

More importantly, the matching wardrobe engaged the public in a city-wide contest, encouraging participation from gamblers like Leith or fussy firstborns with no siblings to root for. The ambiguity served as a guessing game for the audience, and their curiosity—and aching wallets—were eventually satiated at the Revelation, when the victors removed their helmets and revealed their identities to the crowd.

It was a dumb tradition, but a tradition nonetheless.

The cohort measured 150 or so, and I recognized the male students I'd evaluated over the years—plus a few standouts who'd attended other training groups. And while I'd found Frost's public sessions the most easily accessible, and particularly convenient after my father signed me up for piano lessons, I'd eavesdropped on various districts and age groups throughout my adolescence, determined to build a holistic foundation.

My eyes roamed over the boys now, their excited whispers and laughter, their words of encouragement, and it sent a sharp twinge across my breastbone. This could have been *my* year to join the ranks.

Had I been a boy, I could have walked through those doors with ambition in my gait and freedom at my fingertips. As a boy, I could've counted the years, the months, the days until I had the chance to demonstrate everything I'd been working toward.

But I couldn't so much as whisper that intention.

Because I had been born into this world as an opposite. A weak link.

A breeder.

An ugly sensation festered at the base of my stomach, an itch begging to be scratched. It was the feeling that preceded a stupid decision—something capricious and dangerous and outright ridiculous. A feeling I'd experienced many, *many* times before.

And one I failed to suppress.

Cutting through the line of competitors, I marched straight for the opposite side of the gym and my backup entry point: the maintenance room. A combination lock barred the public from accessing the storage space, but the device had lost to my cursed, naked palm during a downpour two years ago. I'd cracked the code in less than fifteen seconds, and I'd put that memory to use any time I was running late to an indoor session.

Scanning for potential spectators, I pocketed the lock and slipped into the room, leaving the door ajar so I could navigate in the dark. I skirted the cluttered shelves and landscaping equipment and quietly opened the interior door, peeking out into the hallway.

At the end of the poorly lit corridor, a group of boys mingled about in the gym, waiting for the other competitors to complete their check-in. Helmets on, weapons polished.

My gaze landed on the boy at the rear of the room, standing apart from the rest of the group. He fumbled with the straps of his armor, wiping his sweaty hands on his trousers, glancing up and down again repeatedly, as if he were afraid someone might barge in at any moment and announce a historical cancellation.

Even with his helmet shielding his face, he looked unwell.

More contestants entered the waiting room, and he backed away to let them pass, stumbling his way down the hallway, just feet away from the maintenance room. He started pacing back and forth, shaking his head. Berating himself and his indecision.

You can't, my conscience insisted. *You can't rob him of this.*

If someone were to take this opportunity from me—steal it right from my fleeting grasp—I could never forgive him.

But I'd also never have an opportunity like this to lose. Because I was a girl, and girls weren't physically capable of fighting men. Our gender would be a distraction in combat, an endless source of concern and disruption. We couldn't *survive* the psychology of war.

Our forefathers told us so. And surely, we had no reason to doubt such sound logic. It wasn't like they'd steered us straight into a territorial war and agricultural doom or anything.

I smothered my reservations, and just as the boy mustered the courage to return to his peers, I raced forward and slapped my hand over his startled mouth—dragging him into the shadows and away from his fate.

6

"Ladies and gentlemen! We come together for a day of celebration and re-
membrance. A day to honor the good men who defend our nation. Soldiers
who embody our most sacred of virtues." The man beamed at the crowd
with his dazzling smile, a hypnotist working his magic. "Soon after today,
our champions will join these brave souls beyond the Rim and devote their
lives to preserving this beautiful nation."

Jacob Gilmore was the head of the local Council and the most influ-
ential politician in Belgate. He always hosted these events, year after year,
and his enthusiasm for the Tournament never waned. With his prominent
chin, striking features, and booming voice, he was the closest thing Belgate
had to a celebrity, and he seemed to embrace the attention.

"Now," he said, channeling that spokesperson charm and exuberance,
"on with the Tournament!"

The crowd cheered and whistled and stomped their feet as the band
burst into our national song. In the stands, sundresses transformed the audience into a colorful, rippling mosaic, while men had traded their work
clothes for something that would complement their partners' palette. Children waved homemade signs and little district flags, offering support to
their siblings, cousins, and role models. And at the bottom of the steps, vibrant banners embellished the court walls, forming a quilted necklace of red
and gold.

I grinned.

Here I was, clad in the armor of some random kid I'd locked in a closet, standing where Tom had once stood. Staring out at the crowd, at the world.

Like an absolute idiot.

But I wouldn't waste this impulsive decision. I'd try my best, give my all, and when I was eliminated, I'd conveniently disappear before the Revelation.

I could finally compare my strength to an entire cohort of boys. I could prove to myself I was capable of fighting, that all women *were*. And maybe one day, I could reveal my accomplishment to my father—the one person whose support mattered most.

I was the turquoise helmet, I'd say. Profoundly, of course.

Thankfully, and perhaps regrettably, I passed for a boy without much of a makeover. My long, tangled hair fit inside the helmet with extra room to spare, and my flat chest and narrow hips finally made up for years of inappropriate comments about a healthy, childbearing body. Add that to a pair of fighting gloves and a layer of recycled armor, and I blended in perfectly.

If I played my part, no real trouble would come of this.

Specs—noxious weeds who gambled on contestants—placed their bets from the sidelines, toying with more money than some of us would make in a month. They watched me bounce on my toes, chuckling amongst themselves as they sized me up, down, and sideways. I realized I possessed less muscle density than most, but in their eyes, I was nothing but a weakling. A runt. A shrimp.

Sensing my scowl, they grinned wolfishly and slammed a few more skits onto the teller's stand. Betting against me.

Welts.

Standing upon a raised platform at the edge of the court, Gilmore motioned for the contestants to move into place, a composer conducting his choir. We lined up shoulder to shoulder along the concrete floor, filling the space from one corner to the other, as instructed. From above, we must have looked like a linear rainbow, or maybe just a long row of push pins.

Gilmore raised the silver mic to his lips. "Contestants, your first trial is a testament of speed and stamina, a tradition we've adopted since the Tournament's inception."

Excitement buzzed in my fingertips. I wasn't great at a lot of things, but being fast, nimble—that was something I'd mastered. It was a learned trait, running from repercussions.

"When the bell sounds, each of you will run to the first red marker, collect it, and return to the starting line. Then you will race to the second marker, retrieve that, and so on. This test proves a soldier's endurance, drive, and agility. And we *Ell* love a good race, don't we?"

My male competitors groaned as laughter filled the ring and echoed off the venue walls.

My eyes ran the length of the stadium. 100 yards and five different markers, each progressively distant. *This is gonna burn.*

"I'm pleased to announce that over a hundred-and-twenty contestants have registered today," Gilmore continued, his voice ringing through the bell-shaped loudspeakers along the court's perimeter. "But alas, not every man is destined for war." He gestured to the panel of male judges behind us, composed of war vets and Council members tasked with tracking contestant performance and arbitrating disputes. "As you know, the true purpose of this event is to evaluate this cohort's skill and athleticism in hopes of supplementing our forces with the most successful candidates. Because of this, the Tournament follows a single-elimination format. Individuals who fall within the lowest rankings of each trial will be eliminated. Those who prevail will proceed to the next round."

My stomach took flight, and I ground my jittery heels into the pavement. *There's no going back, Al. This is happening.*

"Let us begin."

The contestant in the white helmet, 99, cackled from the adjacent lane, stretching his arms above his head and rolling his neck. "Watch and learn, rats."

Mason.

I could've detected his presence a mile away—no helmet could hide that pungent attitude and superiority complex. Granted, he'd also picked the newest and cleanest armor in the bin, and the attire beneath it just oozed privilege.

Will, I presumed, stood to my right in his red helmet, all shadows and taped knuckles. He appeared perfectly poised, and I wondered if he was immune to anxiousness or just completely unintimidated by his competition.

"On your marks," Gilmore declared, and I bent to the ground, my fingertips kissing cool pavement. The world blurred around me as my focus narrowed on the stretch of red tape 20 yards away.

This is it.

Gilmore raised his arm—a beacon that drew the attention of every man, woman, and child in the arena. A stopper in the lungs of the enraptured.

I breathed out, balancing on the pads of my fingers, cocking the hammer.

The second the bell chimed, I flew like a bullet.

***

I moved like a flash flood, a deluge, as if I'd conserved energy for millennia and finally had a chance to discharge it all in one race. One outburst.

I slid to a stop at the first red marker and nearly ate concrete, stripping the red tape off the ground in one fluid motion. I darted back to the starting line and slapped the tape down, pushing off again before I could bask in the glory of being the first to do so.

A smile tore at my cheeks as I pulled ahead of the others, sensing their disbelief and irritation at being left in the dust by the scrawny guy in the blue helmet. My confidence burned like fuel, and I transitioned to a fore-foot strike, becoming faster, smoother, lighter.

I heard Mason curse as I retrieved the third marker. He vanished from sight by the time I reached the fourth, and my racing heartbeat drowned out his trailing footsteps. My own feet pattered over concrete, barely audible, hands pumping, lungs flexing.

Someone was keeping pace with me, but I didn't dare take my eyes off the goal. I reached for it, I drove for it, and after several grueling minutes of stinging hands and burning hamstrings, I got there.

With my lungs on fire and the taste of iron in my throat, I skidded across the painted line, taking in the roar of the crowd and my own thundering pulse. Will finished a moment later, but the others didn't arrive for another seven seconds, wheezing and weak-kneed. Several of them lagged even further behind, jogging back to us with red tape crinkled in their fists.

I'd beaten them all. I'd outrun their biologically superior bodies and boyish adrenaline.

I'd *won*.

"The winner of the first round—the speedy number six! Followed by twelve ..." Gilmore's voice fell away as I drank it all in: the cheers, the band, the bursts of confetti. The push pins here on the floor of the stadium, draftees of entertainment. The Specs who'd prejudged me staring at the giant manual scoreboard in bitter silence.

I angled my head at them, raising my palms to the sky and smiling behind the wire mesh visor of my Corinthian helmet.

That's right.

Watch and learn, rats.

7

"In battle, a soldier's strength is critical," Gilmore said, speaking slowly to draw the crowd's attention. "At any time, he may be expected to carry heavy loads, artillery, or wounded comrades. His capacity to do so reveals the character of a man who's mindful of the stakes he'll face on the battlefield—and diligent enough to prepare for any given scenario. And that, gentlemen, is why our second trial will help shine a light on the strongest and most dedicated contestants in your cohort."

My posture deflated as I recalled the ridiculous, humiliating strongman trials from past Tournaments. Beam tilting, rope climbing, weighted monkey bars, deadlifting, and other resistance exercises had resulted in countless muscle strains, shoulder impingements, and hernias over the years.

Honestly, I'd been hoping this trial would pop up later in the competition, after we'd been given the chance to illustrate our combat skills. Because yes, fitness was imperative for active-duty personnel. But was it really wise to judge a soldier's merit by the diameter of his bicep—and prior to boot camp, no less?

These days, only the wealthy could afford protein-rich diets and personal trainers. Yet the weeds rarely, if ever, volunteered for war; they'd already inherited respect, fortune, and property. They had nothing to prove and no one to save.

By giving prominence to brawn and stamina, the nation was damning the poor, then sending the strongest of us to our graves. All for the honor of serving our country—or the desperation to feed and house a court-ordered family.

The Court spun it as a means of elevating survival rates, but it sure seemed like the perfect way to prevent an insurrection to me.

"For this event, each contestant will move four shots," Gilmore gestured to the furrow of metal spheres along the rear wall, "to the opposite end of the stadium. The individuals who transfer all four weights in time will proceed to the next round."

I scowled behind the visor of my helmet. Seriously? *Cannon balls?*

We didn't even use cannons anymore.

"You have five minutes," Gilmore added with a borderline-evil smile. "Begin!"

The band began playing at an anxiety-inducing tempo, and I stood there for a moment, staring a little dejectedly at the oversized marbles.

Demoralized, I watched Mason crouch and heft the first weight onto his shoulder, fumbling with his grip. He could barely walk, but he made it a few steps at a time. Will fared a little better.

Approaching the row of cannon balls, I used my knees to lift one of the shots about a foot off the ground. My muscles screamed at me, and my arms trembled, but I made some progress, moving forward like an ungainly chimpanzee. Unfortunately, gravity clouted me over the head a few moments later, and I was forced to drop the weight at the halfway point, fingertips aching from the strain.

Okay. Speed was one thing—I was light on my feet, thin, underweight, agile. But there was no way I could compare to these guys and their upper body strength. Even if I *had* spent my whole life on a ranch.

The others had almost finished their first transfer. One larger boy carried his second shot, and I heard him snicker as he passed me.

I couldn't take the embarrassment, so I tried again. This time, I brought the shot all the way up to my shoulder like Mason, balancing the weight between neck and clavicle. But then I began teetering too far to my left and ended up dropping it on the ground in lieu of crushing my head.

The ball cracked the concrete and rolled away.

It *rolled away*!

The crowd bellowed with laughter, and I stared after the projectile in dismay, burning crimson as my dignity abandoned me. It had to be at least 70 pounds of solid, dense metal. Carrying the thing the rest of the way was impossible—forget the other three. I'd never make it in time. Not like this.

My competitors hobbled past me, red-faced and panting. One of the smallest boys had given up entirely. He toed the row of shots but made no effort to pick anything up.

I glanced at Gilmore and silently cursed him for designing such a ridiculous series of tests. He stood there like a god on his stage, overlooking the contestants, towering over his pawns and listing off the minute marks.

My eyes narrowed as the announcer's instructions resurfaced.

Transfer, he'd said. *Move the shots.*

Those were the exact words he'd used. Not carry, lift, or tote. *Move.*

Cautious optimism straightened my spine, and with a deep breath, I banished my loudest, most anxious thoughts from my head so I could flesh out my idea.

Gilmore had compared the weight to a human body, so I couldn't just roll the ball to the other end of the court—you wouldn't roll a wounded soldier across a battlefield. But perhaps ...

I scanned my surroundings, searching for resources, scrounging for clever ways to exploit the technicality. My gaze eventually settled on the colorful banners hanging from the walls of the inner ring, and I grinned. *Perfect.*

I could hear the crowd's puzzled shouting as I bolted for the stands and

yanked a golden strip of fabric off the wall. Outraged protests and enthralled cheers followed me back to the court, where I swaddled the wayward cannon like the world's heaviest newborn. Then, with the corners
bunched in my fist, I took off, dragging the weight behind me.

The sack glided along the slick surface without much resistance, allowing me to sail past my sweaty peers in glee. A few boys paused to stare at me,
including my gloomy neighbor with the red helmet, and I couldn't resist a
prideful strut. They would most likely disqualify me for this, but I soaked
up the feeling while it lasted, snorting at Gilmore's incredulous laughter and
the judges' baffled reactions.

Might as well sparkle if I was destined to crash and burn. I had to lose
at some point, anyway; at least I'd had my fun.

But as I sprinted back to the gutter of cannon balls, a banner tossed
over my shoulder and looped around my waist like a philosopher's toga, it
became clear that my speed made up for what I lacked in quantity. I repeated my projectile-in-a-blanket process for the second shot, and the gap
between Mr. Snickers and me narrowed.

Excitement filled the dispirited cavities in my chest. Maybe it wasn't
over yet. Maybe I could still go out with a bang—a bang loud enough to
damage some eardrums.

My ambition revived, I capitalized on Gilmore's blunder and rushed
to transport the remaining shots in my vicinity. By the time I'd hauled the
fourth cannon ball across the court, I'd finished around 50th. They cut the
contestants off at 80, the others having failed to meet the quota in the
minutes allotted.

Predictably, the boys were not pleased with my trickery, and neither
were the Specs in the stands, if their incoherent shouting and finger-point-
ing were anything to go by. I folded the banner up and set it aside, shooting
the judges an apologetic smile, but it didn't seem to mollify them any.

After a few minutes of intense discourse and betting mayhem, Gilmore returned to his stage and acknowledged that I hadn't broken the rules, strictly speaking. The contestants' parents didn't appreciate the verdict, though, and I could hear their angry reproofs and accusations a whole court length away.

"However," Gilmore stressed, "going forward, I will articulate instructions more clearly, and any attempts to cut corners again will *not* be tolerated."

I made a point of nodding along to show I understood the warning. He'd given me a second chance today, a chance to showcase skills beyond speed and muscle tissue. And I wouldn't take that for granted.

As he shifted gears and launched into the explanation of the third trial, I could have sworn he winked in my direction.

8

It seemed I'd made an impression.

As I advanced, I felt the crowd's eyes on me—a sea of bated breaths and wrinkled noses. But I was pretty sure their rapt attention had less to do with skill level and everything to do with my bizarre, semi-illegal performance.

I was the small one who'd surpassed expectations. The speedy underdog in the turquoise helmet. The twig with thorns.

And so, the Tournament proceeded, weeding out the boys who didn't meet certain physical and mental qualifications through a series of creative and wildly entertaining trials.

For one event, we were told to traverse the playing field while snickering sentinels shot training arrows at us—their soft, bulbous arrow tips soaked in red disqualifying paint. Darting around in unpredictable patterns had served me well, though, and I'd crossed the court unsoiled. In another trial, we completed a wooden obstacle course that involved a small climbing wall, a balancing bridge, and a cargo net. I'd beaten Mason by a handprint in that race, but he insisted I'd had a head start—the milksop.

Eventually, we reached the most anticipated and beloved trial in the Tournament: the Deadlock.

A trial of close combat, it served as a testament to a candidate's swordsmanship and dexterity. Each contestant fought a commissioned officer—

one of three practiced soldiers selected by the judges panel—and if the trainee managed to stay on his feet for two minutes, he passed. If he was knocked to the floor or pushed out of the fighting ring, he was eliminated. And every year, without fail, the Deadlock trials had the crowd foaming at the *mouth*.

Lifting the bottom half of my visor, I chugged an entire canteen of water while the top-ranking contestants kicked things off in the ring.

A merit-based lineup helped even out the fight some. That way, when the consummate soldiers grew weary, they only had the worst of us left to school. But that was fine with me—I'd take any handicap I could get.

In the far-right circle of the stadium, a broad-shouldered boy fought an indestructible force of a man, their swords clanging loudly with each forceful collision.

As a greenie, matching with an experienced soldier was daunting enough on its own; I couldn't imagine facing someone so burly and fearsome in my first and only Deadlock trial.

Still, the boy held his own.

In the middle ring, Mason sparred with an older, smaller, and nimbler opponent than the first. As the veteran lunged for him, Mason reeled back—his foot landing a mere inch away from the border of the circle. But he didn't appear unnerved by the man's skill set. If anything, the challenge seemed to excite him. Dipping his chin, he planted his feet and took the offensive.

Both fights offered entertainment, but the audience hardly paid them any attention. Instead, all gazes were pinned to the third circle and the boy with the red helmet.

This Deadlock opponent was the youngest of the three—exactly what the mind conjures at the thought of a chiseled, active-duty soldier. Every thrust was smooth and vicious, each parry effortless and instinctual. He was so confident in his abilities, he even rejected a helmet.

Despite all that, Will pushed him further and further to the edge of the ring, relentless. He spun and sliced and dipped and whirled, and before any of us could process his phenomenal streak, he'd knocked the soldier to his tailbone.

A bit of water dribbled out of my mouth.

In all my life, I'd never seen a contestant beat a trained and war-scarred soldier. Not until now.

Gilmore shook his handbell, signaling the end of the sequence, and the other contestants sheathed their swords, completely unaware of Will's incredible feat. For once, Gilmore was rendered speechless, and he left the crowd to their screaming as he revised his Deadlock narration.

Well, that confirms it, I decided, allowing myself a small, proud smile. William Tooms was the red helmet, and anyone who'd ever attended training with him surely knew that. Any good Spec would be doubling his wager right about now.

He offered a hand to the soldier he'd bested, and the man laughed, clasping his forearm. When Will pulled him to his feet, his opponent clapped him on the back and congratulated him, and the sportsmanship prompted another round of applause.

Will deserved the praise, even if he humbly skirted the spotlight, and I'd like to think he wore a radiant, toothy smile beneath that visor—a content, prideful expression none of us had ever witnessed.

As he joined the other competitors, my gaze trailed back to the middle ring. Mason stood in the center of his own circle, still as death, and though I couldn't see his face, I knew his triumphant grin had long since faded.

***

I stood across from Mason's opponent, completely regretting my life choices.

Sure, I'd taken meticulous notes on fighting techniques. I'd practiced daily since childhood, attacking wooden beams, sacks of grain, and fictional enemies. But I hadn't sparred with another living soul since Tom had left.

Seven years ago.

I knew I had potential. Nothing in me doubted my capacity to learn, improve, and excel with a sword, and the chance to engage with a trained professional was something I'd always dreamed of. It just never occurred to me that I'd need to unveil my total lack of experience in order to obtain it.

Luckily, I didn't have much time to panic. Before my brain could finish compiling all the ways I was guaranteed to fail, the handbell rang, and a steel blade came flying for my head.

I bounced away, keeping my sword low to protect my knees and shins. I'd seen enough Deadlocks to know soldiers never sought to maim or injure the contestants—they only aimed to knock the boys off balance or drive them out of the ring. Success hinged on defense.

My opponent stalked the rim of the circle, much like a vulture closing in on carrion, and while his sallet-style helmet exposed his aging face, I didn't recognize his wrinkled features, angry eyes, or hairy lip. But I wasn't a big fan.

"Come on then," he taunted after I made no attempt to initiate our bout. "Quit acting like a skirt. Make a move already."

It was sometimes frightening how easily I could be provoked.

Growling, I flew forward, swinging wildly for the soldier's sternum. The clash of our weapons sent vibrations up my arms, and I pushed off our grazing blades only to spring at him again, anger refueling my exhausted body.

The old war vet wouldn't get away with that comment, and I downright *refused* to lose to Mason's opponent. So I fought the hardest I'd ever fought, channeling everything I'd ever learned from Frost and Will and Tom. Chopping the air. Slicing at armor.

A windmill in a tempest.

I really had no idea what I was doing. Jabbing, dodging, parrying—it was like I'd unlocked something inside, some inherent, feral fighting style. But the thrashing, as ungraceful as it was, seemed to keep me afloat, and that was all that mattered.

Do you see me, Dad? I thought between strikes. *Don't you see what I'm capable of?*

I dodged the vet's next advance, and I even managed to scratch his metal tasset—something the crowd thoroughly enjoyed. However, the spike of laughter caused a shift in the fight. The bad kind.

Suddenly, the soldier was no longer holding back, not with his pride on the line. I felt it in the ferocity of his swing, in the swiftness of his step; he was done playing games.

I shuffled back, raising my arms to defend myself as he pummeled away at me, sword striking again and again. Harsher movements and fiercer sounds. Panicking, I forgot to take the breadth of the ring into account, and right before my heel kissed the chalk, some small, inner voice whispered a forceful *stop*!

I wobbled, teetering backward, and just as the soldier prepared to deliver the finishing blow, I reached through the junction of our swords and grasped his breastplate.

And that was when the bell sounded, capturing a picture worth painting—a young contestant bent backward over the ring, clinging to the armor of her opponent.

Both feet safely inside the circle.

9

Should I have been eliminated for the move?

Probably.

The judges certainly frowned upon my actions, glaring at me and my raucous fans. Even the other contestants voiced their disapproval, with Mason boldly making his case for my disqualification.

But Deadlock didn't prohibit hand-to-hand combat. In fact, if a contestant was disarmed, he was encouraged to fight with his fists—whatever it took to survive those two minutes. So, laying a hand on a seasoned warrior was in no way foul play. Taking your opponent down *with* you, however, was another matter altogether.

I watched Gilmore communicate with the judges from his absurdly tall stage, shaking his head, responding in lengthy sentences, shooing their comments away. When he brought the mic back to his lips, he expelled a long, exasperated sigh that hollowed my stomach.

"Number six ..." he began, and the stadium quieted, eager to hear the verdict. "Number six remained within the ring for the entire duration of the match. And although he acted with dishonor in his final moments, I believe his opponent exhibited an unwarranted and unparalleled degree of aggression in this match."

The veteran scoffed, and I shifted from foot to foot, holding my breath.

"You've proven your skill, young man," Gilmore concluded. His voice shifted pitch, almost like he was trying to repress a smile. "You've passed yet another round."

I blinked, uncomprehending.

I'd ... gotten away with it?

It would've taken me longer to ingest if the crowd's cheers and vocal objections hadn't brought the decision to life.

I'd made it.

I'd *made* it through Deadlock.

Chest tight, I walked toward the finalists on the other side of the stadium. Toward my peers, my equals. Mason scoffed as I passed, murmuring a derisive, "Cheat," under his breath, but the word bounced off my ego like a spitball.

Nothing could ruin this high. Nothing could pin me down.

My gaze raked over the stadium, the banners, the people, searching for a middle-aged, dark-haired man. What did he think of all this? Was he blindly cheering for his daughter right now? Was he angry at my alter ego for breaking the rules? Or did the rancher in him find the lawlessness amusing?

I couldn't wait to see the stupefied look on his face when I revealed how far I'd climbed—after the shock and anger subsided, of course. He'd be livid with me at first. Probably try and feed me to the chickens. But he'd come around eventually.

And maybe once he realized how committed I was to escaping our lifestyle, he'd finally support my efforts. Once he saw what I could do, maybe he'd talk to his peers about the stupidity of the Gender Clause and the cons of prohibiting female service. Maybe he'd speak with Gilmore and utilize the man's widespread influence to our advantage. Maybe then we could see a chain reaction in society, even if it hinged on the male species.

That, or chicken feed.

When Gilmore began narrating the next round of Deadlock matches, my eyes fell upon Will, who sat against the rear wall with his arms folded over his knees.

He stared back in my direction, his head tilted curiously to the side. And despite the metal visors shielding our faces, I found his gaze a little too penetrative.

***

Before long, we'd reached the final trial.

Around 50 contestants remained, and to my utter bafflement, I stood among them—weary, drained, and aching. But the fact that I was still here, still progressing, numbed my senses to every scratch, contusion, and pulled muscle.

As far as I could tell, Will, Chinger, Potato, and Mason were the only four from our training group who'd made it this far. Fudge and the others had lost somewhere along the way, and for many of them, that loss had cost them their futures, their dreams.

Yet here I was, basking in stolen eminence.

My heart sank.

I'd taken this too far; I should have deliberately failed along the way, given another contestant a real opportunity to serve our country. But the excitement had swept my conscience away, and I'd forgotten to intentionally lose. And perhaps my ego hadn't wanted to feign inadequacy in the first place.

Now, my options for elimination were far and few between, and exiting this competition on my own terms had just become a whole lot trickier.

Gritz. What if I couldn't escape the Revelation?

What then?

No. I pushed that dreadful thought to the back of my mind—I simply had to fail this time. It couldn't be too obvious, or the Specs might think I'd thrown the bet on purpose. I'd have to fight and lose as authentically as possible if I hoped to avoid a witch hunt. There was no alternative.

On the sidelines, the two Specs from earlier battled the astonishment on their faces. One begrudgingly handed the other a wad of cash, and I resisted the urge to flip them off.

"And now," Gilmore spoke, his voice dropping an octave. "Now we've reached the last trial of the Tournament. A final challenge to see which contestants will join our federates in the fight against tyranny. Let's give a round of applause for the incredible young men who've made it this far!"

Congratulatory shouting fell upon us in successive waves.

"You've all proven outstanding aptitude, and for those of you who do not qualify for enlistment, do not despair. Like many of your elders here today, including your talented, notably handsome host, I'm positive you will come to serve our community in other valuable ways." He looked down at his microphone for a moment, then back at the line of competitors, eyeing each of us, one by one. "Gentlemen, your goal for this round is simple: bypass the guards and ascend this very platform. The first 30 of you to reach this stage will be our champions. That is your challenge."

The contestants shifted, glancing at one another in masked bewilderment. *Guards?*

Before any of us could question Gilmore's demands, the gates at the eastern end of the stadium opened with a metallic shudder. Then three sentinels on city horses emerged from a dark tunnel, hauling a series of wooden crates across the court.

It took me a moment to register what exactly they contained. Because surely—*surely*—they did not harbor lions.

And yet ... there they were.

Cougars in cages.

I didn't know how or why they'd trapped a mountain lion, let alone three, but these creatures were nothing like the predators I'd seen in our textbooks. First of all, they were huge—the size of a farm wagon—and dark veins bulged beneath their fur, weaving over their sharp, bony spines. They reared up against the walls of their cages, heads stooped and shoulders raised, ready to pounce upon the first man to twitch.

"They expect us to fight those things?" someone choked.

"They're just cats."

Chinger snorted. "Enormous, hungry, *devil* cats."

"Why are we fighting lions? How could that possibly correspond to fighting people?" another snapped.

We stood in a line, watching as Tournament officials locked the wheels on the low-lying carts and walked the horses off the court. Simultaneously, the armed sentinels unlatched the cages and dashed away as the enclosures fell open on all sides, the metal slapping harshly against pavement.

I wet my lips as the grown men abandoned the court.

Great. Now the only thing standing between the lions and their canned dinner were the chains binding them to the pad eyes of their cages.

The beasts tugged on their collars and stalked the generous perimeter their chains allowed. Off to the side of the court, the judges leaned back in their chairs.

"We've established boundaries in red tape. Step outside the line and you forfeit," Gilmore instructed, and my gaze flew to the markings that ran perpendicular to the platform. In other words, no skirting around the rectangular playing field. We were fresh out of loopholes this time. "Good luck!"

I failed to stifle my incredulous huff.

Each year, the architects behind the Tournament devised some ultimate test. Some final, nail-biting entertainment that surpassed the previous year in scale, danger, and absurdity. But I wasn't sure how they could ever outclass this one.

While most of us were still processing the task, or in Potato's case, backing away from the spectacle altogether, one boy remained undaunted. He darted into the spectacle at full speed, confidence dripping from his armor like spoiled milk.

"*Mason*," Will and I seethed.

The weed waved his weapon about him threateningly, spitting insults. I'd heard him complaining earlier about the sword he'd been supplied with, that he'd wanted to use his new one. I almost wished they'd permitted it— then the crowd could marvel at something besides his idiocy.

Mason swung the sword around and nipped the first lion to come into his path. The animal pawed at him, and the teen stumbled backward out of the way, taking a second to reevaluate. A few other contestants advanced as well, trying to appear big and threatening, but failing to intimidate the beasts.

Playing predator wasn't working; they didn't *have* any predators.

"We need a plan," I said quietly, voice muffled by my helmet. No one heard me, so I repeated myself in a deeper, manlier tone.

It drew the attention of several contestants.

"We?"

I nodded, knowing I'd need to attempt something radical to convince the crowd of my noble intentions. Sitting this one out would only raise suspicion, but if I appeared to try my best and lost anyway, there was a chance I could leave the stadium pitied and unbothered. "We need to work together," I decided, and that turned a few more heads. For my disappearing act to succeed, a large group needed to advance as one unit and ambush the felines together. Unfortunately, that required a certain degree of cooperation.

"This is a competition. There is no *we*."

One boy shrugged. "Well, this is supposed to illustrate our war-readiness, right? And there's no such thing as a one-man army."

I eyed Gilmore's raised platform—an obstacle in and of itself. We'd have to climb it, and that meant we couldn't have feral lions chomping at our ankles. "We need a distraction. Some way to keep those lions preoccupied."

Will finally seemed to take some interest in the conversation. His dark visor scanned the length of the stadium, his taped knuckles drumming against the hilt of his sword. "If we split into three groups, two parties can approach the stage by hugging the sidelines while the third draws the lions' attention to the middle of the court. The two exterior groups can help each other scale the platform, then pull the last of us up when we get there."

When no one responded, too skeptical of the half-baked plan, too suspicious of an alliance at this stage in the game, I added, "If we move before the others, we should all make the cut, regardless of who touches that platform first. It's the best option here."

Chinger turned to look at the lions again. "So ... who's the kitty kibble?"

The boys held their breaths, hiding behind their masks. Begging for a volunteer to spare them an early death.

I'd expected as much.

"I'll do it," I said. "I'm fast. I can make it."

Will turned to me, and I wondered which of his expressions he was wearing now. "It'll take more than one of us."

10

The lions were already pissed about being there. Prodding at them with a sharp, pointy object didn't lighten their moods any.

They padded toward Will and me, ears laid back, silver eyes pinned to our figures, and I couldn't help thinking they looked more monster than animal.

When one charged at Will and nearly took his leg out, he sliced the back of its neck, causing the feline to yowl and scramble away from the blade.

Keeping his eye on the lion, Will positioned himself with his back to the sidelines, drawing the cat's malicious gaze. Then he flicked his wrist, indicating for one of the groups to start inching its way along the red tape.

Meanwhile, I held the other lions' attention, jabbing at them and dancing in circles to keep them sufficiently furious—anything to divert their attention from Gilmore's platform. Eventually, though, one lion's patience ran dry. It bounded for me, eager to mop the court with my carcass, but the chain tautened, detaining the creature, and my heart plopped back into my chest with a shudder.

Crazy.

This is crazy, Al.

The crowd roared above us, their chants too loud and jumbled to decipher. Were they condemning us for our stupidity? Cheering us on? It was hard to tell.

The boys excluded from our guild watched us from the starting line, visors doing nothing to conceal their awe, their envy. Mason folded his arms across his chest, pouting in true Mason fashion. I knew he'd felt entitled to his triumph here in the Tournament, convinced of his role in the military. Now, that opportunity was fading before his very eyes, shriveling like an earthworm under the muted sunlight.

Beyond our hissing, feral obstacles, our allies helped one another ascend the concrete stage. One. Two. Five at the top. Throwing their hands in the air, waving at the crowd, reaching down to assist the next finalist.

The cats appeared oblivious to the ruse, but I had a hunch they'd already settled on a two-person feast.

"We should hurry," said Will, just as Mason moved forward to partake in our scheme.

"Hurry *where*?" I murmured. We had no distractions, no disposable teammates. Only three outraged felines and too much ground to cover. "They're closing in on us."

This plan sucked big time, and I couldn't just dip out unnoticed. Not without putting Will in jeopardy.

He shuffled behind me, his shoulder blades bumping mine. "Head for the stage, but keep spinning, slowly, and try to parallel their movements. If we turn together, our backs are never open. Once Price and the others approach the lions and draw their attention, we'll have our window."

It was a ludicrous idea, but it helped that he sounded so sure of himself.

He raised his sword, the blade stained with blood so dark it resembled molasses, and I mirrored his stance, begging my nerves to settle. Then we moved for the platform, rotating like some kind of razor-edged Lazy Susan.

The lions watched us progress, waiting for us to stop spinning, waiting for us to break apart from our alien structure so they could pounce. But I didn't dare.

Channeling my inner ballerina, I focused on my footing—slow, elegant, deliberate—while keeping my gaze fixed on the cats. My heart hammered against my ribcage like it wanted out of this body. Like the organ knew I was a dead woman walking, and it intended to abandon ship.

We were about thirty yards from the platform when another lion grew sick of our game and ambushed me, determined to end this charade. I gasped as it moved too fast, too suddenly, and as the lion flexed its paw to rip out my neck, my partner-in-folly raised his foot and kicked it in the face.

In the *face*!

The cat recoiled, and Will stumbled back from the force of the collision. Realizing he'd left his back open, I repositioned myself to face the other predators, deeply unsettled by their premeditated stalking.

These things were smarter than I'd thought.

I thrust my blade in their vicinity, attempting to ward them off without making contact. Still, I managed to clip one on the shoulder, earning myself an enraged hiss or two. And then I did the stupidest thing of all.

"Run!" I yelled, and Will's helmet whipped in my direction, obscuring what I assumed to be a confounded scowl. I jerked my head at the stage and the group of boys crowded along its edge. "Go. You can help me up!"

It was a lie.

"*Now*," I stressed as the lions regrouped.

Reluctantly, my partner sprinted away. As he should have. He was the contestant in this game, not me. I wasn't even supposed to be here. Now was my chance to pull out.

Before Will's lion could follow him, I intercepted it, now one against three. A barricade with shaky legs. A cornered rabbit.

But instead of shredding me apart, the cats approached me unhurriedly, stalking me like doomed prey. Their padded paws fell silent against the pavement, their whiskers twitching with hunger.

Their delayed attack concerned me. And the fact that they chose to ignore the *legion* of boys behind them disturbed me even more.

Cautious, I stepped sideways, away from the goal, away from the win. I just had to move laterally until I crossed the boundary line. Then I was done. Eliminated.

Safe.

But around me, the lions had formed an isosceles triangle—two on either side of me and one at the vertex, dead center. They'd blocked the easy way out, almost like they knew what I'd been thinking. Almost like they understood the rules of the game, and they'd developed their own elaborate countermove.

I fought off a shiver. *Since when did solitary animals hunt in packs?*

I raised my heel, preparing for launch, and the middle lion perked up at my movement. Our gazes snagged like fishing line.

Up so close, I realized there was something terribly wrong with the beasts.

They didn't have eyes.

I mean, they *had* eyes, obviously, but they were blank. No pupil, no iris. Just gray ink webbed in black veins. Just muddied sclera ringed in oil.

A second eyelid, perhaps? Or maybe some kind of disease?

Our breathing fell in time, and my exhale was soft, charged. The cat sensed my fear, and perhaps even worse, my plan.

We both moved at the same instant.

Pandemonium broke loose as I spun on my heels and raced for the platform. The lion followed—its heavy footfalls and breathing too close for comfort—and I pushed as fast as I could up onto the wall, desperate to find grips that didn't exist.

There was only one ledge that cut the stage in half, separating two blocks of slick, solid concrete. Clinging to that single ledge, I heard the chain snag and catch my pursuer, and I breathed a sigh of relief.

I peeked over my shoulder, and the silver-eyed beast sprang again. Only this time, the restraints didn't hold, and the chain snapped a few links from the pad eye.

My assailant was unleashed.

Horrified, I watched the monster rush toward me again, starved and furious. The crowd screamed, and so did the boys above me, which did nothing but exacerbate my fear.

I tried to locate a crack, a ridge, a foothold, but there was nothing. Only flat, unscalable rock. My toes scraped uselessly against the wall, and I felt myself slipping.

Gritz!

The lion lunged for my calves just as Will's hand clasped around my forearm and yanked me out of range—up and away from those drooling, snapping canines.

I clutched tightly to his arm, feet flailing for purchase. Below me, the lion fell back to its crouch and growled, miffed at his wasteful energy investment.

Gripping Will's shins and belt straps, the boys dragged us up and over the edge of the platform, and as soon as my knees hit the surface, I sagged into my savior, panting and shaking from the adrenaline rush.

The audience roared at our success while the band swapped to a victory song, and I chuckled as the distress melted away. Exhaustion replaced anxiety, my muscles unclenching, my heartbeat steadying. I could feel the sweat dripping down my nose and forehead and the back of my shirt, and I closed my eyes as I replayed the last few minutes in my mind.

By a hair's width, I'd avoided death by puma, and I had Will and his pack of welts to thank. I squeezed the boy's forearm in gratitude, hoping he would understand, and a moment later, he squeezed back.

When the rogue lion had been sedated and Gilmore was able to capture the city's attention again, he opened his arms to our gutsy group of candidates. "Ladies and gentlemen, our champions!"

Riotous applause.

Will's hands loosened around my arms, and we rose to our feet, taking in our company.

I quickly counted helmets to see how close I'd placed, and acute panic seized my heart upon my first calculation. *No way. That can't be right.*

10...15...20...

22...28...

My stomach churned. 30 of us, and not a contestant over.

"I have to say, in all my years of hosting this event, I've never witnessed a cooperative effort quite like this one. Shall we take a look at the makeup of our marvelous team?"

Will slowly turned his head, watching me through the sheen of his red visor. Almost like he knew exactly who I was and what was about to happen.

"Let's start with the fan favorite!"

I was sinking.

No, no, no. How could the numbers add up so perfectly? Why did the Fates have such a wretched sense of humor?

Gilmore beckoned me forward, but I couldn't move. My feet were cannon shots.

This...this was the worst thing I'd ever done. The punishment warranted more than a demerit. More than community restitution. I could go to prison for this. *Or worse.*

The boys slapped my back encouragingly, playfully nudging and pushing me toward the spokesman. Because they were idiots.

"I think we all had our doubts when we first saw you," Gilmore teased, feeding off the crowd's laughter. His bright eyes crinkled as he looked at me. "But your victory proves that size and stature account for little. Ingenuity, bravery, selflessness...those traits define a true soldier. And you've reminded us of that today!"

I glanced at the stands. At Will, tense and frozen.

He *did* know. And he knew I was done for.

Because competing was one thing, but I'd actually stuck the landing. Hell, I'd earned their *preference*. If I revealed myself now, I could shatter paradigms and blast the doors of reform wide open. And if the High Court couldn't keep the notion of women in combat out of the public's head, it would certainly do its best to ensure we feared the consequences.

"Off with the helmet then," Gilmore pressed.

I debated running.

I could make a break for it. Through the crowd, out the entrance, all the way back to the ranch and the warmth of my unmade bed. No one would ever know. And I wouldn't be labeled a misdemeanant.

But there were too many eyes, too many people. I'd never make it past the sentinels.

Go out with dignity.

That's all you have left.

My hands shook as I reluctantly slid the helmet off—dark, sweaty hair unfurling over my shoulders.

There was an intake of breath from the entire stadium, and for a few seconds, everything was still. I'd like to think no one recognized me, but only one girl in Belgate was stupid enough to masquerade as a boy in a federal competition. And only one girl was naive enough to think she'd get away with it.

Before I could come up with some brilliant excuse or play it off as a joke, an innocent mistake, the universe burst into noise. Like a teapot screaming and trembling on its burner.

Wincing, I turned my back to the stands, as if that would prevent the whole world from seeing what I'd done.

The boys stood there in a cluster, surrounding me in a dumbfounded arc.

"Kingsley?" Chinger pulled off his helmet, unable to hide the delighted smirk on his face.

The others followed suit, hair plastered to their foreheads as they stared at me. Appalled. Flabbergasted. Amazed. All but Will, who watched on with wary eyes.

Gilmore, ten shades paler than before, tore his astonished gaze from my face. "Attention!" he tried, voice squashed by the thunderous crowd. "Quiet—everyone!"

I imagined my father's expression right now. Eyes shut. Head bowed. Battling immeasurable shame, humility, and disappointment as the parents in his vicinity turned to stare. Accepting their blame and criticisms despite his best efforts to dissuade me.

I would never be forgiven.

Regret and embarrassment carved a deep wound inside me, and tears welled in my eyes. I'd always wanted to make a bold statement someday; I'd wanted to yank off their blindfolds and show them the truth.

But not like this.

The screaming increased a few decibels, and I thought it was just the crowd's escalating outrage at first. The Specs demanding their money. The Council screaming for my arrest. The weeds yelling at one another over the roar of the stadium.

But it wasn't. The clamor came from *above*.

Following my peers' bewildered gazes to the sky, my mouth parted at the strange spectacle overhead. A dark cloud hovered over the arena, as black as chimney smoke. But as the tempest stretched across the ashen heavens like spilled ink, I realized it wasn't a storm at all.

It was a mass migration of birds—a tremendous murder of crows—shrieking as they fell upon us.

11

They dove like acid rain. Abundant. Merciless. Painful.

The corvids swooped through the stadium, talons raking at skin and hair and eye sockets. One flew straight at me, aiming for me like it was bred to end me. It landed on my nape and pecked at my exposed jaw and cheek, breaking skin. Swearing loudly, I shoved the squawking rat off my neck and swung for it with my sword, almost dismembering Will as I did so.

The crowd rushed out of the stands in a chaotic frenzy, pushing each other out of the way, amassing at the exits. A parade of blood and feathers and screams.

Gritz, the *screams*. I'd never heard sounds like that—human pain and horror spliced with harsh, bloodthirsty caws. It was such a violent, haunting shift from the jubilant applause moments ago that I could hardly fathom what was happening.

My gaze pivoted to my immediate surroundings as something heavy struck the stage. Something ... humanlike.

The figure had climbed up the back of the concrete platform and now slowly, deviously rose from its crouch. At first glance, I thought it was a Deadlock soldier. It wore a soldier's uniform and boots fit for the Ellsian military, and the broadsword and dagger it carried on either hip nurtured that conclusion.

This creature, though ... this was like nothing I'd ever seen.

A lattice of black veins and blisters covered its decaying skin, and its male, human face bore two gray, vacant eyes. It suffered from the same uncanny quality as the mountain lions—like a corpse that hadn't stayed dead.

The soldier sneered at me with stained teeth. A black tongue flicked across his lips as he drew a jagged sword from his scabbard, gripping the extended hilt with both hands.

I retreated backward into Will.

Breaching his state of shock, Gilmore stepped between the contestants and the devil birthed of crow feathers. "Boys, get behind—"

He didn't get the chance to protect us. The soldier had already sliced his head clean off his shoulders.

The announcer I'd known all my life—the symbol of the Tournament, the speaker of Belgate—crumpled like a sack of grain. His head hit the platform with a sound I'd never forget.

I dropped my helmet and stared at the blood rushing for my feet, my chest cavity squashing my heart, my breathing stilted. Aghast, the contestants scrambled over the lip of the platform to escape the bloodshed, only to trade one slaughterhouse for another.

Similar creatures poured through the entryways and crawled over the stadium walls like spiders spilling out of an egg sac. Armed and murderous, they attacked the innocent, chasing them down and cutting them open. Others tossed glass bottles into the stands, flooding the event center with scarlet fire and toxic smoke.

I watched, sick to my stomach, as Belgate's entire populace ran for their lives from killer birds and these … these … fictional terrors. Stunned into inaction as my life drastically changed course in less than thirty seconds.

The events unfolded around me too fast—the crows, the decomposing soldiers, the children crying as strangers swept them into their arms and carried them away from their parents' corpses.

It couldn't be *real*. But as ruby blood began pooling around my boots, denial gave way to sheer terror.

We've been invaded.

The homefront is under attack.

War is here.

And I wasn't about to die in the middle of the arena, trying to differentiate fiction from reality. Wallowing in the trauma of it all, rendered useless by shock. No, I wouldn't die here, trapped in my own mind.

In a burst of rage and panic, I broke free from my paralysis and lunged at the ghoulish soldier. But the humanoid deflected my attack with the smallest degree of effort, and he passed me a smile so patronizing it shriveled up my insides. He sprang forward, hacking at my unprotected ribcage, and I barely dodged the blade in time. I backed away, swallowing the icy fear climbing my throat.

Shaking, I prepared to charge again when Will grabbed my wrist and all but threw us off the platform, putting an abrupt end to my duel. I hit concrete and fell forward onto my hands, miffed at Will's manhandling but relieved to be out of the creature's striking distance.

We ran, and I spared a glance at the beasts taking lives around me, slicing entrails, bombing exits—trying to absorb the images and not the emotions they induced.

"What . . . *are* they?" I gasped out.

Crows plunged and swerved around us, blood splattered the walls, and the anguished cries of my elders reverberated through the stadium.

Block it out, block it out.

Seeking cover, we ducked behind the judges' seats and peered out at the mayhem. Crows. Blades. Deranged soldiers at war with their own civilians.

"They're spirits," Will answered, his eyes narrowing on the ghouls chasing attendees out the door.

My gaze snapped to his face. "What do you mean?"

"Disturbed spirits," he tacked on. "The Ancients called them demons."

"*Demons*?" I stood up to get a better look, but he yanked me back down again, exasperated.

"They've claimed human hosts and eaten their souls," he explained, as if that weren't the most ridiculous thing he could have uttered. "These things have been building an army at the Rim for years now."

I gaped at him, tempted to smack the folklore off his tongue.

Did he fall on his head?

"Patrons. You mean the war—this whole time—we've been up against soul-eating *monsters*?" Chinger cried, hunched behind a row of bleachers a few feet away. His sweaty red hair clung to his forehead, and his dimpled chin quivered between labored breaths.

Grim, Will nodded, and my doubt wavered at the threatened and foreboding look in his eyes.

But ... that was impossible.

In no real-life scenario could we be fighting living corpses, even if our enemies looked like they'd crawled straight out of hell. That just didn't happen outside worn pages.

And how would Will even know that? Every citizen was running for his life, completely blindsided. How did a seventeen-year-old boy from the slums have all the answers?

"Who told you that?" I asked, inspecting his unreadable profile.

Onyx-brown eyes locked on the exit. "Get out of Belgate, Kingsley. And try not to die."

And with that, he left me at the courtside, his mission as unclear as his explanation. Chinger darted after him a few seconds later, and before I could think to follow them, the two contestants vanished into a sea of monsters and chaos.

Monsters, spirits, demons … who could be sure?

All I knew was they wanted us dead, and I was *not* on board with that plan. I had too many unanswered questions. Too many goals at stake.

Sculpting alarm into adrenaline, I fled for the exit, my left elbow shielding my eyes from sadistic crows. *Should have kept your damn helmet, Al.*

Frantic bodies pushed and shoved at one another as hundreds of people funneled through the fiery archways, and for a moment, I was more terrified of being trampled to death than beheaded. I could taste the fear around me, smell it on the cobblestone. The mob reeked of it.

As soon as I crossed the threshold and escaped the mass of bloody, shrieking attendees, sturdy hands fell on my shoulders and spun me around.

My father held me at arm's length, wild-eyed.

"Dad?" I clutched at his wrists, desperate to anchor myself to something real and concrete and factual. "What's happening?"

"Alex, listen to me." Harrowed eyes burrowed into my own. "I need you to warn the Interior of an incursion."

I blinked at him, shaking my head slightly. His words made absolutely no sense. "… What?"

"Eastward, Alex. Holly first. They're the head of military operations. They can help us, and you'll be safe there." His grip tightened on my shoulders. "You know your geography. You know where Holly is."

It was a question, not an affirmation.

"I … I can get there," I promised, my throat closing in on itself. Was he really tasking me with this? Venturing into the Range on my own? Finding the Command? "But what about you? You're not coming with me?"

His throat bobbed, and he glanced over my head at the flood of Ellsians pouring out of the stadium, bloody and broken and wailing in pain. "I'll meet up with you as soon as I can. But I need to help the others secure safe passage out of Belgate. And you … I need you to do this for me. For *all* of us." He gazed down at me, too many words on his tongue, too little time. "I know now—I know what you're capable of, Al. You can save us."

The admission pinched the corners of my eyes, and hot tears sprang to the surface. All I'd ever wanted was to know he believed in me, and he was finally gifting me an opportunity to prove myself. Now I just had to find the courage to do it. "Dad, I—"

"Separating is the last thing I want to do. But anyone capable of fighting will stay to defend Belgate; they won't prioritize Holly's citizens or the capital. Everyone else will seek refuge in the south, and they need someone who knows his wild crops, his water sources." He shook his head, and his hand dropped to my own, peeling it away from his forearm. "You need to deliver the message to the Interior that the borders have fallen. Before it's too late."

I wanted to argue, but I also knew he was right. If these soldiers came from the west as Will had implied, then they'd continue northeast where our population was most concentrated. "...Okay," I managed, biting my lip. Nodding to myself. "Okay."

Time drew a long, nervous breath, and save for the dry wind ruffling our hair, it felt like the whole world had slowed to a halt. We stared at each other for a few heartbeats, gathering the courage to say goodbye, seeking the strength to part ways. And there, in the verdure of my father's hazel eyes, was an intensity I'd never seen before. A bravery I'd never noticed.

"Go on." He pushed me away, his expression pained, his eyes wet. "Go."

I took a step back, hesitating. This felt wrong, leaving him behind, putting so many miles between us. "I ..."

"For once, Alex, do as I say." He turned to face a courtyard full of demons, and I watched his spine uncurl, his shoulders straighten. "*Run.*"

Conflicted, I looked him over one more time—his tanned nape, his fall sweater and field trousers, his worn and cracking hands—and then I took off in the opposite direction, blinking away tears.

My father trusted me enough for this task. I wouldn't let him down. *Not again.*

I ran past ravaged festival booths as soldiers with moon-colored eyes swarmed the city, torching every man-made creation in their path. Horses lay dead at every hitching post, preventing a swift escape, and my heart throbbed for the countless animals across town who'd likely suffered the same fate.

So much death and destruction ... for what?

What did we do to deserve this?

Burning buildings blurred red on either side of me: Nova's storefront, Lucky's Liquors, the library. Places I'd memorized to the smallest and most mundane detail, all drowning in flames as bizarre as the creatures who'd unleashed them.

The fire itself was devoid of any yellows, oranges, or blues—just lightless, raging red—and I suspected it promised more harm than its earthly sister if the immediate conflagration was anything to go by.

Families fled into alleyways like nests of mice, husbands carrying two or three children at once, their wives missing shoes or hobbling on broken heels. Meanwhile, sentinels, veterans, and undeployed soldiers fought in the streets, attempting to slow the onslaught. But they were falling quickly from what I could tell. Bodies already littered the ground, feeding the crows, and I wasn't keen on joining this mass burial.

Lungs aflame, I ran past it all—the dying, the endangered, the dead—not pausing for breath until I burst through the front door of my house.

There was no time to deliberate.

I shot upstairs and flung a few spare clothes into my school pack, distant screams bouncing off the windowpane. I slid everything from my desk into the sack with one motion: my old flashlight, a few of my most treasured books, my knife. Then I rushed back down to the kitchen and tossed in a loaf of bread.

After frantically filling a waterskin, I barreled on for the barn to search for potential camping gear. The chickens scurried around my feet, mirroring my stress, while Guinevere and Ophelia huddled together at the far side of the ranch, seeking sanctuary. Richard was nowhere to be found, and I could only hope he'd run far, far away from this place.

I retrieved some cord and a box of matches from the shed, and I'd nearly made it to the fruit trees when a burst of heat and wood chips launched me into the air.

Fire, some primal piece of me recognized, even as my mind failed to comprehend the ambush. *Fire everywhere and all-consuming.*

Sprawled on the dirt, I forced myself into a sitting position, my vision shifting back and forth. When the blurry image sharpened, my nails pierced the earth.

Crimson flames engulfed my house.

A permanent structure, now kindling to destruction. Now fuel for the conqueror.

I stared at the death of a space I'd called home my entire life. The old shingles charring, the wooden foundation splintering under ferocious heat. And as my father's legacy burned to ash before my eyes, I knew this pyre had to forgo a funeral if I had any intention of escaping Belgate.

So I numbly rose to my feet and willed myself to turn away.

To *run* away.

12

I felt for the path with my sword, hoping my blade tasted foliage and nothing else. My left hand gripped the flashlight like a second weapon, fingers clutching the handle so tightly, I wasn't sure they'd ever go back to resting position.

But I told myself I wasn't afraid; I was *determined*.

I had a destination, a mission. And that was the only thing keeping me on two sturdy feet.

The forest swallowed me up the further east I ventured: pine trees taller than buildings, underbrush thicker—and pricklier—than any hedge I'd ever pruned. It was overwhelming and eternal, emanating decades of growth and maturity, and I wondered if these same sights, sounds, and smells had also crossed trails with the Ancients.

Had they too felt like insects beneath the canopy? Or had they taken comfort in the unmade?

I'd never traveled beyond the Gates, even back when the sentinels had allowed public access to the Range. I'd only ever heard stories of the wilderness and the radioactive wasteland beyond the forest. Then, when I was finally old enough to explore the woods, the Gates had been closed to civilians without travel permits. Indefinitely.

I'd spent years trying to convince the impudent adults to let me through the walls, bribing the sentinels with farm food, scheming ways to smuggle myself across. But today, no guards had been there to catch me and escort me home.

Today, the eastern gates were abandoned.

Keyless, I'd climbed up and over the great stone walls—unobserved, unrestricted—and dropped down on the other side with a satisfying crunch of leaves underfoot. And for a brief moment, the despair for my city had quieted as I'd inspected the ugly exterior of my enclosure.

Finally free from you, I'd thought. *But at what cost?*

Something snapped behind me then, blowing out my bravery like a wisp of incense, and I clicked off the light, yielding to darkness as I shoved the device in the side of my pack. My pulse thrummed in my temples as I scanned the trees and the black spaces between them, watching for shaking leaves or shifting shadows.

Begging for a false alarm.

This is what I get for taking shortcuts, I decided. Straying from the winding, weathered road had felt like a smart decision an hour ago. Now, I wasn't so sure avoiding the obvious escape route was a good call.

I straightened at the sound of crinkling mulch, readjusting my sword grip. This time there was no denying it; something was here in the dark with me, and it was getting closer. I spun in a circle, struggling to spot my attacker through the surrounding brush. Failing to pair sound and location. And finally, almost imperceptibly, the air shifted.

Veering 180, I sliced down on my opponent with all my might.

Metal clashed against metal, and when no remise followed, I cautiously opened my eyes.

Through the crossroads of our swords, two black pupils stared back at me, agitated and confused. I yelped and pushed away from him, keeping my weapon between us as I tamed my heartbeat.

"*Kingsley?*" he hissed, and I jolted at the sound of his voice.

Anxiousness thawed into annoyance as I made out the shadows of his face. "Why didn't you say something, Will? We almost killed each other."

"Why are you following me?" he demanded, but it was hard to take him seriously in his competition attire. Like me, he still wore his shoddy armor over his work clothes: mismatched spaulders and bracers, weathered tassets, and a leather torso plated with scrap metal.

"Why would I be following you? I'm warning Holly so they can bolster their defenses." *Dimwit.*

I couldn't see him very well, but I could sense his judgement. "You ... really don't think things through, do you?"

My mouth parted, but words failed me. We'd witnessed a butchering today, and *that* was the first thing he needed to get off his chest? "What about you? Shouldn't you be taking back the city?"

Our sentinels were already few in number, our veterans even scarcer. But Will was a skilled fighter, and despite his Tournament fatigue, I suspected he could tally more kills than most of those men.

Belgate desperately needed soldiers like him right now.

His eyes, like blister beetles, dipped away. "There's nothing left to take back."

The whisper cut me like a knife, and my blade dropped a few inches as I grappled with his conclusion. "Why would you say that?"

He sheathed his sword, his gaze finding the trees again. "Belgate doesn't stand a chance against an enemy like that. They took us out strategically, and we don't have enough men to force them out. Anyone who values his life will flee to neighboring cities or the Southern Ridge. Everyone else ..." His shoulders sank. "Belgate's in enemy hands now."

His statement was a fingernail peeling across glass—painful to hear and almost unbearable to endure. Because if Belgatians were known for anything, it was our proud, stubborn existence. Very few cities could survive isolation the way we had, and even fewer would try. But our rural folk were as tough as shadscale, our city dwellers unrelenting.

And to think that all their homes and livelihoods had crumbled to dust in one evening, that the community had lost everything to an *ambush* ... it was like the wind had swept away all the seeds we'd sown in one abrupt, catastrophic storm.

"There's still time for you to seek safety," Will said, his tone gentler than before. "There's a reservoir about ten miles south of here." He tilted his chin to the right as if I didn't know my bearings.

I shot him a dirty look. "Thanks for the advice, but I've got a message to deliver. So if you don't mind." I imitated his chin-tilt: a gesture for him to politely buzz off.

He stared back at me, taking me in like a map he could hardly unfold, let alone read. And frankly, I pitied him for trying.

"Oh, you've got to be joking." The sound came from the shadows. An awful, whiny sound. "Follow the voices ... *ingenious* idea ..."

My nerves writhed.

"Mason?" I whispered, and the pure dread on Will's face just about summed up my feelings.

"How? How is it *you two* of all—?" A disgusted grunt. "This is just great. Just absolutely fantastic."

Yeah. That was Mason alright.

Two silhouettes stood between the trees, both of them sporting Tournament armor. Mason's arrogant posture was a dead giveaway, and the second figure was distinctly short and elfish.

"Fudge?" I guessed, swinging my pack around and blinding them with the beam of my flashlight.

The freckled boy shielded his eyes. "Alex. You're okay?"

"Hardly." I ran a hand over my face. I couldn't even begin to explain how *not* okay I was. "Where are you headed?"

"East," Mason answered. "Military headquarters. With the Command's help, we can figure out exactly what we're up against."

His voice was steady, but I'd seen enough of his unchecked ego to recognize false confidence. And honestly, I didn't blame him for putting on a show. Hours ago, we'd watched demonic creatures rape our land and set fire to our hometown. If he was anything like me, acting like he had it all together was a last-ditch effort to preserve his fragile mind.

Fudge approached me, and I could see the trauma and fear etched into his face. "Holly's also the closest Interior city. Even if it's still several days out, we're more likely to run into people who can help us if we head that direction."

"And the sooner we find people, the sooner they can evacuate," I added.

We were all eastbound, then—a bunch of teens running from monsters. It sounded like a story arc I'd read before.

But as much as I loathed Mason's company, he wasn't a terrible fighter to have on this journey. And multiple travelers would enable watch rotations, permitting a solid night's rest—something I was unlikely to experience on my own. "There's strength in numbers," I managed, keeping the bile in my stomach like a professional. "... We should team up."

"No," Will and Mason echoed.

Despite their hasty reply, I maintained a low timbre, aware that men liked to accuse women of speaking shrilly when we raised our voices. "Why not? If those ... *things* ... are waging war on Ells, they'll come for the capital. They'll come for the four of us. We have a better chance of surviving together."

It was actually called selfish herd theory, but I didn't think sharing that detail would help my case.

"She's right," said Fudge. "And it's impractical to travel in pairs now that we're all here."

Mason contemplated this for a beat, and then he turned to the daunting expanse of wilderness before us. "Fine, you can tag along."

"You mean you can tag along with *me*," I corrected.

"Yeah right. I wouldn't follow you anywhere."

Fudge stepped between us before I could dent Mason's skull with my flashlight. "How about we prioritize finding somewhere safe to spend the night? It should take the enemy at least 24 hours to secure their hold on the city. Maybe another day to reorganize. We've probably got a couple nights before they move."

"Maybe," Will said. "But if we're making assumptions, it's best to assume they're trailing us as we speak."

Fudge blanched at that, and I opened my mouth to counter Will's unhelpful opinion when the hair on my arms suddenly stood erect, and a cold, unsettling feeling trickled down my throat and into my gut.

Uneasy, I watched a gust of wind kick up needles and leaves from the ground, snatching up the elements and dragging them along for the ride. Pebbles and loose soil joined the debris, contaminating the zephyr that eddied between us.

The warm, unnatural current wove around our group, through our legs, and back to the center of our circle where it formed a baby dust devil. Inside that languid whirlwind, a bright orb appeared, hovering in the air like an unmanned torch.

Fudge gasped loudly, and Mason widened his stance, readying his blade. But Will and I just stared intently at the glowing sandspout, holding our breath.

Then, as though the ball of starlight contained its own gravitational force, rocks and leaf litter began accumulating around it like plates of armor, encasing the liquid sunlight in a cool, rocky chamber.

When the air finally settled, the components formed a human figure.

***

My breath hitched, and I backed into Will for the second time this afternoon.

The yellow orb danced right where the eidolon's heart should be, and the forest particles floated in suspension around it—earthen limbs, torso, and flesh.

Was this . . . a demon? An evil spirit?

"Do you guys see it too?" Fudge whispered. The fear in his voice reinforced my own apprehension.

My hand tightened around the hilt of my sword. This thing didn't emanate violence the way the other creatures did. It seemed different, less reactive . . . less rotten. But that didn't mean it wouldn't hurt us.

"What . . . exactly are you?" I asked.

The head snapped to me, faceless and blank and *creepy as hell*, and I swallowed my next question.

The phantom dissolved, its components dropping to the earth again, and I worried it might have read my mind. But as the pine needles trembled again, and as the warm wind tousled my hair, I realized our guest wasn't finished here.

It reappeared directly in front of me this time, remade exclusively of dead leaves, and I failed to leash my startled flinch.

The living lamp shade cast orange and yellow colors across my body, turning my recycled armor into a vibrant sculpture, my face into a painting. It peered up at me as if it could see me without any eyes, and I leaned away.

"Can you talk?" I probed carefully, trying to remain calm. By the way it behaved, it didn't seem dangerous. Just ill-mannered.

The mummy retreated, and the leaves fluttered, as if that question disturbed it.

"Can you not see that it doesn't have a mouth?" Mason sneered.

The creature dispersed among us in non-tangible form, only to reassemble with a body built of sticks, flora, and pebbles.

"I think *it* might be a girl," noted Fudge.

Now that he mentioned it, the spirit's form did resemble a girl in her early teens: slim, feminine, flamboyant, and void of any pointed corners.

'She' had nothing to say regarding her classification. Instead, her chosen form solidified, and she stepped forward, closer to Will and me. She scanned our faces with her nonexistent one, weeds and stones forming a long braid over her shoulder.

She cocked her head at us inquisitively, circling Will a few times. Riveted by his lack of tact and human emotion, if I had to guess.

"Are you … friendly?" I tried again. As extraordinary as she was, we needed to know if she posed a threat to our group before we assigned her any additional identity markers.

The tween nodded absently, focused on Will, who seemed a little perturbed by the ogling.

Fudge grinned, shedding his guarded disposition. "I think she likes you, Will."

She poked the broody trainee in the arm, seemingly delighted by his subsequent frown, and I highly doubted anyone had ever survived prodding at him like that.

I regarded our new arrival with dread and exhaustion. This all had to be a terrible dream, right? An attack on my hometown, and now a one-sided conversation with a forest nymph? A nymph who seemed to understand English?

Did I die back in the Tournament or something? Was I being punished in the afterlife?

Behind me, a critter scampered across the forest floor and immediately knocked my wits—and vigilance—back into place. "Okay, well, this is … great," I began, tearing my gaze from the underbrush, "but there's an army of monsters down the hill, and we should really keep moving. Unless," I addressed the entity, "you plan on stopping us. Or killing us?"

She shook her head like that was a stupid thought.

"I take it you won't be providing us with any useful information either?" I muttered, sliding my sword back in its scabbard.

The mute ignored me, totally enthralled by Will's presence.

The boy's eyes roamed over her, and it was the only time I'd seen him look genuinely curious about something. "What's your name?" he asked.

The spirit-demon glowed a little brighter, and I had the inkling she was blushing. But she didn't answer him. She just went on observing the trainee, as if *he* were the paranormal variable in this situation, not her.

Mason released an impatient noise. "Okay. I actually agree with the breeder over here. We need to gain some elevation, and fast. We can sleep after we put some tangible distance between us and our enemies."

I shook out my fist. If he called me that word *one more time* ...

"Right," Will said, breaking eye contact with the phantom to study the branches above us. "If you're looking for the Command, it's this way." He veered left and vanished into the dark without another word.

The three of us stared after his retreating figure in shock.

Had he just *declared* himself leader?

...Was that allowed?

After a moment's pause, Fudge jogged to catch up with him, and the ghost trailed after them with a spring in her step, as if she regularly joined travelers on their quests. As if this were a typical weekend in the woods.

I wasn't sure what was most absurd: the four of us running from demon soldiers, accepting a supernatural nightlight into the group, or blindly following Tooms into the Range. Then again, it seemed pointless to rate the nonsensical anymore. At this point, nothing made any sense to me. Up was down, fire burned crimson, and pebbles could float.

Mason and I glared at the stretch of woods before us—the spirit's light fading between branches, the vegetation ingesting our peers.

"Ladies first," he taunted.

"Scared, are you?"

Tutting, the blond followed after the others to prove a point. Just as I'd known he would.

As he trudged into the understory, the valley's dry wind swept through the forest, eliciting a gentle susurrus from the aspen leaves and pine needles overhead. The gust delivered the scent of decaying fruit and autumn harvests to the mountains. But it also brought traces of smoke and wisps of bloodshed.

Heart wrought with uncertainty, I glanced back at the small patch of forest I'd traversed, the edge of city grounds.

My childhood. My home. My cage.

I breathed in deeply, scrounging for the metal I'd need to steel myself. Mustering the courage to trade one unknown for another.

And then, after sparing the city one last glance, I purged myself of the shackles and followed my competition into the dark.

13

The campfire crackled, and the kindling caved in on itself, sending a small plume of embers into the night sky. The image reminded me of the horrid red flames that swallowed our ranch house—and the beasts who'd unloosed the inferno.

"So … those creatures were once people …"

Will didn't respond, but he didn't have to. The haunted look in his eyes said everything.

I rubbed my neck. "And these spirits—these evil, dead spirits—have come back to life to … what, eat people's souls?"

It sounded so surreal, so unbelievably terrible that it was preposterous. Until today, my own curse and Nova's uncanny fortunes were the only supernatural elements in my life, and that had been plenty.

"They must need a sustainable life form. To fight, I mean," said Fudge, tearing off a piece of bread and handing the rest over to Mason, who inspected it the same way he might inspect a cheese wheel for mold. "That's why they possess our dead. Our military."

"So they're using humans … to fight humans?" I clarified.

"That's so twisted," Mason hissed, swearing at the dirt. "They're taking away our army and then using it against us!"

The fire danced in our eyes as we fell quiet, reliving the disturbing events we'd witnessed through, impossibly, a *more* horrifying lens.

How did a day so ordinary devolve into something so abominable?

Eight hours ago, I'd had no intention of competing in the Tournament, let alone fleeing Belgate with nothing to my name but a pack of uncharred possessions. And just this morning, my companions had intended to secure their enlistment, attend boot camp in the spring, and greet war at the Rim. *In that order.*

But ultimately, we didn't go to war. It fell from the sky and buckled the pavement.

"I don't understand why the Court hasn't informed the citizens about this." Fudge waved his bread slice around like a petition. "Why would they keep this information about our enemy a secret? This is sort of vital stuff, you know? Soul-eating demons? They should have been training us for this. I thought we were fighting Rhean dictators, not the undead!"

Will poked at the fire with a long stick, his expression inscrutable. "If they told us we were up against an infinite force that can hijack our corpses, there'd be hysteria. No one would want to join the army. We'd cripple ourselves, and we'd be dead before the Court could instate a draft."

There he went again, popping out explanations as if he'd had years to mull over the forbidden details. "How do you know so much about this, Will?" I asked. "How come you never said anything?"

He offered a half-shrug, but I could tell he didn't appreciate the accusation under my tongue. "My father's a postman. He crosses the Range on a monthly basis, and he's been to the Rim a few times. He's seen and heard things on his travels that the High Court..." He hesitated. "That the Court prefers we keep to ourselves. The rest I pieced together."

My gaze fell to the fire again, homing in on the ruby cinders.

Will moved to Belgate about four years ago with his father, the sum of their belongings confined to the travel packs they carried. After their cabin burned down two years later, they were forced to live in the slums with the other outcasts and one-eyed widows. Only now, I wondered if the burning had served as some kind of warning, a gesture to keep quiet.

Considering the High Court's allergic reaction to transparency, it wouldn't surprise me. Though I doubted anything *could* at this point. Not demon creatures. Or leaf people. Or violent decapitations. I felt adrift among the irrational, and I feared if I stopped to reflect on it long enough, my proliferating questions might bury me alive.

My eyes drifted to the spiritual entity to my right—the living, breathing personification of the unknown. She sat next to the campfire, rocky fingers exposed to the warmth, leafy knees pulled to her glowing chest. And while she hadn't attempted to kill us, she also hadn't tried to communicate again. She'd simply adhered herself to our group, refusing to leave. And now she was stuck to us like dog crap on a boot.

My instincts screamed at me for being so passive. Could we really trust her? If she wasn't one of *them*, then what was she? And were there others like her?

Fudge picked up on my paranoia. "I think she's okay. If she wanted to harm us, she would have."

Yeah—unless she planned to suck out our souls while we slept, or slit our throats and steal our skin. But I kept that happy little thought to myself; none of us needed anything else to haunt our dreams tonight.

The wind blew through camp, turning the embers and pulling at ancient tree roots. Pine trees groaned at the disturbance, and I shuddered at their monstrous vocalizations. The whole forest felt awake right now, as if the mountains themselves were watching us grapple with primal forces, evaluating our coping skills, and betting on our survival. As if we'd unwittingly registered ourselves for another perilous Tournament. One with harsher critics and fiercer opponents.

I didn't like it one bit.

"Anyone else feel like we're not alone out here?" I whispered, eyeing the canopy.

"We're not," Fudge said—so confidently it flipped my stomach. "The Siren's out there somewhere."

Mason slapped his palm to his forehead. "Not this again."

I looked between them. "What's the Siren?"

Blue eyes ignited at the follow-up question. "He's this legend from the Battle of Exeter—a deserter who stopped taking orders from the Command. He wears his own blood around his eyes, like a masked vigilante, and he lives in the trees."

I glanced at Will for validity, but he was scowling at the campfire, probably analyzing the kindling's burn rate or something.

"He can kill an enemy without ever showing his face," Fudge continued. "Rumor has it he took out an entire Rim post with only two of his comrades and a bow!"

His excitement almost had me answering his grin, and I wondered if he truly believed such a thing, or if he'd merely seized the opportunity to steer the conversation away from today's traumatic events—to pierce the shadow of survival's guilt, if just for a moment.

"Bull," said Mason. "There's no way some archer could pull that off. And besides, attacking incognito is cowardly."

I rolled my eyes. "You think it's cowardly to use strategic offense?"

"What would you know about war tactics? Stick to your tapestries."

"My *what*?"

"Anyway," Fudge cut in, "my brother—he's stationed at the Rim—he says the Siren's still out there, fighting from the treetops. Maybe he's got our backs."

"Maybe," I said, trying to sound encouraging, but I had a feeling no such guardian existed, and no hero was coming to save us.

The forest moaned again, and my eyes slipped back to the darkness beyond the fire's radiance. "We should call it a night. If those spirits are stealing human bodies, they're probably susceptible to human needs. And I'd prefer to sleep when they do."

Mason scoffed, making a point of stoking the fire anyway. "Are you actually giving orders now?" His eyes thinned to angry slits. "Quit acting like one of us. We don't need a skirt telling us what to do."

I opened my mouth to spear him with a retort, but Fudge beat me to it.

"Like one of *us*?" he repeated. "Mason, she's just as much a soldier as any of us. You saw her at the Tournament. She fought off lions! She out-performed most of the contestants in that stadium, including me." He gave a chastising shake of the head. "No one here is qualified to lead. We have no idea what we're doing. At least Alex had the brains to bring food and matches."

I could've hugged that kid, but I refused to let him fight my battles. "Forget it, Fudge. I'm used to Mason's chronic sexism."

"It's not sexism," the blond growled. "You say that about everything."

"Pretty sure belittling someone for their sex is the definition of sexism, sexist."

"Just admit it. You're out of your depth here, Kingsley. You're not a fighter."

"Says who? You? You can barely lift that sword off the ground!"

He was glaring so hard there was no way he could see out of his eyes. "Says the law. Girls aren't suited for combat. Never have been. I mean, look at our anatomy! Women are built to have children, to nurture—"

I sprang to my feet. "That's because boys are *boys,* you weed. Can you imagine the life of something so small and fragile in a man's possession for nine months? We wouldn't need a procreation law anymore—we'd be extinct!"

Fudge snorted, and Mason shot him a look of betrayal. "Each sex has its own useful role in society," he explained slowly, like I hadn't spent every school day ignoring the very same doctrine. "Guys are born stronger.

They're born to fight on the front lines *for* women. You should be grateful."

Grateful?

"Are all guys born so idiotic? Or is that just you in particular?"

Will kicked in the edge of the fire pit and buried the flames in soil, plunging the group into darkness, silencing our dispute, and obliterating our efforts to distract ourselves from the crisis at hand.

"She's right. We should sleep while we can." He moved for the nearest tree, running his hands over the bark, searching for grips. "I'll take first watch."

With that, he quickly scaled the conifer and nestled himself in the fork of two sturdy branches, a good twenty feet above us.

I gaped at the raccoon among us, bewildered. Was ... was he going to sleep up there? In the tree?

Boys were so *weird*.

Like children sent to bed, the rest of us settled down for the night, claiming our own patches of pine needles and succumbing to the weight of our weary limbs and muscles. After a while, the spirit girl disappeared into the trees, bored with us, and I tried not to dwell on her possibly evil intentions.

It didn't work, so I tucked my knife up my sleeve.

Just in case.

Will promised to wake one of us up in a few hours, but I had a hunch sleep would evade me anyway. The day's residual terror and adrenaline kept my nerves ablaze. I felt like I could run a thousand miles right now—my mind, obviously, not my body. My body was crippled and sore from carrying outdated cannons for no goddamn reason.

Every time I neared unconsciousness, my brain snapped me back like it knew what awaited me on the other side—like it wanted to spare me from soul-eating soldiers and decapitated celebrities.

I was traumatized, surely—and perhaps still stumbling down the slope of shock. But I was also intrigued by the strange new variables the Fates had introduced to us this afternoon. Spirits. Stolen corpses. Murderous crows.

All the gossip in Belgate about magic and the underworld—could it really be true?

I curled my hand, my nails pinching my palm and its hidden crescent.

Could everything we know about the world be wrong?

14

I ran barefoot through the pines, shoving through branches and stumbling down hillslopes. Demon crows nipped at my face and neck, their claws raking across exposed limbs, scoring my flesh with painful cuts and abrasions.

I ignored my burning calves, the stress on my lungs, the needles in my feet—pushing onward as fast as I could while shielding my eyes from the air raid. (If they claimed my optic organs, my other soft spots stood no chance).

At last, the forest thinned around me, and I choked out a sob of relief. I was almost out. Almost free.

Then something molten sailed through my chest, wrenching my sternum forward and slaughtering any hopes of escape.

My gaze dropped to the gaping wound in my chest, the red soaking a uniform I didn't recognize. I watched the bloody circle grow over my breast, warm liquid dripping down my navel, and I knew this would be the wound that killed me.

Someone—a boy—screamed my name outside the grove, waiting for me to breach the forest line, but I wouldn't get there. And the fact that I would never arrive almost hurt worse than the hole in my flesh. Inside me, there was a desperate, puzzling need to go to him. A deep sense of guilt I didn't understand.

I fell to my knees, hands trembling over the expanding bloody mess.

It's ... over. There's no coming back from this.

I'd *lost*.

The birds coalesced before me, morphing into a singular entity. The shadowy figure bore two gory legs, a torso, and a head—and when the creature's face appeared, I finally felt the raging agony inside my body, the ruptured organs and splintered ribs. I howled in protest, shaking my head as scalding terror flooded my eyes.

The man flashed a cruel smile, a blistered and deformed face replacing the one I knew.

He'd been killed, his soul consumed, his body purloined.

He cocked his head to the side and grinned down at me, hateful and unfamiliar. "Your turn, kiddo."

***

Upon waking, it took me several moments to disentangle dreamscape and reality, but consciousness eventually butchered my nightmare into puny, unrecognizable scraps.

I took a deep, steadying breath and loosened my death grip on my knife. *So that's what sleep looks like now? Trauma not reanimated, but unlived?*

Pushing off the ground, I staggered through the glade in search of a mental reset. Darkness enveloped my surroundings, the shrouded moon barely casting enough light to navigate, and after pacing back and forth for a while, I settled on a patch of grass and stared into the wild emptiness of the night. Tears formed in the corners of my eyes, and I frantically wiped at them to keep the droplets from falling.

Don't you cry. If you cry, you won't be able to stop.

I scolded myself until the urge subsided. Dad was fine. Nova and the others had made it out okay. Even Richard had fled Belgate unscathed. For now, I couldn't assume the worst—not with my sanity on the line.

"Can't sleep either?"

The voice kicked me out of my skin.

I spun around, wide-eyed, and Fudge offered a weak, apologetic smile. He sat down next to me, his gentle presence whisking away my anxiousness like a summer breeze. Strange, how some people were capable of such things; I only seemed to infect folks with headaches, and my shadow was a far cry from soothing.

We sat together for a while, far away in the refuge of our own minds. Processing our circumstances, negotiating with our fatigued skeletons.

"I can't believe this is happening," Fudge said out of the blue, and I found his openness refreshing. "These things—we're completely unprepared for them, totally outmatched."

Understatement.

"Our soldiers don't stand a chance, let alone teenage recruits." He shook his head. "How could the Court send its youth to their death-beds? *Blindfolded?*"

I frowned, thinking back to the training sessions I'd attended. "Didn't you sort of expect that when you auditioned for the army? I mean, all Frost ever talked about was personal responsibility and losing his leg in battle. Seems like we were always taught to see ourselves as disposable pawns."

Bodily autonomy, livelihoods, health—those wants were all inferior to our nation's wellbeing. That was the High Court's philosophy, anyway.

He glanced to the side. "I didn't think I'd place in the Tournament, actually."

I failed to repress my bewilderment. "Why?"

Male students were often encouraged to compete in the Tournament as a ceremonial tradition, but those who intended to pursue apprenticeships or careers in Belgate rarely trained for the competition, and certainly not for years on end. So why had the smallest boy in our cohort?

He started plucking weeds out of the ground. "I never really wanted to be a soldier. My parents expected me to carry on the family title. My brother and my father and his father were all in the military, earned huge honors—so I did as I was told and attended lessons. I mean, at least it got them off my case, you know? But I knew all along I wouldn't make it; I was never built for war."

I thought about my own father trying to influence my decision to fight. He'd dragged me kicking and screaming away from the dangerous path I'd chosen. But Fudge was *thrust* into the fire.

"Knowing I'd flunk out," he continued, "I was so relieved. I thought, well, my parents can't say anything if I just don't have the talent for it, right? It was my ticket out of fighting. Out of *dying*." He hummed, ripping up blades of grass between his fingers. "So much for that."

My mind conjured an image of weary citizens crossing the Southern Ridge—my father at the lead, carving a safe path through the woods.

"Why didn't you go with the evacuees, then? Run when you had the chance?"

"My mother tried to convince me to leave with her and my cousins, but Mason was set on finding the army ... and I just couldn't let him go off on his own." A tired grin twitched at the corner of his mouth. "Not when he lacks every basic survival instinct."

I knew Fudge and Mason were as close as brothers—a friendship that had stumped me for years—but for someone so unfit for war, it didn't justify his decision. "Is that the real reason?"

He looked down. "Part of it. I guess I also didn't run away because ..." He paused, his shoulders falling pathetically. "Because even if I'm useless on a battlefield, it doesn't mean I can just ... stand by and watch other people die for me. I'm sick of being a spectator."

The confession pushed my eyebrows moonward. Our limitations were different in nature, but I understood his feeling all too well—the desire to contribute something, however minimal. The need to be the enforcer of change, not the recipient.

"There's no way I'm going to make it out of this war alive, Alex," he said with a sad tilt to his lips. "But . . . even if I die tomorrow, at least I'll have tried to help. At least I might still make my parents proud, you know?"

His sapphire eyes were so bright, even under a starless sky. Everything about him was vibrant and honest and young and—and someone like him did *not* belong in a world as dark as this.

I patted him on the shoulder. "I won't let you die."

His chuckle was empty. Mirthless.

"Hey, I'm serious, Fudge. I won't let any of you die. I promise."

He looked at me then, contemplative and curious, his skepticism deteriorating with every heartbeat. No one had ever looked at me that way, with wonder parting their lips and hope glistening in their eyes. It did weird things to my heart.

"Okay, I mean, if Mason happened to fall behind, it wouldn't be the most devastating thing in the world," I amended.

The response pulled a small, tired laugh out of him. "Honestly, he's not so bad once you get to know him." I made a face, and he snorted. "Really. There's more to him than you think. He's a different guy under the bravado."

"Well, if he never shows his good side, what does it matter?"

He rolled his eyes, but a smile still danced on his face. He seemed to feel lighter, having shed his concerns, having confided in me about his fears. And despite everything we'd seen today, I felt safe beside him. Safe and *heard*, which wasn't something I could say about most of my male contemporaries.

"So, how did you and Mason even become friends?" I asked, not ready to kill this peaceful feeling just yet. It was a pleasant change, having a conversation with a boy who didn't make me want to pull my hair out, run away, or kick him in the coin purse.

Fudge leaned back on his hands, his oversized breast plate and spaulders overwhelming his petite form. "I guess I saw through his act early on, and as soon as I recognized his insecurities, his behavior didn't annoy me anymore. It just made me sad."

He paid me a hesitant look, probably wondering if he should reveal any more, but whatever he detected in my features killed his reservations.

"The first time I witnessed that vulnerability, we were nine years old. We'd just had our first training session, and when Mason's father came to pick him up, Mason ran right up to him with this big, toothy smile. He started gushing about his day, bragging about how amazing he was and how much better he was than the rest of the class. But instead of indulging him, or even scolding him for his conceit, his father walked away without a response, snapping his fingers at him to hurry up. And Mason's joy just disappeared. Vanished right off his face." He sighed. "I started to realize it was always like that."

I pursed my lips. "So he's just, what, attention deprived?" Made sense why he was always trying too hard and shining too brightly. He wanted his old man's approval, and he'd shoved everyone aside to get to his pedestal.

"That's just scratching the surface."

"Maybe. It still doesn't explain why you tolerate him." Ugly home life or not, it didn't excuse Mason's horrid behavior, even if it did explain it.

"Once you see him for who he really is, it's hard to unsee that, you know?" he said. "Mason has a lot of potential. He just needs some help."

I dipped my chin, smiling at the ground. Leave it to Fudge, the nicest, most harmless kid in class, to take on a project like Mason Price. "Well, he's lucky to have you. Not many people would put up with that attitude this long."

Fudge laughed again, louder this time, and I wasn't sure I'd ever heard a sweeter sound. "I think I've just grown immune." He tilted his head, his expression warm. "It's getting late, Alex. Why don't you try to get some more sleep? I'll take watch."

I tried to argue, but he waved away my protests, and I sauntered back to my circle of dirt in resignation.

Trying my best to sustain the warm, comforting feeling in my core, I curled up in a ball on the ground, pillowing my head on my arm and staring at the cold, lifeless embers.

My gaze crawled to Will, who sat in his crooked tree like an animal native to the forest and her whispers, wide awake.

Had he been thinking about his father too? We all had family back in Belgate, and we had to keep moving—keep pushing—without knowing if any of them were okay.

"Are you worried about your dad?" I asked, casting for a human reaction of some kind. Avoiding sleep for another minute or two if I could help it.

He regarded me for a moment, cautious of my small talk. "Yeah."

"Did he go with the others?"

"Think so."

"…Do you think they made it out alright?" I whispered.

He chose not to respond, but his silence said everything I was too scared to acknowledge.

15

I awoke to the smell of charred hair and begged my temporal lobe to put me out again.

Mason had gone hunting early this morning, and he'd managed to catch something edible, much to my surprise. The small, unidentifiable mammal now burned above the fire. It was charcoal black, and I had to wonder if Mason had dropped it in the ashes by accident, or if he was just allergic to the culinary arts. I lacked the energy to ask.

"What is that?" asked Fudge, fanning the air in front of his nose.

Mason jabbed the meat with a stick. "Your breakfast. What else?"

Fudge glanced at me, dubious, and I grinned. Maybe it was too soon to tell, but I might have just made a new friend. My first *human*, age-appropriate friend.

Bordering the glade, pine trees stood like stoic guardians in the haze, warding off paranormal entities and mysterious gales. Birds squawked obnoxiously from their branches, and I frowned at the peaceful terrain between their podiums, wondering if the demons had moved for Holly yet, or if we still had another day or two before they marched east.

Had they been trailing us last night, as Will suggested? Could their forces be hiding just beyond camp, waiting to strike us down? Or had they sent another horde of demon crows to finish us off?

Mason shoved a piece of meat in my face, cutting off my anxious spiral, and after watching the others devour their portions, I took a small, cautious bite.

The gamey mammal tasted like coal and rust, but my empty stomach didn't protest.

"Exactly how big of a hike do we have ahead of us, Will?" I asked a few moments later, mourning how quickly my helping had disappeared.

"We've halved our traveling time by cutting through the Range. Reaching the Command by road would have taken a week," he said. "But if we maintain a reasonable pace, we should hit Holly in three days. Give or take."

Dark circles bordered his eyes, and I suspected he'd stayed up all night. None of us appeared to have slept enough—or serenely—and I feared the luxuries of deep sleep and clean sheets were far behind us.

The spirit-demon seemed to be the only one undeterred by the lack of rest. She'd materialized in front of the campfire a few minutes ago, waving her leafy arms about and urging us to get going. Her bossiness really pissed me off, and I was about to tell her so when I noticed the impressive height of Mason's fire, the intense heat of the flames. My gaze dropped to the flaking kindling, and my anger burgeoned like a fungus.

"Mason," I said dangerously. "Where did you get that paper for the fire?"

He nodded toward my pack, where my books lay open and gutted upon the dirt.

Rage hit me like a cannon shot.

"You moronic *rat*—" I flew at him, incensed, but Will caught me around the waist and twirled me back around before I could do to Mason what he did to my books.

The weed stepped away, appalled by my aggression. "Whoa, they're *books*. They were just weighing you down. I made good use of them."

I shook off Will's hands, watching the pages shrivel in orange, watching them erode to windborne debris. They weren't just books. Not to me.

They were artifacts that survived the Water Wars. Stories of Greek heroes, revenge in Paris, and murders on the streets of Russia. Ties to Belgate and the library and our nation's origins.

With the slip of my glove, I'd watch the Ancients hold the very same copies in their hands, their eyes darting from margin to margin, their minds converting words to images. I'd study their strange clothes and hairstyles. The way they laughed, cried, or scrunched their noses at plot beats. The speed at which they consumed the content and the strange places they chose to do so. Occasionally, I'd found their vibrant environments overstimulating, their sophisticated architecture overwhelming, but those vast blue skies overhead never failed to soothe my brain—or reinforce how little truly separated our generations.

After absorbing all that I could from the relics, I'd spend days trying to place the memories on my broken timeline, mapping the lost world of our ancestors. Estimating time periods. Investigating inconsistencies. Overturning truths.

The books had become my lens to the world before the Crash, and I'd clung to them in hopes of confirming my suspicions about society: that once upon a time, life didn't revolve around war and marriage and childbirth. That before catastrophe, there'd been *more*.

And Mason had reduced them to combustion material.

I shot him a scathing look and stuffed the violated novels back in my bag. "We need to put out the fire. The smoke will betray our location."

Will shoved past him to bury the flames, and Fudge crouched to help me salvage what pages I could. I thanked him quietly and turned away to finish packing, stifling the frustrated tears that threatened to fill my eyes.

Nope. Nope. Nope. You cry, and you lose all clout.

You cry, and Mason wins.

And that can never, ever happen.

A cool, rocky hand dropped to my shoulder, and I glared at the phantom in wary silence. She didn't have a face, but somehow, she conveyed her sympathy.

Or it's all part of her ruse, my lizard brain supplied. *You don't know her intentions.*

"Don't you have a name?" Fudge asked her, his voice light and mellifluous, as if he were speaking to a child. "Can't we call you something?"

The demon angled her head, but I wasn't sure if it signaled confusion or deliberation. "Don't bother, Fudge." I slipped away from her ghostly touch and pushed to my feet. "You'll get attached."

I didn't want his heart to break after the spirit's inevitable perfidy.

"She doesn't seem to know what we're talking about," he went on, deaf to my griping. "If she's going to follow us all the way to Holly, we might as well give her a name."

"Pest?" I muttered.

Fudge examined the nymph for a few seconds, stroking his chin. "How about ... Sticks?"

"Isn't that a bit frank?"

"No, not Sticks, Mason. *Styx.* Like the river in Greek mythology. The boundary separating the underworld from Earth."

It seemed appropriate—as appropriate as naming any supernatural humanoid could be, anyway.

"Awesome," I said, slinging my pack over my shoulder. I faced our unbidden party member with a menacing scowl. "Cross us and you'll regret it, Styx."

She offered a sarcastic salute, and I knew she'd have flashed me a snarky grin if she possessed a face.

***

After hiking through the morning, we came to the edge of a tranquil meadow. Three enormous slabs of concrete rose from the field like some kind of giant, unoccupied exhibit. I stared at the mysterious art piece for a moment, wondering if the megalith served as a grave marker ... or perhaps an occult ritual site worth avoiding.

I'd always taken the rumors of Rhea's diablerie with a pinch of salt, but after yesterday, my frame of reference for the feasible and the unsound was broken, and I wasn't about to dismiss any explanation, even if the answer involved a coven of witches. For all I knew, Nova wasn't alone in her psychic abilities, and others like me existed in this space between cities, harboring memory-eating limbs under their clothes.

Right now, a closed mind promised a closed casket, so I planned to leave that barn door open.

Tooms the Talkless climbed a tree to assess our herd path, and the rest of us immediately planted our butts on the ground, passing around my waterskin and massaging our calves.

I had no idea how Will expected to pinpoint our location in the middle of the forest. Maybe he could spot the road from the treetop; maybe he had a compass built inside his brain, like a robot; or maybe he'd navigated the Range with his father before moving to Belgate, and he'd memorized the terrain. It was only speculation though—he refused to answer my questions.

I left to scavenge for food before the welt shimmied down his tree and dragged us back into the woods unfed, hoping my knowledge of agriculture and herbology would help me find something edible in our vicinity—or at a minimum, rule out any deadly varieties. My father was the stronger botanist between us, but he was busy putting those skills to use at the Southern Ridge.

At least ... I hoped he was.

I glared over my shoulder when Styx decided to tag along. Befriending me was likely the first goal in her assimilation plan: earn my trust and watch the others follow suit like susceptible guppies. But her paranormal brethren had just destroyed my city and slaughtered my peers. If she wanted my trust, she'd have to work a lot harder than that.

We ventured through the grove, and I struggled to shake off the uncanny feeling bubbling beneath my skin. Maybe it was the open space—we weren't concealed enough, it was daylight, those things were somewhere out there, coming after us. But the weight in my gut told me it was something else. Something worse.

After a brief search, I found a meaty blackberry bush at the base of a gully, and a flood of gratitude drowned my unease. Nova always brought blackberries home from her trips to the Interior, so I was relieved to find an unmistakable bramble. (I wasn't foolish enough to try the other colorful fruit nearby and risk poisoning the whole group. Not without Mason sampling them first.)

Styx helped me fill my pack to the brim, and we made it back to the others just as Will concluded his reconnaissance mission. As expected, he wore a somber look on his face while descending those final boughs, and it had me reconsidering my automaton theory. I'd read about the machines in Belgate's limited sci-fi collection: unemotional, proficient at every task, inability to socialize, no grasp of human kindness whatsoever. And it wasn't like any Belgate natives had witnessed the immigrant's birth; the boy could have very well spawned in a robotics lab.

I offered him some berries, but he just looked at me and sat down on a fallen log.

"You know, you could always say, 'no thanks' like a normal person," I said. "Even Mason knows his manners."

My attempt was met with a tired shrug. "No thanks."

I bit my lip to keep my insults unuttered, my disappointment concealed. After everything we'd faced in the arena together, I thought Will might've warmed up to me a little more by now. I'd been holding out hope that his hard, frozen corners would thaw on our journey east—that his cold exterior might melt away entirely—revealing a more approachable traveling companion.

But if I sought snowmelt, perhaps I needed to strike a match.

I sat beside him, my gaze raking over the meadow and the strange shapes towering above the grass. "What are they?" I asked quietly, so as not to engage Mason and his pretentious answers.

Will observed the crumbling walls with yet another emotion I couldn't decipher. "Ruins."

"...Of what?"

"A bunker vent? Or a logging station, maybe. Something the Ancients left behind."

"A cistern?" I offered, thinking about the water scarcity that drove our ancestors to war.

The smallest tick of his eyebrow told me he was impressed by the suggestion. "Could be."

"You think it was destroyed in the Crash?"

"That, or it was abandoned prior and left to the mercy of the elements."

That was an intriguing theory, but I had a feeling if I asked any more questions, Will might strangle me. I had to probe his android brain slowly, gingerly, like one might approach a wild buck. Any second he could dart away—or maul me with his hooves.

Fudge bumped my knee, raising his brow at the tentative robin a few feet away. The bird hopped forward, eyeing the berries in his palm and gauging the threat he posed. Fudge tossed it a seed, and the robin scrambled away from him with a shriek, fearing an attack on its life.

Snickering, Fudge cupped his hands over his mouth and whistled a complex series of chirps. A heartbeat later, the bird hopped closer with an identical warble, swayed by the trainee's multilingual skills.

"Who taught you that?" I gasped, amazed by his mimicry.

"Oh ... no one," Fudge admitted sheepishly. "I only know a few calls, but I practiced them over and over again until I got them just right."

I blinked at him, suddenly reminded of my mother and our time together in the orchard. She'd always pretend to speak to the birds to amuse me—whistling at magpies and laughing at their replies, exchanging gossip with the sparrows, singing with mourning doves. Sometimes I questioned if it had been an act at all, or if she'd descended from the mythical Dryads I'd read about.

Mason scoffed at his friend. "No wonder you flunked out of the Tournament; you spend all your free time whistling."

"Are you kidding, Mason? I took one look at those cannon balls and tossed the towel in. My bones would've snapped in half." His lips twitched. "And in case you forgot, we *both* flunked out."

He resumed his conversation with the robin, undeterred by Mason's relentless insolence—almost like it wasn't insolence at all, but rather some weird display of affection.

I threw an amused glance at Will, hoping to find him on the same wavelength, but he was just staring off into the meadow now, his brow furrowed. *Typical.*

With a pained sigh, I resumed my blackberry feast, watching Fudge develop rapport with his new little friend. He was so natural at it—being open, building trust. There were times I wished I emanated such agreeableness and honesty, that forming bonds with my peers was easy and safe and uncomplicated. But my curse made that impossible.

I couldn't *be* open and transparent, or my neck would find a gallows garland.

"What's that sound?" asked Mason, regarding the meadow with distaste.

Tense, I listened for signs of danger, but there was only a steady, whir-ring hum in the air—a hum any rancher would recognize.

"Rattlesnakes?" he guessed, fishing for his rapier.

I rolled my eyes. "Just grasshoppers, Mansion Boy. They're friendly."

They're singing, my mother would have said. *Singing for company.*

Fudge threw another berry at his feathered companion, and it vanished into the meadow's hedge. We both chuckled as the robin hobbled after it with comical hastiness.

"Where are the others?" Will murmured.

I glanced at him, unsure if he'd intended to speak aloud. "The other what?"

His dark eyes searched the pines, the skies, and an unpleasant chill kissed my spine at the wary expression on his face.

"...Birds?"

As soon as the word left his lips, the robin squealed from the depths of the grass, flapping its wings chaotically and staggering backward into the dirt. What I thought to be an overzealous game of fetch quickly turned hor-rific, and I watched, baffled and aghast, as a giant insect crawled up the robin's head, weighing the poor animal down and causing it to stumble. Then the winged creature scuttled around the bird's eyeball and forcefully wedged itself inside the socket.

In mere seconds, the robin toppled over, twitching and squawking as the grasshopper digested its brain.

When the insect returned to the meadow, thoroughly satiated, Fudge offered a wobbly, "Did that just ... happen?"

I rose to my feet and approached the humming grass, and as I peered out over the field, my stomach dropped to my boots.

Countless bones littered the meadow—a graveyard of rodent skulls, bird skeletons, and dried up, unidentifiable carcasses. Their flesh and or-gans were long gone, ribs licked clean and meatless. And there, nesting within the remains of the hapless, were thousands of squirming, thrumming locusts.

A plague.

We'd awakened a *plague*.

The ground vibrated beneath my boots, rumbling like the growl of a famished stomach. Then the grass began rustling with active inhabitants, and I spun for Will, hoping my expression would convey the urgent warning stuck in my throat: *run*.

16

The swarm of grasshoppers emerged from the meadow in one giant, rattling cloud of darkness. They formed an impenetrable mass, rolling across the landscape like an avalanche—a wheel of insects leaping, flying, and ravaging everything in their path.

The five of us dashed through the trees, hurdling over boulders, shrubs, and fallen logs. Undisturbed twigs and needles splintered beneath my boots like ancient bones, and the forest became a blur of yellow and green foliage. The swarm nipped at our heels, the backs of our necks, gaining distance on us with every passing second.

"*Just* grasshoppers?" Mason raged, and I smothered the urge to deck him with a pinecone.

A river roared somewhere nearby—a potentially hazardous obstacle we unanimously steered clear of, lest the grasshoppers trap us against the rapids. But if the insects had a ruse in store for us, I feared we wouldn't live long enough to see it. Not if Fudge kept tripping over his half-fastened boots.

As we raced down a leafy dell slope, a devil bug pounced onto my calf and drove its mandibles through my trousers, attempting to burrow into my flesh. Stumbling, I hacked at it with my knife before it could disappear beneath muscle tissue.

The swarm advanced, filling my periphery, and I hated to think I was running from carnivorous critters the size of my thumb. How far would these freaks-of-nature chase us? And how much longer could we maintain this pace?

"We need to shake them off somehow!" I shouted, flinching as another airborne monster sliced my cheek open—barely an inch below the crow's mark. My gaze fell to the pines on either side of me. "You think we can out-climb them?"

"May as well play dead!" Mason hollered back. "A treed animal is a dead animal."

I glared at his straw-colored head. "So is an exhausted one!"

Will veered for a mossy area that smelled like our compost bins back home. "Then let's switch environments."

It was the last place I'd ever consider a refuge, but I didn't hesitate. The four of us plunged into the slough, putting as much distance between us and the tapering ferns as possible. It was sickly warm, surprisingly deep, like a pool of Mother Nature's sweat, and I gagged as I sank to my ankles in slimy mud.

The demonic grasshoppers flew over our heads, leaping from bank to bank, from scalp to shoulder. I sank to my chin and covered my head with my arms, cursing as the locusts tore into me and tunneled through my hair. Will and Mason thrashed about with their knives drawn, and from the shoreline, Styx swung a tree branch around like a baseball bat, warding off the evil bugs and smashing their unlucky pals to hopper paste.

Where's a murder of crows when you need one?

"What do we do?" I tossed at the group, shielding my eyes from vicious mandibles.

Several grasshoppers miscalculated the distance and plopped into the swamp water beside me, frantically paddling for cattails or pitifully sinking into the shadows.

Will grunted, his own face a crosshatch of bloody nicks. He angled his head at me, raising his brow to expose the barren state of his 'sane idea' reserve. "How long can you hold your breath?"

My eyebrows shot up at the suggestion. He thought we could outsmart them by pretending to *drown*? "You think that'll work?"

"Worth a shot."

Mason fisted a pair of locusts by his ear and threw them across the swamp. "I'm not dunking my head in this *cesspool*—"

"On three!" Fudge decided, already halfway underwater. "Hold your breath as long as possible! First one up takes midwatch tonight."

"Are you deaf? I'm not—"

"Three," Will and I said together, and Mason swore as we all dropped into the murky, reedy depths of the slough.

Eyes shut, I listened to the dying thrum of insects overhead, securing a sweet reprieve in the stagnant water despite its unappealing temperature and opacity.

I held my breath long enough to trigger painful contractions in my lungs. Then, just as the pain grew unbearable, Will tapped my arm, and we surfaced together, gulping air.

Without visible prey, the swarm had thinned to all but a few determined stragglers, the remaining locusts waiting patiently at the edge of the inlet. The rest of their colony had seemingly grown bored of us and retreated to their hunting ground.

"Gross," Mason complained, wiping the algae off his face. "Just...gross. How many parasites just shot up my nose?"

"It's a good look on you, Mason," Fudge teased, snickering at his friend's drenched and muddy state. "The outdoors."

Will eyed me suspiciously, and I frowned at his accusatory expression. *What?*

"Is there a reason you're groping my leg?"

I gaped at him, and my innocent hands shot out of the water as fast as rainbow trout.

His gaze swiveled back to the murky space between us, his bothered expression now perturbed.

The attitude shift sent my blood straight back to my running muscles, and something brushed against my own leg a second later—something long and slick and mobile.

My stomach lurched. "Snakes."

The declaration straightened their spines, and Will drew his sword.

"Snakes ... *plural*?" Fudge squeaked.

I nodded. The muddy slough offered incredible camouflage, but the shivering vegetation and colliding ripples told me we had more than one reptile in our bathwater. The real question was if we'd simply encroached upon their territory, or if our bleeding bodies had drawn them away from their basking sites.

"Are you kidding me?" Mason cried, inching his way toward solid ground. "Why is everything out to kill us?"

Ten seconds later, I caught a glimpse of our host species: a black ribbon on brown glass, at least six ugly feet in length. But before I could alert the others, it dove back under the surface to conduct its attack, and fresh terror sluiced through my veins.

Snakes didn't scare me. Few critters did, really. But something I feared more than anything was navigating an invisible threat. I loathed waiting for an attack, unable to see or expect my enemy. And right now, I couldn't see a *thing*.

The water trembled beside me, and I held my breath, apprehension gnawing at my stomach lining. If these snakes were anything like their winged neighbors, we were in for a very dangerous swim.

"Where are they?" Mason mumbled. "I can't see a d—"

He vanished below the surface in one chaotic splash.

Fudge screamed his name, staring helplessly at the crime scene, and I started forward, swearing profusely at Mason's ineptitude. But three steps in, something seized my own ankle and tugged—violently.

Unprepared for the ambush, I lost my footing on the mud and crashed back into the water with a startled gasp.

***

Through a flurry of bubbles, I beheld dozens of jet-black snakes darting around the intestines of the swamp—spurts of ink and oil in a sea of mountain backwash. With Tom's knife, I hacked at the slimy tail squeezing my thigh, and black blood billowed up from the wound, wisps of liquid smoke around me.

Demons.

Mason writhed in a den of snakes a few yards away, completely enveloped in fleshy black coils. They mobbed him like minnows around bait, constricting him, weighing him down, pulling him to the deep.

I swam across a maze of reeds and algae, snatching black bodies and slicing their bellies open with a subaquatic languor. My lungs yearned for oxygen, but I pushed on, muffling my body's protests and ignoring the fire in my diaphragm.

Squinting against suspended sediment, muck, and organic matter, I cut through reptilian flesh as fast as I could, trying not to mutilate Mason as he flailed about. It cost me a few nasty bites on the wrist, but after an excruciating minute of underwater combat, I spied a glint of armor rising up, up, and out.

He'd escaped.

I kicked out to follow him, but the snakes began hounding me in a tangle of long, slick bodies—preventing my pursuit and avenging their fallen. The ones I carved apart were quickly replaced by their brothers, and they latched onto my legs like whip-chains, aggressively biting into my skin.

Not to defend themselves, but to kill.

My eyes stung miserably, and I blinked rapidly to maintain a shred of visibility, converting my experience into snapshots of black mesh, olive water, pressure, and pain. I thrashed to get them off, but the snakes held on, contracting around my arms, legs, and torso. The water itself seemed to drag me down and keep me there, thick and heavy with biofilm. My dark hair hovered above me in suspended coils, mocking my density, and I watched my pack slide off my shoulders and float up without me.

More bubbles escaped from my nose, constricting my chest cavity and placing even more stress on my respiratory system. I twisted desperately to get away, but my vision grew dimmer and dimmer with every passing second, my strength dissipating.

I was pinned to the mud. Sinking into the murk. Dying.

No. My eyes fluttered at the thought. *Not like this.*

You can't die like this.

I convulsed once—twice—and then, against every sensible voice in my head, I gave in to the pressure and let my breath out in a torrent of vapor.

My body tensed in response, preparing for the pain of the inhale. Preparing for the end.

Not like this...

Just as my world began to blacken, a beam of light speared my vision, sweeping over my face and drowning body. Miraculously, the snakes scattered away, and a hand grabbed the lip of my breastplate, pulling me upward.

I broke the surface, coughing and hacking up swamp life.

Will wrapped his arm around my waist and heaved me out of the slough, an irate Mason clearing the path ahead. Behind me, Fudge aimed my flashlight at the snakes keen on following us, and they reeled back at the slightest graze of contact, the briefest sting of light.

Leaning on Will, I thrust my knife back in its sheath and shuffled with my party to the safety of the woods, grateful to be free of the demonic pests. I glanced back at the landmark to curse its existence, but the slough had already reverted to a still pool of water, perfectly normal. Seemingly innocuous.

When we'd gained ample distance, I collapsed onto a patch of level ground, refusing to budge again until the metallic taste in my mouth went away. Accepting my respite, Will propped me up against a tree, and I thanked him with my aching eyes.

It felt like I'd swallowed a clew of leeches, and the thought was so disturbing, I forced myself to speak, if only to kill the notion. "The flashlight really freaked them out," I panted, practically wheezing between every syllable, but grateful for an unclogged larynx. "Who thought of that?"

Fudge removed a tangle of swamp entrails from my hair. "When Styx appeared, the grasshoppers made this weird circle around her. She was trying to hit them with her tree branch, but they wouldn't get close enough, like her light burned them or something. I thought it might work with artificial light too."

"Smart."

"*Lucky.*" He offered a small smile. "Are you okay? You were under forever."

I shrugged, eyeing Styx and her throbbing yellow light. She rocked back and forth on her heels, as if she expected some kind of personal thank you. "I'm fine."

"No, you're not," said Will. He raked the wet hair out of his eyes, exposing his hairline and eyebrows, and I fought the urge to stare. I'd never seen him with his bangs back before; he looked a lot less menacing with a forehead.

He yanked up my shirt sleeves, revealing about a dozen different snake bites and locust wounds—a massacre of my smooth, tanned skin. I hadn't felt much before, riding out the adrenaline, but now that I had eyes on the damage, the throbbing pain hit me all at once.

"Venomous?" I got out.

If they were, I was *so* dead.

Will squeezed my arm, ignoring my flinch. Dots of red pooled in areas of punctured flesh, and a queasy Fudge proceeded to check his own appendages for similar markings. "Not sure. Water snakes in this region aren't typically venomous, and there isn't any swelling or discoloration yet ... but I'd rather err on the side of caution." He took my pack from Fudge and extracted one of my soaking shirts from the berry pile. Then, without a hint of remorse, he began ripping the material into long, ragged strips.

I didn't protest, but it made me question if all boys possessed a penchant for tearing my belongings to pieces.

He lightly wrapped the cloth above my observable wounds and any additional places I believed I'd been bitten. It would limit lymphatic flow, he said, and hopefully, any death-related consequences.

"Do you feel dizzy? Nauseous?" he asked.

I shook my head, wiping traces of demon blood from my brow.

Unsatisfied with my response, Will hooked his hands under my knees and pushed my legs to my chest. Then he draped my arms over my kneecaps to keep them level with my heart. "Are you just saying that?"

"I'm fine," I insisted. "Pester over Mason. He thinks he's got hypoxia."

Mason, voicing some unintelligible dispute, sat next to me so Will could tend to him as well, and we looked each other over. Brown water trickled down the welt's long, angular face, his chest heaving with exertion, and I swore I caught a flicker of humility in his expression.

"You saved my life," he murmured.

It sounded more like an accusation than an expression of gratitude, but I nodded anyway. "Let's not make it a regular thing."

17

The fish squirmed as I removed my custom thorn-hook.

To avoid soaking my gloves in fish guts, I'd stuffed the garments in my pocket, confident I could handle the fidgeting food with the pads of my fingers. But as the blood spilled over my hands, running down my knuckles like the juice of an overripe peach, I knew I'd made a terrible mistake.

Too slick to handle properly, the fish slid into my palm, and I gagged at the sputtering images in my brain. The fear. The disorientation. The torture.

Sympathy pains flared in my bones, in my throat, and I swore at my error. How could I survive a *war* if hunting triggered an episode? How could I kill demons with human faces if I couldn't even gut a fish?

Get it together, Al.

Will stared at me from the riverbank, and I threw him an irritated look.

"What?" I snapped, trembling slightly. The images were too intense, too bright. All I knew in this moment was birth, life, predation, and suffocation—a sequence captured from the harried lens of a survivor.

Will didn't say anything as he approached me. He just grabbed the writhing fish out of my hands, slammed its head against a rock, and sliced its belly open to prepare the filets himself. Calmly and effortlessly, as he conducted most affairs.

I swallowed, backing away from the river.

I was relieved he'd taken over, but my own hesitation disturbed me, and I couldn't let the group see how rattled I was.

"I ... need some air."

"Alex, we're in the woods," said Fudge, his voice tinged with concern, but I was already marching for the pines.

I should've killed that fish immediately, the way Will had, before its pain and suffering penetrated my skin. A quick death, and I could've thanked it for its sacrifice and carried on with my evening. The dead bore no emotions, after all—I'd learned that the hard way.

I turned left, deciding to walk along the meandering river to help calm my nerves. Its pathway mimicked a giant serpent, its thick and lazy currents pushing across the surface like shimmering scales. At its center, deep greens melted into cool grays, the colors glistening with caliginous daylight, and something about the peaceful setting made me want to stop here and paint it, despite my abysmal art skills.

That's exhaustion for you, Al.

Fatigue has deluded you into thinking you could capture this beauty in any way, shape, or form.

After our run-in with demonic wildlife, we'd avoided tall grass and stagnant water at all costs. Toomsday had led our party through the trees, glancing back at Mason and me every half-mile to make sure we hadn't keeled over yet. Fudge, meanwhile, had become the chief of the flashlight, and I was glad he'd found something to contribute, even if it was powered by an ancient saltwater battery.

We'd traveled uphill for hours, and despite the incline's strain on my sore and tender muscles, it felt wonderful to stretch the parts of my body I rarely could back in Belgate. Only two sloped roads cut through my district, and save for the top of the arena staircase, the city didn't offer much of a view. It was like the base of an unwashed bowl: flat, filthy, and crusted by forbidden hills.

So, aside from the near-death experiences we'd acquired thus far—and the sticky, sweaty layer of swamp skin—the forest offered a nice change in scenery.

I craned my neck to peer around a mess of boulders, gnarled tree roots, and eroded riverbank. In the clearing beyond, the group had taken to setting up a fire pit while Will carved himself a cooking skewer. Styx watched him chisel away at the tree branch, enchanted by his handiwork.

"I'm gonna take a dip, so don't come upstream unless you want your eyeballs ripped from their sockets," I announced. They scoffed at the threat, but they unanimously rotated away from me to grant me some privacy—urgently so, in Mason's case.

Wandering to a pool that didn't contain any demonic abnormalities, I began peeling off my armor, and as much as I hated the prospect of wet underclothes, skinny dipping just didn't feel safe here. I had no idea what lurked in the shadows of these woods, and I didn't want Styx's creepy friends watching me bathe.

Half-dressed, I took a moment to inspect my grasshopper wounds and snake bites, worried they might have introduced tetanus to my body—or something equally appalling—but most of the puncture wounds had faded away by now.

Really, I just hoped their rabid donors weren't venomous; I did *not* have the patience to die a slow and painful death.

I subjected my left foot to the river first, testing for hypothermic temperatures or paranormal flesh-eating bacteria. At this elevation, the water was ice cold, but it appeared safe enough to swim in, and the mud on my scalp, between my toes, and beneath my nails made the plunge an easy choice.

I waded in, sucking in sharply at how quickly my body lost all feeling, and after convincing myself that standing there stupidly, halfway in, had no benefits, I sank to my collarbone and dunked my head.

My cells split open, and I screamed into the frigid veins of the mountain.

We only had a small, flat, noodle of a river back in Belgate. It was shallow and muddy and gentle enough for the kids to swim in on summer afternoons—the perfect place to catch fish and tadpoles and bullfrogs. But it was nothing like this.

My muscles contracted, warding off the ice water like a fortress barricading itself against attack. Beyond its shock-inducing temperatures, though, the bath was refreshing, its endorphin-rush rejuvenating, and as I scrubbed the swamp life and fish juice from my skin, I closed my eyes, listening to the stream gurgle and spit and howl around me.

My mother used to sing about alpine rivers. She'd hum the tune when she gardened. When she washed the produce. When she harnessed my wild, tangled hair into a braid before bed.

> *I am the river, the river is me.*
> *I care not for cities, or towns, or levees.*
> *I flow how I wish, and I choose where to be.*
> *Oh, I am the river, the river is me.*

> *I am the river, the river is me.*
> *And many a person comes looking for me.*
> *The humble, the gracious, I share life with thee—*
> *But to greedy exploiters, I show no mercy.*

She'd crafted dozens of unique verses for the song, and building new, creative—and often *ridiculous*—couplets had become our favorite pastime. Sometimes her witty poetry had me laughing so hard my stomach ached for hours.

She'd always known how to turn a frightening situation on its head.

Proposing a silly game. Breaking into song. Making up a story she knew I'd dissect to pieces. She was the giggle that broke up a spell of solemn silence ... and I could really use that giggle right about now.

Just a few hours ago, I'd kissed the grave. I'd nearly died at the base of a slough, murdered by a den of snakes with an untarnished sword at my hip. And what a lousy legacy I'd have left behind—a failed mission the Court would inevitably use to reinforce the Gender Clause and a heartbroken, disappointed father.

Embarrassing.

And though the event hadn't killed me, it *had* unearthed dreadful memories of my childhood traumas. One horrific evening, to be exact.

The blackness sweeping in, the compression, the asphyxia.

The well, the rain, the mud.

I shuddered, beating the memory to shreds with positive affirmations. I was okay now. I wasn't confined to a well; I wasn't trapped in a snake pit. I was living and breathing and bathing in a river, all because of my male peers and a rusty flashlight.

It was odd, feeling grateful for a group of teenage boys. But Fudge and Will had worked together to save me from that hellish swamp. And for some unfathomable reason, I'd saved *Mason*.

I opened my eyes underwater, impressed by the clarity. The gentle current carried golden leaves, riparian debris, and silver flecks of sediment down the winding, rocky channel. Insects and tiny critters swam past me, expressing little to no interest in human flesh, and I envied them for their obliviousness. These river creatures were isolated from the rest of the world, unaware of the chaos on the surface and the horrors beyond. Unable to comprehend the threat of extinction and the perils of war.

In a way, I understood why Ellsian officials kept the nature of our enemy under wraps. Living in ignorance was peaceful, and while that illusion had cost us dearly, it had also spared military families unimaginable pain and sorrow. We thought we'd sent our fathers, brothers, and sons to war, not assured eradication. But Will was right; if we'd known the truth, our mental state would have crumbled, and societal productivity soon after.

Now, with the veil lifted, every red leaf and iron-rich stone reminded me of Gilmore's bloody corpse. Every swooping bird of prey made me flinch. And that old, splintering heartache had returned now that I knew my brother's body was not feeding the soil, but likely serving his enemies. Meanwhile, folks in the Interior still lived such beautiful, clueless lives, totally blind to their impending paradigm shift.

They were lucky to hold on to those dreams a little longer.

I lifted my head from the water, breathing in the crisp evening air and the scent of dying wildflowers. The gray sun had dipped behind the treetops now, leaving behind a smoky haze and an eerie sense of kenopsia. But as a cool mountain breeze tickled the water, I got that uneasy feeling again—the one that revived all the dead butterflies in my stomach.

"Guys?" I called into the quiet. "Is everything okay?"

The world was calm, ostensibly normal, just like it had been moments before the insect attack. And not a soul disturbed its silence.

I swam toward the closest tree trunk, crouching in the shallow water beneath its long, drooping branches. "... *Guys?*"

18

A number of possibilities came to mind:

    A) They were ignoring me.

    B) They took my warning to heart.

    C) The grasshoppers had dined at last.

Then I heard a loud splash a few yards away, closer to our campsite. A grunt. The sound of metal scraping rock. And two more splashes.

I peeked over the side of the tree trunk and swore under my breath. Two armed figures waded down the river, flanking the deep belly of the snake. They wore old brown and navy military uniforms, muddied and bloodstained. Black veins marbled their flaking skin, and like their ruthless brothers in Belgate, they peered through eyes with no irises or visible sclera. Just gray film spanning canthus to canthus.

I pressed myself against the mossy tree roots, struggling to stifle my panic. My belongings remained on the opposite side of the river: my clothes, my sword, my gloves. I couldn't collect them without being spotted, and even if I managed to seize my weapon in time, I had little faith in my ability to defend myself from militant demons.

Gritz. They were wading closer. They were going to find me sitting here, exposed and defenseless. I needed cover. *Now.*

I slid up out of the water, grateful for the rush of the river to muffle my movements.

"He came this way," a new arrival said, his voice gravelly and haunting, like the infernal growl of a thousand hellhounds. The creature appeared across the water, almost in direct sight of me. He hadn't registered my presence yet, but it wouldn't take him long to spot my tan skin against this dark, saturated backdrop. With a weapon that size, it wouldn't take him long to kill me, either. "I can sense him ... and another."

Just when I thought things couldn't possibly get any worse, a monstrous claw clamped over my mouth, silencing my gasp and tipping me backward. My hand flew to my face to pry the demon off, but a second appendage looped around my chest to clamp my elbows down. Within his restrictive embrace, my fingers barely grazed his wrist.

The soldier pulled my body backward into the shrubbery, and after a moment of terrorized paralysis, I tossed my shock to the floor and began thrashing about, shoving, kicking, twisting. Prepared to bite my way through if I had to. *Fight. Fight it off!*

However, I quickly realized the rigid claw was, in fact, a hand. A warm, *calloused* hand with all five knuckles wrapped in fighting tape.

I stopped fidgeting at once and gazed cautiously, and a bit sheepishly, behind me.

Will glared at me from the shadow of the thicket and slowly lifted his palm from my mouth. Holding a stern finger to his lips, he peered around the bush to better assess our stalkers.

My focus deteriorated under the direct heat of his body—his warm hands on my ribcage and bicep, his leather breastplate kissing my shoulder blades. He didn't seem aware of my state of undress, nor the humiliating heat that colored my cheeks. Or maybe he just purposely ignored my sodden underclothes, their mismatched colors and fraying threads.

I *did* threaten to rip out his eyeballs.

A minute later, he restored the distance between us and motioned for me to stay put. Then, like an elusive forest animal, he crept back into the maze of aspens and disappeared without a word.

I stared after him, appalled by his horrendous communication skills. Did I look like an obedient house pet, or was this an "only-child" defect?

I stood there in scraps of poorly sewn linen, dripping wet in the camouflage of the bushes, waiting anxiously to see what Will would do.

Would he attack them alone?

Would he bring Styx?

Where were Fudge and Mason?

I couldn't believe the worry I felt for this endeavoring, ragtag team of mine. But if I lost them now—even with our bonds so unripe—I'd be all alone, and for once in my life, that solitude terrified me.

I didn't want to face this scary, confusing world all by myself. And based on today's hazardous incidents, I wasn't so sure I *could*.

The demons resumed their search, nostrils flaring like hunting hounds who'd lost their scent. The closest beast could have passed for an alien; he boasted a pointed skull, fingers twice as long as human digits, and an abnormally long torso. Even his skin was torn apart by the vile spirit within him, forming a lattice of melted cheese across raw and ruined flesh.

Stretch, I'd call him.

His comrades approached him, and they snarled in low whispers, aggravated by their laborious pursuit. Stretch raised his hand to silence them, then pointed at the riverbank and my suspicious pile of belongings.

Well then.

Time to skedaddle.

I took one deliberate step backward, and those dead, silver eyes instantly zeroed in on my position. *There she is*, the gaze said, and the cruel smile that followed tugged at every hair on my body.

All three demons turned to face me, ready to capture, kill, or consume. I couldn't tell which, and quite frankly, I had no intention of finding out.

I stared them down, my palms clammy, my toes curling into the muddy bank for traction. I'd evaded them as long as possible; this encounter now boiled down to fight or flight. And I was *tired* of running.

Eyeing my things on the other side of the river, I snatched a tree branch off the ground and rushed the triad.

Stretch found this amusing. He swung his sword at my face, and I ducked, feeling the weapon whip past my damp head with a lethal swiftness. Raising my hefty stick, I countered his vicious second blow, and he looked outright baffled when his blade struck wood.

The move offered a temporary victory, but it also brought me dangerously close to my unsightly enemy. Relying on a technique Tom had once demonstrated, I whacked him in the temple with the butt of my tree branch. *Twice.*

The demon stumbled back, dizzy and perplexed, and I dashed away before he had the chance to recover. But his friends were already closing in on me, seeking to trap me here against the current and deliver my flesh to the river trout.

One demon bore a face of inky veins and pulpy, tarnished skin, almost like he'd been boiled alive. He also carried a lengthy spear, and he appeared very ready to lodge it through my skull.

I didn't even realize they still *made* spears, and I had no idea how to fend off such a weapon.

The second, not unlike a hairless Bigfoot, cracked his knuckles so loud I thought he'd dislocated his shoulder.

"The human child thinks she stands a chance," Stretch taunted, wading up behind me. "Isn't that precious …"

My stomach dropped to the slippery river rocks. I was surrounded on all sides and cornered by three apex predators—much like yesterday's trial. Only tonight, I was freezing, barefoot, and fresh out of climbable platforms.

Pulpy looked me over, laughing to himself in a way that was entirely inhuman. "Look at her stance. She thinks she can kill us with her bare hands."

Before I could show them exactly that, a rock whizzed past my ear and lodged itself in the middle of his friend's egregious forehead. The assault knocked Stretch flat—a felled tree crashing into the river—and I let out a squeak of frightened amusement.

I turned to catch a glimpse of Will spinning through the air, a steel blade in either hand. Mid-jump, he sliced the two demons' throats open in one smooth arc and, incredibly, landed on sturdy feet in shin-deep water. As graceful and unruffled as ever.

Their limp bodies splashed into the river, demon blood polluting the watershed like bitumen.

Alrighty.

So much for Pulpy and Titan, then.

I stared at Will, not sure what to say in the wake of his gallant intervention. He trudged through ice water to join me, eyes locked on Stretch and his submerged, unmoving body. Styx stood behind him, composed of mulch and water particles, and a ring of jagged throwing stones swirled two inches above her palm.

You're welcome, her faceless expression said.

Will handed my sword over wordlessly, and I winced at the images the weapon projected. Violent memories and Tournament conquests burned against my bare hands, flashes of scalding white light contaminating my vision. I let the guard rest against my fingertips to alleviate the pain, but fighting this way would be damn near impossible.

"You okay?" he asked, the question accompanied by a cursory glance.

I commanded my senses to refocus before the sword's associated memories triggered tears. "Superb."

Stretch clambered to his feet, wiping the blood and water from his dented forehead. Wet clothing hugged his corpse-like body, weighing him down, and it made me yearn for my armor a little less.

He regarded us first with a timid air, and then his eyes flashed to our weapons, and he smiled. "You can't kill us with your primitive toys."

Will narrowed his eyes, and I mirrored his response. Was he blind? We had swords now—I'd ditched my broken tree branch. There was nothing *primitive* about this altercation.

"What are you—?" Will faltered at the soft splash behind us, and a terrible feeling crawled up my spine and over my shoulder.

I twisted around to confirm my irrational fears, then recoiled at the inconceivable.

The enemies Will had cut down were moving again. Like Nova's mystical poppets, they rose from the water—knees, hips, bellies, shoulders. But unlike the bodies we'd exsanguinated, these soldiers were once again intact, their necks mended and healed, their heads firmly reattached.

And very much alive.

19

Will and I stepped away from the enduring trio, taking in the insanity of this moment and the futility of our actions.

I instantly thought of the snakes in the slough, their numbers seemingly infinite, their energy unyielding. But those serpents hadn't multiplied like single-celled organisms, and I hadn't stumbled into a bottomless nest of demons. They'd been *healing* themselves, regenerating again and again. Never fatally wounded. Never killed.

My heart thundered. Belgate fell as quickly as it did not because of our ineptitude, but because these creatures couldn't *die*.

Will's throat bobbed, and we exchanged tense glances. With him and Styx beside me, we were evenly matched, but how could we possibly defeat immortal beings?

We can't, my brain purled. *There's a reason these demons invaded Ells to begin with. They obliterated our defenses so thoroughly that not a single warning reached Belgate in time. We lost this war the moment they crossed the Rim.*

Styx moved first, surprising everyone. She shot after Pulpy as a ten-foot water avatar, attempting to envelop him in her body and drown him in her chest cavity like a sentient tsunami.

Properly motivated, Will made for Stretch, initiating his duel with a casual sword flourish, like he'd used the weapon for real battles countless times. Like he wasn't a rookie.

That left the large one for me.

Grunting, Titan surged forward, and I sprinted out of the way, afraid to engage in combat with something so massive and indestructible. Each of his steps swallowed two-and-a-half of mine, but I tried not to focus on that disheartening detail as he barreled toward me, removing the colossal scimitar from his back scabbard.

I managed to avoid him for a few more seconds by luring him into my swimming hole, where he sank several feet into the clay and nearly lost his balance. But he was too big, too fast, and I was running out of riverbed. Before I knew it, he'd caught up with me, and without boots to traverse the rockier half of the tributary, I had nowhere left to turn.

Gnashing my teeth together, I brought my sword up to his falling blade, and I dug my feet into the gravel, flinching as steel kissed steel.

Merciless, he drove me backward, his cuts too powerful, too heavy, too deep. My hands burned with old images of past contestants and Tournament trials, and I could hardly see straight.

Eventually, my bruised heels hit the riverbank—the sign of a battle lost—and I cursed the Fates. Mustering a final lap of courage, I kicked off the shoreline to meet Titan's next strike, determined to make him bleed before he killed me.

Our collision sent a violent tremor up my arms, and the angle created a bind between us, our swords at an impasse as they slid against one another with equal tension. Titan leaned in over our crossed weapons, his weight making my bones tremble, and I used all my strength to keep the scimitar from cleaving me in half.

Reduced to a crouch now, I sank into the river margin, one hand on the hilt and one on the blade, its blunt edge drawing blood. My flimsy Tourny sword was the only thing keeping my neck from teeth of sharp steel, and my opponent knew it. He grinned down at his sealed victory, pushing me further into the mud.

I spared a helpless glance at Will, but Stretch claimed his undivided attention. They were both wicked quick on their feet, delivering effective parries and ripostes even in thigh-high water, and I knew any distraction to that blizzard of thrusts and lunges would prove deadly.

I thought about calling for Styx, but she was further upriver and fully absorbed in the task of harassing her foe. She wouldn't get here in time.

I was on my own.

Titan backed off, granting me a second of momentary relief before he brought the scimitar down like a battle axe. My teeth clanked, and the force of his blow snapped my sword three inches above the hilt—a clean and shocking break. His blade impaled the wet earth beside my ear, and my petrified gaze traveled over two halves of a useless weapon.

Just like that, he'd left me swordless, hopeless, and completely defenseless.

No, Al, my defiant heart echoed. *Not completely.*

Titan bent down to yank his sword from the clay, his fat demon hands too close to my face, his wet, grimy fingers clasping the hilt of his curved weapon.

My window was closing. I had no other choice.

In a fit of desperation, I closed my icy palms over his.

***

Searing pain erupted throughout my body, and a flash of blazing light engulfed my mind, overwhelming every sensation, every nerve. Faintly, I heard Titan's roar enmeshed in a scream that might have been my own, and our union burned in my hands and my eyes and the metaphysical. But as the light faded, it also severed all ties to reality and the present moment, and I stumbled down a tunnel of timeless white ether.

Within the blinding nothingness, a series of images passed by too quickly to snatch or construe. A montage of fire, war, and carnage. And just when I thought I might puke from the grotesque disorder, a beautiful woman appeared amidst the chaos—a life raft in a vast, tumultuous sea. She wore a gown that matched the color of my burned retinas, and pink flowers adorned her auburn hair.

She was laughing at something in the distance, her cheeks rosy, her eyes glistening. It was one of those laughs that made you smile without context, without reason. A belly laugh straight from the heart.

The scene changed, and I was now walking away from a tiny brick house, glancing over my shoulder at a group of blurry faces and fuzzy figures. They stood in the yard waving goodbye, young children sitting on their shoulders or clutching their legs. Children who would forever ask themselves, *what if?*

Someone remained off to the side, shadowed by a willow tree, and though I couldn't make out the individual's face, I suspected it was the same woman as before.

Despite its simplicity, the clip was emotionally jarring. So much so, it left a throbbing pain in my bones—a despairing longing inside me. And when the memory finally vanished, I'd contracted a terrible hole in my gut, a hole festering with sadness and anguish and regret.

Crippling guilt, my body translated. You know it well.

I felt a sharp, foreign tug on my sternum then, as if someone had tried to pluck a rib from my torso, and I opened my eyes.

Titan stared down at me, his rotten face just inches away, our hands still linked on the scimitar. Shock and fury swam in his monstrous eyes, along with an emotion I couldn't quite place.

A beat later, black fluid filled his scleras, and he fell backward into the water, collapsing into the riverbed with a heavy, resounding splash.

I sat motionless in the clay, gaping at where the demon had stood just moments before, my hands clutching at air.

"Alex?" Will called, and his voice sent me plummeting back to earth. He and Styx had paused to stare at me in amazement—then my opponent's enormous corpse floating downriver.

I tottered to my bleeding feet, queasy and disoriented. "I think I knocked him unconscious," I lied. "He'll find his way back."

Stretch narrowed his eyes at me, and my whole body shuddered at his perceptive gaze. But if the demon knew the truth, he didn't reflect on it long. He launched himself at Will again, and I ran to fetch my knife and boots from the riverbank.

I hastily pulled on my gloves to hide the pulsing crescents on my palms. To push away the memory of what I'd done. To mask what I was.

Focus, Al.

Will was in trouble. He might have kept pace with Stretch until now, but I could tell he was losing steam. He needed out of this stalemate, and he wasn't alone. Despite Styx's waterboarding regimen and finned projectiles, a river trout could only inflict so much damage upon a self-healing demon.

This wasn't going to work. We couldn't hold them off forever, and my curse had all but drained me of cortisol. If I attempted that stunt a second time, Titan might not be the only one kissing the current.

I glanced at Will again, watching him chop off his opponent's arms before the demon could grow them back again—anything to run the clock while he reevaluated his approach. Somehow, he'd managed to stay relatively dry and uninjured, but his movements had grown sluggish, and a black layer of demon blood coated his skin and clothes.

As he pivoted to avoid a river boulder, I noticed my traveling pack slung over his shoulders, and I jolted.

"Will. Backpack!"

He ducked, avoiding a fatal slash to the forehead. "*Now?*"

"Now!"

He didn't bother pushing me for details. He simply shrugged the pack off his shoulders and tossed it my way so swiftly, so adeptly, he was already back to maiming Stretch by the time I caught it—too busy torturing his opponent to notice my awestruck expression. Sloshing out of range, I yanked the bag open and plunged my arm into a mushy pit of waterlogged books and blackberry jam.

The problem we faced was our inability to kill our opponents, but we didn't *need* to kill them. We just needed to evade them long enough to survive our trek to Holly.

I held up the tangle of rope for Will to see, and his eyes brightened. He nodded at me, agreeing to my unspoken plan, and a few parries later, he drove his sword through the demon's armpit, puncturing his poisoned heart.

Wasting no time, we seized Stretch's limp body and dragged him through the water to an adjacent tree. Styx, catching on to our ploy, drowned her victim one last time and sent Pulpy's bludgeoned body downriver for delivery.

"Bind them!" Will shouted, and the two of us pinned the groaning demons to the tree trunk as Styx untied the hank. She promptly dissolved into river mist and sped around the tree in stormy circles, fastening the demons to the bark with multiple knots and hitches. In seconds, our enemies were anchored to the cottonwood, spitting up water and fish food.

Stretch writhed against his restraints, attempting to break free, but the rope only tightened further, mocking his efforts. I retrieved his weapon from the pebbled river floor, winking at him over my shoulder, and his vengeful snarl made me grin.

I followed Will to the demon-free side of the river. "Do you think that'll hold them?"

"Not sure, but it should buy us some time." He cast me an approving side-eye. "The rope was a good idea."

His praise was as startling as it was flattering; a compliment from William Tooms was scarcer than sunshine. "Well, I'm full of surprises."

"I wasn't surprised," he corrected. "You're resourceful."

My cheeks warmed, and I stashed his comments away for future rumination.

Honestly, I'd lucked out with every *resource* thus far. The flashlight had mere minutes of life left, and I'd packed the bundle of rope on the off chance I'd have to rappel down a cliff or fashion a lean-to. I never thought I'd use it to apprehend demon soldiers.

Correction: *immortal* demon soldiers.

I was afraid to ask the question, but I needed to know. "Fudge and Mason?"

"Captured. They were out collecting firewood when the demons found us. I heard a scream, but I was too late." He tossed me my clothes— a stark reminder that I'd just fought off a group of river demons half-naked—and my face grew even hotter. "The party split. A group of them took Fudge and Price, and the others stayed to hunt us down."

"Where did they take them?"

He tipped his head at the pine trees. "They headed back the way we came. Probably have a camp set up a few miles west of here."

A few *miles*?

I stepped closer, my heart bleeding at the thought of those evil creatures holding Fudge captive—or worse, killing him so they could turn his corpse into an unrecognizable combatant. "We have to go after them."

He glanced at me again, grim, and that single look conveyed a thousand rational arguments.

I knew the risks. I *knew* the boys were likely dead by now. But I made a promise to Fudge, and I wouldn't abandon him to a bunch of decomposing barbarians. "We can't just leave them behind," I appealed. "And I know it's stupid and dangerous, and that we're running out of time, and that

Holly is depending on us, but we *have* to—"

"I know."

My speech disintegrated on my tongue, my lips twitching without sound. I really hadn't expected him to agree so easily. Not when it came to saving his infuriating rival.

He stared at me with another inscrutable expression, and I couldn't tell if it was exasperation or respect that shimmered in those brookite irises. "We're wasting daylight, and that demon is still somewhere down-river." His eyes flicked impatiently over my damp clothes and away. "Hurry up and get dressed."

20

Will and I crouched behind a thick manzanita bush, peering through its twisted red bark to the campsite beyond.

The demons had chosen a small glade for the night, the wild grass flattened beneath discarded travel packs, weaponry, and firewood. At the center of camp, a large fire boasted the same crimson flame they'd torched my home with, and I didn't appreciate the cat-shaped carcass that roasted above it—or its stench.

A dozen soldiers occupied the base, arguing with each other and sharpening their blades. There was a sense of accomplishment in the air, and no one seemed particularly concerned about the three huntsmen who'd failed to return before sundown. Perhaps they couldn't fathom a scenario in which their comrades had lost, or maybe they just didn't care.

"There," I whispered, pointing to a head of soft curls protruding from a tree stump. Shuffling as far as the manzanita crown would allow, I could just make out Fudge and Mason's profiles. Their limp bodies were slumped against one another, their hands and feet bound with rope. But I couldn't detect any movement from here, and it shoved a stone down my throat. "Are they ... alive?"

"They shouldn't be," Will said, and I passed him a dark look. "I mean ... what's the incentive? Why spare them?"

"You think it's a trap?"

"Maybe."

A large ghoul skirted the edge of the camp, axe in hand. He looked like he'd made his own concoction of leeches and potato beetles and slathered it all over his face, basking in his title of the Ugliest Demon on Earth.

As he approached our hiding spot, Will and I ducked in tandem, pressing ourselves to the floor of pine needles. The shadow paused in front of the shrubbery, and I heard him sniff the air like an animal. Scrounging the perimeter for fresh meat.

Catching wind of something, he moved closer, glaring into the forest. One more step and he'd spot us. One more step, and my journey ended with a question mark.

Keep moving, Hideous...

Frigid water dripped down my spine—the consequence of swimming in snowmelt—and I had to hold my jaw in place to keep my teeth from chattering. But after several painfully long seconds, the demon moved on, and I released a loaded exhale, unclenching every muscle in my body.

"What do we do with them?" a crew member demanded. He jerked his chin at Fudge and Mason, and my heart skipped a beat.

Alive, then.

A demon with a shredded ear waved his hand, as if he were shooing away the subject. He was not the oldest corpse among them, but he carried the weight of authority, and the others looked to him as he spoke. "We should send them back."

"What, back to *Belgate*?" a third creature balked. "That's too much effort. Why not dust our hands of them?"

"He told us to capture all the able-bodied," Earlobe replied, his voice pulled taut like a tug-of-war rope—unwilling to give an inch.

"*He* isn't here. He wouldn't know."

"Exactly!"

Earlobe scoffed at his subordinates. "You're fools if you think he doesn't have eyes on all of us. The skies are watching."

Yeah. I did *not* like the sound of that.

Hideous turned to face his comrades. "He sent us to find the escapees and scout the area, and that's what we've done. We're not responsible for contender output."

I glanced at Will, puzzled by their jargon. *Contender?*

As they bickered on about the fate of their hostages, my brow furrowed at their evident anthropomorphism. Our enemy followed a chain of command. They spoke our language. They even spoke of strategy. It dawned on me that these evil spirits were not storybook monsters on the loose. They were organized—sophisticated. And that meant they were far more dangerous than we'd been led to believe.

A warm breeze tickled my shoulder, and I scowled, pivoting to acknowledge our new arrival and her conspicuous light source. The nymph squeezed herself between Will and me, taking up an unnecessary amount of space behind the bush, and I rolled my eyes.

"Nice of you to join us," I praised, shoving my pack into her chest to conceal her glowing heart.

She flickered once in response, returning my sass, but she looped her leafy arms through the backpack anyway, wearing the bag backwards to block out her eternal night light.

It might've been endearing if she weren't so obnoxious.

"Who cares if we lose a few," another demon grumbled, seizing my attention once again. His white eyes glowed like gold coins in the firelight. "Let's dust our hands of them; the lions need to feed."

My lungs shuddered on my exhale. The *what.*

My gaze soared across the campsite again, begging for a lie. But this time, I spotted the huddle of tan bodies I'd previously mistaken for a pile of furs. The three demon cats lounged beneath a pine tree at the far end of camp. Chained and collared. Bored and hungry.

Why?

Why had these dummies brought those feral beasts along? To track us? To eat us? Or did they plan to unleash them on the citizens of Holly?

My gaze swerved back to our peers with fresh urgency. "Let's go."

Will snatched my wrist before I could rise from my crouch, huffing at my impulsivity. "We need a plan."

"Okay, so a distraction then? Like in the arena?"

"Maybe, but all twelve won't storm off for some bait."

Part of me wanted to run in there with the flashlight and hope for the best, but I was pretty sure Fudge's "Holy Beacon of Light" wouldn't get us very far this time around. Somehow, we'd have to save our companions from unkillable enemies with no climbing rope, no sloughs, and no *deus ex machina*.

And to think that just a few hours ago, flesh-eating bugs had been our biggest problem!

My eyes widened. "The bugs," I breathed, swatting at Will as two trains of thought collided. "The killer crickets!"

He shushed me, exasperated.

"I can lead the demons to the hopper field," I explained, the plan stitching itself together and forming an appealing, achievable pattern. "They'll get minced. Then, while I've got their attention, you can free Mason and Fudge."

Will blinked at me a few times like I'd just smacked him across the face. "What? How will you get them all to follow you? Grasshoppers might not feed at night...they might not attack other demons." He shook his head, adding up all the unknown variables. "Do you even know how to get back to that meadow in the dark?"

I opened my mouth and shut it again. The truth was, I could sense the bizarre spiritual energy less than a quarter mile away from here. The meadow, Styx, every demon so far—I could identify their presence with the same nervous prickle in my spine, the same yawning hole in my gut. And that hole expanded the closer I wandered to the supernatural.

Maybe it was another curse, or just a sixth sense of sorts. I couldn't explain it, especially not in the time we had, and definitely not to someone as shrewd and skeptical as Will.

"You're just gonna have to trust me," I decided. "Unless you have a better idea?"

"No," he ground out, scrutinizing our demonic foes, his eyes darting from side to side like a robot homing in on his targets. "Just try to get as many to follow you as you can. Styx and I will take the camp."

The thrill of transition offense displaced my fear, and I looked him over, grinning slightly. "Right. Don't die or anything."

He dipped his chin at me, but his gaze was still pinned to his opponents. "Not part of the plan."

The three of us split, and I dashed back to the pines for cover. I took a moment to study my obstacle course, sketching my path in my mind's eye, and then I bent down to secure my boot laces.

Finally, a race worth racing.

A moment later, I was in position—hair tied back with a bloody cloth bandage, one glove stuffed in my rear pocket to expose my right hand, and adrenaline dancing down my femoral artery. Ready to prove myself. Ready to change the script.

I couldn't think of a cool, effective way to seize the demons' attention, so I just started yelling invectives.

"Hey boys!" I shouted into the quiet, watching their heads swing in my direction. "You forgot about my squad! We killed your buddies up-river. We didn't even break a sweat." I sighed dramatically, expelling the nerves in my throat. "You thought you could beat us with only three of your crew? I'm embarrassed *for* you."

The group rose to their feet, abandoning their tasks. They lifted their chins, baring their neglected teeth and flaring their nostrils, as if I reeked of false confidence.

While I sprinted around the camp's circumference, Styx rustled the branches with her wind powers to paint the illusion of sufficient manpower. "We're out here, bored sick with such easy victories!" I taunted. "Come on, welts. Catch me if you can!"

Peeved, the demons looked to their leader for permission to permanently shut me up, and Earlobe examined the foliage around the camp, successfully goaded. "Get them," he snarled. "Kill on sight."

Half the huddle charged in my general direction, their weapons drawn, their eyes ablaze. I tore into the trees, trying my best to lead them away from Will's position with my vociferous laughter.

"Too slow!" I cackled.

It was a lie.

I followed the rhythm of the forest, and the steady hum of the earth pulled me forward, closer and closer to the source of my anxieties. I heard the horde of demons on my tail, just out of sight, and I whooped, changing directions on them to drag the fun out a little longer.

Carving through an aspen grove, I grazed my palm against the low-hanging branches on my right. The contact sparked memories of our group crossing the terrain earlier today, and glimpses of our expedition skated over my vision like passing fireflies.

The clearer the images, the brighter the colors, the closer the trail.

I altered course, and within a minute, the ancient ruins graced my field of view.

Heart racing, I slipped my glove back on before scaling Will's ponderosa, and just as I looped my legs around a sturdy tree branch, the evil spirits came bursting out of the forest into the field of nightmares.

"Wait!" one shouted, and the group halted, their chests heaving from the chase. "We went too far. Their scent is weaker here."

They stood at the edge of the meadow, but the killer crickets were nowhere in sight, and their haunted symphony had fallen silent.

No buzzing. No clicking. No *threat*.

Gritz.

"Maybe your Sense is just failing you. Wouldn't be a first."

"Quiet."

They glared at one another, and my hands were sweating so badly I almost slid down the tree bark. Thinking quickly—or perhaps not at all—I snatched a pinecone off a branch and pricked my finger on a scale. Then I launched the blood-scented cone into the meadow.

The demons' gazes turned on me with startling precision. Their silver eyes reflected the hazy moonlight like tarnished skits, and I swore the soldiers had never looked more *soulless*.

As they began marching my way, my doubts resurfaced. Maybe Will was right, and the bugs were diurnal. Maybe they were full, or they refused to kill other demons. Maybe they'd migrated to another hunting ground.

Maybe I'd doomed us all.

But before the demons could reach my tree, a familiar thrumming filled the air, and then—like graywater flooding farmland—a mass of insects materialized in the grass.

The demon-men didn't stand a chance. A cloud of wings, claws, and mandibles had already enveloped their party, and their screams tangled with the murmur of locust wings.

Hoping the carnivores had their sights set for the evening, I sprang from the tree and ran back to Will as fast as I could.

21

It took me several minutes to find my way back, and my concern had sharpened into urgency. Five demons had followed me to the meadow, and I feared the remaining seven were right where I'd left them, ganging up on Will.

Will, who'd already wasted his energy dueling Stretch. Will, who was severely outmatched by a troop of invincible ghouls.

Had I teamed up with anyone else in our cohort, they'd surely be dead by now.

But you didn't, the optimist in me interjected. *Will is the best fighter you know.*

He's fine—which means Fudge is fine. And Mason too ... so long as his ego didn't get him killed.

At last, I spotted streaks of red flame between the tree trunks, and beyond the ring of manzanitas, a scowling 17-year-old drenched in demon blood. He was still fighting—thank the skies—and a relieved breath whooshed out of me at the sight of him on his feet.

I stumbled out of the shrubs and paused at the edge of camp to gauge the state of our extraction. Two demons were sufficiently incapacitated, moaning and twisting on the dirt as their limbs labored to reappear. Styx dropped a large boulder on their bodies each time they attempted regeneration, and I decided then and there I should avoid taking up residence on her bad side.

Will faced four demons at a time, swinging his sword around in wide, deterrent arcs to keep the monsters away from Fudge and Mason. But our enemies were closing in on him now, backing him into a corner with a useless pair of hostages.

The plan hadn't worked particularly well. Not that they ever did; we were like 0 for 3 at this point.

I jogged up to Styx and retrieved the flashlight from my bag, murmuring a quiet, "Nice work," to appease her aggressive nature—just in case. And while she didn't possess any lips, I was pretty sure she smiled.

Eager to join the fight, I used Stretch's sword to behead an unsuspecting demon creeping up on Will's left. The tactic required much more force than expected, though, and it took a few tries to get a clean cut.

When the soldier's decaying body finally hit the ground, I shot Will an embarrassed grin. "Sorry I'm late."

He looked at me briefly, acknowledging my presence and affirming my efforts with a subtle nod, and it was oddly satisfying, the way he didn't seem relieved to see me. It was like he'd expected my arrival, like he'd had ... confidence in me or something.

"Help the others," he said, right before a demon tried—and failed—to impale him with its glaive.

I dashed for the tree stump where they'd deposited our defenseless duo, only to find that Will had already cut the boys' bindings. They were free to run, free to fight, but they still hadn't budged an inch—hadn't even opened their eyes—which could only mean one of two things.

I pressed my hand to Fudge's neck, fearing the worst, but the world found its axis again when his pulse kissed my fingertips. *Just unconscious, then. And likely drugged.*

Good. I'd take nightshade poisoning over a concussion-induced brain injury any day.

I shook the smaller of the two boys, but he merely groaned and slumped against Mason's shoulder, leaving me with the least cooperative human on this planet.

I patted Mason's face with the back of my hand. "Wakey, wakey, Mansion Boy."

Gray eyes fluttered open, then squinted at me, as if he couldn't believe I had the audacity to slap him around. "Where . . . ?"

"Get up. We need to move."

Dazed, the blond blinked dumbly at his surroundings before jerking upright, recalling the string of events that had landed him here. The sudden motion made him clutch his head, though, and he scraped his tongue against his teeth and spat at the ground. "Gritz, what did they *feed* me?"

"Mason, take Fudge—"

His gaze flew to something above me, and he recoiled. "Look out!"

My heart in my larynx, I spun around to greet the seventh member of the demon gang, mid-ambush.

I watched his sword fly toward me in slow motion, its trajectory bound for the meat of my neck, its shaft reflecting the fire pit like a scarlet ribbon on a funeral casket.

And then Will was there.

He pushed me aside, taking the full brunt of the impact against his blade—or most of it, anyway. When he threw my attacker off, I noticed a fresh streak of blood beneath his battered spaulder.

He glared at me and said, through gritted teeth, "Can you *try* to pay attention?"

He chopped through the demon's torso cleanly, and a fountain of black blood burst from its chest. The ink spattered my cheek and temple, and I flinched at the unpleasant stinging sensation.

The gore burned like acid. It burned like it didn't *belong* here.

Two more demons approached us, and the one I beheaded wasn't far behind, its tendons and epidermis melding and mating, its black blood co-agulating. Will, unperturbed by this resurrection, positioned himself between me and the enemy—his sword steady, his boots shoulder-width apart. Relaxing his shoulders, he gazed at his opponents with such poised intensity that they readjusted their stances.

They came for him then, one after another. And one after another, he delivered flawless, fatal blows . . . or what *would* have been fatal blows, if someone hadn't rewritten the laws of nature yesterday.

Still, he kept them at bay.

In fact, he fought with far greater skill than he'd ever displayed at Frost's sessions, and not even his Deadlock match compared to this. But perhaps that was because I'd never seen him truly *fight*. Not with his life on the line.

At the river, I'd only caught glimpses of his swordsmanship, and by the numerous hits Stretch had taken, I'd just assumed the demon was an unremarkable fighter. But it was obvious now, why Will had outperformed his cohort, why he'd walked away from the river unscathed, and why he hadn't hesitated to cross this spirit-infested forest alone.

He was fast, adroit, and he never miscalculated. Every swing struck true, and somehow, he could always anticipate his opponent's next move, then render it ineffective—all within a matter of seconds. Never stumbling. Never missing. Never losing.

I was dazzled.

I was *jealous*.

"Use the flashlight to keep safe," I told Mason. He snorted at the absurdity but didn't argue when I tossed the tool his way.

I entered the fight, cutting and thrusting in a series of unrehearsed maneuvers. I wasn't great—sloppy at best, and awfully inconsistent—but my ugly thrashing kept me alive. I even managed to inflict injury, though it wasn't too difficult when I received the demons secondhand. Will put enough holes in them to knock their proficiency level down a few pegs.

With each blow we dealt, I felt the bite of black poison on my face, the burn of a demon's bloodstain, as if Will and I were plowing through a garden of stinging nettle. But gritz, at least stinging nettle would stay down when cut.

The longer we fought, the worse we fought, and the corpses just kept recharging and regenerating, over and over again.

As I waited for my opponent to heal himself—for the third time—I briefly wondered if the other demons had escaped the hopper hellions as we had, and the frightening thought almost cost me a blade to the face. Because I knew the second those angry goons returned to this fight, we'd be done for.

Mason yelled something nonsensical behind me, and when I finally had the opportunity to pull away from my opponent, I saw him standing at the edge of camp, holding a forever-unconscious Fudge off the ground. "My sword!" he snapped, tilting his head at the pile of belts and scabbards by the fire. "Use my sword!"

I didn't ask. Fetching and unsheathing the rapier, I felt something strange spark to life in my veins—a feeling lost in an ocean of adrenaline. But based on the way the demons regarded the weapon with renewed caution, I sensed we'd reap better results this time around.

With two weapons drawn, I redirected my attention to Earlobe, the squad leader, limping toward us, dragging his severed foot behind him—courtesy of a spunky forest spirit.

He met my first swing with a firm, unyielding block. The force sent me straight to the ground while he stood there perfectly resolute, like an oak tree I had foolishly kicked. I gaped as he loomed over me, sneering at my pitiful fighting skills. Then he brought his saber down for my head, and I rolled aside at the last second, watching the metal sink into the dirt with the velocity of lightning.

I stood from my crouch and attacked again, recalibrating. This time, I lunged for the chink in his armor, and the rapier skated beneath Earlobe's weapon, slipping behind the monster's breast plate and piercing the meat of his ribcage. Upon impact, the demon exploded in a plume of black powder, leaving nothing behind but his sword and a pile of armor.

Poof.

Gone.

Disintegrated.

I coughed, blinking against the cloud of ash that enveloped us. Will appeared behind me, wide-eyed, and I stared down at the sword in my bloody glove.

Had I just ... *cremated* a demon?

Will grabbed the hilt of the rapier below my fist, voicing a smoky, "Can I have a turn?"

My fingers disentangled from the guard. "Do your worst."

As a team, we pushed onward, executing another undisclosed plan. Seamlessly, I engaged from the front, drawing them out, holding their attention, while my coordinated partner destroyed from the back—a silent wraith in the darkness. The demons howled as they vanished into the rapier's tip, filling the night with cries of unbridled rage.

Within minutes, a layer of black ash buried the forest floor.

Within minutes, we'd won.

I grinned at Will, and although he didn't return the smile, he didn't scowl either.

Fudge, having roused from his slumber, whistled loudly from the sidelines. "Mason, *where* did you get that sword?"

Mason stomped over and jerked the magic weapon out of Will's hands. "I told you it was first-class!" He left to retrieve his scabbard, grumbling to himself about being saved by a breeder two times in one day.

I moved to pummel him for using that word again, but I staggered into

Will halfway there, struck by a spell of dizziness. The warrior wrapped his arm around my middle and frowned. "What's wrong with you?"

What's wrong? Patrons, where did I even begin? Everything today—the running, the drowning, the fighting—it was all taking its toll. And using my curse so much in the span of a few hours was bound to leave me woozy.

I'd pushed my limits this evening. Dangerously so.

"I'm good," I lied, though I didn't move from his support.

He was not convinced. Not even a little bit.

"Well, I don't know about you all, but I'd like to get the hell out of this place," Mason declared, fastening his belongings to his belt and grimacing at his mud-caked buckles.

Will's hand tightened on my waist like he could sense my body's impending collapse. "I second that. We failed to kill the three demons who pursued us, and half a dozen more are still out there. We should keep moving."

I decided my charade wasn't worth it anymore, and I leaned into Will's side with my entire body weight, sliding my hand up his spine to grip his armor. Thankfully, the robot didn't bat an eye at my plea for help, and for once, I truly appreciated his impassive nature. "Agreed. Let's steal their travel packs and bounce."

"Whoa, hang on a second," said Fudge, his gaze sliding to the other end of the campground. "What about the lions?"

We stared at him blankly, bewildered by his question. "What *about* the lions?" I asked, worried he'd received too much nightshade after all.

"We can't just leave them here, chained up. They'll starve."

Mason screwed up his face like he'd tasted something sour. "Fudge, you try and free those things and you'll get your throat ripped out. Just leave them be."

Fudge gave a disappointed huff and walked over to the demon cats anyway, an appalled Mason gaping after him. Will and I exchanged looks again, a *who's-gonna-take-this* kind of look, and it occurred to me he'd suddenly become my brain's backboard on this quest. A person to bounce ideas off of, a place to cast my concerns. And I wasn't sure how to feel about that, considering this backboard wasn't exactly … springy.

With a defeated sigh, I slid out of Will's grasp to follow my little white knight and his humanitarian impulses.

Fudge crouched a few feet away from the lions, and they blinked at him with cold, hooded eyes. They looked twice as spent as we did, and I almost felt a granule of pity for the beasts, but then I remembered our last playdate and took it back.

"Fudge, be careful," I warned, lowering myself next to him. Ready to yank him backward at a moment's notice.

He ignored me and crept forward with his arm outstretched. Circumspect, the lions righted themselves, growling and purring at low levels to scare him off, but their throaty vocals didn't work.

As he reached for the chains, the hair on their backs rose in sharp bristles, and I almost passed out. "*Fudge,*" I cautioned again, fingers brushing my hilt.

But he kept moving—steadily, calmly, fearlessly. "It's okay, guys. I'm gonna get you out of here. So, you know, if you could not eat me, I'd appreciate it." His fingers curled around the restraints, and three pairs of demon eyes snapped to his hand. "See … I get it. You may be demons on the inside, but you're still stuck in an animal's body. You're animals *first*. And animals hate chains. Cats most of all."

His hand rose for the steel collar around the first lion's neck, and all three felines shot to their feet at once, prepared to defend themselves, prepared to attack.

My stomach seized up.

Fudge stood on a tightrope in these woods. He knew the lions could pounce on him at any moment. The chains offered enough slack for them to seriously maim him—an event that promised certain death in a place like this, so far away from anyone capable of piecing him back together. He recognized this, but he still didn't take his eyes off his goal. He didn't lose his balance, not for one second.

Gingerly, his hand traveled closer, *closer*, until he finally had the first collar in his grip, his wrist exposed. But somehow, Fudge was able to remove the band from its neck untouched, and as the collar fell to the ground, the beast shook its head, ridding itself of any phantom confinement.

Fudge repeated the process for the next two lions, speaking to them in quiet, soothing tones, just as he did with Mason and other belligerent males.

Once all three cats were free, they considered Fudge for a few seconds, as if communicating their gratitude—or, more likely, debating his nutritional value—before bounding off into the forest. Never looking back.

We rose from the ash, and I stared down at the animal whisperer, a good ten inches shorter than me. He may have been soft and kind and … small, but he was anything but helpless.

"That was really brave of you."

"Not really."

"Yeah, *really*," I said sternly, so he'd believe it.

He smiled up at me, dimples and freckles and bruises, and I realized I'd never felt this protective over anyone before. Not anyone *human*, anyway. My first duckling was probably his biggest contender.

"Nice. That's not going to backfire at *all*," Mason complained as we joined the group again. "What if they turn around and stalk us? What if they eat us in our sleep?"

Fudge just rolled his eyes, grinning to himself like the querulous brat was endearing or something.

Will eyed me peculiarly, traces of suspicion and concern in his pupils, like he could tell I was using my sword as a cane. Like he could tell I was moments from kissing ash.

"Let's find some shelter," he said, throwing my pack over his shoulder. He scanned the circle of gray sky above us, the swaying tips of the pine trees. "I think there's a storm brewing."

Our party returned to the forest, my flashlight illuminating the dark terrain ahead, and my gaze swept over the empty campsite one last time — lingering on seven piles of Ellsian armor.

22

The rain drenched us in less than thirty seconds. It came down hard, relentless, and within five minutes, the shower that had so graciously washed away the ash and demon entrails had become a hazardous inconvenience. Mud painted my legs, rain blinded me, and I couldn't remember the last time I'd hated the sky so much.

To make matters worse, thunder and lightning shook the world off its hinges, denying me sleep. Decompressing at all was impossible when my heart splintered at each bellow, when my muscles clenched at each flash of violet electricity.

It was the sound of revenge, accompanied by a foreboding, anxious silence.

Sitting on the floor of an abandoned mine, I wrapped my arms around my damp legs, shivering as the temperature dropped another ten degrees. Hugging myself as I glared into empty space.

The rain hadn't just killed my victory high tonight; it had also forced me to stop and reflect on my actions. Actions that had *killed* people.

And sure, those people may have lost their souls. They may have been nothing more than empty vessels of evil, but they still resembled and spoke like people. There was life there—a breathing creature capable of complex thoughts and emotions. And yet, when it came down to my life or theirs, there'd been no hesitation. I'd chosen manslaughter.

I'd even … enjoyed it. Because in the heat of the moment, it felt like I'd won a competition. Like I'd proved something.

But now?

Now it just felt like I'd lost my own humanity.

Admittedly, I'd signed up for that feeling when I picked Tom's career path. War required callousness, and killing other humans was the staircase to victory. But the aftermath of those choices, the mental warfare we'd grapple with *post* battle, that was all fine print.

Thunder rattled my thoughts, spooking me so badly I jumped an inch off the floor. In my panic and embarrassment, I lost my grasp on guilt and shame and a colder, darker feeling.

Mason peered at me with blatant judgement. "Seriously? You'll charge a group of demons, but you're scared of thunder?"

"I'm not scared," I grumbled.

Will pressed his lips together, and in the briefest flash of lightning, it almost looked like he was smiling.

Almost.

We'd found an old mineshaft inside a rocky alcove of the mountain, and we'd quickly shuffled inside the ancient structure to escape the downpour. We had no idea if the mine was safe or toxic or unoccupied, but we were all so sick of trudging through mud and rain that we'd decided to take our chances.

A gradual peal of thunder hit this time. It began as a mild, distant roar—then escalated into a horrific tremor that shook the whole mountain. Dust floated to the floor, and pebbles danced on the ground.

My hand flew to Will's knee in search of an anchor.

It was just rain. Just a natural phenomenon. I was safe here, and I had no reason to be scared. In fact, I recognized how irrational the fear was, and it still didn't matter. Every time I encountered a thunderstorm, my insides coiled like conductive wire, and I forgot how to breathe.

It was just…at any second, a bolt of lightning could zap me out of existence. In an instant, it could fry my nervous system with 300 million volts of electricity. I couldn't fight it, I couldn't outrun it, and if I happened to be at the wrong place at the wrong time, I was very unlikely to survive it. No amount of training would change that.

Those kinds of odds were scary.

It was the same underlying fear as the water snakes. When I couldn't see my enemy, I couldn't prepare myself. I had no control over the situation; I had to guess.

And I *hated* guessing.

Like the fear of drowning, my astraphobia could be traced back to the well incident, and those subsequent rainy seasons were *rough*. But I'd also had Tom back then, and he used to make the phobia chase its own tail. He used to tell me that every clap of thunder was a god in Olympus trying to prove he was more powerful than man. So when the storms hit, he'd gather all the pots and pans in the house, and we'd start banging on them as loudly as possible. Eventually, the thunder would go away, and he had me convinced that we'd outdone the sky. That we'd won some kind of divine battle against the gods.

To be louder than fear, that was the goal, and the strategy never failed, even after Tom had perished. He'd left me with that gift—a way to fight back.

Only right now, I was short a few skillets.

As soon as I realized I was still gripping Mr. Untouchable's kneecap, I yanked my hand away, avoiding his gaze and any collateral humiliation that followed.

"This mine goes forever," Fudge marveled, shining the flashlight down the tunnel and exposing way too many cobwebs for my liking.

Mason swore behind us as he attempted to light another wet match. When it failed to ignite, he threw it to the ground with the others and glared over his shoulder. "Don't wander. You don't know what's lurking down there."

Fudge aimed the flashlight at his own face so Mason could see his eye roll. "Wouldn't it be better to know what's *down there* before you lower your guard and go to sleep?"

"Whatever. When you contract rabies after some demonic rodent eats your foot off, don't come crying."

Fudge just laughed.

***

Will offered to take first watch again, albeit unenthusiastically, but Styx volunteered instead. She insisted she could take the shifts—*all* the shifts. At least, that was how we interpreted her ambiguous sign language. And because she'd fought beside us consistently today, I agreed, though I blamed my leniency on my complete and utter fatigue.

Fudge and Mason wandered to their respective sleeping areas, leaving Will and me at the mouth of the mine.

For a while, we just listened to the storm. The thunder and lightning had ceased, and the rain that followed was softer. Not of lesser volume— the sky still bled in buckets. But it came with less intensity. Less anger. It fell like a gentle caress, repairing any damage the storm had inflicted upon the earth in one long, apologetic kiss.

I examined my new sword. The rain had cleared the blood and ash from the blade, revealing the dips and chips along its edges, the battle scars and rusty patches. It was an older model, and heavier than I would have liked, but I'd also never practiced with a battle-ready sword before—my arms weren't used to the weight. Not yet, anyway.

I wondered ... if my palm were to graze its surface, would I see how much destruction Stretch had brought to Belgate? Would I see my father's face? Or Nova's?

It was tempting, in a twisted way. To know. To stop agonizing over their wellbeing. But if I saw what I dreaded to see, how could I possibly recover?

Stop it.

He's alive, I told myself, tossing the thought away. *Dad said he'd meet me in Holly. He'll be there.*

He has to be there.

"If the material in Mason's rapier is the only thing that will kill demons, then seven of them are still out there," Will reflected, his voice breaching the quiet roar of the rainstorm. "Plus the one you knocked unconscious."

Right. I swallowed thickly, instinctively curling my fists. *Unconscious.*

"Even if they come after us, I think we can take them now." I sent him a sidelong glance. "Well, *you*, mostly. But I'm happy to play jester again."

He looked at me, and we made solid eye contact for maybe the first time in our lives. The kind of contact that watches, measures, and learns. The kind that stretches on long enough to encode the details into memory.

Will's eyes were thin, hooded ovals—a shape that, like most of the country's lower class, pointed to his mixed ancestry. In this lighting, his irises were obsidian black, deep and rich with melanin, as if they harbored a thousand truths and sorrows. They melted into his pupils like two long, dark tunnels transecting his brain.

Two forbidden tunnels taunting you with their ominous pathways and hidden secrets.

Heat crept up my neck at the prolonged exchange, and I tore my gaze away. "You think there are a lot of old mines like this?"

He nodded absently and leaned over to assess the snake bites on my arm.

"How do they look, doc?"

"Fine."

"I'm not going to die?"

"Not from *them*."

I frowned at him. "How do you know?"

I wasn't talking about his medical expertise. This kid from the slums of Belgate fought like a well-trained soldier. He could navigate the Range as if he'd lived here his whole life. And he even knew about ancient ruins and snake bites and evil spirits.

Something wasn't adding up.

He withdrew from me. "You ask a lot of questions."

"I only ask so many because you respond with six words or less," I retorted. Minimal information necessitated further probing.

He scanned me critically, and after a pregnant pause, he said, "You should eat."

What. Where did that response even come from?

Did he just reboot?

Then I remembered the look on his face when I'd nearly passed out earlier. The seed of concern I'd planted, then ignored. He must have thought I was malnourished or something.

Jeez.

He dragged my sopping backpack over and excavated a pile of blackberries from the outer pouch, grabbing hold of my wrist and dumping them into my palm.

I glared at the abomination in my gloved hand. I was hungry, but not *that* hungry. The berries were all smashed and waterlogged and gross.

My face twisted. "Pass. I'd rather eat killer crickets." Far more appetizing than crushed and swampy grapes.

"You could always say, 'no thanks' *like a normal person*," he said.

My disbelieving eyes rose to his deadpan expression. Had he just mocked me with my own criticism? Had William Stone-Faced Tooms just ... made a joke?

Styx trembled from the edge of the cave, her luminous heart flickering, her leafy arms clutching her stomach.

The nymph was *laughing*.

My mouth lifted at the corners, but when I glanced back at Will, he was already on his feet, walking away from me before his ears started bleeding. He settled within a narrow depression of the tunnel wall, tucked between two wooden beams. Mostly out of sight.

He must have liked to sleep in confined places—hidden, enclosed, out of reach. Not unlike a moody cat ... or a psychopath.

I gagged down the mouthful of berries and planted myself between Fudge and the mine entrance.

We'd lost ground today, rounding back for him and Mason. Crossing this terrain, battling nature and its shadows ... it was taking longer than we'd anticipated. Longer than we could afford. I could only hope the news of Belgate had reached Holly by now.

Maybe a messenger had made it by road, or perhaps a merchant had arrived on the scene and turned on his heels to alert the capital. Perhaps humanity's fate did not rest on the shoulders of four teenagers after all.

A girl could dream.

Fudge lay slumped against the side of the mineshaft, his knees to his chest and a flashlight in his hand. With every exhale, a strand of ashen hair trembled against his forehead, and I had the strangest impulse to brush the curl away from his face.

"You came back for us," he said, his eyes still closed.

"You thought I wouldn't?"

"I wasn't sure."

Sadness pierced my chest. "Fudge, I meant what I said. I'm not gonna let you die."

I'd bargain with Death himself if I had to.

He sighed, opening one blue eye to peer at me. "Considering I became a hostage on the first day of our journey, I suspect that will be a difficult promise to keep."

I smiled and reclined against the cavern wall. "The best promises always are."

23

"Can you teach me how to fight?"

Will didn't even look up from his knife. "No."

I bit back a curse. To think I deigned to ask. "Why not?"

"Because it'll encourage you to engage with every opponent you come across, regardless of skill differential."

"But I already do that."

We waited near a brook while Mason caught lunch. That welt might have driven me out of my mind, but he did know how to set a trap—I'd give him that. Whatever god had built that boy must have dumped all the foulest ingredients into one human and then decided to make him a skilled hunter so society would still tolerate his existence.

My hands found my hips. "Teach me how to protect myself, then. I'll learn offense from someone else." I had the gist of it down from years of notetaking, just no one to practice with. Not since Tom. "Please."

Will didn't answer, and I thought it was a lost cause, but then he sighed at me and rose to his feet. "Stand over there."

I grinned broadly, and he shot me an impatient look, so I quickly shuffled to where he indicated.

"Simple defense should keep you alive long enough to escape. A parry you can handle—I've seen you do it." He raised my sword at an angle, holding it out in front of me, level with my torso. "Those demons might be stronger than you, but you're faster. You can use that to your advantage if you master your footwork."

I shot my feet a withering look.

"Your problem is that you swing for anything that breathes, and you give each blow your all. It leaves you exhausted and exposed." He walked behind me and readjusted my shoulders and elbows. "Control is key. Stay on the balls of your feet, keep yourself loose but compacted, and remain perpendicular to your opponent. The idea is to shrink their target as much as possible and simultaneously protect your vital areas." He gently tugged at my shirt sleeve, pulling my sword inward a few inches. "Maintain a tight radius. Don't worry about feints or ripostes until you've studied their fighting pattern and identified a weakness to exploit. Let your enemies tire first, just like you did with the river demon. Then strike where it counts."

This technique directly opposed Frost's training curriculum. With him, it had always been "strike first and strike hard"—kill them before they can kill you. But this ... this was conservative. Condensed. I felt like a spring built to pounce but not permitted to.

Maybe that was a good thing. I wasn't sure.

"I could tell you what I know, the tricks, the tips. But words won't teach you anything."

His hand curled around the hilt of his weapon, and before I could fully process his disconcerting statement, his sword came flying for my jugular vein. Stunned, I brought my blade up to block his advance—instinctively, the way he'd shown me.

Steel clipped steel, and I swallowed the knot of terror in my throat.

He nodded with approval. Like it was normal to suddenly *attack* people.

I spun the weapon off mine, gaping. "A warning would be nice. You almost took my head off."

"I didn't."

And with that, the lunatic lunged at me again.

This time he swung top-down, quick as wind, and I panicked. I raised my sword parallel to the ground—a last-ditch effort to parry the blow—but his momentum carried him forward, and I wasn't strong enough to push him off, nor lithe enough to dip away.

The impact of our weapons bent my elbows inward, and he looked at me through the junction of our swords, eyes of scorched earth pulsing with amusement and impish delight.

I didn't even know he could *make* that face.

He stepped back for a heartbeat, granting me a second chance, only to tip his blade at my stomach. I couldn't think of a way to deflect his succeeding thrust, so I jumped aside and groaned at my own stupidity.

My loss of balance granted him the perfect opportunity to grab hold of my arm and reel me in like a ball of twine, sword at my throat, and I failed to comprehend how he'd moved so quickly.

"You hesitated," he said, disappointed.

"I didn't know what to do next."

He let me go. "Figure out the flow. It isn't about knowing. It's about thinking."

That was literally the least helpful advice I'd ever heard in my life. "Will, if a demon's charging me, I can only defend myself for so long before I have to resort—"

He flew at me again, and I readied myself, trying to think like him, fast like him.

Our swords collided, and he forced me back along the hillslope.

Sword fighting was like swimming, I decided. I had to make consistent movements to stay afloat, had to work with the water, not against it. Remember to inhale. And just like swimming across an alpine lake, there were no breaks; I was always treading water.

Or drowning, in this case.

He drove harder, and I frantically attempted to deflect him. Splashing chaotically.

Rage sprouted in my chest. This muck-eyed jerk was enjoying himself! He was toying with me, hardly exerting himself. And I knew, behind that fine line of his mouth, he was laughing.

"Stop it!"

"Stop what?" he asked, casually snipping through one of the strings in my armor.

I lost it.

Exploding with impatience, I threw my sword at an upward angle, grazing his chin. And it was at that moment I realized he'd been waiting for this transgression all along. For me to fight back, to take the offensive, to lose control.

Because with an opening there in front of me, my victory just a solid strike away, I couldn't help myself. I brought my sword down over my head, aiming for the top of his shoulder, and I watched my glorious redoublement go down in flames.

Will deflected my sword with a speedy vertical block, and with his free hand, he punched the air to the left of my hilt. He then twisted his torso and dropped his forearm over mine, pinning my elbows under his armpit and forcing my entire body clockwise. With my balance in ruins, he was able to kick my right leg out from under me and flip me over.

I landed on my back with an *oof*.

From a distance, I could hear Fudge and Mason's loud guffaws, and I wanted to sink into the gurgling brook. *Dammit.*

So I wouldn't have to see his smug face, I grabbed hold of Will's ankles and yanked. He fell to all fours, but he caught himself before eating grass.

He blew a strand of black hair out of his eyes and gazed back at me. "Satisfied?"

"This is stupid."

Not stupid. Just hard. Harder than it had ever been with Tom.

That being said, I'd had confidence Tom wouldn't actually stab me in the face.

"You were doing fine until you threw a fit," he said, and I scowled some more. "You can't expect to be an expert right off the bat. We'll keep practicing."

I tossed my curtain of tangles aside, gaping at his serious expression. *Keep*?

As in ... a commitment?

"Really?" I whispered, afraid to believe that a boy outside my family would risk such a thing. In Ells, training a woman to fight was as felonious as her passion to do so. Never in my life had a soldier offered to help me attain my dream.

Not until now.

Will nodded, and I beamed at him, truly grateful for his words—in part because I knew he wasn't the type to waste his breath on empty promises—but also because I enjoyed his company, even if I didn't always speak his language.

He blinked back at me, visibly confused by my blatant appreciation, as if he'd never been the recipient of a genuine smile before.

Fudge and Mason approached us, snickering at our expense, and I clambered to my feet. Obviously, Will hadn't offered to help me off the ground, the welt.

"I almost had him," I insisted, and Will rolled his eyes.

"Are you kidding?" Mason exclaimed. "Tooms was running circles around you. Then you got your feelings hurt and flipped yourself upside-down." He froze, realizing the insult had cost him a compliment, and he turned to Will to rectify his slip up. "Took longer than expected though. A girl wouldn't stand a chance against any qualified soldier."

Will tilted his head at the blond, almost like he couldn't believe Mason was that stupid.

"That's funny," I said. "Because I recall fending off plenty of soldiers last night on my way to save your useless butt."

"Please. Those demons are not trained soldiers," he said. "Just because you lack combat skills doesn't mean the enemy is competent."

It took all my willpower not to strangle him, and I shoved the anger back down my esophagus. "Well, try not to get kidnapped next time, and you can put your many *qualifications* to the test."

Pure loathing filled Mason's eyes, and I expected Will to step in and diffuse the situation before we started throwing fists. But instead, he just raised his eyebrows at Mason in a, *'Well, what's your countermove, Price?'* sort of way.

He just wanted to see me pound Mason into the ground. I was sure of it.

"Uh, Alex?" Fudge cut in, his laughter gone, his tone nervous. "She's ... uh ... waving at you ..."

"What?"

"Turn around."

I stared at the boy for a bewildered beat before whipping around in confusion.

She?

And there she was, impossibly, her gray hair braided back in a loose bun, her pink dress stark against the conifers.

"Alex!" Nova barked. "You're late!"

* * *

"When did you get here?"

Nova set a second teapot down on the pinewood table, despite my disclosure of our perilous time crunch. "I left the evening we last spoke. Took an old city mare and the buckboard, as usual. I arrived just a few hours ago. Biscuits, anyone?"

Fudge raised his hand, and she disappeared into her kitchenette.

Nova had brought us back to her little getaway home: a log cabin tucked away in the trees, encased in vines and forest weeds like something straight out of a fairytale. Then she refused to answer my questions until we sat down and ate something—not that any of us starving kids put up a fight.

Mason gagged into his cup. "This tastes like water with dirt in it."

"Have you never had tea?" I hissed.

"Have you never *shut up*?"

I kicked him in the shin.

My restless gaze flitted about the cabin, and I took note of the strange trinkets and bottles on the shelves, the wooden grilles on the windows. Cobwebs inhabited the corners of the slanted, sunken ceiling, and I was pretty sure I'd heard a family of rodents in the walls.

The old woman returned with ten slices of shortbread, and the glorious scent of honey, butter, and lemon zest had me salivating before the platter even touched the table. Once she'd divvied up the servings and poured herself another cup of tea, she finally sat down and folded her hands on the wood. "I sense that something tragic has occurred. Something … prodigious."

The four of us exchanged weary looks, and I heaved a long sigh. "Belgate was attacked."

We filled her in on our chaotic evacuation, and with each passing sentence, the lines of her face deepened, sinking with dread and sorrow and emotional fatigue. In several minutes, she'd aged a decade.

"I feared something like this would happen," she said after a lengthy pause. "You must get word to Holly immediately."

I blinked at her, searching her face for hidden sentiments.

Was that ... it?

I'd expected more from a woman who'd lived in Belgate for eight decades. Stunned silence, a slew of follow-up questions. Maybe a few tears for the place she'd once called home. But her mind was already racing for solutions, much like my father's.

No time to dwell on the past when our futures hung in the balance.

"Do you think we're the only ones who've made it this far east?" I asked, though I wasn't sure I wanted an answer.

"To my knowledge. I didn't encounter a single soul on my journey. The roads were barren."

Great. The city depended on us, then.

Two kidnap-prone boys, a cursed ranch hand, a robot, and a pile of rocks.

Holly was *doomed*.

I fixed her with a serious look, tired of tiptoeing around the subject matter. "Nova, do you understand what's going on? These creatures ... do you know where they came from?"

She dragged her long, thick nails across the tabletop, absently tracing the wood grain. "You're well aware of our conflicts with Rhea," she began, waiting for us to nod along. "About a decade ago, the war shifted. My psychic abilities heightened, and there was suddenly an abundance of spiritual energy in our realm. Soon after that, I discovered a portal had opened in the West. A mechanism that acts as a bridge between this world and ... others. It serves as a gateway for spirits, demons, and the occult. And it promises victory to its keeper."

Victory?

"Wait. You're saying someone did this on purpose," I whispered.

"The world does not simply fall out of balance. Someone or something broke through the natural barrier and is now using that breach to wreak havoc on mankind."

I stared at her, struggling to comprehend the fact that someone actually wanted this. Someone sought this awful future. This devastation was *orchestrated*.

Fudge stared at the shortbread in his hand. "But who would do this? Who would deliberately kill and defile so many people? So many innocents?"

Nova smiled sadly. "My dear, revenge is a terrible and powerful thing. Men will go to great lengths to right a wrong."

Her response only left me more bewildered. "Which wrong warranted *this*?"

"War is ugly, Alex." She added another spoonful of honey to her cup, gazing at the auburn liquid so intently, it made me think the tea leaves concealed another ominous fortune. "Years and years ago, Ells attempted to seize the habitable areas of the continent."

"For natural resources," I recalled. Primarily, the remaining water reserves and irradiated farmland.

"What they don't tell you in school is the means by which they did so," Nova explained. "Ells acquired its territory by burning entire villages to the ground. We contaminated sparse water supplies and inflicted terrible epidemics. Anything to condemn the colonized." She offered a reproachful head shake. "Some rumors even boast of targeting children to wipe out an entire generation of foot soldiers."

Will and Fudge blenched, but Mason didn't look convinced. He was too patriotic to identify the bloodied flag we hoisted, too blind to see Ells for what it really was: a shiny pot of lies.

All those polished history books they'd forced us to read—filtered fables. The chronicles of an honorable, wiser civilization born from the ashes—pure fantasy.

At our core, Ellsians were greedy imperialists, just like our ancestors before us. And deep down, I'd always known it to be true.

I'd seen the redaction all along.

"Rhea is the last of the unconquered West, and because of that, we've fought the Sterling bloodline for centuries," Nova continued. "It was only a matter of time before the kingdom turned to dark magic in retaliation—though I suspect the responsible party did not fully comprehend the ramifications of a Blackbourn Bargain."

"So *Rhea* opened the portal?" I clarified. "With ... dark magic?"

I'd entertained the gossip of a Rhean alliance, but I never imagined the kingdom had partnered with body-thieving demons. Two days ago, such things weren't even found in my lexicon.

"I don't know who has unleashed such evil, or how, but only the utmost abhorrence could channel the netherworld, and Rhea harbors great hatred. Most notably, the royal family."

Mason leaned forward. "I get why those rats wanted to convert Ellsians into G.I. Jinxes, but why are so many of the animals affected? The lions. The snakes. Even the bugs? That doesn't make any sense."

"I'm not entirely sure," Nova confessed. "I believe when the portal was initially created, an alarming number of spirits and demons were inadvertently released, like a silent gas leak. Before that valve was closed, much of our natural world felt the impact—the animals, the plants, the air you breathe. It's why our cities shut their gates to the Range; they had to keep the mystery out."

The revelation killed my appetite.

That was the reason I'd been locked in a cage? For my own good?

"You keep referring to demons and spirits as unique entities," Will remarked. "Are they different?"

She dabbed at the corners of her mouth with an embroidered cloth napkin, contemplating her answer. "In short, a spirit is the essence of a deceased organism. But for a sentient creature, many would consider it a soul or a postmortem consciousness. These unbound energies are only harmful if their mortal lives were deeply perverted—or if they have unfinished business to attend to, I suppose. Demons, conversely, are the byproduct of evil. They're soulless and infinite, born from our wrongdoings, our cruelty, and our selfishness. They're humanity's sins incarnate, if you will. They are indeed distinct creatures, but not always different."

My gaze slid to the window.

Styx must have been a spirit then. She hadn't tried to kill us yet, as far as we knew, and she'd fought against our enemies three times now. On the other hand, she was a faceless mute, so how could any of us truly know what sinister objectives she concealed?

I caught a glimpse of her twirling in the breeze, dissolving angelically into a cloud of dandelion florets, and I scowled.

. . . Still suspicious.

"So what now?" I pressed. We were wasting time, sitting here and drinking tea as if the world had stopped spinning.

"Now, Alex, your journey finally begins, and it is far from solitary." A slow smile spread across her face as she inspected her visitors. "All of you play a crucial role in this fight. I can see it."

Mason opened his mouth to comment on that last bit, but I kicked him in the shin again, and he bit his tongue.

The merchant's eye shifted to Will, her expression wary. "You will have to make a choice, William. One you've dreaded all your life, but a choice that will make a vital difference in the world. Your past is a tool, not a curse. Remember that."

Will's gaze didn't falter, but his hands tightened around his cup.

"And you two," she said to Mason and Fudge, "you will turn the tables in this war. Together."

Mason glanced skeptically at Fudge, who choked on his shortbread.

"And me? What's the usual?" I said, trying to play it cool even though my throat had twisted itself into figure eights.

Nova placed her hand on my forearm and gave it a reassuring squeeze, which, given the context, was anything but comforting. "It's a dark path— one riddled with smoke and imperceptible detours, and you will face many truths and many obstacles. But you will also eclipse your namesake, Alexandria. That, I am sure of."

24

The old woman smiled like she hadn't just struck us between the ribs. "Well then, I'll go pack you some supplies. You're all in want of a little zinc."

I let out a strained chuckle. *Nova and her damn beans.*

Gathering up the empty plates, she wandered into the kitchen, and Fudge turned to me with a feeble grin. "She's ... nice."

"She takes some getting used to," I admitted.

I don't suit everyone's palate, she'd once said. *To be an acquired taste is to be thoroughly and uniquely appreciated.*

Mason pushed his cold tea aside. "My grandpa used to tell us she was crazy. He said the witch stuff was all an act so she could swindle gullible kids out of their chore money." When all three of us turned to glare at him, he raised his brow. "I never said I agreed with him."

I almost praised him for developing some critical thinking skills, but I decided the argument wasn't worth it. Instead, I rose from the rickety table and stretched my arms over my head. "Do you guys want to wash up? Nova won't let us leave without a care package—or a few inapt requests on her end—so we might be here a while."

Fudge and Mason examined their earth-stained clothes, raspberry joints, muddy boots, and bloody armor. And while the rainstorm had cleared away most of the grime, the hostages had seen better days. Plus, Mason had an ugly bruise on his head that warranted attention.

They shrugged, heading off to the restroom in tandem. "And gargle some soap while you're at it, Mason! You have fish breath," I said as an afterthought.

"We never even ate the fish!" he shot back, outraged. He ranted on, but his voice was squashed by his friend's hearty laughter.

Will was glaring at me when I turned around, and I huffed. "What?"

"Eat," he said, sliding my plate to the edge of the table. "You're not eating, and if you pass out later, I'm not going to carry you."

I snatched up my half-eaten pastry with a theatrical flourish. "Happy?"

"Lucid?"

I smacked him on the shoulder, and he winced, sucking in sharply through his teeth. My brow creased at his reaction, my lips curling with suspicion, and he averted his gaze.

"I'm fine."

As I reflected on yesterday's madness and the many foes we'd encountered, I recalled his timely rescue at the demon camp. He'd taken a bloody gash beneath his shoulder spaulder—an injury meant for me—and apparently, he'd decided to keep its condition to himself for some stupid, inexplicable reason.

Hell, the dingus was so desperate to hide his vulnerability, he'd *sparred* with me.

"Shirt. Off," I demanded, nudging him toward the bedroom.

"What."

"Take it off."

"No."

"It's going to get infected."

"It's fine," he insisted.

"Will! Do you want me to take it off for you?" I hissed. "Even the smallest graze needs to be sanitized. We don't know where that creep's sword has been." Or in *whom.*

There wasn't time to be shy. He'd seen me in less.

He stalked to the bedroom and untied his leather armor. Then he yanked his shirt and breastplate over his head—aggressively—and when he turned to face me again, my heart sank to the floorboards.

Suddenly his reluctance made a lot more sense.

A series of raised, jagged lines covered his chest, white and fleshy with age. The scars spanned from rib to rib, clavicles to hip bones, creating strange geometric shapes on his torso. I didn't recognize the pattern of triangles, circles, diamonds, and squares, but it was clearly *designed*. Which meant the thick pale gashes had been carved there, the features chiseled from flesh. Perhaps even burned.

It joined plenty of other scrapes and bruises on his skin—including a few fresh nicks from the killer crickets—but none of that compared to the symbol engraved across his breastbone, the branded permanence wrought by another's hand.

My eyes traveled south. Tattoos stained his wrists, the scripture too small to interpret at a distance, the ink too light, as if it were intended for Will's eyes only. The backs of his hands were done as well, and intricate black symbols and text embellished his tendons, then vanished beneath taped knuckles.

Until now, I'd never seen him bare-chested, even on summer days when the boys swam in the river or competed as shirts and skins. And he'd always worn such long, scraggly sleeves that I'd never noticed his ink before. But if he'd managed to conceal illegal tattoos and ghastly scars all these years, what other secrets had he successfully entombed?

My gaze flicked back to his shoulder. At some point, he'd dressed the wound with strips of my ruined shirt. Dry blood soiled the cloth, and now, ruby liquid pooled at the center of the gash—a result of our training session, no doubt.

I took one last bite of shortbread to appease him, and then I hurried past him in search of sewing supplies, scissors, and alcohol.

Just as I'd hoped, there was an entire first aid kit in the bedroom closet, and beside it, a bottle of gin.

Nova was an aging merchant; it didn't shock me that she'd built a commuter's lodge to make her journey to and from the Interior less grueling. But all these provisions . . . it was like this place had become her second home—almost like she'd predicted the invasion years ago and gradually established residence here in the Range.

Only, if she *had* predicted this outcome, then why hadn't she said anything to the Council? Why hadn't she warned Holly herself?

I motioned for Will to sit on the bed, and he didn't argue this time. He sat still as granite as I began sterilizing my tools, and I was glad to have something to distract myself from his peculiar scars and markings.

When I finished prepping my workstation, I handed him the gin bottle, and he stared at its contents for a moment before shooting me a bewildered look.

"You're gonna need it," I said.

He seemed suspicious, but he took a swig of the stuff anyway, wincing at the flames it left in his throat.

Taking a seat next to him, I set the needle and hemp pad aside and reached for his upper arm. My exposed fingertips brushed the swollen skin around the dressing, and he flinched.

I immediately snapped my hand back. "Sorry."

Even with my gloves on, I wasn't sure how to touch people properly— I'd never learned how—and adding an injury to the mix didn't help any.

"Your fingers are just cold," he said. "Unhealthy cold."

The comment tugged at my lips, and I gently unwrapped the makeshift bandage. "My dad always made fun of me for having cold hands and feet," I admitted. "I'd tease him back by touching his neck or shoving my hands up his shirt to smack his belly. He'd scream like a child, even when he saw me coming."

The memories ached, and I tried not to think about the very real possibility that I'd never see my father's reactions again. For now, I just kept telling myself that he'd made it out alive, that he was leading our people to safety across the Southern Ridge. I couldn't afford to believe otherwise.

He was, quite literally, all I had left.

Beneath Will's bandage, the wound gleamed a sickly red—raw and irritated and completely unhealed. He needed stitches, just as I'd feared.

"I can't believe you didn't say anything. An infection could've killed you out here! Then what? What would we have done, Will?" I angrily dabbed at his wound to punctuate my distress.

It was no joke. If something happened to him before we reached Holly, we'd be done for. We'd end up lost in the Range, following the broad glow of the hidden sun. And if another demon squad hunted us down without Will here to fend them off? Dead. All of us.

"We need you," I whispered, wiping away the bloodstains. "So don't keep potentially fatal injuries to yourself. Okay?"

He mumbled his submission into the lip of the gin bottle, then kicked back another shot.

Aiming to synchronize the effects of his beverage with my operation, I pierced through inflamed skin without warning, and his hands coiled into tight fists at his sides. His eyelids fluttered at my violent anchor stitch, and his face twitched a few times at the pull of the needle, but overall, his pain tolerance impressed me. The laceration was long and deep, and without eugenol or a neurotoxin to numb the area, he was in for a rough afternoon.

A few stitches in, Will took a third gulp of gin, and I wondered how much alcohol it would take for him to actually let his guard down.

I had a feeling he'd probably die first.

His goosebumps kissed my frigid fingertips, and he appeared to fight a shiver. "Maybe you should go to the doctor," he said. "I don't think that's normal."

"Sure. I'll add 'cold hands' to the top of my list. Right above saving humanity from sin incarnate."

His eyes sought mine, but my gaze didn't stray from his wound. I refused to puncture some vital artery by losing myself in his cast-iron eyes—*not* that they were captivating or anything.

I made quick work of the sutures, and when I finished, my hands lingered on his bicep, savoring the human contact they were so frequently denied. "You shouldn't have taken the hit for me, Will."

He shrugged without really shrugging. "If I hadn't, your skull would need stitches, not my arm."

I couldn't argue with that, so I bound the wound tightly and hoped my medical care would make up for the inconvenience I'd caused him.

He stretched his arm out and rolled his shoulders, adapting to my handiwork. "You're good at that," he said. "I didn't know you sewed."

"Core curriculum."

He glanced at me bemusedly—dare I say, *fondly*—before throwing his shirt back on.

As he donned his armor and tightened his lacings, I noticed a bloody scrape on his chin from where I'd nipped him earlier. Mindlessly, I swiped at it with my thumb, but his hand instantly shot for my wrist, jerking it away from his face with a shocking sense of urgency.

His grip was painfully tight, his body rigid, as if he thought I'd attempted to gouge out his eyes or something. As if he didn't know human touch either.

He saw the blood on my hand then, and his expression returned to its normal state of boredom. He released my wrist. "... Thanks."

His reaction stunned me, and I struggled to respond right away, knocked off balance by the blatant fear that had just skittered across his cold, stoic face. "No problem. Just make sure you keep the wound clean—"

"Actually," he cut in, "I meant for not asking."

I must have looked lost.

"About the scars." His eyes absorbed the shadows in the room, and it felt like I'd just encountered a hazard sign warning me not to venture any closer—a lattice of boundary rope telling me to proceed at my own peril.

I gave a small, stiff nod, and he moved past me for the door.

"And Alex," he said, pausing under the head jamb to look at me. "Finish your pastry."

***

"What about you, Nova? What will you do?" I asked as she handed me another sack of mystery beans. She allegedly purchased them in Averly—a wagon-full every harvest—but her gifts always came in a variety of colors, sizes, and textures, and it made me wonder if she led a double life as a bean dealer or something.

"Oh I'll stay here in the forest. Feed the flowers and drink my tea."

"All by yourself?"

"Don't fret over me, child. I'm never alone. Not in a place like this."

Mason made a face, and I sympathized. Nova was a wrinkled puzzle, always speaking in riddles and obscure fortunes. Half the time I didn't know what she was talking about. But maybe that was the key to intellect—speaking in gibberish to elicit awe and respect.

"You'll be okay, then? I don't need to worry about you inviting demons over for tea?"

She waved the thought away. "They wouldn't dare confront a sister of the Fates."

I smiled and hugged her tightly, but I failed to kill the hollow feeling in my chest. This goodbye felt too conclusive, too permanent, just like my last conversation with Tom had been. The world was changing rapidly, and

Nova's weekly psychic readings already felt obsolete and irretrievable.

As we embraced, her minty breath tickled my ear. "You're special, love. Know that. Don't *forget* that." I frowned into her collar, but I didn't pull away, sensing another omen. "My parting advice to you is this, Raven: let your heart rule your head, and give when all is taken from you."

Before I could ask her to repeat herself—less cryptically, this time—she spoke again, soft and insistent and a little fearful.

I stepped back to look at her, but she just shooed me along as though nothing had transpired. "Go on now. Save the world," she teased, winking at me with her good eye. "It's waiting for you."

As we walked away from her little house in the heart of the Range, I carried her whispers with me.

"*Know that if you do these things, Alex,*" she'd said, "*the sun will shine again.*"

25

As we resumed our trek to Holly, I kept the morbid thoughts at bay by reminding myself that we had a spirit guide and a magical sword at our disposal. It also didn't hurt that the demons trailing us were now dispersed among a thousand evil grasshoppers' hindguts.

Things were looking up.

"What's that?" asked Fudge, who'd chosen to keep pace with me for the past two hours, occasionally pointing at wildlife or offering me dried fruit from Nova's snack sack. "That you're humming?"

I paused, realizing the old river lullaby had slipped through my lips. I swallowed, too embarrassed to explain its origin. "It's just something my mother used to sing."

He froze in place, and the eavesdroppers ahead slowed to a halt, their revolving gazes unsure, timid, and inquisitive.

I'd grown accustomed to that look by now. It was a look that said, *"We've indeed heard the rumors about the Kingsley Household tragedy, and we've been instructed not to pry."*

Fudge's eyes wilted slightly. "My parents told me about her. She earned twelve stars at the Institute, and everyone thought she would succeed Gilmore. Thought she'd be the first woman on the Council. Then she left the city to marry your father, right?" At my rigid nod, he grinned. "What was she like?"

Will's eyes snapped to mine, throbbing with empathy, and that singular exchange confirmed my suspicions: he'd lost his mother too, then.

I'd gathered as much, seeing as he lived alone with his father. But now I knew he'd seen Death—he'd either witnessed her passing or endured the guilt of his absence. He'd known her and lost her. And he knew how painful it was to remember.

Still, I never passed up an opportunity to whisk away the cobwebs. "She was amazing. Always kind and gentle. But intelligent too. And independent." I thought of her beautiful olive skin and deep-set eyes. Her thick hair, lashes, and eyebrows—dark and shapely—as if she'd been drawn in oak gall ink. "She smelled like apple blossoms, and her hands were always covered in soil. I mean, *always*. She had to clean the dirt out of her nails every night. And she loved people. She really loved people." I turned my head to the sky, mostly to keep the tears from pooling.

I didn't talk about her often; it hurt too much to vocalize, and it was impossible to summarize the maverick's character in such a concise manner.

"It was so long ago that everything's a bit blurry, but I do remember how she could make anyone feel better, just by the way she spoke ... or *sang*," I added with a small grin. "Her voice was special. Not just a mother's voice, but a voice that belonged to a teacher and a leader and a minister. Hearing it gave me strength, footing. And I guess, through memory, it still does."

My peers had their heads down, their eyes on the ground as they absorbed my words, and even Styx appeared moved.

Fudge was the first to look up, and he smiled softly. "Must run in the family."

My chest tightened at the sentiment, but something rattled in the underbrush before I could object, and my lips clamped shut.

The four of us reached for our swords and knives and flashlights, and we faced the threat together—instantly alert and battle-ready.

The leaves quivered before us, but the vegetation was too dense to identify our enemy.

What now?

What else could possibly want to kill us?

But I didn't have to wait long to find out. The beast lunged from the bush, crashing into my chest, and a startled scream erupted from my throat as I fell backward.

I hit the soil with a painful thud, expecting the sharp kiss of steel or the fatal canines of a hungry mountain lion. I did not, however, anticipate a slobbery tongue on my cheek and the stench of damp, muddy fur. A stench I knew all too well.

Richard.

The mutt licked my face elatedly, his paws keeping me flat on my back while his heavy tail thumped the earth. Laughing, I hugged him to me— buoyed by his presence and amusing entrance.

"Well, aren't *you* infinitely better than the creature I anticipated?" Fudge cooed, crouching to pet the whining crossbreed. Richard nuzzled into the contact, flopping onto his back and sticking out his tongue. The boy chuckled at the dog's antics and granted him a belly rub.

My fellow delinquent looked fantastic considering his age and the perilous terrain he'd crossed. His lonesome journey warmed my heart, and it also renewed my hope in my father's evacuation plan. Perhaps more citizens had escaped Belgate than Will presumed.

"This is Richard," I announced, standing up and brushing the forest floor off my pants.

Mason gave the mongrel one dainty pat on the head—wary of flees, probably. "Who names their dog *Richard*?"

The mutt made his way over to Will, who considered him with lukewarm interest. Richard sniffed at his boots, then sank to the ground and, much to my dismay, began gnawing on Will's leather soles and ratty laces.

Will merely sighed, like he'd finally hit rock bottom. "I don't know," he muttered. "I think *Dick* is fitting."

***

I sat by the fire, chuckling as Richard stole yet another twig from Styx's body and spat it out at her feet. The spirit slumped over her knees, resigned, but she still accepted the offering and threw it into the woods for the millionth time that night.

With Nova's set of matches and the confidence of four youth, we'd lit a campfire large enough to cook Mason's kill and two dozen hawk's wings. They were my father's favorite mushrooms to harvest as a kid, back when the Gates were open. And, lucky for me, they were easy to identify and bore few toxic lookalikes.

Mason didn't trust my botany knowledge, though, hence the gray squirrels turning on a spit.

I rubbed my aching forearm while tending to the mushrooms. Will told me the muscle would build quickly if I kept practicing with the demon's blade, but when I'd shot him a dry look, he'd said I could always sleep with my arm in the river if the pain was so bad.

I stopped complaining after that.

Since Nova's, our taciturn leader had retreated into his shell again. He was back to business, speaking only to hasten our water breaks or to warn us of loose soil. Worst of all, he was anxious, and his unease was contagious.

If Will was worried, *all* of us should have been worried.

Fudge sat beside me on a fallen tree, offering a piece of charred squirrel, and I graciously accepted. "I can't believe we went a whole day without something trying to kill us," he marveled.

"Easy. The day's not over yet."

He chuckled tensely, and we ate in comfortable silence, listening to the rustling forest and Richard's incessant whining.

"Can I ask you something?" he ventured a few minutes later. He waited for my slow, wary nod before proceeding to ask, "What do you plan to do when we reach the Command?"

My lips parted to provide an obvious answer, but I closed them again to reflect on my logic—or lack thereof. My only objective so far had been surviving long enough to deliver a message. Any plans beyond that were still blueprints and fantasies. "I don't know. I guess ... I'll try to enlist."

The fire popped loudly, and all three boys turned to stare at me. Even Styx looked skeptical, and she didn't even own a face.

"I know it's illegal," I said, glancing away from their scrutiny. "But we've been invaded by *demons*. We need to bolster our forces and recruit as many fighters as possible. Gender shouldn't matter at a time like this."

Mason frowned. "They haven't allowed a woman in combat since the Crash. Since a woman *caused* the Crash. You think they'll suddenly make an exception for some untrained girl who broke the law?"

I'd read stories about the terrorist who'd brought humanity's final empire to ruin. The Mad Commander, they'd called her. She'd launched a rebellion at the crest of the Water Wars, and her following had sabotaged the largest reservoirs, then slaughtered the heads of state. Chaos ensued, and with it, nuclear warfare.

One woman had climbed the ranks, achieved power, and annihilated 70 percent of the human population in the Northern Hemisphere.

Her legacy became the Court's underlying motive for the Gender Clause—the law that prohibited female service. It was her example, compounded by the deep-rooted sexism and misogyny of our central government, that prevented me from participating in this war.

And yet ...

"She might have destroyed civilization, but she did cripple the strongest military in the world," I said. "The Command can't ignore what woman are capable of just because they don't like the implications."

Mason rolled his eyes. "Figures. Should've known you'd idolize a sociopath."

With poetic timing, Richard swept in and stole Mason's squirrel meat right out of his hands, darting away with the speed of a practiced thief. Mason called after him indignantly, and when he turned on me, livid, I passed him a close-lipped smile.

"It's no question that you're capable of fighting," Fudge agreed, "but if you show up in Holly and declare your right to serve in the military ..."

"It's dangerous," Will concluded, and my smile faded.

"If I tell them what I've done, what *we've* done—"

"Stories won't buy you a ticket into the military," Will said. "Not when they can only be validated by three teenagers."

I puffed my cheeks. What, should I have towed Stretch's body to Holly? Documented each of my kills like a crime scene investigation?

"I placed in the Tournament," I insisted, "there were thousands of witnesses."

"You can't admit that openly. They'll imprison you for competing and ignore your merit."

"Why are you being so pessimistic?" I snapped.

Irritation flared in Will's eyes, but so did something that resembled injury, which was even more perplexing. "I'm being realistic."

"*Realistic*? When the demons come for Holly, the Command won't be checking gonads at the gate," I argued. "We fight, or we die."

"Fine. But going to the Command now and asking for a uniform is a death wish."

I glared at him, and he glared back with equal intensity. Styx looked between us timidly, her light dimming a few hundred lumens.

"Then what would you have me do, Will?" I hurled back. "Hide in the woods? Wait until another city is wiped clean off the map? Do I have your permission to enlist then, or do I have to wait until there's no one left to save?"

He clenched his jaw and said nothing.

I threw his gaze away. *That's what I thought.*

"Hey." Fudge touched my arm gingerly. "I only brought it up because I'm worried about you ... about where you'll end up if the three of us are sent back to Belgate or the Rim. I just ... I wanted to know if you had a backup plan."

My brow softened at the genuine concern in his eyes.

No. I didn't have a backup plan. I didn't even have a *plan*.

I'd just assumed I could assimilate myself behind the scenes. Make a difference in this war while no one was looking, then ask for forgiveness. But I hadn't stopped to think about my ultimate destination, just like I hadn't stopped to think about my Tournament debut.

Stopping and *thinking* weren't exactly my strong suits.

"Don't worry about me," I said, slipping Fudge an easy smile. "I'll find a way in. I have a talent for worming my way into male-dominated spaces."

He smirked at me, shaking his head fondly. But when I glanced over at Will again, he was watching me with that cold, unimpressed expression. And maybe, with just a crumb of solicitude.

26

We hiked through the morning and eventually reached the eastern slope of the Range. The vegetation was easier to traverse on this side, the pines shorter and evenly dispersed, the undergrowth less dense. When we reached the peak of another hill, I climbed a pile of lichen-mottled boulders, eager to get a good look at the terrain below. But what I saw in the valley made my entire body go still.

At the base of the mountain, the tree line spat out the weathered road we'd chosen to avoid. The roadway hugged a meandering river between grassy hillslopes, then vanished into the meadow beyond. Past that, several acres had been cleared for a gravel lot, and in place of an aspen grove, a small set of buildings and canvas tents had taken root. Inside this plot, Ellsian flags rippled like the flames of a candle—torches of red and yellow battling the wind.

We'd reached some sort of base camp. For *soldiers*.

I was running before my mind could catch up.

"Patrons—wait a second, you welt!" Mason yelled after me, but I was moving with downhill momentum, and I couldn't stop.

I wouldn't.

We'd found people. Civilization. *Refuge*. Which meant I could finally carry out my father's request. I could finally prove to him that I was more than a girl to be sheltered, more than a curse to be hidden. And the sooner we alerted the Command, the sooner I could save him.

A few minutes later, I burst through the trees, taking in my surroundings with unbridled enthusiasm. Men in navy military trousers and white t-shirts collected in small groups, saddling horses and speaking in loud tones. They snorted at one another, passing jokes or custom barbs—many of them one and the same. Their demeanor was less formal than I'd anticipated. I'd only seen soldiers passing through Belgate on their way to the Rim, disciplined and valiant. And I'd only met veterans with sober expressions or pompous attitudes like Frost.

I'd never seen soldiers act so ... boyish.

When they saw me standing there awkwardly, hands on my knees and panting, they abandoned their tasks and drew their swords, knives, and hatchets. I straightened, raising my hands in the air to signal my pacific intentions. Smiling so widely it hurt.

My reaction was freaking them out, but I couldn't help it. We'd beaten the odds and made it to a military base, and Stretch and his demon crew had failed to hunt us down. We'd *survived*.

"It's a girl!" someone yelled, which only spurred more confusion.

"A what?"

"Hold your positions!"

The voice tugged on my spinal cord, and my head jerked violently toward its source.

A young man approached from the rear of the crowd, wearing a half-buttoned army jacket with several badges sewn into the sleeve. The manner in which the others parted for him pointed to his authority—and the respect he'd garnered.

"State your identity and allegiance," he demanded.

I blinked back at him, mesmerized by his voice, consumed by the itch of familiarity. "You first."

The man cocked his head as he drew closer, his features becoming sharper and more distinct with every step: a lean build and broad shoulders, dark hair cropped short around his ears, scarred olivewood skin that hadn't seen enough sun.

Narrow, deep-set eyes.

"Identity and *allegiance*," he repeated, his words seared by aggravation. But the curiosity nestled in his tone detracted from his intimidating character.

He halted five strides away, stock-still as he looked upon me—as I stared back at him in astonishment.

"Al?" he breathed, barely a whisper.

My tongue was leaden.

"… Tom?"

***

Save for his eye, the right half of his face was burned featureless, nearly unrecognizable. Pink and ragged scars marred him from temple to jugular vein, turning his skin into a quilt of crinkled foil and melted flesh. It was a badge of service. A badge of pain.

The left side, though, remained unscathed.

And unforgettable.

"Tom?" I tried again, louder. My voice cracked against the ceiling of incredulity.

How?

How could he have been alive all this time? A mountain range away?

Tom smiled his crooked grin, and I rushed forward, shocking his subordinates as I jumped into his open arms. He caught me with a startled laugh and lifted me off the ground like I was ten again, spinning me round, holding me tight. Tears were already streaming down my face, and I burrowed into his embrace, tucking my nose into his collar and breathing him in.

Nothing made sense. This had to be a dream.

Alive. My brother was alive.

My brother.

Questions piled into the space behind my eyes until I could hardly see straight. How could this be? Why had he let us think he'd been lost to the Rim? What the hell happened to his face? When did he lose his baby fat?

Tom set me down and held me at arm's length. "Look at you, Al. You're so tall. And beautiful. *Patrons*, you look just like Mom." His gaze dipped to my shoulders and the leather pads beneath his palms. "Except for the armor. Why are you wearing armor?"

I might have laughed, but I couldn't be sure. I was too emotional to be sure of anything right now.

Between us, Richard wagged his tail, sniffing Tom's boots and whining at the smell he'd forgotten. But the way his tail pelted me in the shin over and over again confirmed that I wasn't crazy; Richard saw him too.

This was real. *Tom* was real.

Tears rolled over my cheeks. "How—? When did—" I punched him in the arm, and his comrades tensed. "I thought you were dead! Where the hell have you been?"

His smile wavered. "Al …"

His men unsheathed their swords again as Will emerged from the forest with Fudge and Mason at his heels. Our raven-haired leader slowed as he weighed the situation, then stopped just short of our huddle.

My brother straightened, and when I looked back at his face, I was stunned to see that all traces of joy had drained from his expression. His jaw was set, and his eyes had become dark, murderous slits in a matter of seconds.

It was not a Tom I recognized.

"You *rat*," he breathed, and he charged at Will.

27

And, as usual, I didn't have a clue what was happening.

Sword in hand, Tom sprang at Will, who had no choice but to draw his own weapon in defense. They engaged in a fierce rally before I snapped out of my stupor and ran between them.

"Whoa!" I yelled, waving my arms. They broke apart only to avoid skewering me, and I stepped beside Will to glare at my brother—a man seemingly unhinged. "Tom, what's wrong with you? Will is with us."

"Wait. Thomas *Kingsley*?" Mason said, his confusion palpable. "I thought..."

Fudge looked at my brother with wide, disbelieving eyes. "Me too."

I felt that bewilderment in my soul. It was hard enough to wrap my brain around Tom's resurrection, but now he had to go and attack a teenage boy? Like a psycho?

I didn't even know where to start with that. All I could do was scowl at him and gently nudge Will in a safer direction.

Tom sighed through his nose, his eyes pinned to Will, his sword grip as firm as ever. "Alex, get out of the way," he commanded, his voice dripping with hatred. I'd never heard him speak that way. Or make that face. "He's dangerous."

... What?

If anyone was a threat right now, it was *Tom*.

"Will is a good guy, Tom. He's a trainee from home. An ally." I looked at Will for a little help, but his gaze remained leveled at my brother.

Useless.

"He's no ally." Tom snatched my wrist and pulled me away from Will with a forcefulness that told me he wasn't playing games. "I'd know that face anywhere. His fighting style confirms it. You pull those sleeves up, and you'll have all the proof you need."

The sentence drained my gut of blood, leaving my stomach hollow and uneasy. His sleeves? How did Tom know about Will's tattoos?

"What are you saying?" I asked.

"That his family is military. *Rhean* military." My brother narrowed his eyes at the silent boy before me. "And he's directly responsible for this war."

I felt my own face contort at the absurdity.

Rhean?

Responsible?

Tom wasn't making any sense. His accusations were ridiculous and entirely unfounded, and I couldn't help feeling humiliated by the entire exchange. Perhaps his return from the afterlife had left him with a few too many screws loose.

"What are you talking about?" I hissed, struggling to remove myself from his vice grip. "How could Will, from *Belgate*, be responsible for any of this? We're fighting demons, Tom."

Angry brown eyes slid my way. "And how do you think they got here in the first place?"

At that, I stopped trying to wriggle out of my brother's grasp. I thought back to what Nova had said about Rhea, that someone had to have opened a bridge. Most probably, a member of the royal family.

Warily, I turned to Will.

He wouldn't look at me—only my brother—but his entire mood had transformed. And when he spoke, it was a ripple in ice water.

"It's true," he said, his voice low and even and eerily foreign. "I broke ties with my family eight years ago and immigrated to Belgate. When I discovered their forces had tripled, I decided to compete in the Tournament for a chance to leave the city and enter the Interior unnoticed." Something akin to shame marked his face. "I was planning to desert."

"*What?*" I cried, marching forward, but Tom dragged me back.

"Tell them who you are," he ordered.

A muscle flexed in Will's temple, and for a second, I thought he was going to make a break for it and dissolve into the shadows of the Range. But after a long pause, he swallowed and lifted his chin. "I'm the second son of Godric Sterling, an heir to the throne." He hesitated—took a breath. "My father's the king of Rhea and the commander of its army."

My heart sank to the bottom of my ribcage, and it took all feelings of hope and friendship and trust along with it.

The soldiers stepped forward, raising their weapons, but one stern glance from my brother had them halting in their tracks, stewing with revulsion and blatant odium.

Will paid them no attention, his gaze still tethered to Tom's. "Ten years ago, my father opened the portal with the assistance of the Seventh Order." Lignite irises finally met mine. "Your brother's right. This is all Godric's doing."

I closed my eyes as if that would shield me from the truth.

I couldn't process it. And gritz, I didn't want to.

Sterling had built the bridge. He'd had help from the Seventh Order, one of the most notorious cults on the continent. He'd become a mass murderer.

And Will was his *son*.

Will, who'd acted ignorant. Who'd lied to our faces. For days, for *years*.

"Why didn't you say anything?" I whispered. He gazed back at me, perpetually silent and impassive. "You could have told us after Belgate. After Nova's. But you lied." And gained nothing.

Will's reaction was stone, like I'd shot a dart at a granite statue. Fudge and Mason, on the other hand, bore the faces of betrayal and disappointment. And I was positive my expression was ten times as potent.

Will's father had been responsible for snatching Tom away. For destroying our city and murdering our neighbors and nearly getting all of us killed. And Will had just stood by, waiting for the invasion to happen, waiting for his father's minions to pick us off one by one. He was a wolf in sheep's clothing who'd heard his pack howling.

I thought I'd finally started to figure him out, but I couldn't have been more wrong. I knew nothing. *Less* than nothing.

"Is your name even Will?" I spat bitterly, and I hated the wounded sound of my voice.

He pressed his lips together, guilt flashing in his eyes, and I looked away in disgust.

Tom eyed Will with unadulterated loathing, then nodded for his men to detain him. "Congratulations, Sterling. You have the honor of being Ptarmigan's first prisoner of war."

PART 2: Trials & Tribulations

28

I felt like I'd been trampled by a horse.

My insides were bruised, and my mind had turned to sludge, incapable of demolishing and rebuilding Will's identity so quickly.

"Sir...the Interior," a soldier said awkwardly as a group of men took the Rhean prince away.

Tom heaved a sigh and placed a scarred hand on my shoulder. "I'm sorry, Al. I don't have time to discuss this any further right now. I was just about to leave for Holly—it's urgent."

I shook my head dismissively, slipping out of my shock, my residual anger. "Tom, you've got to deliver a message. The demons have taken Belgate. There are more on our tail, just west of here. We've been invaded."

His face turned white, and as my words traveled across camp, wooden crates crashed to the ground, heads swiveled, and an entire company tasted the aftershock of a task fulfilled.

"They broke through the Rim?" someone asked fearfully.

"It can't be ... Belgate's fortified ..."

"Are there other survivors?"

"We're not sure," I admitted, and several men blanched at the devastating news.

Most of them hadn't felt the pain of chronic anxiety since early childhood, when their fathers and uncles and cousins had gone to war. These young soldiers had left their homes to *protect* their families—only to have the homefront gutted in the meantime.

It couldn't have been an easy thing to hear.

Tom cleared his throat and the panic welling there. "When did this happen?"

"Three days ago."

His eyes leapt to the tree line. "How many hostiles were there?"

I shook my head, unsure, so Mason chimed in. "It was hard to get a sense of their forces. But I'd say three hundred, minimum."

My brother glanced between us. "And you said you were pursued?"

"We *were*," I said. "They sent a small team to find survivors and map the terrain. Half of them are dead now, but the other half are unaccounted for."

Tom ground his molars, staring into empty space, forecasting and calculating. Just like our father did when he faced inadequate crop yields or precarious pest problems.

"Dad told me to warn Holly so they could bolster their defenses and evacuate civilians," I emphasized, eager to pluck him out of his musings. "Can I pass you the baton?"

He blinked away the haze of machinations, then nodded. "I'll inform the Command. You and your friends stick with Rover until I get back." He exchanged looks with one of his subordinates, and the 20-something blond dipped his chin, passing me an easy grin. "And don't ... wander. Okay?"

"Okay."

I hugged him once more—before he disappeared on me again, and before I woke up clutching thin air. His arms instantly enveloped me, and I curled my fingers into his uniform, clinging to a ghost in a grown man's body.

"Is Dad okay?" he whispered in my ear.

"I don't know."

He kissed the top of my head and released me, fighting back the emotions in his eyes. The fear and vulnerability there.

Dazed, I watched him bark a few orders to his comrades, mount his horse, and speed off into the valley with four other men. When he vanished into the rolling hills beyond, I let out a long, bewildered breath. I could still feel him on my fingertips, his physical presence, his tangibility, and it sent another storm down my cheeks.

After six years of grieving, my brother had emerged from his grave.

***

"We call them Pans," said Rover.

Mason wrinkled his nose. "Why?"

"Short for Paranormal, Type A classification." The soldier smiled, opening the door to the armory. "Don't look at me like that; I wasn't around when they named the things."

Rover reminded me a lot of Tom—or at least, the Tom I used to know. He was charming, mellow, gregarious. The kind of man who could work a crowd and brighten any atmosphere. He also looked like someone who didn't take military policies too seriously, despite serving as my brother's first lieutenant. Against every protocol I was taught, scraggly blond hair curtained his face, and thin stubble framed the broad, mischievous smile he wore between breaths.

"Type A?" asked Fudge. "There are different … breeds?"

"Sure are. Type A is the kind of demon that wears a human body. They're the moon-eyed soldiers you've encountered in Belgate and the Range. Type B, which I reckon you haven't seen before, resembles a plume of smoke. B's are the raw energy forms that enter our dead soldiers, pre-host. Also known as Pots."

Pots and Pans.

I wondered if there was a psychological component to the names. If perhaps calling the demons inanimate objects helped quell the soldiers' fears. Or maybe, like most military slang, the shorthand terms stemmed from a niche, humorous situation that spread through the ranks like influenza.

"Pots are confined to the West, near the portals," Rover went on. "They can't travel far from their source. Not without a body."

"Wait." Mason paled. "Did you just say *portals*? With an S?"

Rover nodded. "There's a monstrous portal within Sterling's stronghold. It's the first one ever created—the Queen Bee and her wretched beehive. But the Pans can produce other gateways on a smaller scale, all along the Rim. Last I heard, there were twelve geysers on our border spewing demons all day and night."

Thirteen portals. Thirteen demon factories.

"Can you destroy them?" I managed to say.

"We can dismantle 'em when we get close enough. Break the magic seals on the ground, and the portals wink out like candlesticks. But it doesn't take long for the enemy to open another portal the second we destroy its sister."

Great. These demons were infinite *and* coactive.

"And this queen bee portal," said Fudge, "have you tried bombing it?"

Right. Take out the mother ship, and maybe we'd see a domino effect. Maybe we'd buy ourselves enough time to end this war if Sterling couldn't manufacture more soldiers.

"Unfortunately, we've never had the opportunity to do so. Our troops haven't hopped the Gorge in ages; we've been stuck at the Rim for years now." Rover pointed at the weapon on my belt. "Also. You'll have to ditch that sword if you plan on killing anything, Kingsley."

Stretch's weapon grew heavy at my side. I'd fought my first few Pans with that thing; it was kind of special.

"In case you haven't noticed, demons don't die easily. The only thing capable of killing a Pan is vanadium."

"Vanadium?" Mason echoed.

"It's a rare metal," Fudge clarified. "In ancient times, it was used in Damascus steel. But our ancestors used it for nuclear reactors and jet engines."

I glanced at Mason's magical rapier and its ash-rendering blade. I supposed that explained the weapon's price tag; it contained the one ingredient capable of ending this war.

"We use vanadium steel in our combat weapons. It's easy to work with and tough as hell," Rover elaborated. "But like Freckles pointed out, it's rare. We've sucked our deposits dry of vanadium ore, and we've melted down ninety percent of the scrap metal in our reserve. That scarcity made a firearm resurgence impractical too, much to the Command's dismay. Even if we made enough guns to kill the demons more efficiently, we couldn't recover our vanadium-laced ammo."

"So you can't just blow up a bunch of Pans? Bomb them in a giant land mine or something?" Mason proposed.

Rover jutted his chin at a giant pile of bloody swords, helmets, and shields in the center of the room—battle trophies ripe for a vanadium finish. "We can. Bombs made of vanadium shavings and shrapnel are incredibly effective on the Rim. But vanadium combat weapons are the only way to conserve the stuff long term." He eyed my stolen blade. "Three years ago, the Command sent a mining party to scavenge for more resources in the South, but we never heard back."

Three *years*? "I thought the Southern Ridge was safe?" I said, thinking of my father and the evacuees who'd fled there.

He looked at me through eyes of turbulent seawater. "So did we."

Richard licked my fingertips to keep me out of the depressing rabbit hole I'd just uncovered, and I scratched his head, grateful for his company. Good boy.

"Why hasn't anyone come to help us?" Mason asked indignantly. "Other territories across the continent, I mean."

"Ells is Godric's target. The rest of the world doesn't know what we're up against," Fudge reminded him.

"Even if they did, no one would come to our rescue," I said. "Not after the Water Wars. Not after all these centuries."

"Assuming those territories even survived the Crash," Rover added. "The world's gone dark. We could very well be alone."

It wasn't an outlandish thought—that our warring nations were the very last of humanity. But given our current situation, I'd never heard a more terrifying theory.

Rover went on to explain that Ptarmigan had become a central rendezvous point for the military personnel stationed at the Rim. It served as a rotation wing where soldiers could recover for a month or two before deploying again. A home away from home.

Once a year, for six months, the base also hosted a boot camp to train the young Tournament champions from each province. They prepared the fresh recruits for war and, it now occurred to me, equipped them for a total nightmare. The camp's other main purpose was to protect the Interior and the densely populated areas of Ells—doubling as a garrison of sorts.

Rover led us to the main workshop area, where several men crouched over a glowing pot of molten vanadium. Others hammered or chiseled away at steel, filling the building with a cacophony of horrible, deafening sounds that did *not* appeal to Richard. I was half-tempted to plug my ears like Fudge, but my ego wouldn't allow it.

We approached a man sharpening a battle axe, and Rover slapped him on the back with an aggressive playfulness, not at all concerned about startling his armed victim.

The snickering man didn't even flinch, and it made me question if this was one of Rover's close friends, or if the lieutenant simply behaved that way with everyone. "Sol, this is Alex, Tom's sister. These are her travel buddies, Fudge and Marcus."

"It's *Mason*."

Sol peeked over his shoulder at me with storm-gray eyes. His skin was the color of freshly tilled soil, and a wing tattoo spanned the base of his shaved head. "Ah," he said, looking me over like a weapon he'd never seen before. "A girl with holes in her pants and two blades on her person. I smell trouble."

"Good nose," I commended.

He shot me a bone-white smile and scanned the rest of our crew. "How'd you lot get to the Interior from Belgate? It's got to be a fifty-mile trek."

The three of us traded glances, and I shrugged. "We walked."

Sol took us in, reassessing. Then he spun in his seat to fully face us. "You walked through the *Range* with a group of Pans on your tail?"

"There was some running involved," I amended.

He lifted his eyebrows. "Pans hardly sleep. They consume only what they need to keep their human bodies from falling apart, then fight or travel for days at a time. You must have moved pretty damn fast if they didn't catch you."

"They didn't catch *her*," Fudge interjected. "But Mason and I were captured on the second day."

Rover whipped his head around, suddenly intrigued. "They took you prisoner?"

Fudge nodded. Mason pretended he wasn't listening.

"*Gritz*. How many were there?"

"Twelve? No . . . fifteen altogether."

The men's eyes widened, and Rover shook his head, his lips splitting into a wide, wonderstruck smile. "How'd you get out of that one? I would have pissed myself as a grunt."

"Ask Alex," Fudge said. "I was unconscious for most of it."

Rover and Sol looked at me expectantly, like two children waiting for a bedtime story, and the piece of me that had once been so eager to showcase my capabilities shriveled up like a spoiled potato.

"Rope … river trout … and demon grasshoppers," I answered, blowing a stray curl out of my eyes as I recalled Will's swordsmanship and bravery. There had also been a magical spirit chick involved, but I was hesitant to reveal that ludicrous detail. Styx had vanished into the woods, and I had a feeling she did so for a reason. "It's sort of a long story."

The two men stared at me for a moment, and then Sol jerked his thumb at me, flashing another wolfish grin. "I'm gonna like this one."

It wasn't the reaction I'd anticipated, and it pulled a slow, coy smile out of me.

When Mason began showing off his rapier to Sol, hungry for attention, Rover led me—and therefore, Richard—out of the workshop into the gravel courtyard. Two dozen soldiers unloaded supplies from the wagons or busied themselves with other chores, but as we passed, every man did a double take, then immediately muttered something to his companion.

Okay. Not subtle. At all.

Rover slung his arm over my shoulder. "Don't mind them. We just don't see too many girls around here, you know? Give 'em a day or two to adjust." He passed me a cheeky grin. "That said, your grand entrance didn't help any. Barging into camp with a sword in hand and an enemy of mankind at your side … it's rumor gas."

"He's not—" I bit my tongue to kill the rest of my sentence.

Why was I defending Will? He was Rhean, through and through. Just a Rhean whose personality I'd come to enjoy.

"I'm just sayin', right now you embody everything society forbids, kid."

"Yeah," I murmured, "it's a bad habit."

29

After leaving Richard by the chicken coop with some well-earned scraps, we entered a brick building next to the barracks, and I was startled to find it packed with soldiers. They crowded the tables and bar, laughing too loudly and drinking too much.

Rover's whistle cut through the din. "Boys, this is Alex Kingsley. She's a guest here—" He was disrupted by a chorus of hoots. "*And* she's your captain's baby sister! Act accordingly."

The catcalls dwindled.

So Tom really *was* a big shot, then. That would come in handy.

As we made our way through the pub, men greeted me with cordial smiles and welcoming head nods, others with suspicious once-overs. A few scoffed and traded sexist jokes.

"What has this country resorted to?" one growled. "School girls in the army ..."

He reminded me of Titan—huge and Yeti-like. Illegible names spiraled up his brawny arms in ugly, faded ink. Five of them were crossed out, and I didn't want to think about what that could mean.

Rover smiled warmly at the brute. "Grismond, this is Alex. Alex, Grizzly."

"I know her. She brought that Rhean trash here," the giant hissed, needlessly stentorian, and the room quieted to a hum of murmurs.

My eye twitched at the accusation. "*Trash*? Have a whiff at your underarms, Neck-Rolls."

It sparked a few snorts of delighted surprise, but Grismond didn't find my quip very amusing. He let loose a terrifying guttural sound as he stood from the table. "You—"

Rover placed himself between us before someone got his crotch kicked. "Let me handle this, Fuse." He wet his lips and patted the man on the bicep. "Sergeant, I'm sure you can understand how excited the Captain is to see his sister after seven years. She's made it all the way from Belgate, on foot, to alert the Interior of a raid. She also survived a demon attack. And she even brought us a war prisoner to use as leverage. As far as I can see, she's deserving of a warm welcome, no?"

Grismond shrugged Rover's man-hug off. "That boy's an enemy. And she defended him. She could be a conspirator for all we know."

"Gris, Gris, *Gris*. You don't really think a seventeen-year-old girl is conspiring against the Ellsian government, do you?"

The titters around the room only further agitated the man. He glared at Rover and puffed out his colossal chest. "Girls don't belong here, Wright. Skirts don't fight, and they have no business totin' steel." His gaze flicked to my sword in disgust. "She might share his blood, but that doesn't mean we'll blindly accept her. His demands ain't law."

Rover's expression remained good-humored, but something dangerous churned in his eyes—an ocean receding from the shoreline. "You've forgotten your rank, my friend. We respect our captain and those he deems trustworthy."

"Respect oughta be earned," the man spat.

Exasperated, I brought my knife down on the weathered table, forcefully piercing the wood and startling the men in my vicinity. "Let me earn it, then."

I was so sick and tired of men debating my worth. If they wanted me to prove why I deserved a place here, I'd prove it, even if I had to work twice as hard.

Soldiers' backs uncurled in surprise, and a few mouths twisted up into curious smirks. But Grismond only sneered. "Put away your toy, girl. This is no place for you."

"Why? 'Cause the weeds on the High Court told you so?"

He and his peers laughed at that. "Aside from genetics? You're just a child. You wouldn't last a day in the belly of war."

Was that a challenge? "You willing to put money on that? Or are you scared you might lose all your skits to a *school girl*?"

Grismond moved forward threateningly, and Rover pressed his hand against the man's sternum—holding him back calmly, but with intention. "Why don't you get some fresh air, Gris? Before this gets ugly."

The Bear's muscles went taut, and he leaned forward, invading Rover's personal space. "And if I prefer ugly?"

An excited grin tugged at Rover's lips, and I suddenly regretted pushing the envelope. I didn't want him to *die* on my behalf.

"Oi! Break it up, you two!"

I pivoted, baffled by the angry, feminine voice behind the bar, but my ears hadn't deceived me: strands of silky black hair curtained the woman's angular face—the bulk of it tied back in a soiled orange bandana. She wore a man's collared shirt with the top buttons undone, exposing her cleavage, and she'd even pierced her nose. But it was her bright red lipstick that really drove the point home.

This was a woman of authority, and she reveled in her success.

"There'll be no fighting in this building, you hear me? I just had the windows fixed from the last dogfight." She pointed a bottle of whiskey at the men. "I'm not mopping up any blood tonight. If you can't play nice, get out."

Grismond narrowed his eyes, but the aggression subsided. Holding

Rover's gaze, he slowly leaned away.

"There, see?" the bartender purred, and Grismond sent a hostile look her way. Her ruby lips quirked up at the edges. "It's not that hard to act like a civilized human, is it, Gris?"

Vexed, he marched for the exit, waving at his posse to follow him. "This is why we don't let breeders run a man's establishment," he snarled. "They don't know fun if it's slapping them in the face."

When he slammed the door behind him, conversation returned to a normal octave.

Rover threw his hands in the air. "You won't let me get into a single fight, will you, woman? No matter how hard I try, you'll always be there to save the day!" He collapsed onto a barstool to cap off his theatrics.

She shrugged, lifting a pitcher off the counter and filling his shaker. "You know I'd let you throttle Grizzly if I thought you could handle him."

Rover gaped, snatching up his cup before she was done pouring. Alcohol dribbled over the edge of the table, and she tsked. "What's that supposed to mean, Jay? I could take down twenty Grizzlies if your life was at stake."

"My hero."

They shared a grin, and Rover beckoned me over. "Jaden, this is Alex."

She smiled, her big brown eyes warm and doelike—a stark contrast to the belligerent attitude she harbored. "Nice to put a face to name. Your brother talks about you all the time."

I faltered as I slid onto my stool. "Really?"

Rover huffed. "You kidding? It's constant. *Al used to do this*, and *Al always did that.* The man is obsessed."

"Are you two . . . close to Tom?" It was weird hearing people talk about him in present tense. I still didn't know how to process him *existing* again; the thought of him living out his military dreams and reminiscing with friends itched and oozed like a fly bite.

"Yeah, and we get crap for it," Rover complained. "People think I'm a sycophant because of how he treats me. Lots of backlash."

Jaden slapped him with her towel. "That's because the shoe fits, Rove. Now suit up, I need help."

"Apologies, Fuse. Duty calls."

The blond jumped over the counter, leaning in to kiss Jaden's cheek. She intercepted his stubbly face with her hand, shoving him away—naturally, like she did this often. But they were both smiling.

***

As Jaden tied Rover's apron around his waist—after he'd failed to do so correctly, twice—the two made eye contact over his shoulder. Their gazes lingered, perhaps a few seconds too long, so the lieutenant murmured something offensive to shock them out of it.

Jaden pushed him away in mock outrage, rolling her eyes as the buffoon giggled through his teeth.

"Nauseating, isn't it?"

I jumped in my seat, turning to the man who'd seemingly appeared out of thin air.

He was older than most of the soldiers here, bundled in a heavy black coat with too many pockets. His hands were covered in scars and calluses—proof he'd been at war a long time. Proof he'd survived it. "Those two lovebirds have been dancing around each other since birth, basically. Always flirting in our faces. Hard to stomach at times."

His husky voice was like a gust of mountain wind—worn thin from too many years in too many places.

"They aren't together?"

"Friends, they say."

My eyes settled on the pair again, and I reexamined their interactions.

Jaden asked Rover something specific, and he launched into a tangent, cursing and changing his voice to suit the characters in his story—glancing at her every few beats for the reactions he sought. Jaden scoffed and shook her head at his dramatics, visibly unimpressed with his tale. But they both breathed easy.

"I'll admit, it's refreshing to see young love, though," the stranger conceded. "Even in its prickly stage. It has you reflecting on your choices. Makes a man ask himself what he's really fighting for—and for *whom*."

I glanced at my gloved hands.

The military had always been my calling. It was something Tom and I had bonded over since we were children, and after his passing, it became a way for me to honor his sacrifice, to live as he had lived. Eventually, that dream had grown to encompass several other goals, including a ticket out of Belgate and a chance to do something. To *be* something.

But now I had Tom back in my life, and I'd escaped Belgate's towering walls, so that left me with new and shifting motivations.

What *was* I fighting for?

I didn't have a Jaden to protect; I wasn't even sure I had a family to support, least of all a home. And the High Court was the last thing I'd die for. So, would I fight for justice? Revenge? Peace?

Freedom, as Frost had campaigned? Or mere survival?

Was I just . . . trying to prove a point?

Now that I was finally here, I couldn't pinpoint my purpose, the concrete motivation propelling me forward, and it bothered me.

"Do you think they'll ever admit their feelings?" I asked, trying to bury my discomfort.

The man took a swig of his beverage, swishing the contents around in his mouth for a few moments as he considered my question. "Undoubtedly. War makes the heart grow fonder—and obnoxiously raw. One day he'll come too close to losing his head, one of them will break, and the next thing you know, we'll have a whole family of glib, egotistical rule-benders."

I grinned. This guy was something else.

He stuck out his hand. "Beckett."

I grasped his forearm in favor of his bare palm, surprising him a little. "Alex."

"The one who brought the enemy," he said, although his tone was jocular.

"He's not an enemy."

"Then just a bad person."

"No … not that either." Just apathetic and deceitful.

"Then what is he, exactly?" Beckett stroked his chin. "Because he sounds to me like someone people make up their minds about the moment they have something to call him. Thrown into a sea of prejudice and told to swim upstream."

He watched me with perceptive, forest-green eyes—eyes that made me feel childish and small … and maybe even unjustified.

Was I really judging Will so harshly? Even though he'd lied?

My father once told me I shouldn't judge people solely by their actions. That sometimes people have the right intentions. But Will's actions were noble; his *motives* were the screwy part.

"Haven't you been fighting Rhea for years?" I asked. "How can you be so …?"

"Tolerant?" He chuckled and took another swill from his pint glass. "For the last ten years, I've been fighting monsters, not people. Before that, I fought a monarch, not his kingdom. It's an important distinction, and I believe Rhean citizens shouldn't be punished for what their leader has done, nor should Rhean soldiers be condemned for their service." He gave me a small, sad smile. "We tend to forget that when we taste the sword, we all bleed red."

His comments surprised me. I hadn't heard anyone speak so sensibly in a very long time, especially when it came to Rhea.

In school, we read texts on Rhean's deviance from democracy, its adoption of despotism and witchcraft and other medieval practices. We read horror stories of human sacrifice and execution by flame. We were taught to hate the culture, to perceive its people as prehistoric and savage and murderous.

But Will didn't seem like the type of guy to go around lighting people on fire. He was intelligent. Rational. And perhaps ... perhaps even considerate, if you peeled back enough of those stiff, frozen layers.

"They'll kill him."

My heart thudded so painfully I thought it might have tumbled from my chest struck the rum-splattered floor. "What?"

"Vengeance, fear ... they run deep among us." Beckett watched the crowd, his gaze sweeping over Grismond's abandoned table. "Your friend's not safe here."

My mouth turned to sand, and I struggled to swallow. *Kill him?*

Realizing he'd just knocked a rib loose, Beckett poured me something from the bottle he'd hijacked. "Here. While you ruminate."

I peered down at the foamy liquid in my cup. "Alcohol?"

"There's nothing else here, kid."

"... Will you tell Tom?"

He flashed a mischievous row of teeth. "Tom who?"

30

Mistaking nervousness for hunger, Jaden insisted on feeding me, and despite my respectful vetoes, I'd ended up with a large plate of food I had no intention of consuming. Thankfully, Richard had snuck his way into the pub after befriending the federates, and he now sat beneath the counter, happily munching on my discarded table scraps.

Jaden, blissfully unaware of my deception, was finally a happy hostess, Rover was thrilled to see Jaden satisfied, and Beckett watched my symbiotic relationship play out with a knowing smirk.

Fudge and Mason had just joined the party as well, wrangled in by a short, burly man who proceeded to drag them around the pub and make introductions. Fudge looked a little overwhelmed and slightly terrified, but Mason, to his credit, stuck to the boy's side, periodically squeezing his shoulder to keep him calm.

When Fudge and I brushed gazes across the establishment, I raised my brow. *You okay?*

He shrugged, eyes darting to their stocky tour guide, who'd begun chugging a pitcher of alcohol, and back to me.

I stifled a laugh.

When darkness filled the windowpanes, a fresh slew of men arrived, making their way to the bar and eliciting a rumble of friendly greetings and jubilant cries for more alcohol. Among the last to trickle in was Tom, and his presence stole my breath away.

My brother was back from his travels—back from the *dead*—and once again walking this earth like a phoenix scarred by its own flame.

"Debrief in ten," he announced to the room, and a few individuals bobbed their heads.

Rover elbowed Jaden. "Mom's home. Hide the whiskey."

Tom grimaced at their snickers, pulling off his jacket and throwing it over a chair. "This is why no one takes me seriously, Rove. You never address me properly."

Rover gasped and bowed comically low. "Apologies, Captain Crater-Face."

Jaden poured Tom a drink with mock sympathy. "May this appease you, Officer Man-Child."

My brother huffed at their antics, reaching for his lager to put an end to his misery.

"Come on, guys," Sol chided, throwing an arm over Tom's shoulder before he could claim his beverage. "We address His Majesty as King Kingsley on Tuesdays. *Manners*."

An impish grin lit Sol's face, and my brother chuckled, shoving the man away with the same boyish vigor as fourteen-year-old Tom.

It made me happy knowing he'd forged quality friendships in the last seven years. That he'd found people who saw him as an equal when the sun went down and the armor came off.

I was glad to know he hadn't been alone. Not like I'd been.

Tom passed them his crooked smile, and it widened when he saw me waiting for him.

He moved for me then, his strides quickly eating the distance until we stood toe to toe. Those sturdy hands found my shoulders again, and his honey eyes flitted over my face, cataloging the changes in my appearance under auburn lamplight.

I knew it ached, reuniting at the curtain call of my adolescence and suddenly meeting the replica of our departed mother. I felt the same way looking at Tom; he was the product of the two people I loved most in the world. The living memory of Mom and Dad. And if that wasn't bittersweet enough, our aging features only emphasized our time apart—all the milestones we'd missed, all the highs and lows we'd experienced without each other.

It was a slap to the face ... but if that slap meant Tom's revival was real and incontestable, then the sting was certainly worth it.

"Al, thanks to you, Holly's sent riders to every small town and citadel in the country," he said. "They're calling in the army, rallying the troops here in the Interior. When the Pans come for us, we'll be ready."

I let out a breath so big, it felt like some of my soul slipped out. "That's ... really good to hear."

He leaned in close and sniffed. His brow creased. "Have you been drinking?"

"I'm seventeen."

"Yeah. What's your point?" He glared at Rover. "You gave her alcohol?"

Rover gaped, eyes flying to Beckett murderously, and the older man grinned behind the lip of his bottle.

I tugged on my brother's shirt to claim his attention. "Tom, where is he?"

His smile vanished. "Who?"

"You know who."

He didn't answer me right away, and I could practically see the gears spinning in his head as he scrambled for a clever way to avoid my question. Wary of the curious eyes on us, he dragged me to the side of the pub. "Al, I don't want you anywhere near him. He's an enemy. In fact, he's quite literally *the* enemy."

"Would people stop with that word? He may have withheld infor- mation ... a lot of information, but he's done nothing that warrants that title. He saved my life. And I'd like to see him." *Before it's too late.*

I was suddenly desperate to get Will out of this situation. I was still angry with him—furious, actually. But Beckett's words burned beneath my skin, and I needed to set things straight. I needed to see that liar and speak my mind. Throw my punches while I still could.

Tom ran a hand through his dark mane of hair. "You really haven't changed at all. I think you've actually grown more stubborn in my ab- sence."

"*Tom.*"

"He's in the stables."

I arched an eyebrow. "The stables."

"We don't have a proper detention facility here. We weren't expecting delinquents. *And* we knew if we took him to Holly, he'd be executed with- out a trial," he explained when I shot him a dirty look. "I'm serious, Al. Don't go near him again."

I pushed past him, ignoring the prying gazes that followed me to the door.

Apparently, Tom hadn't changed much either. He still knew how to piss me off like no one else. He still thought he was the boss of me. And he still thought he held a candle to our father's preeminence.

But he was sorely mistaken.

***

Breaking the rules was easy as breathing, and slipping past the drunken guard wasn't difficult by any means—he'd been half-conscious when I ar- rived anyway. My biggest challenge was deciding what to say to the puzzling boy inside the barn.

Was Will even the same person I'd come to know? Or had everything been an act, down to his clipped diction and hermit behavior?

Who was this boy of jagged corners, stripped of his mask?

The Rhean sat alone on the hay-strewn floor, bound to an empty horse stall. He leaned against the stable, carving something into a block of wood. Each time he raised his knife, the chains rattled, and the horses grunted or swished their tails at the disturbance.

He wouldn't stab me if I startled him, would he? And what *idiot* had failed his pat-down?

As I crept closer, I realized he wasn't doing anything particularly menacing. In fact, it looked like he was busy sculpting a small wooden figure. The toy soldier had limbs, a shield, and even a sword at its side, and I almost scoffed at its quality. I'd never seen any of Will's projects when he apprenticed at the carpenter's shop, but he clearly had a talent for woodwork—like everything else he tried.

"It's good."

He looked up, but he didn't seem surprised to see me—or relieved or hopeful or even slightly intrigued. It was like he knew I couldn't tolerate the unknown and unanswered, so he'd been waiting patiently for me to cave. And that annoyed me, because *I* didn't even know I would be here, and he sure as hell didn't know me better than I knew myself.

He continued whittling his wooden soldier, and I watched him work for a while, shuffling my feet and thumbing my leather tasset. "Did they let you keep that knife?"

"No. I had it stashed in my boot. They weren't very smart."

I crossed my arms—mostly to keep myself from fidgeting like a student in detention. "Will…you had the means to escape this place, but you didn't. You could be miles deep in the Range by now, but you aren't." He didn't even have to run after me when he did. He could've vanished into the trees when he spotted camp, just like Styx. And he most definitely could have killed the soldiers who brought him here. But he hadn't.

He shrugged, and I bit my cheek. He had to know his life was in danger. So why risk it? Why follow me into the belly of the beast?

I watched him silently chisel away at the block of wood. He'd shed the tape on his fingers, revealing strange symbols and foreign iconography across his knuckles. I wondered if he'd acquired them before moving to Belgate, or if he'd found an artist in Ells who was willing to tattoo an underage client. "Are those runes? On your knuckles?" I asked.

He paused, flexing his fingers like he'd forgotten the marks existed. "Not runes," he said, as if that was the stupidest thing he'd ever heard. "They're the crests of the ten clans in Rhea. A teaching tool for monarchs."

"How old were you?"

"Nine."

I winced, and he resumed his carving. *Stop acting like the one who needs to explain herself, Al. Confront him like you confront everything else: head-on.*

"So, your father," I forced through my lips, "he's not the man you lived with in Belgate."

He sighed through his nose, and it must have occurred to him that I wasn't leaving without an explanation because his weary gaze finally rose to mine. "The man back home was a guard I trusted. He got me out. He's not my father."

Got him out? That painted a much different picture than 'breaking ties.'

"But Godric Sterling, the king of Rhea, *is.*"

He nodded, surrendering to my inquiries—if only to end them as soon as possible. "He and my siblings are protecting the portal. They've kept it open for the past ten years, and they've measured their success in rivers of blood." He stabbed the little soldier boy through the chest, and when he looked up at me again, his expression was beaten and resigned. "I don't want this war, Alex. I never wanted to bring those creatures into the world. That's why I left."

I studied the sincere expression on his face, trying my best to place myself in his shabby boots. Trying to understand him fully, marred chest and all.

He'd been thirteen or so when he first moved to Belgate, even younger when he'd left his family behind. Then, upon fleeing to the land of his enemies, he was forced to listen to our prejudiced school lectures, our Rhean slurs, and Frost's cruel, inaccurate portrayal of his homeland. And yet, in the face of so much hatred, he'd never so much as *uttered* a refutation.

"You weren't sent to Belgate undercover? You weren't involved in the invasion?" I asked, though it sounded more like a conclusion than a query.

"No. I only ever wanted to escape. First Rhea, then Belgate."

Escape. As if he'd worn the same phantom manacles as I had—trapped in a city that barred him from his own identity.

The puzzle was finally coming together now, piece by piece. At the moment, I had nothing but the outer frame to work with; the inside was left barren and imageless, and I had no reference, no expectation. But for some reason, this feeble foundation was good enough.

Crouching, I unlocked Will's shackles with the key I'd nabbed off the guard. The bracelets fell to his lap, and he stared at them for a few heartbeats, then at me. "You trust me?"

"I don't know," I said honestly. "But I forgive you."

He was expressionless. No gratitude. No roll of the eyes. Nothing but brooding silence.

I stood again, clenching and unclenching my fists as I restructured the speech on the back of my tongue. "It's not fair to judge you because of who your family is—or for hiding the truth from people who would have likely killed you. I hate that you lied, but I understand why you did." My shoulders dropped, my ego dissipating. "I'm sorry I didn't give you the benefit of the doubt. I was just … angry."

Unreasonably so.

Because really, what should he have done differently? Tell his travel companions he was directly linked to their demon assassins? Tell them his father wanted to eradicate their society? He gave us as much information as he could without exposing himself, and he protected us on a treacherous journey that, upon its completion, would guarantee his persecution.

We could not have asked for a better outcome, and had Will confessed any earlier, I wasn't sure I'd be standing here today. Not if Mason had allowed the revelation to destroy our fellowship. Not if he'd split and taken his rapier with him.

Besides. I hadn't been wholly honest either—with any of them. Who was I to demand transparency?

I turned for the door, wondering if this was the last time we'd ever speak, when he blurted, "Asa."

I peeked back at him. "…Sorry?"

His eyes dipped to the chain draped over his thigh. "My name is Asa. William's my middle name. Will just became my nickname—my *real* name for the past four years." He frowned at his own fractured dialogue. "But that's who I am now. I *am* Will."

A delicate smile pulled at my lips. His awkward admission was kind of endearing. "Thanks for telling me," I said. "But I would've called you Will regardless, just to tick you off."

Starlight returned to the night in his eyes, and it was the same look Fudge had worn in the glade. A look that evinced a sense of renewed hope, as if he'd just encountered a fork in the route he'd yielded to.

"So?" I prompted. "What will you do?"

He rubbed the tender skin of his wrists, his gaze flicking to the door, then back at me, uncertain. "What do you *want* me to do?"

Stay, I thought mindlessly, and I scolded myself for stumbling into his trap. "It's up to you. If you want to stay, I'll stand by you and defend your right to serve. If you want to leave, I'll turn a blind eye. But this is about what *you* want, not me."

He needed to make a choice, and I needed to see him clearly—muddied motives and all.

He ran his thumb over the faded tattoos, scowling at the ink. I was tempted to ask him if the markings triggered fond memories, or if they served as a constant reminder of the legacy he'd left behind. But we could hardly classify ourselves as friends at this point—I had a few more walls to pierce before I could get away with a question that invasive.

"Then...I'll stay," he decided, and the astonishment on my face had his nostrils flaring with amusement. It still wasn't funny enough to evoke a smile, though. "I have a part to play in this war. I realize that now," he added with a little more confidence. "Running will just prolong things."

"You're saying...you'll fight? For Ells?"

"With," he corrected, pushing himself to his feet and brushing the dirt and hay off his pants. "*With* Ells."

I could sympathize with that distinction. I didn't want to align myself with this country and its bloody roots either—not after everything Nova had revealed.

"Do you have a plan?" he asked as he followed me down the corridor of restless horses.

"For what?"

He halted beside me with a stern, disbelieving glower on his face. "For convincing an entire military branch to accept Godric's son?"

I stole a glance at the stable entrance, happy to see the drunken guard still very much inebriated. "Well, my brother's in charge here, and I just happen to know his greatest weakness."

"Which is...?"

I winked at him. "A *whom*."

31

We were brainstorming ways to smuggle Will inside the barracks when I heard muffled voices from the matrix of canvas tents behind us. *Sober* voices.

Will didn't seem inclined to investigate, but I followed the alluring sound to its source: a four-walled tent that glowed with the muted yellows of a private counsel.

The shiny slit in the door beckoned me forth like a treasure chest inviting me to unearth its secrets, and I couldn't help myself. Furtive, I lifted the tent flap to peer inside, and it transported me back to those summer evenings I'd spent eavesdropping on Frost and his trainees.

Inside, Tom and his subordinates sat around a wooden table, analyzing the crusty topographic map bedecking its surface. A lamp dangled from the ceiling, attracting an eclipse of moths, and it cast just enough light for me to see the flip charts, roller maps, and typewriters stored along the inner perimeter of the room.

"Are you suggesting we attack them inside a *mountain*?" a man inquired.

Tom released a violent huff of air. "No, I'm 'suggesting' we lure them inside the mine and trap them there. We can blow up the entrances and rid ourselves of a couple hundred at once."

"And that's supposed to kill them? There's no vanadium left in that place."

Rover rolled his eyes. "I feel like they'd have a hard time regenerating when they're crushed by a thousand tons of shale and sandstone. The goal is to buy ourselves some time, not eliminate an entire brigade."

"And the Command approved this mission?"

"It's a go," said Tom. "Considering I omitted the bits about the mine, the dynamite, and the expenses—it's definitely a go."

The men traded grins at that, and I had a feeling this was typical Adult-Tom behavior: pushing limits, seeking loopholes, and leaving out details that would've had executives frothing at the mouth. And that knowledge planted a warm, feathery emotion in my belly. Because even though we'd spent so many years apart, we'd managed to grow parallel to one another, bursting through sidewalks and circumventing other man-made obstacles in our path.

He was, undoubtedly, my kin.

Beckett, capping his metal flask, observed the map again. "This one will be difficult to pull off, Kingsley. Lives will be lost."

Tom's jaw rippled. "Manipulating the Pans won't be an easy task. But nothing has been easy for the last six months. We're running out of ideas."

"And time," Sol pointed out.

"And now they've invaded Ells, and we don't have an army assembled to stop them." My brother tapped a spot on the map, nodding to himself. "This is plan Z. But it's all we've got."

The room sobered at that, and no one offered any rebuttals this time.

"Hey, Cap?" Rover cut in, and I could hear the smile spreading across his face. "Looks like we've got ourselves an audience."

Before I had the chance to fashion an exit plan, the flap flew wide, and I fell face-first onto the sandy tarp—like a nestling chucked out of its nest.

Gritz.

Perched on my forearms, I glanced behind me worriedly, but Will had already vanished into the shadows ... and perhaps a little too quickly for my liking.

"Alex," Tom said, voice flat. "What are you doing?"

I clambered to my feet, standing tall and shameless as I adjusted my armor. "I heard you talking about the mission, and I want in." I reflected on my statement and said, "Actually, all four of us do. Will included."

The men stared at me, wide-eyed and slack-jawed at my complete disregard for titles, formalities, and decorum. Tom, to his credit, was entirely unsurprised. "Not a chance."

"*Tom.*"

"Alex. You don't understand the way things work here. I'm the captain of this company. And I'm saying no. That's it. End of discussion."

I scowled at his tone. I realized he had to act all macho-manly around his underlings, but we hadn't seen each other since I was a kid, and he was already talking down to me like I was some unwanted, unhelpful nuisance.

He was addressing me the way men had spoken to me all my life, and it burned.

"But we've come this far," I pushed. "We deserve to be included in something, even if it's grunt work. Don't you need men, anyway?"

"Yes. We need men. Not teenagers who haven't attended basic training—or even meet our qualifications, for that matter. You don't know the first thing about killing Pans."

"I—"

"No, Al. Like it or not, you're young, you're inexperienced, and you can't jump straight into battle like it's a sporting event." The shadows deepened beneath those hardened eyes, and his gruesome scars only sharpened his dispute. "You aren't ready."

I drew a breath to fuel my scathing objections, but his subordinates' expressions gave me pause. Rover and Sol eyed me like uncles by marriage who genuinely sympathized with their troubled niece. Beckett's gaze fell to

the ground, heavy with pity. And the others just stared at me in confusion—or worse, they stared at my brother, who hadn't countered the most
ludicrous proposition of all: a woman fighting among them.

Challenging him here in front of his team had been a foolish idea.

When I said nothing more, Tom whirled me around and ushered me
toward the tent flap. "We'll figure out what to do with you in the morning.
We can talk about this—about *everything*—then. For now, take my quarters. I'll be up all night planning anyway."

"But—"

"Don't, Al. If you want to pretend you're in the army, then start minding direct orders." His glare cut me to pieces. "Now get some sleep. And
please, for the next 24 hours, just … stay put."

And with that, he threw me out of the tent.

***

A black snake slithered up my bed and over the mattress, moving slug-
gishly across the sheets and my motionless body. When the demon serpent
reached my face, it slipped through my parted mouth like poison and disappeared down my throat in its entirety.

My eyes snapped open, and I sighed, reaching for Richard's warm belly
to ground me.

I'd always battled nightmares, but they'd grown progressively worse
lately. To the point that I actually dreaded sleep—one of my favorite hob-
bies.

"Are you still awake?" I whispered to the darkness.

Will shifted next to the mattress. He'd positioned himself between the
bedpost and the dresser, his feet pointed at the door. For the fourth night
in a row, he'd chosen yet another awkward and uncomfortable sleeping position, and it had me wondering what his sleeping arrangements looked like

back in Belgate.

"Nightmare?" he guessed.

I fiddled with my fingers, peeling at the skin around my cuticles. It was a habit my brother had successfully rid me of before his deployment, but I'd picked it up again in his absence. "Yeah."

Will didn't ask me to elaborate.

After a long stretch of silence, I figured he'd fallen asleep, but then he spoke again—this time, with a softness that surprised me. "Your brother loves you. That's why he's acting that way, why he's holding you at a distance. The last thing he wants to do is involve you in this war."

It was such an unusual sentiment to come from Will that I dug my nails into my arm to make sure I wasn't still dreaming. "I guess. But it's irritating how everyone always underestimates me, constantly. My own family tries to shield me from the world. I don't need that."

And I definitely didn't *want* it.

"Did you ever think that they might?" he ventured, and I flopped onto my side to read his shadowed face—or attempt to, anyway. "Sometimes the people who care about you need to feel like they can protect you, keep you safe. Older brothers most of all."

He didn't say it pretentiously; he said it from the heart. A heart that bled a little with every word he uttered. "You mentioned your siblings," I recalled. "You have a sister?"

He didn't reply for a moment, and I worried I'd overstepped. But then he expelled a long, mournful breath from his throat. "Lucille, though I call her Lou. She's fourteen now."

"Were you close?"

"She was three when my mother died," he said. "After the funeral, my father immersed himself in the war and the Order's dark magic. We hardly saw him at that point—he became a name to fear and nothing more. So, Lou became my responsibility . . . until I left her."

I sank back into the warmth of Tom's sheets. "At least she has your brother."

"That's what worries me."

I wanted to look at him again, inspect the vulnerability I could hear, but I rejected the compulsion. There was still so much I didn't know about the boy beside me—so much I would never know. And as tempting as it was to pry Will open, some things weren't meant to be disentombed.

Some things couldn't be.

32

I sat with Will and Richard in the dining hall, trying to ignore the conspicuous gap between us and the other soldiers at the long breakfast table. Will
didn't seem to mind the extra space, nor the whispers, murmurs, and
pointed glares sent our way.

Rhean snake ... spy ... that breeder ... that skirt ...

I watched my food drown in a puddle of syrup.

After seventeen years, mudslinging rarely affected me anymore. I'd always been an outcast who liked to stir the pot—and proud of it. The last
thing I wanted was to be like everybody else, even if the snide remarks found
their way under my skin every now and again. But Will didn't deserve the
blind hatred. They were all snarling at him like he was a Pan, like he wasn't
even human.

Snake.

Spy.

Breeder.

Skirt.

Will draped his hand over my own, and my thoughts instantly turned
to sand. My gaze flew to the point of contact—his palm on the most lethal
part of my body—and every alarm in my head began screeching at me to
rectify the situation.

Calmly, he tugged the steak knife out of my white-knuckled grip and used it to cut his sausages. A relieved breath exploded from my lips.

"Don't let them get to you," he said.

I tried to ignore the lingering heat of his touch. "They're calling you a spy." *Among other things.*

He glanced at me. "Do you think I'm a spy?"

"No." I couldn't. Not after everything he'd told me.

"Then that's all that matters."

Shaking my head at him, I began picking at my unappetizing breakfast. How could he be so docile? I was about one insult away from lodging Tom's knife into someone's thorax.

It was only when Fudge set his tray down across from us that my anger receded. The refugee had changed into a fresh set of trousers and a T-shirt, and the soft, nervous look on his face subdued my murderous spirit.

"Fudge, you don't have to sit with us," I assured him. He didn't have to make a statement and spoil his reputation before he'd even established roots. "It's okay."

"You say that as if I *want* to sit somewhere else." He tossed Will an apple, and the Rhean stared at the fruit in his hand for a beat, taken aback by the simple gesture and the endorsement it promised.

Fudge's amiability was unsurprising—his heart was basically three sizes too big for his body—but I was glad to see he'd arrived at the same conclusion I had: Will's character was not defined by his heritage or his desire to hide it, and even a Rhean heir deserved a clean slate.

Mason, however, was less accepting.

He'd just finished piling a mountain of bacon on his cafeteria tray when he caught sight of Will. He stomped over to us, rage pulsing in his eyes. "What are you doing out here with the rest of us?" he hissed, his entire face contracting in disgust.

Will glanced at the blond with casual disinterest and kept chewing.

Met with no response, Mason turned to Fudge and me. "How can you sit with him? He trained with us. He pretended to be one of us. And he's *Rhean*."

"He's also an ally," I offered.

"Since when?"

Our conversation had drawn attention, and I shifted in my seat. No one knew I'd released Will against Tom's orders. No one knew I'd bunked with him all night in Tom's private chambers. Except maybe Beckett, who'd winked at me when Will and I showed up at breakfast together.

I lowered my voice. "I know you're intrinsically bigoted, Mason, but Will saved your life. He's also committed to fighting this war alongside the idiots who chained him up with horses. Let it go."

Mason sputtered out some nonsense, but he was interrupted by a bout of commotion outside.

"He's gone? How did that happen?"

Gritz. That was definitely Tom's voice. Tom's *enraged* voice.

"—this *morning*?"

Sighing, I dragged Will with me out the door before things could escalate. The Rhean didn't resist, but he did bring his tray and silverware with him—determined to finish his breakfast on his deathbed.

Tom, wearing the same clothes as yesterday, stood next to the stables. He looked distressed, and he was waving his arms at the sheepish, hungover men in front of him. Behind him, Rover scratched the back of his head, trying not to laugh.

"Tom!" I called, marching for him.

My brother sighed deeply when he spotted us. He turned on me, and *Patrons*, if looks could kill. "Did you let that criminal out?"

"He's on our side," I deflected. "And he's not a criminal. You'd know that if you'd just hear us out."

He looked like he wanted to argue, but he was too agitated to form the right words. "What is it then, Al? Before I have him arrested. Again."

There it was again—the ugly mask of a man in power. A boy lashing out at his loved ones, unwilling to listen to anything that might vanquish his radical hatred. I couldn't stand it.

But if the welt was giving me room to speak, I'd *speak*.

"Tom," I said, and his front wavered at my tone. "We want to help. We *can* help. We defeated a dozen Pans on our own, and we made it out alive because of Will. Please just take a chance on him. On all of us."

This mission was my only chance to set things in motion. I had to make a stand today, or Will and I would be swept away by the chaos of war—silenced and buried by the avalanche of Ellsian conventions.

Tom's eyes scanned my face, then Will's. He was rummaging through scenarios and repercussions, and when Rover realized he was actually considering my proposal, the lieutenant chuckled uneasily. "Cap ..."

"You know what it means if I let you take up a sword," Tom said to me. "You know the consequences."

"I know."

If he signed off on this, it would change the course of history. He'd become the first officer to arm a woman. I'd be the first woman to join the ranks. All of it illegal.

"We might get killed for this," he said.

"We might get killed anyway," I countered, tilting my head at him. "Don't tell me the fancy title you carry has shattered your spine, Tom."

He looked to the heavens as if he were asking my mother for help. But she must have denied his prayers, because his shoulders slumped, and he nodded. "Alright. I'll give it a trial run."

I exhaled at the same time Rover sucked in a disbelieving breath. "*Captain.*"

Tom pointed a finger at me. "You do exactly as we say, no buts, no questions, no flaunting, and I'll allow you and your friends to participate in this operation." He scowled at Will. "But not him. The others won't accept it."

"Let him work alongside you," I insisted. "If he steps out of line, I give you permission to kill him."

Will released an incredulous puff of air through his teeth, but I ignored him, hoping he would understand my intent. This was a chance for him to prove himself—to both my brother and me. If he passed this test, he was in. He was *safe*.

"He's skilled at fighting, Tom. Better than anyone I've ever met. He defeated his opponent in the Deadlock, and he's saved my life four times already. He could save others too, if you let him." I leaned closer, begging for him to reconsider. "One chance, that's all I'm asking for."

My brother's exasperated gaze fixed on mine, and in that moment, I saw each of my parents in the soldier, summing and subtracting my actions before delivering judgement. Mom's stern countenance as she reprimanded us. Dad's heavy gaze as he determined a fitting punishment. It was jarring, seeing that look on his face; we'd always been on the same team, the two of us, but now he'd become the authority figure in my way.

"You can't expect me to trust him," he pressed.

"I don't. I expect you to trust *me*."

His mouth tightened at that, and I could tell I'd landed a good punch.

Tom knew how selective I was when it came to accepting strangers into my circle. I *had* to be choosy if I wanted to keep my curse a family matter, if I wanted to achieve my goals in a society so prejudiced. What he didn't realize was that after losing him, I'd closed myself off to everyone but Nova, too afraid to form new attachments. Too afraid to hurt again.

Will earning my advocacy was damn near miraculous.

His gaze swept over camp. "My men—"

"Won't think any less of you for putting your prejudice aside," I said, ignoring Rover's dancing eyebrows. "Think about it. If this works, you'll go down in history as the man who turned Godric's own son against him.

You'll have intel no one else will. You'll have Rhean—"

"Stop," Tom said, waving me off. He cracked an exasperated smile—an old, dusty one that warmed my heart. "I'll let him fight if he's so inclined. I'm more worried about you disobeying me anyway."

"I won't."

He squinted at me. "Willing to bet on it?"

Like I'd back down now. "Stakes?"

This kind of territory was familiar. Betting, gambling, pushing buttons and kicking shins.

It was a comfort to know it still existed between us.

Tom scratched his chin. "If I win, you have to do one thing I say with absolutely no fuss. If you win …"

"If I win, we all become federate soldiers, enrolled in training and everything. We get to be involved, and we get to know what's happening."

He shook his head like I was too predictable. "Deal."

We watched each other for a moment longer, taking in the similarities, the differences. Then Tom's crooked smile faded, and that precious minute of kinship slipped away from me so fast—it was like it never happened.

He turned to leave, and I blurted a beseeching, "Tom, wait."

He looked at me.

I still had so many questions, so many fears. "When can we have that talk?"

His face hardened once again. "Soon."

He left me with that empty vow, and Rover followed after him, swearing at him in high octaves. *A girl*, I heard him cry, *and a Rhean heir*!

"Look at that," I said once the sting of dismissal disappeared, "problem solved."

"You just sold my soul to your brother," Will complained.

I stole an apple slice off his plate. "It's better than the stables."

"*Is* it?"

***

After showering with harvested rainwater and changing into suitable work clothes, we spent the afternoon preparing the ambitious demon trap, or as Rover liked to call it, Plan Z.

We waited until Tom forbade any of his subordinates from cutting Will to pieces—an order that raised a few brows, to say the least—before following Sol and Rover down a dimly lit mineshaft.

Around us, wooden beams preserved a narrow channel in the earth, the supports bowed and splintered from the weight of the hillside. White-hot carbide lamps flickered from niches in the rock, and I swore the gas made the adit smell like honey garlic chicken, though my near-empty stomach might've had something to do with it.

Dirt trickled down on us as the mountain swallowed us whole, and I stepped imperceptibly closer to Will.

"What about light?" Fudge asked, probing for more information about the Pans and their limitations. "The demons are sensitive to light stimuli, aren't they?"

Sol looked impressed by our discovery. "Natural light works best. We think that's why the sun's gone, actually. It seems to be an Achilles heel of sorts."

So Leith had been right after all? Rheans really had blotted out the sun?

"Your family sucks," I murmured to Will.

His lips thinned to a grim line. "I'm aware."

"But you're right, Freckles," Rover said. "It's no secret that Pans despise flash powder and strobe lights. Problem is they blind me too."

"But they *can* tolerate fire," I said, observing one of the fiery lamps overhead. "At least ... red fire."

Rover grinned back at me. "Isn't that a doozy? Your brother and I spent four months experimenting with different chemical compounds. We tried our damnedest to reproduce that color and intensity. Had no luck." He ducked under a low-hanging prop. "Tom thinks I'm superstitious, but I don't think that fire comes from this side of the chimney, if you know what I mean."

Interesting.

We hooked another turn down the skinny tunnel, and I shot a worried glance behind me as the exit faded from view.

Just how deep was this mineshaft? And how long ago did such operations—and maintenance—desist?

A hand found the top of my head, gently shoving it downward, and I stumbled over my feet, peeved at being manhandled. Then I realized Will had just prevented me from smacking my face into a dislodged wooden plank, and I grumbled my thanks.

"So what's the plan exactly?" he asked as I fell into step behind him.

Sol hesitated, exchanging a distrustful look with Rover, and I rolled my eyes. "He has to know what you're up to if he's going to be of any help," I reasoned, perhaps a bit too tersely. "We all need to know."

Sol dipped his chin, reining in a chuckle. He faced us then, matching our pace as he walked backwards along the iron rails. "Well, the Pans will be searching for a population to kill or capture. That's their goal, right? It's not to advance, it's not to overthrow. It's to kill every last one of us."

"So..."

"*So* if we can trick them into thinking the mines are still active, that we've built our base *within* the mountain, they'll coordinate an ambush."

"Then we're using ourselves as bait?" Mason deduced unhappily.

Rover snapped his fingers. "Exactly, Matthew."

"It's *Mason*."

"But how do we lure them here?" I asked, frowning at the neglected adit. "How do we convince them to chase us into an abandoned burrow?"

Rover held up his lantern, splashing our clothes and faces in vibrant oranges. "We'll have to beef up our acting skills. Get some props, pack the stage. This mine used to be a huge resource for us—we can make it look alive again. Vanadium or not."

"As for logistics . . . we've got a team of runners," Sol elaborated, seemingly well-accustomed to Rover's metaphorical detours. "These soldiers will draw the Pans to the mine and divert them away from Ptarmigan. We'll need numbers to fool them. Numbers, and the illusion of activity." He tapped his knuckles against an empty, rusty minecart as he passed. "Our mission is to convince them it's a worthwhile pit stop—especially if they're interested in boosting recruitment."

"Nothing entices a Pot more than a young, fit soldier," Rover agreed, punching a hole in my stomach. "Pans never leave a fort unprobed."

Sol held his hand out to stop us from walking any further, and for good reason; the tunnel abruptly ended. In fact, the adit dropped off altogether—like an underground cliff giving way to a sinkhole.

Or in this case, a giant . . . *crater*.

The pit spanned a few hundred feet in diameter, and it formed an enormous pocket of musty air in the mountain. It was like a bubble of magma had hardened and cooled within the earth, attracting miners to its vanadium base millions of years later. Leaving us with a rocky cavern hollowed out by nature, and below it, a chasm hollowed out by man.

A wooden staircase spiraled down the quarry of doom, and I inched closer to peer over the ledge, where dozens of climbing bolts pierced the rock and ejected rope into the darkness. In my periphery, I watched Will cautiously do the same.

Deep within the cavity, a group of soldiers worked under lantern light, carrying maps and tools and shovels. Some stood at its distant base, adjusting lengthy ladders or flaking rope, while others stripped away the winding staircase, mopping their brows and passing jokes. Around the lip of the crater, the tunnels resumed, leading to different mining routes through the mountain, and, according to Rover, the six other exits.

So quickly Tom had orchestrated a plan, and so quickly he had brought it to life. It was astonishing to witness.

A soldier appeared behind Rover then, marching up the staircase, and just as the lieutenant detected heavy footfalls, the man smacked him over the head with a rolled map. "Running a daycare, Wright?"

I recognized him as the same man who'd accompanied Fudge and Mason to the pub. He was short and stocky—the type to brag about how many cannon balls he could carry at once—and his face was covered in grease, pooling at the dip of his chin in a thick, oily goatee.

Rover sighed as he massaged the back of his skull. "This is Claus, our bomb specialist. He's not much good for anything but blowing Pans to bits."

"He's just saying that because I don't have my axe to rip him open," Claus growled, throwing an accusatory look at the blacksmith.

Sol tutted. "I can't prioritize weapons destroyed behind the wire, Greco. Maybe don't host an axe-throwing tournament on a granite playing field next time."

Ignoring Sol's comment, Claus turned to me and squinted. "So, you're the broad everyone's buzzin' about." He looked me over. "How old are you?"

"Not old enough," Rover said tersely, and he violently shooed the man away before I could answer.

Will didn't find the exchange as amusing as I did.

"After the runners lead the Pans here, then what?" Fudge asked a few moments later, staring down at the glowing pit of deceit.

Smiling, Sol crouched at the edge of the crater. "A countdown. We blow the adits, one exit at a time, until every federate makes it out. Then we bury these Pans alive."

33

I pulled the leather armor out of the bin and took a deep, steadying breath.

Platoons were spotted five miles west of camp this morning. Tom had intended to finish Plan Z preparations this afternoon, but we'd run out of time. The demons were coming for the Interior, and without the Rim troops assembled, we were Holly's last hope. We *had* to intercept them.

Despite playing nothing more than a mascot in this operation, I was wrought with nerves, and my fingers trembled as I fastened my gear.

This was my first and only shot at enlisting in my brother's company; I had to prove myself to Tom and his men that I deserved a seat at their table. I needed to show them who I could be today, or I'd be shunned and unheeded. Titled a breeder, then forced to climb a ladder without rungs.

I needed to blend in, but impressively so.

When I glanced up, Will was watching me from the other end of the canvas tent, assessing me, as always. He crouched to tie his boots and asked, "What do you hate?"

The question came out of left field, and I didn't mask my bafflement.

"What do you hate more than anything?" he revised. "Besides thunder."

I scowled at him and resumed my search for the smallest leather breastplate in the bin. "I guess ... I hate the word breeder. I hate that I don't know if my father is okay." A less patent answer popped into my brain a second later. "I hate not knowing in general."

"What do you mean?"

I tried to gather my thoughts, the chaos outside pressing in at the seams. "I don't like being kept in the dark, and it's even worse if I'm cloistered because of my gender. It's like all the redacted information in the library—the censored history books, the skewed memoirs, the incomplete series. The missing pieces drive me crazy."

So many story arcs I'd never finish. So much dead-end character development. So much context expunged from intriguing nuggets of history.

"Or like … when a story ends with unanswered questions." I yanked my third set of armor over my head and shoulders. It wasn't a perfect fit, but it would have to do; they were transporting teams to the mine already, and I planned to be on the next wagon. "I read this one story where a slave crosses the desert seeking freedom. But at the very end, we don't know if he reaches the oasis or if he's just hallucinating from dehydration. That's how the author leaves us—on a cliffhanger. I nearly threw the book in the river."

"There's no closure," he translated into robot speak. "You're left guessing."

"It's the worst."

It felt better talking out my nerves, and I wondered if that had been his motive all along—to make me less anxious in his own humorless, roundabout way.

"What about you?" I tried. Maybe with this new mood of his I could skim a few of those private pages. "What do you hate?"

He pondered the question for a moment and rose from his crouch. Then, after careful deliberation, he said, "Luck."

I waited for the joke to surface, but it didn't. "Are you serious?"

"It conflicts with karma," he defended.

"… That sounds like something an unlucky person would say."

Had he never once felt the bubbly giddiness of good fortune? The sweet relief of fortuitous happenstance? Each time I'd received nothing more than a stern warning for my seditious tongue and masculine disposition, I'd sent my love and thanks to Lady Fortuna.

"I've had good luck before," Will replied—ambiguously, of course. "But it doesn't mean I deserved it. Most people don't."

I rolled my eyes. "You're so gloom and doom."

He looked offended by that. "I'm not gloomy."

"What kind of twisted person hates luck?"

Propping his foot on the bench between us, he leaned forward. "You're throwing out a lot of adjectives today, Kingsley. Gloomy, twisted . . . ?"

"Cheeky," I added.

The edges of his mouth quirked upward at that, and my breath hitched at the miracle.

Patrons . . . I'd just made Will *smile*.

Me, all on my own.

It disappeared a second later, but as brief as it was, I'd never forget it. It was like a great flash of lightning—bright, sudden, fleeting—leaving you with a marvelous afterimage. Leaving you with your hands on the windowpane, begging for more.

Strangely enough, the expression fit him perfectly, as if he had once been the most cheerful child in Rhea. It was like joy had been engraved in the bedrock of his features, and happiness had always been his natural state of being.

It made me wonder what horrible things had made that joy cower beneath a mask of cold indifference.

"Why hate?" I asked him. Why had that been his conversation piece?

He looked me over, his gaze lingering on my side where I'd hastily tied the knots of my armor. He reached toward me and began undoing the strings, shaking his head at my incompetence. "Hate is undervalued. It can be a catalyst for action. Fuel for the fight."

I arched an eyebrow.

"Sometimes a victim of abuse has to learn to hate her husband enough to terminate a marriage contract. We teach soldiers to hate the enemy so they don't lose their own lives in their hesitation." His fingers re-threaded the strings with appalling dexterity. "Sometimes all it takes to survive is petty antipathy."

He dropped his hands, and I examined the flawless knots along my ribcage. "Why not ask me what I love? That's just as powerful as hate, isn't it?" And less corrosive.

His eyes found mine, and they were so blackened by sorrow, they nearly flooded my own.

"Because we *die* for love," he answered, handing me my belt and scabbard. His prolonged grip summoned my gaze. "And no one's dying today."

***

I sat with the lookouts a few hundred feet above the primary adit, eyes peeled for demon crows and creeping Pans. I was armed to the teeth, and my dark hair fell in a heavy braid over my shoulder, pulling a bit too tightly on my temples.

Dusty minecarts sat on the tracks that wound deep inside the mountain, brimful of ore. Hand tools and other props littered the site, and a steam-powered mining drill sat to the side of the entrance, still warm from use.

The old mineral deposit looked like an active workspace—a *living* space. And, astonishingly, a promising trap.

Tom, Will, Claus, and the other runners had left an hour ago to their assigned outposts, aiming to draw the fast-approaching Pans to the vale below. Rover had encouraged Tom to sit this one out, albeit unsuccessfully.

He'd argued that, should Plan Z fail, Holly would need someone of Tom's caliber to lead an evacuation effort, and his subordinates were inclined to agree. But my brother had been obstinate in his decision.

"How can I expect my soldiers to put their faith in my plans if I'm not willing to partake in them?" he'd said. "My rank is worthless if it's built on nothing but dead and dated achievements."

Rover had looked to Sol for help, but the blacksmith merely closed his eyes and sighed, aware that Tom couldn't be dissuaded of anything he'd set his mind to.

The two of us were cut from the same cloth, after all.

While they executed subterfuge, I studied the east-facing hillside opposite me, watching the stagnant shadows between the trees. It killed me, playing such a minor role in this mission. I wanted to confront the demons who'd destroyed my home, take part in the action—the glory. But I promised Tom that I'd obey his chain of command; I swore to him I'd stay out of the way today, and I would.

Another excruciating period of silence passed before we heard the cacophony of snapping twigs, crunching mulch, and rattling armor. Heartbeats later, I spotted Pans across the way, slinking down the hillside like a sluggish earthflow, their navy uniforms embellished with leather and steel.

It was the same company that had taken Belgate, and now they'd come for the Interior Company, lured by Tom's men and the stench of mortal blood.

Pivoting, I ran up and over Goddard Mine, dashing through trees and swerving between boulders, eager to watch a real-life military operation play out before my eyes. And when I finally descended the shrubby foothill, I crouched beside Rover, Fudge, and Sol at the valley floor.

The four of us were responsible for triggering our tunnel's bomb when the runners emerged—tasked with sealing the demons in a tomb of soil. The blasting machine, a device capable of collapsing the exit in one go, sat at Rover's side, primed and safeguarded. It was one of seven plungers that we'd use to inhume our enemies, and it was absolutely essential to our success.

And, ultimately, our *survival*.

The wait was shorter this time, and I almost bit through my lip when the first bomb detonated, signaling the destruction of the primary adit and our men's staged retreat. The explosion also indicated the demon's gullible pursuit, which meant they were now trapped in the body of the mine with our runners.

At this very moment, Tom and his subordinates were climbing out of the crater, collecting their rope and torching their ladders. Their combined efforts would strand the demons at the adit drop-off or in the stony dungeon below, sentencing them to a fate worse than death.

The apprehension of crouching in place, waiting patiently for their triumph, was agony. But sitting here, knowing the creatures who'd slaughtered my neighbors and destroyed my house were just within reach—it was absolutely unbearable.

I picked my cuticles to squash the anxious, vengeful knot in my stomach.

Minutes later, two men staggered out of the tunnel to our right, gasping for breath and shouting at their teammates to destroy the exit.

My resolve frayed when no one else trickled out. Four runners were assigned to each tunnel, so where the hell were the other two?

"They should be out by now," Sol whispered.

We watched our own mineshaft, begging for a flicker of light, a patter of footsteps, *something*. But there was no activity in our tunnel. Not a puff of dust. Not a whisper of movement.

If we didn't bomb the adits soon, the mission would be pointless. And, considering the fate of the Interior, potentially catastrophic. But our runners—the strongest and fastest of the company—hadn't emerged yet, and we couldn't just seal the exits and name them martyrs.

"Someone should go see what's wrong," I suggested.

Rover pinned me with a deterrent look. "Don't even think about it, Fuse. If you get blown to bits, your brother will murder me."

Another minute passed, then another, and I glanced helplessly between the adit and the advancing minute hand of Rover's watch.

Three minutes.

Four...

My intestines had all but twisted themselves into malrotation when the darkness finally ejected a short, stubby figure. The individual barreled out of our tunnel at full speed, distressed and cursing.

"Blow it up!" Claus panted, crashing into our group. The soldier was covered in a sheen of soot and sweat, the whites of his eyes blown wide with horror.

The last time I'd seen such a disturbed expression on a man was the morning my father encountered my mother's corpse, and I dreaded his next words.

"We underestimated them—it didn't work," he got out. "The others are holding them off. Wouldn't leave."

Rover's body went taut. "Underestimated them how?"

"They knew. They knew it was a trap! They've flipped the script on us!" Claus gripped his knees, struggling to oxygenate his blood. "The Pans came from outside. Intercepted the runners in the northern tunnels. The plan went to hell."

The news squashed my windpipe. Tom and Will had taken the northern access, which meant they now faced enemies on either end of their adit. Penned in by demons. Victims to their own elaborate gambit.

Claus wiped his brow and looked up at us expectantly. "Go on. Blow the damn thing!"

Fudge glanced at Rover. "But the runners—"

"They're as good as dead!" Claus snapped, spittle flying from his lips. "If you don't do it now, you'll waste their sacrifice."

No…

I'd just gotten Tom back; I couldn't lose him again. And Will was only in that mine because of *me*. I'd sent him to perform at Death's doorstep.

Pained, Rover positioned himself over the plunger. "We'll wait for—"

I ran into the mine before I could hear the rest.

34

Among bouts of urgent shouting, the sound of pure torment echoed down the tunnel: a terrible discord of groans and screams and raging voices bleeding through the walls. Accompanying the eerie noises were traces of acetylene, smoke, and—most alarmingly—the smell of burning, rotten flesh.

With a firm grip on my sword, I ventured into the mountain of misery.

At the end of the passage, where the seven tunnels dropped into the crater like the inside of a ghoulish teapot, a nightmare unfolded. The pit itself was spitting flames, and dozens of demons crawled out of the smoky deathtrap—creatures covered in burns, bloodthirsty monsters haloed in embers. Above them, our runners fought wildly to keep the enemy at bay, kicking Pans back into the pit or turning them to ash with their vanadium weapons.

At the threshold of my own tunnel was Grismond, the colossus male chauvinist. He battled a pair of demons who'd seized one of our burning ladders, forfeiting their outer layer of skin to breach our defenses.

Two soldiers lay on the ground between us, moaning atop a bundle of climbing rope. One lightly armored runner, having favored agility over protection, bled profusely from a blow to the clavicle. The other clutched his leg and cursed our Patrons.

Steeling myself, I approached the fiery pit that had nearly claimed their lives.

Inside the furnace, the Pans roared with vehemence, closing their eyes and shielding their hideous faces from the sun they'd awakened. A handful of soldiers hadn't made it out of the chamber at all, their corpses trampled by the demons who now blindly climbed the walls of their tomb. Runners struggled to keep the demons out of their adits, failing to inflict enough damage to guarantee a head start in this perilous race.

In the northern exits, men stood back-to-back—several soldiers warding off the Pans in the pit while their comrades fought the demons blocking their escape.

But there was no sign of Will or Tom.

"It's time to go!" I shouted.

Grismond jerked his head around, taking notice of me for the first time. "What are you doing here? You'll get in the way!"

Was he deaf?

"Go on!" he insisted between maneuvers, bleeding heavily from his brow, his fighting labored. "It's too late for us."

Too late?

Had he really planned to stay here at the crater's edge while we bombed the tunnels? Had he already accepted death by burial?

I threw my hands up. "I'm stalling to save your life, moron! We need to get out of here. Help me!" I motioned to the injured men at our feet.

A new demon clawed his way to the rim of our adit, and Grismond and I swung in unison, chopping his head off in two separate places and cremating him neck-down.

The Bear didn't ask questions this time. He whistled loudly, and the brave stragglers around the pit repeated the signal, filling the chamber with shrill chirping.

Run.

Run like hell.

All at once, the men broke into a sprint down their respective adits.

Pushing demons out of the way or hurtling down vacant railways. Determined to outrun their enemies, lest they join them in this blistering communal grave.

In my attempt to contribute something of value, I yanked a torch from a sconce in the wall and chucked it into the crater, adding fuel to the blazing hellscape. *For Belgate,* I thought as the Pans wailed in anguish, *and the fertile land you scorched.*

Grismond and I each grabbed an injured runner and shot into the dark. But as we hobbled for the exit, I heard demons scaling the pit behind us, using one another to climb the flue like an army of fire ants. Grunting and hissing at the gradient. Metal armor clanging against rock. Flesh burning and oozing and sticking to the molten surfaces they clasped.

It was the most haunting thing to ever plague my ears.

We twisted through the tunnel's maze, slowed by the weight of the wounded. And then, just as we cleared the final bend in the tracks, we came to an abrupt, grinding halt.

Three Pans blocked our exit, smiling like victors.

***

My breath stuttered at the sight of our leering obstacles, and I looked to Grismond and his stoic expression for answers. *How?* How had they evaded Rover and the others?

Had they ambushed my team while I was away? Had they slaughtered Fudge to get here?

"Humans … and their inflated sense of cleverness," a Pan rasped, standing before us with his sword confidently sheathed. As if our lives were struck and discarded as trivially—and effortlessly—as friction matches. "It's lamentable …"

The bleeding soldier I supported freed himself from my grip, and I frowned as he stepped in front of me, one hand nudging me away from the Pans, the other fishing for his blade.

"Go back to hell," he snarled at the demons, bravely brandishing his sword.

In the dim lighting of the carbide lamps, he didn't look a day over nineteen, and I resisted the urge to tug him back into my embrace.

His defiance made the Pan's ghostly eyes crinkle in amusement. Then the demon sliced the soldier's throat open in the beat of a crow's wing.

In the flick of a wrist.

I stumbled forward to catch the boy, appalled by the swift deathblow, and with trembling hands, I eased him to the ground. I could feel my throat drying out, my tongue sticking to the back of my mouth as I realized what was about to happen—and just how helpless I was to stop it.

The soldier's blood coated my hands, dark and sickly warm, and he choked, gasping for air through his severed windpipe. Eyes wide and frightened as he gargled his own blood. In less than thirty seconds, his hold on me slackened, and his eyes fluttered shut.

He was dead before I could even *think* it, and I didn't even know his name.

Behind us, another two Pans appeared, singed by the tongue of flame, and I knew more were sure to follow. It was only a matter of time before the rest of their fire-resistant platoon emerged from the pit.

I swallowed the desert in my mouth, forcing myself to breathe, to push back against the surging panic. Reining in my fear, my devastation, I rose from my crouch and retreated to Grismond's side.

The Bear gnashed his teeth, and the federate he supported moaned in pain, his boot twisted the wrong way entirely. If we abandoned him now, we might have stood a chance in this fight, but I knew neither of us could do that. Gris may have been illiberal, but his willingness to perish for the greater good told me he wasn't cold-blooded.

"Smells different," one of the demons noted. It sniffed the stale air and grinned at me. "*Succulent.*"

The others shifted on their feet, eyeing me with the same yearning hunger as their friend, the same sinister curiosity. And then, to my utter dismay, they began closing in on me—famished lions preying upon an isolated idiot.

Had I somehow personally offended every product of the netherworld? Or had the councilman been right when he'd said my audacity would appeal to "no man?"

Perhaps I was catnip to an even crueler creature.

The largest demon stepped toward me—a single stride that brought him much too close to my nostrils. He smelled like expired market fish, and he looked like it too.

"Nowhere to go, child," he taunted, his voice like a slow, painful incision across my cochlea. "Brace yourself for death."

I raised the vanadium blade Rover had lent me, and I hoped no one could see how badly my hands were shaking. *Be brave*, I told myself. *Be brave and die brave.*

The Pan's lips twitched as if he could read my mind and the pitiful mantra I'd invoked.

I tensed, preparing for his first offensive strike, but as he moved to engage, the entire mountain gave off an enormous, guttural roar. The walls shook, and the old carbide lamps fell to the ground, restricting our light source to the orange glow of the inferno and a distant circle of daylight. Several more tremors followed, and the sound of crushing rock and exploding soil traveled down the tunnel like a war drum.

I counted four detonations total, which, had they been executed successfully, made us one of two adits still accessible—and the last two exit routes in the entire mountain.

"Grismond!" I whispered harshly, accepting the only course of action left. "Get your runner out of here."

His protruding brow furrowed in outrage, blood drenching that mean, massive forehead of his, and I found the expression all the more petrifying in the orange and silver ombre. He looked like a man torn between heaven and hell. A man, quite literally, pinned in place by his sins.

"They're after my head," I insisted. For whatever reason, I'd become the Pans' target—a sick source of fascination for these welts—and there was no sense in wasting my enthralling properties. "Get him out of here and see this operation through." My fingers tightened around my hilt. "*Hurry.*"

Without a second glance, the Bear slung the wounded man over his shoulders and barged through the wall of demons like a cannon shot.

Leaving me to fight alone.

To *die* alone.

Finding some inner courage—or more probably inner fear—I used the distraction to stab Tuna Melt in the stomach. The demon howled in pain before exploding in ash, and as another Pan rushed forward to skin me alive, my instincts took the wheel.

I rolled away from a direct hit to my diaphragm and somersaulted beneath the Pan's second swipe. Bracing my hands on the ground, I kicked the demon in the knee and slashed his wrists when he joined me on all fours. Putrid smoke billowed out of the cuts.

Sheathing my sword, I scrambled off the rails and darted past the two Pans recovering from Grismond's body slam. Adrenaline rushed through me as I fled, and I barked out an incredulous laugh when I realized I might be home free.

My brief celebration ended when a hot, metallic sensation tore through my side. The force wrenched my whole body to the left, and I violently crashed into the wall, smacking my head against a beam with too many nails.

A fuzzy picture flashed in my mind—*a bullet wound, a bloody forest floor, a moon.* Then it was gone, and I was staring down at a skinny pole protruding from my ribcage, its spearhead wedged deep inside my body.

It took a few seconds for the pain to hit. But when it finally registered that I'd been *impaled*, the weapon became molten shrapnel in my veins, the wound a chemical fire inside my liver. I couldn't breathe without inflicting more agony, couldn't see beyond the tears flooding my eyes.

I'd just been dealt a fatal blow.

In seconds, I'd become a *fatali*—

A hand snatched my braid and yanked my scalp backward, forcing me to stare at the lumber overhead. Holding me still, my assailant wrenched the spear out of my gut, and I choked on my scream.

He released me, and I sank to the ground like a straw-stuffed training dummy, battling a blackout. When the splotches in my vision finally disappeared, I spat the dirt out of my mouth and glared up at my killer.

The demon's eyes shone like silver marbles in the dark, both rows of neglected teeth on full display. My wet eyes latched onto that familiar, pointed skull, then fell to a gaze of unmistakable hubris.

Stretch.

The same Stretch I'd tied to a tree and left for dead. The same Stretch whose sword I'd stolen, leaving him ripe for an archaic weapon.

"Hello again, river sprite," he cooed, angling his head at me. "I almost didn't recognize you without your conceit."

I said nothing, but my fingers slid, ever so slowly, toward the knife at my belt.

"Let's draw this out, shall we?" He raised his bloody spear, prepared to brutally finish me off, but another bomb—closer and sharper than the others—claimed his focus for one short, crucial moment.

I aimed for his legs.

The motion sent an agonizing spasm up my torso, and the monster's acidic ankle blood splattered across my face—hotter than boiling water. But the lacerations brought Stretch to his knees, and with my hand pressed firmly to the right side of my body, I staggered to my feet and backed away.

Draw this out, you said? I pivoted on my heels. *If you insist.*

As I tottered for the exit, I rejected the instinct to examine the hole in my ribcage, nor the red liquid gushing through my fingers. I could feel my intestines sloshing against my palm—that was all it took to keep this plow turning. I didn't need to puke up my breakfast while I was at it.

Escape was just starting to feel attainable when I suddenly tripped on a carbide lamp. The twist sent a horrible jolt through my body, and I collapsed to the mine floor. *Hard.*

I tried to carry my momentum into a forward roll, hoping to break my fall and find my footing again, but I functioned as well as a fish out of water, and I fell back to the rails in a painful crunch.

Gritz . . .

Pressing my cheek to the dirt, I fought off another wave of nausea, narrowing my eyes at the dead lamp beside me. *Which of the six bombs knocked you loose from the wall, huh?*

The primary adit? The four bombs that enabled Grismond's escape?

Or the detonation that saved me from Stretch?

The clamor of a violent skirmish traveled down the tunnel, and I raised my chin to scowl at the small circle of light in the distance. Was Rover still waiting for me to emerge after Grismond's brutal tidings? Or was he busy fighting for his life, crippled against the demons who'd outsmarted us?

Could he even access the blasting machine?

. . . Was he still alive to do so?

Using the rusted railway, I pulled myself forward, dragging my body across rocky soil and splintered mine ties. Pebbles and planks scraped against my wound, my face, and I growled into the darkness—as if that might expel some of my pain.

Commotion stirred in the rear of the adit, and I knew the demons had identified their only means of escape. If we didn't destroy the exit now, Plan Z would be futile.

Rover had no choice: he had to blow the tunnel with me inside. And if he couldn't bury his captain's sister, then Grismond would have to detonate the blasting cap.

It was now or never.

Dirt rained down on me, and I rolled onto my back and closed my eyes, halted by blood loss. The volcano inside me had cooled, and my entire body throbbed in pain—like my heart was screaming and wailing for help as its fleshy prison frosted over.

The Pans' snarls and footsteps were audible now. My enemies were almost here.

This was it.

I was going to die alone in a mineshaft, labeled a breeder who let her emotions get the best of her. Immortalized as a cautionary tale in the case against female service.

It was not the end I'd anticipated, and it was nothing like the meaningful life I'd envisioned.

Nova had told me once that my name held great significance—that the Alexanders and Alexandrias of the human pedigree had accomplished many wondrous things. She claimed these name-bearers were conquerors, rulers, generals, and revolutionaries. Scientists and inventors. Authors and poets.

But *me*? This Alex?

I suppose she'd won a watermelon-eating contest for five years running. She'd nearly murdered a boy for throwing rocks at Richard once, and she hadn't felt a crumb of remorse for it. She was on a first-name basis with Belgate's entire Corrective Discipline Committee. And it seemed she'd made a few friends—and evolving acquaintances—along the way.

I felt a sharp pang of guilt for leaving Fudge behind. I'd made him a promise, and that task now fell to Mason, whom I barely trusted to survive at all with his Icarus complex.

Will would be livid with me for dying on him ... and incredibly disappointed in my lack of self-restraint. I could already picture his dissatisfied glower, and the thought of it almost made me laugh, even in a moment as dark as this.

And then there was Tommy ...

Tommy, whom I'd finally reconnected with after all these years. Tommy, whom I'd begged and pleaded with to participate in the mission—a mission that would, inevitably, take my life.

He'd never forgive himself for granting me that wish.

The thunderous footfalls and jangling armor told me the Pans were just thirty seconds away now, and the welling tears spilled over my cheekbones, running down my temples into my ears.

I'd thought my life was so ... important. And maybe it was just Nova's influence, but I'd truly believed my existence had meaning. Had *purpose*. I'd thought I was born in this time and place for a reason—that I'd been granted this small, narrow window in the universe to mend and transform the world in my own way, with my own unique flourish. I'd planned to live profoundly and die honorably with my signature in the great Book of Life.

But maybe it was pure coincidence, mankind's debut on this planet. Maybe we had no purpose, no fate. Maybe we were all just ephemeral creatures trying too hard to be legendary.

Ten seconds.

A gust of warm wind swept up the loose strands of my hair, ticking my forehead, as if the universe were attempting to soothe me in my final moments. *You did your best*, the breeze said. *Now pass the torch.*

But then it occurred to me that a gust of wind didn't belong inside a mountain, and I nervously opened my eyes.

Styx crouched over my body, dust and dirt and wood chips swirling inside her body like an anthropomorphic snow globe. Her yellow heart shimmered in the darkness, and her ethereal presence pushed a few more tears down my face.

She came back to us when we needed her most. She's the only star who ever did.

Gently, she pulled me to my feet, steadying me with hands of solid stone while I focused on keeping the bile out of my throat, refusing to leave this life covered in vomit. I was already drenched in blood as is, and I couldn't tell which of it was mine or the young soldier's anymore.

The demons rounded the corner then—an army of sizzling flesh and pearly eyes—and I tightened my hold on my spirit guide, glad to have Styx here for my closing act. (I figured there were worse ways to die ... probably.)

As I took a long, final sip of this tragic life, I froze on my inhale.

Apple blossoms.

Styx smelled like ... apple blossoms.

I glanced at her with disbelieving eyes, denying the impossible, refuting the insane.

There's no way.

I'd lost too much blood; I wasn't thinking straight. And yet, as Styx stared back at me with that expressionless face of raw courage and stubbornness, I couldn't help but see it: the woman before marriage and children. The younger, unfettered, and unclaimed version of my first true friend.

"...*Mom*?"

Her chest flickered in response, and she nodded at me, softly brushing my cheek with her hand. Affectionately, sorrowfully.

My heart dropped to my feet at the tender confirmation. She was really here with me? She'd *been* here with me the entire time?

Her rocky hand fell to my shoulder, squeezing it tight, and though I couldn't read her face, I understood her body language just fine:

This was goodbye.

She positioned herself in front of me, blocking me from the pack of demons just several yards away now. Her heart swelled, brightening and shivering with mystical energy as pure celestial light filled her body. And then, like a dying star—a supernova—she erupted in a blast of air and stones and blinding heat.

The explosion was so intense, it catapulted me toward the light end of the tunnel. And for one brief, absurd moment, I was distinctly aware of being airborne—of flying through the mineshaft like some kind of useless, incapacitated bird—before I hit the ground, skidded like a rock over water, and slammed into the earth.

The dark end of the adit bellowed at my mother's lethal eruption, and the tunnel began collapsing in on itself, smashing the army of demons in a torrent of mountain rubble. The support beams splintered in all directions, and I swore as loose rocks began falling down around me.

My watery gaze swiveled to the exit, just out of reach.

But close enough to try.

Spitting blood out of my mouth, I clawed my way toward the opening, pushing against the dead weight of my inoperable body. *Almost there*, I convinced my shrieking skeleton, *keep going.*

Styx—my mother—had just destroyed herself for me, and I knew, deep in my bones, she wasn't coming back this time.

I had to outrun the subsidence. I had to survive this damned mineshaft.

For her.

As soon as the exit grazed my fingertips, the earth laughed at me, shaking and trembling at the dramatic irony of it all. Then the sky came crashing down on me, and I watched a tintless world of gray turn the darkest shade of black.

35

I'd sprained my ankle and suffered a head injury. *A severe concussion*, the doctors told us later. *She's lucky to be alive.*

The rain came down in sheets, filling the old well that had swallowed me whole. Frigid black water consumed my shins, my knobby knees, my waist. Rising higher. Rising *rapidly*.

I could swim—Dad had made sure of that—but I couldn't tread water forever, not with my screaming ankle. I would drown; that much was certain.

I frantically scraped at the stone walls, watching the sky turn dark and ominous above me, but my wails of confusion and terror were snuffed out by the earth and her husband.

No one could hear me.

No one was coming.

I couldn't remember which chain of events had led me to the abandoned well. I couldn't remember my parents' names, or Tom's. I knew I had a family—just as I knew my own name—but the details were blemished and foggy. Too challenging to retrieve.

The thunder drowned out my cries, my pleas, and murky water splashed against my chest, my neck, my chin. I shivered and coughed and screamed as my density lifted me off solid ground.

Hopelessness, fear, desperation, and fatigue. They were just as deep, just as deadly. But I never stopped clawing at the walls. Never stopped kicking. Never stopped fighting for buoyancy.

Finally, after what felt like hours of dwindling faith, dwindling energy, a silhouette appeared in the circular skylight. They yelled my name, and a long rope was flung into the well.

"Grab hold of it, Al! We're gonna pull you out!"

"Hold tight!"

***

It smelled like a grave, and my ears rang so loudly, I feared my body was trying to discourage my soul from persevering. I swallowed a few times, hoping to kill the high-pitched alarm in my head, but the note didn't falter.

The next sense to return was touch, and the rails digging into my spine told me I was flat on my back with my hands palm-down on either side of my body. My exposed, blood-caked fingers curled into the earth, seizing the soil, the rocks. I savored each pinch of grainy sand.

Alive, my body sang. *You're alive.*

Thanks to Styx. Thanks to my mom's ... ghost.

My mother had been with me this entire time—watching over me, comforting me, fighting demons with trout and boulders and tree branches—and all the while, I'd thought she was a teenage forest nymph hitting on Will.

So unbelievably wrong about *that* one.

It was just as Nova had said: the world was out of balance, and the dead were among the living. They inhabited the air, the earth, the seas. And, apparently, the foothills of Belgate.

Styx was my fallen angel, and I'd lost her for the second time.

I opened my eyes to a binary world of black and brown. Rocky soil pinned me to the ground, and I couldn't move a muscle below my waist.

On a positive note, it didn't feel like my legs had been crushed—just trapped and buried under the rubble of Goddard Mine.

From my torso up, I was encased in a wooden fort. The adit timbers had sheltered my brain from the collapse, providing a sizeable pocket of air, and about ten feet to my right, a small crevice of light provided access to the outside world.

A shrunken exit, assuming I could exhume myself.

Beyond my feet, a wall of debris and blasted sandstone sealed off the tunnel of nightmares. An entire platoon of Pans, if not more, had been crushed and buried alive, their soulless husks condemned to an eternity of immobile anguish and suffocation.

Just a glimpse of that cruel fate had stirred up something unpleasant in my gut—something darker than guilt, something uglier than remorse. But then I thought of Stretch and the nameless soldier who died in my arms, and I stashed the feeling away.

The sibilance of falling sand gave my heart a kick, but I quickly traced the noise to a pair of blurry hands frantically removing dirt and gravel away from my window. Gradually, more light seeped into my tomb, and I felt a sob building in my throat.

Someone was trying to dig me out.

My rescuer moved a broken beam out of the way, and the rubble mountain groaned above me, dirt trickling down onto my face and neck. The hands paused, then vanished.

I'm here! Don't quit on me, I wanted to say. But when I tried to voice my request, I couldn't produce enough sound to reach him—my chest was too heavy, and I'd swallowed too much dust.

The hands reappeared, and this time, they fashioned a plank on either side of the window to keep it from collapsing in on itself. Then, upon rein-forcing his exit and clearing away the remaining stones, the soldier crept through the hole, headfirst.

He came into focus as he drew nearer, and a patch of dusty black hair set a shaky breath free from my lips.

Will.

His charcoal-brown eyes were wide, panicked. I'd never seen him that way, so openly vulnerable and discomposed. The unfiltered concern made him look younger—softer. And for once, painfully human.

He crawled to me and hurriedly pushed away the wreckage on my thighs, eyeing the fragile beams above us. He was covered in demon ash, and though he hadn't suffered any visible lesions, his movements were stiff and awkward—a sign of a more serious injury, if his undetected shoulder wound had taught me anything. When he'd finished rearranging the obstacles in our path, he chanced a glance at my face, almost like he'd been afraid to do so until now.

Our eyes met in the dusky lighting, and I grinned feebly, shedding fresh tears. "Whoops," I croaked.

The dread dissolved, and he huffed at me, releasing a strangled, "You're out of your mind."

It was hard to hear him over the ringing, but I could read his lips, as well as the relief that unraveled his scowl.

A bit of strength returned to my voice. "... Tom?"

"He's fine. They're all fine."

The fist around my heart loosened a bit.

Will's gaze flitted back to our exit. "This pocket won't last, though. We need to hurry."

I pointed to my bloody ribcage. He nodded, like—*Yeah, I can see that huge gash on my own, thanks.* Then he grabbed my hand and pushed it firmly to my wound, giving me a stern look that I interpreted as, *Pressure.*

Murmuring an apology, he positioned himself behind me and pulled my limp body toward the exit. The motion freed my legs from the rubble, but it also revived my pain, and I almost retched from the strain it caused on my injury. Hot, fresh blood coated my fingertips, leaving a slime trail of youthful reds along the mine floor.

How did I even *have* more blood to lose? And gritz, how long did it take to bleed to death? Hours? Minutes? Did it happen slowly, or all at once?

I considered asking Will, but I didn't want to rush him. He was doing his best.

With limited space to work with, the Rhean hooked an arm around my chest and dragged my body backward with his own—the way a capable swimmer might rescue a drowning child. As we shuffled for the light, our weapons caught against the sand and battered railway, making the feat twice as difficult, and I clamped my mouth shut to contain the yelps of pain on my tongue.

We'd almost made it to the window when a plank gave way, and the unstable mountain shuddered around us. Soil dusted our faces, and Will shielded my head as a few rocks tumbled loose from the crumbling ceiling.

I flinched at the prelude to certain death, my nails digging into his wrists so hard they probably drew blood. "Hey, it's okay," he whispered, his lips brushing against my temple as he spoke. "You're okay."

I kept my eyes closed, muscles taut.

"I'm getting you out of here," he assured me. "No matter what."

Despite the many lies he'd uttered in his second decade, I believed him. And despite what I'd said in the stables, I *did* trust him—and not just in the face of traumatic asphyxia, either. I trusted him to keep me alive, to save me.

Perhaps more than anyone else.

He tightened his hold on me and dragged us onward, rolling aside as a boulder crashed just inches from his head. But just as the panic threatened to overwhelm me, we'd reached our light source, and Will didn't waste any time hefting me into the narrow hole. Gripping my breastplate, my hips, and my leather tassets, he slid my body up and over his own, past his chest and shoulder. Saving me first, just as he'd promised.

When I surfaced on the other side, a new pair of hands clasped my forearms and pulled me out the rest of the way—my body uncharnelled, my soul resurrected.

The gray sky blinded me, and I squinted down at my feet to make sure Will had followed, furiously blinking away the silver dots. But he didn't let my anxiety simmer long; the Rhean rolled out after me just as the remaining beams gave way, and the tail-end of the tunnel collapsed like a dying beast, spewing dust and splinters upon its final, defeated exhale.

Fudge's bloody, tear-streaked face was the last thing I saw before darkness claimed me for the second time.

36

I woke up a day later at Camp Ptarmigan.

My first thought was how unbearably dry my mouth was; it felt like a goose-feather pillow had been stuffed down my throat when I wasn't looking. The right side of my torso ached terribly, and though my leg muscles were taut from bedrest, my arms were sore from fighting—and crashing onto rusted railways.

But I wasn't bleeding to death inside a rocky tomb, so there was that.

As I slowly came to, the number of familiar faces at my bedside multiplied, and by the time I was fully awake, Richard, Fudge, Mason, Rover, and Tom surrounded my cot. Will, sporting a fresh bandage on his shoulder and a wrist brace on his nondominant hand, stood in the corner of the tent with his typical somber expression.

A handful of male patients joined me in the hospital, but their wounds weren't fresh. These were the men sent away from the Rim with injuries that required long-term care—amputations, spinal injuries, and an array of invisible wounds.

I was fortunate not to belong here.

"You know, you should sleep more often. Your face is a lot easier to look at when your mouth is off," Mason observed.

"…It's nice to see you too, Mason."

Fudge smiled at me with wet eyes. He'd taken a blade to his cheek and the bridge of his freckled nose, and a wave of unbridled fury shot through me at the sight of his ruptured, inflamed skin.

Who had dared lay a hand on *Fudge*?

"We're glad you're okay," he told me, his voice so raw and delicate, it almost brought me to tears. "When the mine came down, and you were still inside, we all …" He swallowed, stooping to scratch Richard behind the ear. "We thought you were gone."

His blue eyes slipped to the stewing boy in the corner, where Rover's gaze had, coincidentally, also traveled.

All except one, perhaps.

"What happened, exactly?" I asked the room. If the six of us were still kicking, it couldn't have ended too tragically for the federates, right? "The sequence of things is a bit … blurry."

Tom sat at the edge of my cot with a thin smile on his lips. "The Pans followed us into the mine, just as we'd planned, and once we destroyed the primary adit, they had no choice but to dive into the pit and incur injury. While they healed, we set the mine on fire and fled into the remaining exits, but we faced unexpected company." Sadness darkened those honey irises. "The enemy had already slaughtered the northern posts; success hinged on our survival."

"They attacked from the south, too," Mason added darkly. "Fell from the trees, and they didn't seem too keen on preserving our bodies for future Pans. We didn't even have the capacity to blow the adit until our runners arrived."

I felt a stab of sympathy for the prick.

The haunting realization that your best efforts weren't good enough—that even your death couldn't mitigate casualties—was a terrible feeling to endure in the heat of battle. I'd tasted that strain of despondence for the first time yesterday, and I never again wished to experience such despair.

Rover crossed his arms over his chest. "That's when a *certain* someone disregarded orders and sprinted into a war zone." He frowned at my apologetic wince, but his expression lacked any real malice. "If you wanted in on the action so badly, you should've stayed put. There was plenty to do when the second wave of Pans spilled over the hill."

Gritz. The enemy had soldiers pre-positioned in three cardinal directions? How many platoons did they *have*?

"Next thing I know, we're fighting like hell to now keep enemies *out* of the mine," Rover went on. "The Bear joined the group, insisting we blow the adit. But I'd left the blaster with Fudge, and he was under strict orders not to do a damned thing without my explicit permission."

Oh, Fudge …

I could still see traces of distress on his face at the prospect of having to use the plunger—or refuse someone as frightening as Grismond. "And then?"

Rover grinned. "And then we made history, Fuse."

The comment had Tom rolling his eyes. "Don't make it out to be so dramatic, Rove."

"We brought down a mountain. How is that not dramatic?"

My brother caught me side-eyeing the glass of water on the bedside table, and he winked at me as he fetched the beverage. But as I reached to cure my cotton mouth, I froze.

My glove was gone, replaced with meager strips of medical gauze.

It was *gone*.

I slipped my other hand out of the sheets and gasped at its nakedness, scrambling backward. Amidst my overwrought response, the glass rolled off the cot and shattered on the dirt. "Where—where are—?"

"Whoa! Hey, easy." Tom moved to console me, but I scooted away, shaking my head vehemently. "Al! It's okay. Your gloves were in bloody shreds."

"Who—"

"I did. *I* wrapped your hands," he answered. "We'll get you new gloves when we go to Holly, alright?" Brown eyes burrowed into mine, silently pleading with me to rein in the trauma response, and I was suddenly struck by the nostalgia of it all.

Curse-induced episodes that sent me spiraling.

Emotions only Tom could address.

Solutions only Tom could offer.

At the peak of an anxiety attack, Tom used to sit me down and tell me it was all going to be okay—then help redirect my attention to hinder the escalating panic.

Look around you, Al, he'd say. *Name something you can touch. Name something you can hear.*

With my hands locked behind my neck—a self-soothing position I'd discovered shortly after my mother died—I focused on the sporadic pulse leaping against my palm. In addition to my thundering heartbeat, I could hear a thriving military camp just outside the tent: snorting horses, swearing men, creaking wagons, and Jaden's distant laughter.

Tom's eyes softened, realizing where my brain had gone, and the others gawked at me, visibly alarmed by my outburst.

Name something you can smell ...

I could smell the soap they'd used to clean the gore and grime from my body, the dried blood beneath my fingernails, the ashes in my unwashed hair. The medics had also replaced my uniform with a sweater and oversized trousers, but the part of me that felt embarrassed by that fact was also grateful to have avoided the messy aftermath of my exsanguination.

I didn't want to know how much blood I'd lost. I didn't want to see how close I'd come to hypovolemic shock.

"Overall, I consider it a success," Tom continued, trying to spare me from the startled looks of my company—and their inevitable line of questioning. "We lost eight good men, but we trapped over a hundred Pans in that mine and killed another thirty on the perimeter. Survivors scattered into the Range, but we eliminated a fat percentage of their forces."

My brow jumped at the numbers. Over 130 dead or permanently detained in one day—and it cost him eight devoted men.

Eight soldiers with families, lovers, and dreams.

Eight martyrs who'd died for their country.

When had my brother learned to gamble with human lives? And how on earth did he cope with the guilt?

"Sterling dug you out after the collapse, and we fixed you up here at camp," Tom explained, and though he didn't spare Will an appreciative glance, I detected a change in tone—and less venom coursing through the Rhean's surname. "It was the second most reckless operation I've ever orchestrated." At Rover's pursed lips, he huffed. "Okay, *third* rashest, then. Regardless, the mission would not have been possible without every federate going above and beyond the call of duty, and that includes you four." His gaze hopped from trainee to trainee, lingering on Will's blank face for a few extra seconds. "You have my sincere gratitude for the preparation time you've gifted us, as well as your active participation in this operation. Your efforts are duly noted."

Warmth blossomed in my chest, and the boys smiled at the praise—or frowned less, in Will's case.

For the first time since our reunion, Tom looked exactly like the brother I remembered: young and overconfident, boyish and sweet. And, just as I'd hoped, he finally saw us for the seventeen-year-old refugees we were: bold, passionate, and surprisingly adept.

"This afternoon, I want each of you to attend a debrief session on your experience yesterday. You'll review achievements and mistakes, assess the enemy's performance, and discuss any personal reflections you have. But first," his gaze swiveled back to me, "I'd like to know how my little sister brought down the seventh mineshaft all on her own."

They all stared at me expectantly, and it did nothing to soothe my anxious heartbeat.

"It's just that Rover never gave the command, and I never used that plunger," Fudge offered—a gentle nudge for answers. "So how were you able to ignite the dynamite and still survive the blast?"

I lowered my hands to my lap, exhaling through my nose as I recalled the tragic events under the mountain. "It wasn't my doing. A forest spirit sacrificed herself for me—for *all* of us. She used her life force to bring down the rest of the mountain, and the energy wave pushed me away from the blast point." I fought the prickling sensation behind my eyes. "I'm here because of her."

The boys exchanged shocked and solemn glances, taking a moment to process the ninth casualty of the day. Fudge looked especially distraught, and I wished I could take away his pain; he'd grown fond of Styx.

We all had.

I didn't mention the identity of the aforementioned spirit—it was too fresh in my heart to share right now. Too personal to reveal. Too baffling to explain.

Tom narrowed his eyes at my vague response, but I gave him a look that said, *I'll tell you later.*

"Well, if her actions spared your life, then she has my thanks," he said. His voice sounded a bit strained, though, as if he were repressing the magnitude of his relief, and I couldn't imagine the horror he'd felt when he discovered my absence, when he'd learned I'd gone running into a death trap. "Frankly, it's astonishing you made it out with nothing but a scratch."

My brow sailed skyward at that. A scratch? *Ha!*

But that wasn't Tom's teasing face; he wasn't joking.

My bewildered gaze brushed Will's, and I was relieved to find someone just as confused as I was. Because sure, I suppose taking a spear to the gut wasn't the *worst* of injuries in the league of demonic warfare, but still. I'd fully expected to die from that blow.

I lifted my new sweater—and the cloth bandage beneath it—to examine a small, anticlimactic mark beneath my floating rib. The sutured wound was dark red against the tan of my skin, and a nasty bruise haloed the stitches. But the damage was otherwise minimal.

"Yeah," I muttered, blinking down at the scabbing flesh. "Stretch got his revenge alright."

Fudge tilted his head at that, bemused. "Stretch?"

"One of the demons Will and I captured when you were taken. He had a personal vendetta after we strapped him to a tree."

Will's scowl deepened at the news of his opponent's resurgence, and Tom couldn't seem to tell if I was pulling his leg or not.

I placed the bandage back over my scar, perplexed by the seemingly uncomplicated surgery. Had I hallucinated the extent of the injury? Or was I just . . . overdramatic?

I had some *serious* questions for my medic. And Will.

Tom sighed deeply then, the kind of sigh my father heaved on a daily basis, and I cut him a wary glance. "Despite my being so relieved at your recovery, Al, you defied orders. I told you not to disobey me, and you did. Blatantly. You ran straight into the adit without permission. You risked your life and the entire operation." He lifted his chin. "Do you know what that means?"

I held my breath, meeting stern brown eyes.

Our mother's eyes.

"It means you'd make one lousy Spec."

37

"I refuse to go to a meeting in this thing," I declared.

"Holly won't let a girl past the wall with that war getup. And forget the Command Center—they'd arrest you on sight," Tom insisted from the other side of the door. "Besides, these welts won't take you seriously if you show up in a ragged pair—"

"No one will take me seriously in a dress, Tom! I look . . . I look like a *handkerchief*."

Why did Jaden even own this immobilization garment, anyway? I thought she was on my side. But the moment Tom stated his request, she squealed like a startled sow and dragged me to her quarters to retrieve this yellow monstrosity.

"Did we have a deal or not, Al?"

"We did."

After my behavior at Goddard Mine, he could have asked anything of me—to leave the garrison, to clean the latrines. But instead, he chose the most effective, most reformative penalty in his arsenal, and I suddenly remembered all the cons of having an older sibling.

I grabbed my belt and threw it around my waist, setting both my sword and my knife in their proper places. *There—a compromise.*

I opened Jaden's door, and Tom smiled brightly at the wardrobe, laughing a little at the scabbard fastened to my hip. But his face, alive and openly joyful, made me lose track of what I was so mad about.

Damn him.

Behind my traitorous kin, a giddy Jaden cupped her face like she'd never seen something so delightful, and I held up a hand before either of them could say anything that sent me spinning on my heels.

A debriefing with the Command. Dressed like this. *Unbelievable!*

Tom pretended like the outfit had safety implications. *Men will hesitate to string up a girl who appears innocuous*, he'd said. He also argued that the dress would make a stronger statement—orthodox femininity juxtaposed by military experience. He said the image would be jarring enough to chip away at their denial, but I was pretty sure he just wanted me to suffer.

And really, he could not have had worse timing. I needed the Command to have open minds tonight, and if I showed up looking like a goddamned lemon bar . . . I might as well have walked in naked.

At least nudity would seize their attention long enough to speak on my experience.

We descended two sets of rickety stairs and joined the others in the pub. Mason was the first to spot me, and his expression shifted from confusion to outright revulsion—like he'd just stumbled upon a new mutant creature that was never intended to walk the earth. Next to him, Fudge did his best to kill his awed smile, but I could see the joy dancing in his eyes, and Will just appeared slightly amused in his frowny-face way.

Richard, who waited for me at the bar, seemed perturbed by my feminine getup, tail stiff in the air and upper lip stuck on his canines. I gave the derp a kiss on the noggin and moved to greet the boy in black. "You're coming?"

Will offered a tired shrug. "I think I'm on parole?"

I looked at Tom for an explanation, and he glanced to the side like he found the topic of Asa Sterling entirely bothersome. "After his performance in the mine, I think his attendance is justified," he said evenly. "He's still under military custody, but he's no longer considered a hostile."

Will fiddled with his brace, and I squinted at him. Something between the two soldiers had shifted in the 72 hours since the mining incident. The atmosphere wasn't the same as before—there was a new source of tension here, one I couldn't place.

"You think Will's safe in Holly?" I asked, ignoring the Rhean's insulted snort. "I thought you said they'd kill him."

"Only if they know who he is," Tom replied. He raised his brow. "Would you rather leave him here with Gris and crew?"

Definitely not.

I crossed my arms over my chest, feeling far too exposed. The universe endowed Jaden with much larger breasts than me, and I feared one wrong move might have the off-shoulder dress plummeting to my waistline. "Fine. Can we please just go, then? I'm counting down the minutes I have to wear this egregious parachute."

Tom shook his head at me, but he still had that stupid, lopsided grin plastered on his face. "I'll get the horses ready. You think you can survive such cruel, torturous conditions until then?"

I gave a despairing sigh. "Only time will tell."

His snickers followed him out the door, and I sucked on my teeth. I was *so* getting him back for this—the welt had no idea how wicked I'd become in seven long years.

Fudge tapped my shoulder, and my gaze dropped to eyes of twinkling sapphire. "For what it's worth, I think you look really nice, Alex."

Mason scoffed at him before I could mumble my thanks. "*Nice?* She looks like a boy stuffed in a sundress. Look at the way she's standing. No girl stands like that."

I squeezed my folded arms so I wouldn't wallop him. "I *am* a girl, bird-brain."

"Tell that to your posture," he countered and promptly walked away.

Fudge padded after him, scolding the blond for his comments, and I frowned at my favorite pair of army boots poking out beneath my dress.

I turned to Will with an arched eyebrow. "What's wrong with the way I stand?"

***

Hours later, I discovered that wartime meetings were, in fact, terribly boring.

And sure, debriefing a slew of military personnel wasn't on anyone's bucket list, but these insipid reporting methods had me doubting if human lives were ever at stake. These geezers spoke about military accomplishments and death tolls like this was all just "business as usual."

Objectives, policy adherence, resource allocation, performance stats—*gritz*, where were the patriotic speeches? The medals of honor? Our newspapers made the military sound like a glorious career, but this was as dry and monotonous as a mathematics course.

We'd assembled in a large, octangular room on the second floor of Holly's Central Command Center. The space was guarded by a dozen sentries, and the chamber itself doubled as a bomb shelter—eight windowless, concrete walls and a single point of entry reinforced by a steel door. Oil lamps burned in every corner, and a candle-lit chandelier hung above an oval table. Five rows of chairs, occupied by an ensemble of military officers and advisors sipping beverages or smoking various tobacco products, encircled the wooden centerpiece.

It was as every bit pretentious as I'd expected.

For the next half an hour, Tom drizzled honey over our mission, highlighting notable achievements, commending his subordinates' dedication, cushioning errors with intel and demon casualties. Then, like a chef setting fire to his figgy pudding, he introduced his little sister.

"This is Private Kingsley," he said, motioning for me to stand. Just my being here broke about a million laws, but Tom wanted to make a statement tonight—and that statement included a visual so alarming, so absurd, that his reactionary superiors wouldn't know what hit them.

Jolt them loose from their mycelium, he'd said. *Force them to perceive a living contradiction.*

I rose, adjusting the sweeping neckline of my prescribed attire. The men squinted at me through the cigar smoke, and a few of them even seized their spectacles to rectify the impossible hallucination before them.

"Nine days ago, Kingsley and three Tournament contestants survived the attack on Belgate. Putting country before self, these young graduates parted with their families and traveled eastward to inform headquarters of the invasion, as I relayed to the Joint Chiefs of Staff earlier this week." His warm eyes swept the room. "In addition to their advanced warning, this same group—all here in attendance tonight—also contributed to our success at Goddard Mine, and we owe these brave recruits a debt of gratitude."

The crowd did not share this sentiment, however. Several men coughed up their liquor in disbelief, a few echoed Tom's speech with contemptuous *"recruits?"* under their breath, and others just glared at me, deaf to my brother's sugary presentation.

Better to inform them of your participation now than let it find their ears, Tom had said. We could mold facts into pleasant shapes that way. Though, based on these initial reactions, I suspected facts mattered little in the shadow of disobedience.

"Captain, you *are* disclosing that you have allowed untrained refugees to partake in this operation, yes?" questioned the man at the head of the table. He wore a gallery of pins and medals across his breast, and his voluminous eyebrows and mustache resembled healthy fir branches more than facial hair. "Furthermore, disregarding a host of military codes and federal laws, you permitted a teenage girl to engage in combat?"

Tom didn't even waver. "Yes, General. And they performed exceptionally well."

My eyes widened at the officer's title. This grouchy, bushy-lipped man held the highest rank in the nation's armed forces?

This was the famous General Iver? The man who'd crippled Rhea so badly, they'd resorted to dark magic?

Iver scanned me with a critical eye, and I waited for him to sentence me to death or banish me from the country, but he didn't. He said nothing at all, which concerned me even more.

"What about the boy?" he asked instead, and his secretary, realizing we'd just switched agenda items, rushed to eject the page from his typewriter and insert a new one.

Skimmed over, I thought, affronted. *Brushed aside.*

Did he not perceive me as a threat? Or had he already determined my fate, and he'd simply skipped ahead to unsettled matters?

"We've heard rumors of Sterling's heir among the ranks. What can you tell us of that?"

Will leaned against the steel doorframe to my right, peeved at the inquiry, and despite my festering agitation, I nearly laughed. Even in a room full of people who, if aware of his identity, would probably hang him from the ceiling fixture, he wasn't the least bit anxious.

"That individual remains under my team's exacting scrutiny … but so far, he has demonstrated staunch allegiance to the Interior Company," Tom responded vaguely—and far more eloquently than I would've done. "As a matter of fact, I would not be standing here today if it weren't for the son of Godric Sterling and his timely intervention."

Oh?

This was news to me, though I supposed it explained their new civility. I refrained from casting Will a meaningful look and responsibly stashed my questions away for later.

"I see," Iver ground out, making a note of something in his journal. "I must say, Kingsley, your methods have become much more ... liberal these past six months. Results aside, the Command finds your spontaneity and loose interpretation of standing orders ... concerning, to say the least."

Tom just smirked at this. "Spontaneity lends itself to golden opportunities, sir. At this point in the war, I believe risk and adaptability are advantageous—and absolutely necessary when the populace of Holly is under threat. Wouldn't you agree?"

The general narrowed his eyes at the speedy rejoinder, but I swore his lips twitched under that colossal, bushy mustache of his. The other officers seated at the table glanced at one another, conveying a range of opinions in their silence: scorn, disapproval, amusement, assent.

On the ride over, Rover had explained the Command's conflicting perceptions of Thomas Kingsley. He was the youngest captain they'd seen in two centuries—climbed the pyramid early and remarkably fast. But those who didn't respect him for the scars he'd earned envied him for his advancement. The rest just despised his audacity.

It was under Tom's command that Ellsian forces stopped the first breach two-and-a-half years ago. He'd prevented a national emergency, and he'd bought us at least two winters to reinforce our border security. After that, he'd been promoted to Captain of the Interior Company, and now he stood here among these officers with enough experience and esteem to voice, unapologetically, his decision to override his superiors' instructions—much to his peers' chagrin.

"How exactly was the final stage of the mining operation carried out?" asked another member of the Command. He held up the incomplete report with his brow raised. "Be precise, Captain."

Tom glanced at me again, bringing attention to the fact that I'd refused to sit down after the general's flagrant snub—towering amongst seated officers like a yellow parasol. "There came a point in the mission when Private Kingsley abandoned her post in search of missing comrades. Those stationed outside the mine waited for her return, and therefore, failed to detonate the explosives for the final exit."

The officers turned their heads to pointedly glare at me, and I winced.

"However," Tom continued, "her intervention also saved the lives of two highly decorated soldiers and indirectly spared countless others. After inflicting injuries upon the Pans in her adit, she proceeded to set off ammunition that brought down the tunnel, and consequently, our enemy."

He grinned with pride—an infectious reaction—and the men's disgruntled faces uncreased a bit. "It's apparent that Private Kingsley is fully capable of serving her country, and with a little more training and discipline, she and her fellow refugees could become pivotal assets in our Defensive Recovery Initiative." Before anyone could interrupt him, he appended a barbed, "They've experienced firsthand what it takes to defeat these creatures in combat, which is more than I can say for many of our veterans— and many of you in this room."

My chest swelled with love and admiration for my audacious older kin, and I wondered what our parents would think if they could see us now— one sibling platforming the other, laws and rocky reputations be damned.

The general took a silent sip of water, skewering me in place with his unflinching gaze.

But as I stared back, inspecting his hardened features, I couldn't tell if he was angry, concerned, or intrigued. Like Will, he only emoted what he intended to share; he only reacted if he wanted that reaction to serve a purpose. And right now, he wanted us irresolute and unsettled by that cold, inscrutable face.

"I take it this account was provided by the female in the room?" asked a bald man with a square jaw and a long, unnaturally sharp nose. "Are there any living witnesses who can attest to her ... performance?"

Tom's smile dimmed. "Sergeant Grismond provided a testimony of the events that transpired in Goddard Mine, including Kingsley's coura-geous decision to distract the enemy while he transported a wounded com-rade to safety." He flicked his hand at Rover, who promptly weaved through the chairs and dropped a stack of written notes on the table. "After that, Private Kingsley was left to her own devices."

Judging by the sneers that followed, the Command didn't appreciate the way Tom skirted around that question—nor his persistent use of a mil-itary address when referring to his sibling. They doubted my skills, and now Tom's credibility. Pair that with undeniable nepotism, and my story lost all substance.

I glanced at Tom again, unable to discern any chips in his confi-dence—even as mine rapidly deteriorated. What if he was wrong, and this mission wasn't enough to change their minds? What if this transparency only backfired?

What if they hanged us *both*?

"Private," Tom said to me as I spiraled into paranoia. "Why don't you explain to the Colonel how you brought down the adit?"

I'd told him what happened in the mine, and he'd believed me. But he'd decided the Command should hear it from me directly, insisting a writ-ten report wouldn't do it justice. They'd have laughed at the account and dismissed any merit.

They still might laugh...

I rubbed the space between my thumb and the palm of my right hand. It often ached there, beneath the gauze, like a constant reminder of who I was and what I was capable of. But the pain also reminded me just how far I'd come—and how much further I had to climb.

Here goes nothing.

"Since leaving Belgate, my peers and I have interacted with two distinct paranormal entities: spirits and demons," I began, sticking to my preap-proved script. "On our trek to the Interior, we befriended a forest spirit who fought beside us each time we encountered demonic forces. She could not communicate verbally, but she was genial and loyal. This same spirit appeared inside the mine when I was incapacitated ... and she sacrificed herself to implode the surrounding tunnel."

The men looked at me like I'd just read them a fairytale, but Tom gestured for me to go on.

I felt like I was melting beneath the heat of the chandelier—like a candle destroyed by her own luminous flame. "We communicated briefly before she died. And based on this interaction, I now believe that this spirit ... that she was my mother, who passed away prior to Godric's retaliatory measures."

I heard Fudge's soft gasp from my left, Rover's muffled swearing, and Mason's skeptical tut behind me. Tom had reacted similarly at first, but after I'd explained the lengths Styx had gone to aid us in our journey, the way she'd defended me in her final moments, he'd accepted my hypothesis.

"This explains her affinity for me and my peers, and why she sought us out the moment we set foot in the Range," I added.

Styx never could have appeared to me inside city limits without raising alarm—probably the same reason she'd avoided Camp Ptarmigan altogether. So she'd waited years for the invasion to happen, and when she'd finally seen Belgate spewing black smoke, she'd known it was time.

"I can't take credit for anything beyond assisting Sergeant Grismond and buying the runners a few more minutes. And if I'm being honest, I didn't even trust my mother's spirit up until that point. Really ... if it were up to me, we wouldn't have partnered with an obnoxious, supernatural entity in the first place," I admitted, and Fudge passed me a small, watery smile. "But that's the truth. And that's how we managed, collectively, to protect Holly."

Tom nodded at me, pleased with my delivery. His lieutenant, however—visibly concerned for my welfare—moved to stand next to me, as if his presence might prevent an arrest ... or a lynching.

"Well, that is quite extraordinary," General Iver stated, putting an end to the awkward, lengthy pause that followed my synopsis. "We appreciate your candid recap, Miss Kingsley. I'm sure Administrative Services would be happy to offer you a job in their department, should you wish to pursue a career in the military one day."

I held his stare, unblinking. *Administrative Services?*

As in, administrative desk work here at the Command? Away from the action? Away from a position of influence?

His condescension had a ripple effect, and I glanced at the bored, distracted faces of his council. Men holding conversations among themselves, whispering, chuckling, smoking. Men who held nothing but disdain for little girls acting like men. They perceived me as a liar seeking recognition, and at best, a happy accident they'd burn from the records.

I was merely a breeder in their eyes. A handkerchief, now and always.

"Anything else you'd like to share with us?" Iver asked when I remained standing yet again, unwilling to adhere to his defenestration. But the dismissal was clear this time; he'd even painted me a bleak portrait of this dead-end pursuit, expecting me to scurry back to Tom's underwing like a child.

But I did not come here to be ridiculed and criticized. To be willfully ignored, my accomplishments downplayed, my dreams rejected.

No. I came to sow a little chaos.

"Actually," I said, and Tom whipped his head around. "Yes."

There were curious murmurs at that, and the sidebar conversations quieted around me.

"Private," Tom cautioned, but it was too late. The seed was in the ground.

"Isn't it strange that these Pots, as you call them, don't possess the dead?" I questioned, commanding attention of the room, just as I'd done before the Council every time I publicly spat upon their rules.

The circle of officers looked at me, irritated I was still speaking or surprised I took the liberty to do so.

"Pans leave the dead behind. You collect bodies after each battle." Military coffins showed up weekly in Belgate—so frequently, in fact, that we'd run out of graveyard space several years ago. Unless you had the privilege of burying a soldier on private property, family members were cremated or, in some cases, left at the Rim to rot. "But Pots don't possess these perfectly empty vessels, right?"

"That's the whole point of possessing humans, isn't it?" a big-boned officer replied. "They need to inhabit a sustainable life form. They need a living, sophisticated weapon to execute orders."

"Exactly. But if they can heal mortal wounds—excluding those inflicted by vanadium—why do they need a living host at all?" I pushed.

The mean, long-nosed colonel crossed his arms and leaned back in his chair. "The running theory is that demons require human souls for sustenance. They leech the energy out of our men until there's nothing left."

"It's true. Our federates claim you can see the Pots suck the life right out of a man," another officer supplied. "They say a man's soul spills out of his eyes when a demon eats his heart."

The preternatural gossip flattened my lips. "But how do you know they consume their souls? Is there science to support it? Evidence?"

A few sharper knives detected my patronizing tone and scowled.

Tom rubbed the space below his left eyebrow as if I'd just unleashed the mother of all headaches. "Al, I know where you're going with this, and we've been down this road before. Demons hijack human bodies. When the Pans die, so do the humans they possess. Hell, they turn to *ashes*. If our men were still alive, their conscious minds would resurface the moment the demons perished—not combust."

His counterpoint gave me pause.

Why *didn't* our soldiers remain in their bodies after a Pan was killed, unless some vital part of them had been devoured? Unless demonic parasites had destroyed them, mind and soul?

Sweat dampened my palms as I altered course. Arguing hypotheticals with men who'd analyzed every facet of our enemy was pointless; I knew what I had to do.

"When we crossed the Range, a scouting party attacked us," I said, turning to address my fuming brother. It was now, in a dignified way, or later, as I burned at the stake. "I wasn't wearing my gloves at the time, and when a demon tried to kill me—I touched his skin. I saw his memories, Tom."

He stared at me.

"*Human* memories."

38

Out, my heart breathed. *Finally out.*

Tom gaped at me. He couldn't believe I'd gone there, and to be honest, neither could I. But I was done building relationships on a bed of lies. Done hiding who I was beneath gauze and gloves and lace.

The revelation was not how I'd imagined it—and definitely not here in the presence of the general and my fragile friendships. But a picture-perfect moment might never have arrived. War was on the horizon, and these fools assumed I was some innocent damsel raised in the country, not a killer with a groundbreaking exposé.

Tonight, I could show everyone what I was capable of in one sitting. One earthquake to shatter the windows and upheave their foundations.

"What is she on about?" demanded Long-Nose.

Tom and I stared each other down, and the room looked between us, confused, wary. But I wasn't backing down; I'd already plunged headfirst into madness.

Vexed, Tom set his jaw and turned to his superiors once again. "Private Kingsley has the ability to … touch any object and descry its past affiliations." His gaze roamed over puzzled faces, and he wet his lips. "At the brush of her palm, she can observe histories and memories like the Ancients' cinema. I've witnessed it myself."

Rover, who'd placed an admonitory hand on my back when I chose to speak, went perfectly still at this.

His hand fell away, and without glancing behind me, I couldn't tell if he'd distanced himself out of self-preservation, or if he'd clasped his sword to protect me from a witch hunt.

The Command peered at us in skeptical silence, as if they were waiting for Tom to reveal an elaborate prank or deliver a gratifying punchline. But when no admission came, wide eyes narrowed in scorn.

"You expect us to believe that?" Long-Nose cried, and the room promptly exploded in protests and offhanded remarks. Men scoffed, reaching for more liquor, while others attempted to leave the room entirely, unwilling to hear another irrational word from the Kingsley bloodline.

"Is it really that far-fetched when we're discussing demons here, Colonel?" Tom countered, blocking two deserters in his aisle. He might have argued on my behalf, but I could tell I'd crossed a very bold line. He was not pleased with me.

"This is nonsense," hissed one of the many balding men in uniform. He shook his hand at me in disgust, as if I were a stray dog wandering through his abode unannounced, mucking up the hardwood. "Someone escort this child from the room."

I glared at his invisible eyebrows and thin, turtle-like lips. His features looked like they were growing invertedly—toward his round, squat skull—as if his eyes, nose, and mouth were being sucked into a black hole of idiocy.

I supposed he would do.

"Your pocket watch," I demanded, stepping forward.

He bristled, eyeing the object he'd set on the table. "Excuse me?"

"Pocket. Watch."

"What about it?"

"Give it to me."

He looked at me like I'd grown another head. He'd probably never been spoken to with such insolence before, certainly not from a woman, and I reveled in his outrage.

Beckett, who'd sat quietly and obediently in his chair until now, was fresh out of patience, though. Standing, he plucked the watch off the table and tossed it to me, shrugging at the officer's appalled expression before collapsing back into his seat.

Making my way to the heart of the chamber, I unwound the strips of gauze on my hand like a spool of secrecy, acutely aware of the tumultuous path I'd carved. But if these men wouldn't respect me for my accomplishments, then perhaps they'd accept me for my faculty.

After an apologetic glance in Tom's direction, I took the watch in my bare palm, wincing at the sharp twinge of pain it induced—and the fascinating memories it harbored. "Your wife bought this for you in Lawrence, and she gifted it to you maybe twenty years ago, back when you still had hair." I paused, closing my eyes to enhance the glowing image in my head. "A wedding present, it looks like. There's an engraving on the inside in Latin. I can't read Latin, and neither can you, but she told you it meant '*yours, until the end and long after.*' She had the dial refinished for your anniversary this year."

The man sputtered, flushing. "I've never told … this is … *how?*"

"You lost it recently," I continued. My hand burned, and I thought the metal might be eating away at my flesh as the memories flooded my brain. "Left it at the bar. Or *was* it a bar? That's what you told your wife, yet—"

"That's enough!" he cut in, ashen. I slid the watch back over the table, grinning at his distress.

I'd never been able to show off before, not like this; it was the first time in my life I hadn't loathed my curse.

"Who's next?" I dared, and the room fell quiet again. "I can do this all night if you'd like to keep wasting time. My ability isn't limited to objects either, if any of you fancy a palm reading." That was a risky bluff, but it didn't matter; my stunt had its intended effect.

Speechless, the Command looked from their wide-eyed general to me and my hands. Fudge and Mason gaped at me, but I couldn't focus on them right now—nor on Will, whose dark eyes I could feel burning holes in my shoulder blades.

Tom cleared his throat. "Private, if you can see these images, a dead body isn't any different, is it? At the river, you likely perceived the memories of the soldier's corpse. Nothing more."

I shook my head. "It doesn't work that way. I can absorb the memories of any object. But I can sense the *feelings* of living things. Thoughts, emotions. And I felt the happiness and anguish inside that Pan." That *Pan* I'd sent down the river rapids before slaughtering the rest of his troop. "The memories I saw came from a living thing, Captain. That's undisputable."

"A living thing?" Beckett repeated, and his fellow officers turned to him in disbelief. He swished his auburn drink around, frowning at the liquid like *it* might be the thing consuming *him*. "You must've seen the demon's memories, then. Or maybe a ghost steered that Pan—same as the phantom that saved you. Perhaps Sterling commands spirits too, orders them to do his bidding." He lifted the glass to his lips. "Who knows? But my guess is you saw the possessor's past, not the federate's."

My shoulders dropped.

Could spirits possess human corpses? Was it even possible to peruse a spirit's mind inside a foreign body?

"It was a demon," I decided, recalling the creature's blind, ghoulish eyes. "And I don't think Godric Sterling has influence over spiritual energy—if that were the case, my mother would have tried to kill us too."

"Unless evil spirits enlist voluntarily," Beckett reasoned. "I don't imagine all ghosts are as gracious as the missus."

"Nova did imply that some spirits are perverted and vengeful," Fudge said, and I tried not to take his contribution personally. When the officers glared in his direction, he sat a little taller in his seat, his gaze lifting to mine. "Maybe not every Pan we face is a demon. And that would explain your ... visions."

This sparked another debate among the Command, while other attendees, like Mason, remained flabbergasted by my supernatural revelations—abandoned in the dust cloud of denial and incredulity.

I huffed at the derailment. All this debate was diluting my argument, and I could tell I was losing my audience. I had no choice; I had to voice my theory sooner than later, even if saying it aloud promised a military ban and a psychological evaluation.

"Circling back to Beckett's point about spiritual possession," I cut in, kneading the fading crescent on my palm, "the initial leak in the portal's construction might have affected more than plant and animal life. Like demons, unbidden spirits may have found human husks more resilient than twigs and forest mulch."

This captured their attention once again—briefly—and I hastily continued.

"In the mine, five Pans ignored my comrades and cornered me instead. They said I smelled different, and they appeared transfixed." My pulse quickened in my palmar arches. "I think demons and spirits, and perhaps *all* paranormal beings ... can sense each other."

General Iver sat forward, sliding his dry, veined hands across the table like sheets of glasspaper. "What are you suggesting?"

They thought I was nuts, surely, and I very well might have been. But maybe madness was the key to seeing beyond the logical conclusions we'd accepted as reality. Maybe a little insanity would shine a light on the clues we'd dismissed.

"I think ... there's a spirit *inside* me."

***

The Command capsized in a sea of arguments, and I struggled to speak over their rising voices. "It would explain the supernatural abilities I have— the way I attract Pans and demonic wildlife." I battled the impulse to hike up my dress and flash my scar. "In Goddard Mine, I'd taken a spear to the abdomen, but by the time I received any medical attention, it was reduced to a scratch! That speedy recovery was nothing short of unearthly." I thought of my demon-induced stomach aches and the way Mason's sword sent shivers down my spine. "And the fact that I can sense a demon's proximity and the potency of vanadium—there's got to be a reason for it."

It was coming together now. This unrehearsed verbalization had transformed my scattered thoughts into strings of pearly beads, and I was ready to voice my proposition.

I was ready to rupture dogmas.

"I believe a spirit tried to possess me when I was a child," I shared, earning a sharp glance from Tom. "The force knocked me into a well and gave me a terrible concussion—at least, that's what the doctor attributed my memory loss to. My abilities first surfaced after that incident." A decade ago, Godric opened his portal and released countless spirits and demons into the world like toxic particulates. A decade ago, my life changed forever. "Somehow, I was able to master my control over this energy. But every now and then, its power slips through the cracks. Just like it did when I killed that demon at the river."

The men squirmed under flickering oil lamps like earthworms plucked from the ground. I could sense their unease, their agitation, their unwillingness to listen. This news was raw and unrefined, and it directly countered their ideology, their established creed.

"If I can withstand a possessive force like this, then that means our men—these federate soldiers overwhelmed by evil and thereby labeled an enemy—might still be alive," I concluded, urging them to listen, pleading for their comprehension. "I'm telling you now, *that's* what I sensed in that

Pan. A human soul, a human consciousness. Not eaten, not destroyed, not perverted."

"Hold on a minute—"

"They're being used," I stressed, determined to finish my point. "If we kill these Pans, we're likely killing our own men. And we're killing them in droves."

The general held up his hands to the room, and the clamor died down with an impressive swiftness. When it grew so quiet that I could hear the fizzling liquid in Beckett's glass, Iver addressed me directly. "Tell me if I understand you correctly, Miss Kingsley," he began. "In short, you agree with the notion that demons seek out live, human vessels because they rely on our souls—or some unique form of stored energy—for sustenance. You also believe that our soldiers are still alive inside these Pans, suffering through their possession. And you're offering yourself as proof, assuming you are indeed a ... spiritual cocktail, for lack of a better word."

I released a loaded exhale, relieved that at least one man in this room had listened well enough to summarize my points. "Yes, that's correct."

He chuckled at this, and my excitement withered. "As your brother mentioned, this is not an unexplored topic. Troops revisit this concept every few months, claiming their comrades aren't *really* gone. In their hearts, they believe their friends are still present, still kicking. But sentimentality clouds judgement, and as a military unit, our decisions are rooted in logic, not emotion."

"We don't dabble in ideals, either," Long-Nose tacked on. "Take your fictional world to the publishing house, *Private*."

Fudge rose from his chair, prepared to argue on my behalf, but Mason shoved him back in his seat before he could get himself killed.

Taking his place, a second officer stomped my case into the ground. "Even if what you say is true, we have no way of separating demons from their human hosts anyway. In the early years, we experimented at the Rim, searching for a remedy, but it's useless. If someone's turned, he's as good as dead—assuming he's not dead already."

The defeatism jolted me out of silence. "You'd just give up because you haven't found a solution yet?"

Long-Nose sneered, and I'd never wanted to punch someone's teeth in so badly. "Don't you think if we could salvage the fallen, they'd hate themselves for everything they did? For all the people they slaughtered?" He raised his chin and blew a puff of smoke at the ceiling. "If you ask me, killing the possessed to spare their neighbor is an act of compassion. Soldiers would go mad if we managed to exorcise their demon counterparts. Suicidal."

"You can't assume that," I argued, quaking with anger. "We can't just...decide when to end their lives; they're our *soldiers*. People willing to fight and die for this country. For you! And you want to write them all off as collateral damage because what, it's too much to think about?"

"That's just what we need, isn't it? A child preaching to us about the morality of war."

"Did we learn nothing from last time? This is what happens when a breeder steps out of—"

"That's enough," Tom interjected. He turned to me, wrath throbbing in spheres of brown. The room was chaos again, discourse ringing in every corner, and I was, undeniably, the catalyst to blame. "Alex, you've made some interesting points, but it's only speculation at this time. We have no evidence that you're harboring two spirits inside you. And even if we did, spirits and demons are different, like you said—there may be no correlation between you and the Pans. Right now, we have no proof that human souls and demons can coexist in one body. Until we do, we stick to protocol."

My mouth turned to dust—foul, weightless dust. "How can you say that? We could be killing and maiming our own people."

Long-Nose scoffed. "That's hardly novel, girl. For millennia, we've killed our fellow man for things as insubstantial as honor or legacy. But this ... this is a matter of extinction. It's us or them in this fight. No cogitation. No dithering. No mercy." His gaze bounced to Tom and back. "Our soldiers acknowledge that risk when they don a uniform. If you can't fathom that choice, then you don't belong here."

The fear in the room had reached a lethal concentration. All of these men—these directors of war, these composers of carnage—too afraid to change the play, to draft a new melody. Too stubborn to even consider a revision.

Lazy, arrogant bastards.

Tom nodded. "Burroughs is right, Al. We can't risk the safety of our people over if's and maybe's." His tone shifted. "We're going to wrap up this meeting now, and I think you should wait outside." *Before you say or do something I can't smooth over,* his gaze emphasized.

I gaped at him, dismayed. But he was my commanding officer, and I refused to undermine him here among his superiors—not again. Hands clenched at my sides, I stalked out of the room without further comment, brushing past Will's studious gaze.

39

I needed some space from that stupid mass of men.

No veteran sought solutions from a greenie—nor a witch garbed in egg yolk yellow. No man on earth wanted to change his plans and admit he was wrong. And granted, neither did I, but I still knew when to hear a contester out. I knew how to hold a civil conversation without throwing a fit. I knew how to speak without blatant condescension.

But I also valued progress, and like most federal institutions in this country, the Command sought stagnancy.

If demons didn't kill their hosts, then I'd murdered my own countrymen all week. I'd been responsible for silencing a hundred men inside that mountain—*gritz*, I'd condemned them to a lifetime of subjugation in the dirt.

It also led me to believe that a second spirit lurked beneath my skin, just...reposing there, apparently, which I found both terrifying and incredibly interesting.

The idea had sprouted in my mind after dreaming of the well incident. It was like my near-death experience had triggered the memory of our initial fusion: my body colliding with a foreign soul. And when I looked back on my paranormal timeline, there were just too many matching pieces to write the whole thing off as coincidence.

Admittedly, I had not intended to discuss my condition with the

Command, not like that. But when they'd dismissed me like some brainless doll—like some guileless child who'd never endured the harsh whip of reality—I'd snapped.

And as humiliating as my debut was, maybe they'd needed someone throwing old facts and debunked beliefs in their faces. Maybe they'd benefit from an outsider auditing their thought process and forcing them to reexamine their protocols.

Hoping to lose any sentries sent to babysit me, I scaled the water tower next to the spartan Command Center. I'd ditched the bandages as soon as possible, irritated by the makeshift gloves and the underlying message they told. But I managed the climb just fine without them, and the images of rusting metal, hairy knuckles, and boot soles offered the perfect distraction from my demon-soldier conundrum. Simultaneously, the burning pain in my palms kept me mindful, focused, and deliberate.

Some might call the self-injurious behavior masochistic, but it was simply a means of exerting control over my body. I did it to remind myself that my hands didn't limit me in all aspects of life, and this curse was only as powerful as I permitted it to be.

It wasn't a punishment or a cry for help; I just liked to battle the intrusive memories on my own terms, and I *really* liked to win.

When I reached the top of the tower, I spotted the pale sun dipping past the horizon—a splatter of gray light sinking into an ashen curve of nothingness—and it made me think of outer space and Tom's legendary stars. Seven years later, I still found it so enthralling, the sheer number of celestial objects salting the night sky above us. Beyond reach. Beyond perception. Sometimes I even dreamt of the mesmerizing landscape, though I couldn't tell if it was a memory or just my imagination hard at work.

Sitting at the edge of the water tank, I looked out over the city, watching the merchants prepare their booths for the night market, the men socialize outside their workplace, the women scurry home with groceries or bundles of fabric in their arms—always roaming in pairs or packs. Never unaccompanied.

Unlike the rural boundaries of Belgate, Holly was densely populated from wall to wall. The blight of civilization spread as far as the eye could see, forming a shady maze around inviting features like parks, schools, and a groundwater-fed marina. Bikes and wagons cluttered the roads, and merchants and artisans obstructed the walkways.

At every city block, buildings rose several stories high, taller than the facilities back home—and much older. Beckett told me the city planners had built Holly's structures on the bones of the Ancients' architecture, determined to salvage the functional sewer system and unwilling to clear the debris.

From an aerial view, the city resembled a healthy, breathing organism, but down on the ground, poverty nestled in every alleyway. Struggle reared its head on every street corner. And it wasn't hard to miss—or smell.

Holly was about to surpass its era of proto-industrialization, something the High Court flagged as a national emergency. We couldn't afford to destroy the planet a second time, after all, and mass production hinged on cheap energy sources. So, paralyzed by fear and resource scarcity, the city remained stuck in its developmental stage, just as its people remained stuck in their principles.

"Hiding in high places. You haven't changed."

Tom leaned against the top of the ladder with a timid smile on his face. He was so tall now, and handsome, even with his scars. His hair was cut short and evenly, so different from the wavy curls that once dangled over his ears. But his dimpled cheeks and messy locks wouldn't suit him anymore anyway—he'd become a man chiseled by war. A man burned by it.

"Sorry I can't say the same," I said. "The brother I knew wouldn't blindly murder his own soldiers."

"*Alex*," he whined. "Can we just … talk? We haven't shared a moment alone together since you strode into camp. The last time we caught up on life you were ten years old."

"And whose fault is that?"

His smile faded, and he climbed up onto the water tank and perched himself on the rim beside me. Tense silence stretched between us, and I could hear the wind currents swooshing through the air, feel the city water churning beneath us.

"I've missed you, you know," he breathed, piercing the quiet. "I've never stopped missing you."

The confession should have thawed my heart, but it only reinforced the wall I'd built beneath my skeleton. I'd been waiting to speak to him for days now, desperate to talk one-on-one, to get some answers, but he'd kept pushing the discussion aside. And I knew we'd had pressing matters to attend to, bigger threats to deal with, but the fact that he was only taking the time to reconnect with me after I'd almost died on him ... that stung.

If he wanted to open that box now, he could, but like anything set aside too long—ripe and unattended—its contents had become deeply unpleasant.

My eyes slid to his. "What happened to your face?"

His chuckle was soft and unoffended. "Let's start with you. How was life in Belgate before all hell broke loose? Were you faring okay at the ranch?"

"Yeah, really well. Losing a kid does wonders for a family."

He brushed off the comment like harmless flint, and I wasn't sure if the hypertrophic scarring had thickened his skin, or if he just recognized how justified my sniping was. "I'm sorry, Al." His eyes were frosted firewood in the setting sun. "For everything."

I'd wanted an apology. I'd wanted him to express remorse for never coming back, for deceiving us. But for some reason, his perfect words fell flat and echoless.

Where was the hurt? The grief? The regret?

Why did my cutting remarks brush over him like sawdust?

Betrayal bled from my tongue. "Why didn't you come home, Tom? We mourned you, we—*gritz*, we fell apart. And all this time, you've been running a boot camp south of Holly, a week's journey away? Did it not occur to you to write us and tell us that?"

I hadn't realized how furious I'd been with him until now. And maybe I wasn't just angry at him for lying—maybe I was angry at him for leaving me in the first place.

Tom draped an arm around my shoulder, and he pulled my resistant figure toward him. It was difficult to show my discontent with my body forced into an embrace, and I despised the new tactic.

"I couldn't abandon my men," he reasoned, but his voice was packed tight with an emotion I didn't recognize. "They needed me just as much as you did. Arguably more. And after the accident ..."

He paused, and his shaky exhale disturbed me. Tom had never sounded so *brittle*.

"There was an explosion at the Rim, a bomb that detonated before we could clear the area. I barely survived the blast, and two days later, I woke up at a demon outpost." He kept speaking before I could chop up his story with startled exclamations. "They were gonna turn me into one of them, Al. Into a *Pan*. I watched them do it to the others—flush their souls right out of their bodies—and I really thought that was the end of the line for me." He swallowed the node of feelings in his throat. "Fortunately, I escaped that hellhole in time, but when I made it back to the bivouac, they'd already declared me dead. And by the time I realized the postman had come and gone in my absence, I figured you'd be better off not having to worry about me anymore, so I didn't return to fix things."

I frowned, trying to free myself from his hug. "That's ridiculous."

"There's no way I could have left the Rim, not as a grunt, and the next postman was six months out. Even if I wrote to you, you wouldn't have heard from me for another year, maybe two. And in the interim, I could've died for real, putting you through that pain all over again. You and Dad didn't deserve that." He squeezed my shoulder. "There had to be a little sense of relief, knowing what had happened to me. No longer having to wait for an update. You could finally stop *guessing*."

I crossed my arms. Even if a small part of it were true, I refused to admit it.

Sure, I'd hated worrying about him. I'd hated anticipating a knock at the door from one of the local sentinels. But in the end, I'd lost my best friend. My *brother*. There was no comfort in that, despite the dread and anxiety I'd felt beforehand.

"You were wrong. Not to tell us," I whispered.

"...I know."

We sat in the residue of our emotions, simmering in a puddle of angst and exhaustion after seven years of pent-up grief had boiled over. And as an awkward silence enveloped us, another painful thought bubbled to the surface.

An old, ugly inkling from the past.

"Do you blame me, Tom?"

Is that why you left? Is that the real reason you didn't come home?

I'd asked him the same thing years ago, but now that I was older, I could handle the truth.

"Absolutely not," he answered, far too quickly for an honest response. He pulled me in closer, but I leaned away.

"Why not? How can you still love me after what I did to you?"

"Alex," he sighed, twisting to face me, "I don't know how many times I have to tell you this. It was an accident. You were a kid. I don't blame you, okay? I never have."

My nails dug into the flesh of my biceps. "How?"

How could he look past something like that? How could anyone?

"Because you're my little sister, and I love you. I'll *always* love you, okay?" His eyes searched my own, so genuine, so tender. I couldn't remember the last time someone had looked at me like that, as if I were the center of his universe.

"Dad loved me too, but he still resented me." I'd never spoken that gnarled suspicion aloud before, and it tasted rancid.

"He didn't resent you, Al."

"You weren't there. He changed."

He'd tried so hard to fight it, to keep the accusations out of his eyes. But I'd always seen the fracture in the glass.

"Dad loves you," Tom said firmly, and his use of present tense didn't escape me. "He loves you so much, I'm surprised he didn't lock you up in a tower to keep you from ever stepping foot off the ranch."

I wiped at the tears threatening to fall. "…It wasn't for a lack of trying."

A grin tugged at his lips, and he slid his hand across my spine to ensnare me in another hug. "I'm sorry I wasn't there for you when you needed me. But that's gonna change. We're a team now, okay? It's you and me from here on out. You and me till the bloody, bitter end."

"…Promise?"

He kissed the crown of my head. "On the stars."

He snickered again, and the steel melted right off my bones.

It was so strange, reinserting Tom in my life like he'd never left to begin with. Hearing him laugh, feeling his body heat. It was like everything I'd ever known was built on false foundations: Will was a Rhean prince named Asa, Pans didn't eat human souls, and brothers didn't stay dead. Next thing you know, Mason could turn out to be a decent human being.

"I won the Tournament," I revealed, and Tom stiffened.

"…What do you mean?"

"It's why I was wearing armor the day I found you. I competed in the Tournament with Will and the others. Pretended to be a boy." I peeked at his open-mouthed expression. "I made it through all the trials, Tom. I made the *cut*."

His gaping smile split his face in two. "You're joking."

I shook my head, happy to have someone I could share this news with. Someone who understood what it meant to me—and who, conveniently, wouldn't punish me for it, either. "I almost died in the final trial. And when my helmet came off at the Revelation, I think they all wished I *had*."

He shook his head at me and laughed. "You're unbelievable."

I knew this, but I elbowed him anyway. "What, for breaking stupid rules?"

He tutted. "For always getting away with it!"

We sat knee to knee as I filled him in on the surreal experience back home. I gushed about the first two trials, bursting with glee when I recounted the cannon ball loophole. Snickering at his reaction to my Deadlock story. Rolling my eyes at his expletives and dramatic body language. Healing inside, sentence by sentence.

"Come on, victor," Tom said a while later, nudging his head against mine. "If we leave those rats unsupervised for too long, they'll raid the pub."

"Don't they do that every night?"

His smile crinkled his eyes. "You've seen nothing yet."

40

Back at camp, the soldiers had, in fact, raided the alcohol supplies. It was necessary to celebrate their victory, they'd said. They'd earned a lively bonfire bash after putting up with Tom's shenanigans all week—and what was a proper bonfire without liquid fuel?

My brother gave a deep, disappointed sigh when we confronted Sol and his mischievous underlings, but Tom wound up snickering at their justifications by the end of his lecture.

"Clean up after yourselves," he conceded.

They cheered and dragged him into their cluster, shoving a drink in his hand and patting him on the shoulder, embracing him like a beloved king who'd shed his crown for the night.

After losing sight of him, I retreated to his room—a space that, per Tom's orders, had doubled as my temporary lodgings for the past few days. Finally alone, I swapped my dress out for normal, human-friendly clothes: fresh, unapologetically male undergarments and socks; full-length trousers; and one of Tom's long-sleeved crewneck shirts.

Better.

Never again would I ride a horse in a dress—or a horse, for that matter. The anxious mounting, the chafing, the restricted movement. Not to mention the stubborn grazer who preferred scratching fly bites to keeping pace with the others.

Hell, I'd rather walk barefoot.

Fudge, on the other hand, had absolutely adored the experience, immediately bonding with his tame and well-mannered steed. Likewise, Will made horse-riding look totally effortless, perfectly at ease on a beast 16 hands tall.

As a royal, he'd probably been *raised* on horseback, the spoiled welt.

The ride back to camp had been uncomfortable on all fronts, really. I'd smoothed things over with Tom, but the others spent the entire journey inquiring about my "powers." Rover was especially interested in the memories I'd unearthed from the river demon, while Fudge and Beckett wanted to know what a memory feast felt like, how it functioned, and what it cost me. Mason just didn't believe me at all, unimpressed by my "pocket watch spectacle" and suspicious of my convenient, timely revelation.

Still, as exhausting as it was, I'd brought this interview upon myself tonight, striking my peers with a secret so absurd, they'd struggled to reconcile the farmer's daughter and her newfound abilities. Their interest was the natural consequence of transparency, and transparency was the ticket to forging real, honest friendships—like Nova's. But it didn't make it any less awkward, explaining things about my curse I'd only ever shared with family and a trusted physician.

It didn't make it any less difficult, either.

Perhaps Will had felt the same way when I'd grilled him with questions the other night—though I wasn't sure the Rhean felt much of anything…ever. He hadn't asked me a single question since we departed Holly, and I couldn't gauge whether he was angry with me, reflective, or simply indifferent to my supernatural faculties.

But perhaps building honest friendships wasn't a priority of his at all, despite digging me out of the ground, offering to train me in combat, and informing me that my opinion of him mattered. Transparency had been forced upon him, after all, not deliberately accepted.

Eventually, I returned to the courtyard to watch intoxicated men make dumb choices. Jaden, sympathizing with my sobriety, filled my mug with bitter, frothing ethanol, but thirty minutes later, I was still trying—and failing—to finish the meager serving.

I didn't understand how people could authentically enjoy alcohol and the fiery path it carved through the body. Did they merely tolerate the stuff and convince themselves they liked the flavor? Did the alcohol burn away their taste buds? Or did they just prefer their survival instincts on holiday?

A thousand mini sips later, a large hand fell upon my shoulder—heavy and meaty and crosshatched with scars. I spun around with a wary frown, only to flinch at the massive individual looming over me.

Grismond.

He was all cut up from the mining operation—his fat head covered in bandages and tape, his arms bruised and scratched—but if anything, the wounds just boosted his menacing reputation. Quite honestly, I couldn't think of anything that would *weaken* the image of this monster...except underestimating female prowess, maybe.

Grismond frowned at me like a zit he couldn't pop. "You...are a dumb kid," he said matter-of-factly.

I glared up at him, trying to arrange a fitting insult to throw back in his face, but the man wasn't finished.

"Dumb, but brave. You risked your life for men who don't even want you here." His cold eyes thawed a little, like he no longer considered himself a founding member of that club. "You've got guts—for a toothpick."

I gawked at him, concerned I might be hallucinating the whole exchange, and he threw his head back and cackled. He slapped my back a few times, seemingly grateful for the laugh, and I nearly spilled my drink at the powerful cuffs. Then he trudged away in his scary, hulking manner, probably to identify—and bully—the latest weak link.

I stared after him, blinking at his boulder-like back and cartoonish trap muscles. Was ... was I already *drunk*? Or was that some warped and scanty olive branch?

When the shock faded, I dragged my eyes from the Bear's departure to the heart of Camp Ptarmigan, searching for a blob of darkness in a sea of white shirts and navy jackets. With no luck, I shifted my attention to the perimeter of camp and the furthest possible point from human activity. It was here that I spotted—and nearly overlooked—a patch of silky black hair and a wardrobe comprised solely of gloomy, somber hues.

I rolled my eyes. For someone with so many secrets, Will sure was predictable. He sat on the sandbag wall next to an apple tree, his attire blending seamlessly with the shadowed landscape behind him. Richard was curled up at his feet, chewing on his leather boots with comical ferocity.

"Enjoying the party from a respectable distance?" I teased, sitting down beside him.

"... That's one way of putting it."

We watched the soldiers amass at the bonfire, singing and dancing and trading jokes. A fair number of them tried to woo Jaden, who politely disregarded them all as she refilled their pitchers, and Rover observed her with a fondness that would've had Beckett dry heaving.

Beneath a canvas tent, Sol recounted a story to a huddle of soldiers who spat out their drinks with laughter. Claus was red in the face, yelling and shaking his head in protest, and a few men tried to placate him with more alcohol, which, admittedly, seemed to do the trick.

Fudge's mirthful voice rippled through camp, and I recognized his small frame at the edge of the courtyard. He was begging Mason to join the ensemble of various instrumentalists, but Mason fiercely refused, swatting Fudge—and his borrowed harmonicas—away. Meanwhile, Beckett had just won another round of backgammon outside the pub, and Tom threw his checkers at him in mock outrage.

"It's nice here," I decided, cradling my mug through Tom's elongated shirt sleeves. It surprised me after everything that had occurred tonight, but I meant it. There was a sense of belonging here, a kind of brotherhood I'd never experienced before.

Granted, I wasn't part of that fellowship yet, but if I proved myself to the Interior Company once more—this time, without jeopardizing their plans—I bet I could be.

Will looked at me with an expression that either said, *go on*, or *go away*.

I pretended it was the former.

"Belgate and Holly feel like cages. Too many rules and restrictions exist inside those walls. But here ... there's a sense of freedom and individuality. There's unity without uniformity, you know?" My eyes found Tom and his first lieutenant, who'd teamed up against Beckett for another backgammon game. Then my focus swiveled to their company of federate soldiers. "Plus, a lot of the guys seem to accept me now."

A few younger men waved at me cheerfully, tipsy, and Will's uninspired gaze slid to mine. "They're attracted to you. They'll accept anyone who entertains their flirtations."

I waved back. "It's better than being irrelevant."

I had to be on their radar if I expected to upgrade their worldviews. And if that meant tolerating a few lecherous stares and uncomfortable flirtations when Tom wasn't around, then so be it. I'd dealt with worse back home.

"You think you can change their minds?" Will asked. "About women in the military?"

"I don't know. But my brother just so happens to possess power and influence here, and he's granting me the opportunity to make a difference." I set my half-consumed beverage aside. "I'm not sure if I can correct your gender's social conditioning, but I've been afforded the privilege of *trying*."

He scowled at a pair of soldiers focused too intently on Jaden's cleavage. "That's a lot of pressure to put on yourself."

"Maybe," I admitted. "But if I don't fight for us, who will?"

I didn't plan on waiting around for the men of this world to take that leap, and I'd never met, seen, or read about any woman actively seeking to dismantle the Gender Clause. If one existed, she'd likely been killed or threatened into silence. And now that I was here at the fringe of necessity—now that I'd witnessed the Command's rigidity for myself—it was clear to me that if unmarried, childless women were to someday be considered valuable assets to society, it fell to the Kingsley family to construct that bridge.

I'd leave it to the High Court to decide whether that bridge should be built on corpses or not.

A pensive look softened Will's features, and he dropped his hand to scratch Richard's ear. The mutt blinked up at him with pure adoration, tail thumping joyously against the dirt.

It didn't surprise me that the two of them had become fast friends. Will always struck me as the type of person who preferred the company of animals to humans, and I feared that, had he not joined the war effort, he would've become some nature-dwelling recluse that faraway townspeople fabricated horrific stories about.

"I have a question," I declared.

His sigh, perhaps unintentionally, resembled a shallow laugh. "Do you."

"It's just…if you planned on jumping ship from the get-go, why didn't you? You had plenty of chances to ditch us on our way here. You could be way, *way* east by now." My eyes slipped to his shoulder, then his wrist brace. "With a lot fewer injuries."

He gave a half-shrug. "I was on my way to Averly when I ran into you."

I huffed. By *ran into*, he must have meant blindly attacked, then insulted.

"I agreed to meet my personal guard there if Rhea ever invaded. But I knew if I left it up to you and Mason, you'd all be dead before dawn. Then

Styx happened, and the demons found us ... survival just got in the way."

"And you saved my brother's life because ...?"

He glanced away. "The Pans blocked our escape route—we were sand-wiched. The two of us fought our way out together and cleared a path for the others. I didn't do any saving."

"Uh-huh." He could downplay his valor all he wanted, but it sounded to me like somebody cared.

He frowned, reaching for my navel and casually lifting the hem of my shirt. I was about to break his only functioning wrist when I realized he was checking my wound. Or rather, its absence.

"It's healed over," he said, awed confusion sticking to the sides of his throat and stripping his voice of its trademark conviction.

"Weird, right?"

Onyx-brown eyes peered at the scar, then my face. "You really think there's a spirit inside you?"

His tardy interest in my abilities soothed something inside me—some-thing I wasn't ready to unpack. "Well, it explains why I can harvest memo-ries and sense other paranormal entities, even if Mason thinks it's a ruse to secure a military job." I tugged at my shirt sleeves to cover my naked palms, folding my fingers over the fabric to pin them in place. "Also ... the timeline matches up a little too well."

The same day Godric Sterling opened the bridge to another dimen-sion, a leaky portal infected the natural world and its clueless inhabitants. And, if my theory proved true, that included a small, concussed child sud-denly capable of the supernatural.

Will dropped my shirt, shaking his head as if he were arguing with the rational half of his brain. I didn't blame him for his skepticism, though; it was a lot to take in—the memory voodoo, the self-healing magic, my spir-itual copilot.

That is ...

"You believe me, then?" I asked, hoping he couldn't detect the desperation on my tongue. "About the Pans?"

He squinted at the bonfire and, after a prolonged pause, nodded ever so slightly.

Warmth pooled in my chest, and I battled the flood of tears behind my eyes. Will believed me and my outrageous claims. My lack of evidence. My intuition.

He *believed* me.

"But it doesn't change the gameboard," he said after a beat. "Those demons are bent on killing us; we have to fight back. If we don't—if we *lose*—we can't save anyone, innocent or complicit. For now, we don't have a choice. We have to keep playing."

His reality check transformed that pleasant warmth into acidic heartburn, and I scowled at him.

Unfortunately, he was right on the money, and that meant the Command's hasty verdict was also judicious. We couldn't stop fighting, not unless we acted collectively, brainstormed as a people, and put our heads together to find a solution. Which was, ultimately, an implausible phenomenon.

Until then, I couldn't expect anyone to sheathe his sword.

"Did you know?" I asked quietly, not entirely sure I wanted to hear his answer. "About the possession?"

He set his jaw, and a muscle in his temple pulsed with anger. "No. I only knew what my father told me, which was minimal, to say the least. If he knew Ellsian soldiers were captive to his commands, he never shared that with me."

He wrinkled his brow—the way he always did when he was thinking too hard—and I had the unwarranted impulse to smooth out the worry lines. It was, undoubtedly, a ridiculous notion, and based on his volatile response in Nova's cabin, a surefire way to lose a hand.

Still, if it got him to smile again…

"You know, it's pretty incredible I wasn't crushed by the debris," I drawled. "Some might even call it…lucky."

He gifted me a begrudging smirk, and I congratulated myself. "It *was* lucky. It's a miracle you made it out alive."

"Then I guess you're a miracle worker," I said, "because you're the only reason I'm still here."

I'd thanked him for his heroic efforts days ago, but this candid acknowledgement was overdue. Will had risked everything digging me out of that mine. He could have left me for dead when he saw me bleeding out beneath a mountain, half-consumed by the earth. But he'd crawled into that hole and saved me, just like he'd promised.

I expected a flushed face or a modest deflection, but instead, the color just vanished from his eyes, leaving behind cold, lightless obsidian. "When I made it to your post, Fudge was in hysterics. Rover had just…shut down. Everyone thought you were dead."

I didn't want to envision their reactions, their pain. It was hard enough reliving mine.

"I came pretty close," I admitted, thinking about those last few moments in the adit, knowing my time had come, grieving my new relationships. "I thought I was going to die there…for nothing. And Patrons, I was in so much pain. I just gave up. I stopped *fighting*—"

Something painful struck my forehead, and it took me a second to realize Will had just flicked me. In the face.

"But you didn't," he said, and despite the humorous tilt to his lips, his gaze was stern. "You didn't stop fighting. You ran until your body gave out, and the instant you glimpsed a chance of survival, you seized it." His voice shifted to something more gentle and sincere. "I saw the dirt under your nails, Alex. You clawed your way to the exit. Some integral part of you wasn't finished here."

The consolation tickled my ego, and it stirred up that warm, gooey sensation again, only deeper in my body—closer to my soul.

There was a lot to dissect there, to analyze, but all I could think about was the fact that this stone statue of a boy had just struck me in the forehead with the pad of his nail.

Gaping, I reached over to get him back—to extinguish that playful gleam in his eye—but his hand intercepted mine before I could land a hit.

Too late, I remembered my gloves lay at the bottom of a dumpster. Too late, I realized extending my arm had retracted my shirt sleeve and exposed my palm. Too late, I screamed at him to release me.

A white world, a yellow field.

A boy. A woman. A podium.

A floor painted red with youthful blood.

I tore my hand away and fell to the ground, breathing hard. My palms smacked the dirt, sending white sparks across my vision. Yelping in pain, I backpedaled toward the tree, but mid-retreat, my hands brushed its exposed roots, and I shuddered as petrichor filled my nostrils, as wet grass coated my throat.

Gray sky and cold, empyrean darkness played on a vicious loop in my mind, accompanied by birds and squirrels and other hungry visitors.

Blossoms. Fruit. Rot. Frost.

Growth. Disease. Decay.

I slapped my hands to the back of my neck. *Stop! Make it stop!*

My eyes shot open.

Tom and Rover stood over me, arms outstretched to keep the gathering crowd out of harm's way. The music had died out, and people were staring at us—and the dead tree splintering behind me. Shriveled apples fell to the ground around me. Brown leaves twirled through the air and landed at my feet. But I didn't pay the murmuring crowd or the fruit tree any attention.

My eyes were pinned to Will's body and his unmoving limbs splayed across the dirt.

"...Will?" I whispered.

My nails dug crescents into my nape when no answer came.

Piecing together what had happened, Tom rushed over to inspect Will's body, and I trembled at the sight of my greatest fear, my worst nightmare, my darkest memory.

This couldn't be real. This couldn't be happening.

Not again.

I watched them intently, linking my fingers together to keep my hands away from the earth and her creatures—weapons I never sought, tools of entropy I couldn't dispose of.

Tears filled my eyes.

No. No. No. No.

How could I have been so stupid? I never forgot about my curse. It was always lurking there in the back of my mind, a burden, a sentencing, a perpetual weight. Up until this very moment, I'd been cautious, using only my fingertips to hold and grasp the reins, to open doors. I'd kept my sleeves pulled down over my palms, hands clasped tightly together—a conscious effort to shield the world from my skin.

So why hadn't I been more careful with Will?

How had I let this happen?

"Alex, he's okay," Tom said.

The words sent sweet relief coursing through me, and I released a broken exhale. He's okay.

He's okay.

Across the way, Will rose to a sitting position, rubbing his chest as though I'd merely knocked the wind out of him, and I ducked my head, pressing my mouth to my kneecap to smother the whimper on my lips.

Not again.

41

The bonfire crackled, sending violent sparks into the autumn night. No one moved a muscle, too bewildered to form a sentence, too afraid to rock this mysterious boat.

Claus, emboldened by the liquor in his fist, was the first to speak. "So nobody's gonna explain what just happened? Should I start guessing, or what?"

I could feel my brother's eyes on me. All of their wide, wary eyes.

"Al," Tom said quietly, "let's get you inside."

As appealing as that sounded, we couldn't kick this family secret under the rug and wish away the army's interest. We'd set the truth free tonight— it was already feasting on the crowd.

"Cap, your sister...she just murdered a *tree*," a man spluttered. "What's going on?"

I cringed, lifting my head from my knees. Four dozen army boots circled the crime scene, some toeing at rotten apples, others as stiff as granite, and I wanted to crawl beneath the dirt and die there.

"You don't owe anyone an explanation right now," Tom assured me, taking a protective step in my direction.

"No," I said, finally mustering the courage to look at him—then his apprehensive subordinates. Rover, Grismond, Beckett. Fudge and Mason. Anyone but Will, who sat ten feet away from me, dreadfully silent. "I do."

The truth needed to come out. The *whole* truth.

I'd tried to get away with sharing only the gilded edges of my ability—the super-healing elements, the paranormal detection, the memory osmosis. But those were just pretty ornaments on a bloodied weapon, and if I ever wanted to belong here, belong *anywhere*, my peers needed to see me for the monster I was.

Rover looked between Tom and me, sensing the weight of my reveal, and as the garrison's staunch pillar of support, he offered me a platform. "Well, we know you're some kind of passive memory vacuum. It's why you're always wearing gloves." He arched a nervous eyebrow. "What else is there?"

I swallowed the fear and shame weighing down my tongue.

"I absorb the memories of everything I touch," I explained, trying to ignore the rapid pulse thrumming in my palms. "With inanimate objects it's a one-way channel. It's just a little painful. But with living things—with people—I don't just take their *memories*."

Fudge drew a startled breath when the realization hit, clutching Sol's harmonicas like apotropaic charms. "You kill them."

Hearing someone say it aloud was both relieving and dreadful, like a twister sweeping through town. Fear and anxiety died with the tempest, but now there was wreckage everywhere—wreckage and devastation, and I had no idea what came next.

I had no idea if I could repair this.

I nodded and lowered my gaze again, too afraid to see the horror settle in his features. Too afraid to watch my friend's admiration for me crumble like ancient ruins.

The circle of soldiers grew a few feet in diameter, and I didn't blame them for backing away from a death sentence. If I could run from myself, I would.

Rover's voice was fragile when he whispered, "Fuse, how do you know that?"

Tom's sorrowful gaze locked on mine, and hot tears warped my vision. "Because it happened to my mother."

***

Nightmares had hijacked my brain, so I'd run straight to Mom—like any child scared of the shadows. She'd carried me back to my room and crawled into bed beside me, holding me while I wept, humming her lullaby until she'd vanquished the intrusive memories of the orphaned well.

And her strategy was, as always, efficacious.

I'd quickly succumbed to her consolation, weaving vivid faces, landscapes, and fascinating stories into peaceful dreams as I nestled further into her embrace. But when I awoke, curled up against her loving frame, she was, inconceivably, inert.

The unstoppable, vibrant woman of the household was now as pale as the bed sheets, her arms as stiff as tree roots. Motionless. Colorless.

Dead.

I hadn't understood my role in her passing, not at first. I thought I'd dreamt everything I'd seen. I thought I'd imagined it all. But that night had served as the cruel inception of my curse—and the harrowing consequence of stolen memories.

I'd tried to wake her that morning, but when I touched her cool skin and shook her rigid muscles, I was burned by her life experiences once again. Unlike my stimulating dreamland, though, all I perceived was a portfolio of static artwork. All I absorbed was an album of ancient, emotionless photographs.

Because that's what happens when something dies—it loses its essence of life, its emotion and vitality. It becomes an object and nothing more. And I'd done that to the person I'd loved most of all; I'd snuffed out her spirit.

Dad thought she'd died from an illness, killed in her sleep by some unknown contagion. He hadn't believed my incoherent tale of memories and magic.

Not until I killed the calf.

Days later, I was helping Guinevere deliver when I was attacked by a montage of foreign memories and sensations. When I awoke an hour later, I was told she'd suffered a stillbirth, and I'd cried myself into a fit.

That was the day it took hold of me, this curse.

That was the day it *stayed*.

I could no longer touch anything without imbibing memories and inflicting death. Plants, animals, people—it didn't matter. They all died at the brush of my palm. And I'd suddenly become a living poison at seven years old.

My father called a trusted doctor, and he put me through a series of arduous experiments, placing different items, organisms, and living animals in my bare hands to test his hypothesis. Watching as I cried in pain or passed out from exertion, over and over again. Jotting down notes as I murdered countless victims.

His prescription? None. Only gloves to hide what I'd become.

The weeks that followed became a blur of self-isolation, stress, and fear. And unfortunately, my volatile emotions made everything worse. There were times, at the height of a breakdown or a panic attack, when my gloves stopped working altogether, and I had to hold on to myself to avoid brushing the walls or the doorframe. If I set my palms free, I'd absorb every memory attached to those objects—even glimpses of my mother leaning on the kitchen counter or touching the oven handle. Every graze was a thousand cuts. Every handprint, a motley of hidden bruises.

It was then that I realized what I'd done to her. That I'd lost control of the curse bestowed upon me, and it had cost me a loving parent.

In a way, it had cost me two.

By my third year of grade school, my life had forked from the vanguard. Trailblazing was off the table, and so was any semblance of normalcy. Instead, I was to lead a life of loss, lies, and loneliness, and—if society had any say in it—*lowliness*. But despite my unearthly attributes, I was still painfully human. Human enough to adapt, to acclimatize. To master what little control I had over this power.

With Nova's guidance, I began practicing on random objects she possessed—at my own pace, on my own terms. Eventually, I stopped fainting, and I learned to interpret what I'd seen and adjust my technique accordingly. After that, I began experimenting alone: collecting river stones born from erosion and compaction and discarding ones with boring origins; seizing book spines and transporting myself into the Ancients' world; plucking a wilted rose, revisiting its budding stage, and noting the metallic taste of well water as it shriveled in my palm.

The rest of the time, I kept the gloves on, and they kept my curse at bay—and my peers oblivious.

But my father had never looked at me the same after my mother's passing, and my brother had left for boot camp before the self-hatred could manifest. I'd suffocated in that sea of guilt and tragedy ever since, and I suspected it would never truly evaporate.

Worse yet, I feared it *shouldn't*.

Because yes, I hadn't known any better at the time. The onset was sudden and unprecedented—my syndrome was absurd and beyond our understanding. I was just a kid.

But that didn't change reality.

The truth was, I'd killed my mother. My birth was an order, and that order had killed her.

She was dead because of me—*twice now, I guess*. And as horrifying as that was, her death had also engrained several vital lessons across my hippocampus, lessons I'd abided by until this very evening.

First and foremost? To keep a safe distance—both physically and emo-tionally—from the people I crossed paths with, lest I take them down with me. Second, to never underestimate my own lethality, and to only expose my palms with the utmost caution. And finally, should someone like Nova come to care for me despite my antisocial approach, I vowed to disclose the danger I posed to their safety. To show them the blood on my hands and let them decide for themselves if loving me was worth the risk.

***

Even after the morbid story escaped my lips—and a reluctant Tom filled in the gaps—I still couldn't lift my gaze from the ground. I couldn't bear their judgement, so I watched Richard instead, because he'd witnessed my broken sorcery before, and he still wasn't afraid of me.

There. The rest of my ugly secret, stark naked before the jury.

Rover struggled to identify an appropriate response. "That's ... the whole thing is ..."

Jaden stepped in, taking his hand. "Absolutely devastating."

The sympathy stitched up the gaping hole in my gut. *Devastating.* Much better than deplorable or detestable, and much softer than the adjec-tives I used to describe the affair.

"So, you have to wear gloves ... like, all the time ... or people die?" Fudge asked. He sounded more alarmed than disturbed, and perhaps a bit too curious.

"I thought you were just a hypochondriac."

—Mason.

I tried to smile, to prove to them I was still human, still *Alex*, but I failed. "It's true. I'm sorry I didn't say anything sooner, I just didn't know how—" I shook my head. "I never wanted anyone to get hurt. I'm sorry."

"You don't need to apologize," Will insisted, his voice soothing and solicitous.

Hearing him speak gave me the confidence to pay him a bashful, cursory glance, but the engrossed look on his face was too much to bear, and I immediately severed eye contact.

I massaged the palm of my left hand, assembling shreds of dignity and bravery as I finally worked up the nerve to face the Interior Company. But it wasn't fear, pity, or disgust that greeted me tonight. It wasn't even anger, as I'd anticipated. It was sorrow, concern, and understanding. Appreciation and amazement.

"It's not your fault, Kingsley," said Sol, his gaze tender as he sat upon the sandbag wall. "You've been through a lot for someone your age. You're stronger than you look."

"I'm *dangerous*," I corrected.

Grismond nodded approvingly. "Even better."

I frowned at them, bewildered by their responses. Perplexed by their kindness. This warm reception was the last thing I'd expected, and when I turned to Tom, he grinned at me—confirming that this was in fact real life, and I wasn't about to lose the only home I had.

Rover cut a glance at the circle of somber faces and cracked a smile, slapping Claus on the shoulder. "I think Fuse drops bombshells better than you do, Peaches."

A few people laughed—timidly, like they weren't sure it was acceptable to do so—and just like that, the tension started breaking apart like sea ice. Turning to slush and melting away.

"Who the hell are you calling *Peaches*, Wright?" Claus growled, smashing a meaty fist into Rover's ribcage—hard enough to make him buckle. The lieutenant groaned loudly, and Jaden rolled her wet, shimmering eyes as he tugged on her hand.

I smiled without effort this time, blown away by the normalcy Rover had just reinjected into the crowd, the absence of affectation. Upon hearing my history, these men hadn't run for the hills. They hadn't fetched the witch-burning kit. They were intrigued, but not repulsed, and I . . . I had *not* predicted this scenario.

Beckett picked up on my confusion and snorted. "You think this is too much for us, kid? We've been battling monsters for ten years now. We spent three weeks fending off demonic squirrels on the Rim. Trust me, this doesn't faze us." He raised his flask to me. "Quite the origin story, though."

Fudge smiled across from me, all warmth and reassurance, while Mason studied me like an animal he didn't know how to trap. Not anymore.

Tom chuckled at my side. "B's right. It takes a lot more than *deadliness* to scare off my men." He mussed my hair—an action that showed such little disregard for the prevailing topic, I almost kicked him in the ankle. "That's not to be taken as a challenge, by the way."

I scoffed at him, and as he wandered off to deescalate another looming conflict, I revisited Will's dark, patient gaze. His affirming smile was subtle, nearly imperceptible, but it instantly assuaged my concerns and stifled apologies. I also spotted an undercurrent of approbation there, flirting with the corner of his mouth, but I wasn't sure if it stemmed from my capacity to knock him flat or my decision to open up about it. All I knew was that I didn't hate . . . impressing him.

As the night progressed, Sol played the harmonica, and we paid tribute to the eight soldiers we'd lost in the mine. Stories were told. Songs were sung. Sentiments and eulogies were drunkenly presented. We tossed colorful powder into the bonfire, and as it burned tendrils of blue and violet— hues of early departure—I watched the fearless and honorable soldiers of Ells become the very thing they were forbidden to be.

Human.

The ocean began to recede, taking with it my outer walls and sentries. Stripped of my lifelong armor, I felt vulnerable, exposed, and unassured, but I also felt liberated from emotional encumbrance—and stronger for it.

Alongside my new comrades, alongside new *friends*, I celebrated the lives of our fallen: the victims of Belgate, the Rim troops, the men slaughtered at Goddard Mine, and runners like Beau, who'd died in my arms.

And as I stared into that twister of blue flames, leaking tears, I promised justice.

42

I followed Jaden up to her private loft on the pub's second floor, Richard's nails tip-tapping behind us. Her bedroom, a renovated fermentation area and storage closet, accommodated a single bed and a narrow dresser, but very little else. While snug—and a tad malty—the attic's colorful fabrics, buttery candles, and low vaulted ceiling made the space feel cozy and inviting and refreshingly feminine.

I made myself at home on the plush window seat, reclining against the woman's excessive pillow collection. It was the most comfortable thing I'd sat on in days, and my adductor muscles thanked me for it.

Richard didn't have any qualms about our sleeping arrangements either; the mutt passed out on Jaden's fluffy rug before we'd even kicked our shoes off.

My brother had offered me his quarters again—the barracks were off the table, apparently—but Jaden suggested I bunk with her. It would be safest, she'd said, and would allow for plenty of "girl talk." Whatever *that* was.

While Jaden washed up across the hall, I inspected my new fingerless gloves, pleased with the way they comfortably sheathed my knuckles. Visions flickered and died as my palms grew accustomed to the material, adjusting to the fresh garments and their associated memories.

No glovers were still open by the time the debriefing had ended, so

Tom left a few men behind to search door to door for willing vendors—allowing them to indulge in Holly's night markets as recompense. They'd arrived back at camp an hour ago, and I'd never been happier to receive a pair of leather accessories. I'd gleefully kissed the soldiers' cheeks, praising their shopping skills and thanking them for their gallant services, only to be scolded for my "extrinsic motivation."

But Tom's reprimands and Will's judgy side-eye didn't faze me: I had my gloves back. I had my *safety blanket*. And that meant I could operate like a normal human being again.

Earlier tonight, I'd shed my bandages as a means of exercising self-discipline, but Will had almost died from my folly. I'd endangered active-duty soldiers because of my arrogance and negligence, and I refused to slip up like that ever again.

My mind circled back to the resilient Rhean prince. He'd slept in Rover's chambers until now, and this was his first night in the barracks with the other federates. I wasn't there to supervise him—or knock any teeth out, should someone act on their nationalism—so I'd told Fudge and Mason to keep an eye on him. Just in case.

"I'm sure the boy will be fine," Jaden chuckled as she reentered the room.

I gaped at the telepathic.

"Oh, come on! It's written all over your face." She pulled her covers aside and stole a conspiratorial glance at me over her shoulder. "What's *really* going on between you and Sterling?"

"I dunno. What's the deal with you and Rover?" I countered. She smiled, allowing the topic to die, and I almost patted myself on the back for avoiding that catastrophe of a conversation.

When we'd both settled into bed, I turned on my side and tucked my arm beneath the largest pillow at my disposal. "Jaden, how exactly did you end up at a military base?"

She looked up at the ceiling as if her past was hiding between the timber beams. "I grew up in Holly, and my dad owned a popular tavern downtown. It was a real lively place, full of music and historical art. It attracted folks from all walks of life." She knit her brow. "After he died, my younger sister and I inherited the business, but ..."

"But women can't run a bar in Ells," I guessed. "Not alone."

My teachers would've labeled it an *improper* occupation for a young lady, and it was the furthest thing from a motherly trade. How would Jaden raise children in a place like that? What kind of example would she set for her sister?

Working alone was frowned upon in and of itself, but an owner of a pub? Licensed to sell liquor? Capable of doing so well, she'd have no need for a man's income?

Yeah right.

"No, but I still gave it my best shot," she said, punctuating the statement with a mischievous glance. "The locals didn't mind me taking over the establishment. My mother died giving birth to my sister, so I'd spent a lot of time there as a young girl, you know? Doing schoolwork, mopping floors, bussing tables. That kind of thing." She closed her eyes and smiled, reliving the fond memories beyond her eyelids. "Our customers watched me grow up, and they knew I loved the pub as much as my father did. So, after his funeral, they kept quiet—for the family's sake. And they continued to patronize the pub like nothing had changed."

It threw me off guard, her feathery tone juxtaposed by such heartbreaking events. I would've never guessed that she'd lost her parents so young. She conducted herself like a woman untarnished by tragedy and unruffled by patriarchal constraints.

"Things were going great. *Business* was great. But eventually, my ownership status reached competitors, then the High Court, and they took the pub away from me." Frustration laced her words. "As compensation, they offered me a sum of money to attend school and make a living doing something noble. Something they deemed more fitting for a woman."

"So you built your own pub outside the Interior," I finished, snickering.

She beamed wickedly. "Rove had earned his place as first lieutenant by then. It took one meeting with your brother before I was stationed here. Now I run the bar, the cafeteria, and the shop out back."

Brilliant.

Jaden's courage extended far beyond crushing bar fights and putting bratty soldiers in their place. She was a renegade.

"Why here?" I asked. "Why not take that subsidy and build somewhere else? Somewhere your business could flourish?"

She hummed in response, like she wasn't so sure herself. But when she began twirling that silky black hair around her finger, I rolled my eyes. "Rover."

Her lips rose into a coy smile. "Well … in part, yes. He's been my best friend since grade school. Our home lives were never great, but we'd found family in each other. And when he went off to war? Gritz, it was like he took a vital organ away."

A twinge of sympathy ripped through me. "I get it."

All too well.

"When he was finally notified of my father's death, he came home from the Rim to see me, only to find out I'd lost the pub too. I was a mess, and Rove … he was ready to fight the bastards tooth and nail for the place. He even told me he would elope with me. Said I could use his salary and his name to start my own pub—that way the Court would never know." She sighed, and it sounded so wistful, so affectionate, I felt like I was right there with her all those years ago, hearing her gently deny the proposal. "But I'd seen the man he'd become, and I knew he loved his place in the world, his friends. *Tom*. He loved being a hero—always has." Her brown eyes wilted.

"I wanted him to run away with me and live a child's fantasy, but I couldn't let him leave; he'd come too far. So I decided to pack up my life and run away with *him*."

I sank into the pillows, sympathizing with Beckett's frustration. Rover had offered to elope because he loved her, and Jaden loved him too much to let him do it.

Were they really blind to that fact? Or did they just ignore it?

"But Rover ... he was just part of it," Jaden confessed. "I wanted out of the Interior. I wanted out of that pretty vase the Court had planted me in. I wanted a challenge. And I got one, thanks to Tom."

My gaze traveled over her side profile and her sloped, feminine nose, taking in a woman I'd egregiously underestimated. But she wasn't the only one; apparently, my brother had warped the rules long before I'd ever stepped foot in Camp Ptarmigan. He'd been championing an equal world years before I had, and I loved him for that.

"You like it here," I gathered. "Even though you're surrounded by idiots."

She snorted. "I do like it, but I didn't always. When I first arrived at Ptarmigan, most of the company treated me like glass. Fragile, pristine ... practically inhuman. New recruits always balked at me like they'd never seen a woman in such close proximity to alcohol."

It wasn't hard to picture Chinger and the other Belgate boys stumbling upon the female bartender for the first time and struggling to digest her vocation. Mason was *still* trying to rectify his perception of women, even after I'd saved his life. And despite growing up in a world where women expertly managed households and their inhabitants, the prospect of them running a business or adopting a man's duty befuddled the males.

For what was a woman divorced from childrearing, housekeeping, and wifely tasks? What was her purpose?

"It was disheartening to learn how many bigotries I'd have to stomp upon. But as the years come and go, I can see it in their eyes—that subtle change in how they perceive me. Perceive *us*." She crossed her hands over her stomach, lacing her fingers together. "I may not take up a sword, but I'm fighting a war of my own, Alex. And someday soon, I'll have my army."

I stared up at the slanted ceiling, the wooden planks just low enough that I could run my fingers across them and imagine them splintering at my touch.

Jaden and I were both castaways in a sea of male dominion, kicking and thrashing to stay afloat. Boldly, and perhaps a bit foolishly, we'd chosen a new path for ourselves—a terrain plagued with turbulent conditions, dangerous obstacles, and maritime piracy. But however long and exhausting this journey might be, we'd still choose dark, damning waters over a slave ship.

And maybe someday, if we kept pushing forward, we could build a boat of our own. A boat big enough for the women who were never taught to swim.

PART 3: Phoenix

43

I was finally on the Command's radar, and while no sentries had dragged me away to the gallows yet, the spotlight suddenly had my brother walking a fine line—a line that, day by day, started to resemble a tightrope spanning above one giant, sexist circus.

Unfortunately, High Wire Tom was the only thing standing between me and prison, so I reluctantly heeded his orders. *Lie low, give the weeds some breathing room, and blend in as well as any spirit-human hybrid is capable of,* he'd said. *Got it, Al?*

For once in my life, I *did* get it. And I did as I was told.

Like any trailblazer, I'd expected to loathe subordination, but I soon realized that grudging obedience was paramount in the union of refugees and low-ranking officers, and as the weeks flew by, the deliberate space on the cafeteria bench began to shrink.

Now that I'd shed the reputation of a sheltered schoolgirl riding on her brother's success, I'd grown quite popular at Camp Ptarmigan. My life story had transcended gossip, finding its way into songs, journal entries, and campfire stories blown *way* out of proportion. Men grew comfortable enough to challenge me to memory games, betting on my ability to date specific tools or recount how a weapon was inherited.

As for Will, those less inclined to trust him could, at the very least, admit that he was probably *not* a backstabbing traitor.

To nurture such tolerance, the Rhean had offered up pertinent military secrets and cartography corrections, as well as his own crossing route as a child. He'd volunteered to craft and repair wooden field weapons, equipment, and barricade materials, essentially appointing himself Company Carpenter. And it didn't hurt that his fellow runners had loudly praised his battle skills. They said they'd never seen a grunt fight so well under pressure, claiming that Will hadn't hesitated to put himself between cornered Ellsians and demon pawns.

Meanwhile, Fudge and I gushed about Will's Deadlock trial and heroic rescue in the Range—commendations that evoked tears of jealousy from the boy's self-declared nemesis.

Before long, Will's swordsmanship and bravery had overwritten his name, and in the span of one menstrual cycle, he'd become the outsider who turned against his Rhean heritage. The rebel prince. The wayward son.

Still, if anyone shot him a dangerous look, I returned it with equal menace, and given my name and supposed superpowers, it proved incredibly effective.

With our soil turned, Will and I joined Fudge and Mason at basic training—or its closest equivalent, anyway. The Command had understandably cast its boot camp aside to prioritize national security, so an official training program was off the table. It didn't stop us from learning the ropes of a functioning garrison, though. Tom's unit brought us up to speed on military operations, strategies, and protocol, and we attended drills and briefings like everyone else.

I absorbed as much as I could, taking in the vocabulary, the geography, and the configuration of a breathing army. And as I sat between grown, stubbly men, listening to them debate over the projected location of our Rim troops, I'd never felt so *included*. And that alone made me feel accomplished.

Between these sessions, Will and I routinely sparred in the courtyard, where he ruthlessly crafted a new and improved fighting style for me. Each time we practiced together—and each time he publicly humiliated me or put another dent in my armor—I grew stronger, quicker, and more proficient. My reactivity improved, as did my arsenal of defensive maneuvers.

I was becoming a master of deflection, even if the Rhean would never admit it.

After hours, Jaden tutored me on spirits (of the alcoholic variety) and the science behind each poison. She told me what to order if I was trying to impress and what to order if I actually wanted to enjoy myself. She also taught me to keep an eye on my beverage at all times, and to never, *ever* accept a drink unless I watched the bartender pour it myself.

I'd made the move to her loft permanent after she insisted on becoming roommates, and we'd quickly found solace in one another. There was something indescribably refreshing about female companionship. At the end of the day, talking to her was like a warm bath and a good book—a kind of mental release I rarely found in human form.

The way she so easily understood my emotions, my irritation that stemmed from the flood of testosterone outside our window—it was equal parts relieving and unnerving. She could sympathize with my many grievances and braid the inexpressible into cohesive sentences, and I wondered if all women shared a kind of universal experience that allowed them to do so.

It wasn't something I'd experienced before, that bond. My relationships with my mother and Nova had offered similar benefits, but this was the closest thing to sisterhood I'd ever encountered. And apparently, it was a connection I'd desperately needed in this life, even if I didn't understand Jaden's love for lace and jewelry and expensive hair clips.

On the rare occasion that I wasn't training with Will, venting to Jaden, or losing to Beckett at backgammon, I sought more information about the war and its rotten roots. And First Lieutenant Rover Wright, with his loose tongue and easygoing attitude, was my go-to resource.

Corroborating Nova's tale of retribution, he explained how our dev-astating intrusion prompted the Rhean king to unleash his demon army. He detailed how, in the bloody decade that followed, the Pans pushed us back over the Rim, hounding the Ellsian perimeter until we disintegrated—or buckled. The pressure finally fractured our defenses, and now our scat-tered forces were racing for the heart of this nation before the enemy ar-rived.

"If the demons hopped the Gorge, what does that mean for all the men fighting there?" I asked, sitting crisscross on a worktable cleared of metal shavings. "You think they wiped out a whole sector on the demarcation?"

I usually found Rover in the armory distracting Sol, so the two of us had become the blacksmith's longest and loudest disruptions of the day. And this afternoon was no exception.

"Decimated. Or the Pans stole enough bodies to cross unburdened," Rover responded.

Sol, who'd spent a good chunk of his service commitment at the bor-der, swiveled on his stool and frowned. "It's not looking good for any Rim troops, but it's possible the outposts neighboring Belgate were baited."

Claus rolled his eyes from his work bench. "Ever the optimist, Solo-mon."

"I do my best."

I looked between them. "*Baited*?"

Sol rubbed the nape of his neck and the base of his wing tattoo. "If our southern troops hadn't seen any activity this season, a sizeable ambush might've drawn their forces north, leaving a hole in the Rim. A diversion might also explain why Belgate saw zero warning and why our federates didn't chase the intruders down—it's not like you can chase something you never laid eyes on." He shrugged. "That being said, our postmen haven't returned from the Rim, and the clock is ticking. Holly may have requested emergency aid, but at this point, I don't know how many reinforcements to expect."

Rover's grim expression suggested he wasn't expecting any at all, and Claus scoffed like they wouldn't need the assistance anyway.

"What was it like?" I pivoted. "The Rim?"

Shadows pooled in Sol's round eyes, and he breathed a deep, mournful sigh. "Horrible. There were bombs going off all day and night. Ash in your eyes and your teeth. Black snow. Chemical fires to keep the Pans away, and *gritz*, they reeked like nothing else. But the turnings ..." He swallowed, and his hand fumbled for his silver necklace. The pendant resembled the letter "t"—a religious token I hadn't seen in ages. "The Rim is like a massive bee-hive, Alex, and it's *swarming* with Pots."

"The raw demon energy," I recalled.

He nodded. "They circle replica portals like fish in a pond. Except these fish are fishing *us*, and every so often, they drop down from the sky and steal another soul."

I didn't ask for any more details—not because I lacked interest, but because I didn't want to stir up any trauma. Instead, I peered closer at the symbol dangling between his dog tags.

"I didn't realize people still believed in God." At least, not an omnipotent and omnibenevolent god. Not after the Crash.

"Most didn't before Godric's retaliation," Rover said, sitting down on the floor. "Sol was raised with his faith. Other soldiers, though—they'd never seen a Bible verse in their lives—and with demons arriving at our doorstep, it became a whole lot harder to deny an afterlife. Now everything's up in the air; no one knows what to believe."

Claus scowled, speaking around a mouthful of pine nuts. "Yeah, well, the extremists would beg to differ." When he registered my confusion, he harrumphed and spat out a few shells to make room for his tongue. "That's right. Some boots think this war is the Rapture. They think God's responsible for all this supernatural crap, and he's wiping out all the nonbelievers or something. We've had deserters take to the streets, trying to warn people about the end of the world. *Dupable dodgers.*

"Then we have the idiots who can't see what's standing right in front of 'em. They refuse to believe in magic, portals, demons, or anything unmade. They think the Pans are suffering from prions or some fictional contagion, while the other half claim it's psychological torture. They're all nonbelievers until their blood runs black."

"People are divided," Rover summarized. "They're questioning God, consciousness, and death, and no one has any real answers." He frowned at the stone pavers between his legs. "This entire war has forced us to reevaluate everything we know. It's another reason we haven't gone public with it—civs have got enough to worry about with resource scarcity and an agricultural crisis. Last thing they need is a spiritual reformation."

To be honest, I hadn't spent much time thinking about the theological implications of body-sharing spirits and soul-eating demons. With so many concrete issues to process, I'd hitched religious ideology to the fencepost this month.

"If you ask me, it's all irrelevant," Claus muttered. "Don't slap names on it. Just give me a Pan to throttle."

"You mean like all the Pans you throttled when you came running out of the adit, pissing yourself?" Rover teased.

Claus threw his saliva-soaked hulls at the blond, and Rover swore in disgust, kicking at his comrade from the floor.

"What about the Seventh Order?" I asked. "Will said they helped Godric build the portal. Can't we talk to them and figure out how to shut it down remotely? Or ask them to perform an exorcism for our soldiers?"

"Sure, if you can find a living member," said Rover, irritably flicking the shells off his shirt.

"There was a mass suicide," Sol elaborated as he resumed operating his grindstone. "Those involved in the scheme took their own lives after Godric forced their hand."

The blood drained from my cheeks. "How did he force them?"

"Prohibited them from reversing their magic. Threatened to kill them and persecute their families," Rover said over the grating sharpening sound. He scrunched his nose. "They couldn't live with themselves."

"Cowards," Claus grumbled. "They let the world fall to hell …"

"They brought *hell* to the world," Sol corrected.

Rover rolled onto his back, folding his arms under his head and propping his feet against the cabinets beneath me. "After that, the Order was dissolved. We have no clue if the remaining members survived Godric's wrath—or where they might have fled if they did. But if they haven't tried to end this chaos a decade later, they're no ally of mine."

Fair point.

"Couldn't someone else replicate the magic? Reverse it?" I pressed. "There has to be some sort of spell book or reference material, right?"

Spells, magic. What was I even *saying*?

How was this real life?

Sol shook his head as he inspected the honed broadsword in his lap. "They were a secretive bunch. Only passed their knowledge down verbally, member to member. But even if we miraculously came upon a cure-all ritual, it might not be enough." My brow furrowed, and he grinned at my imminent follow-up question. "The Order believed a gene was required to perform magic—a gene found in mediums and witch doctors and other spiritualists. A trait shared only between blood relatives, and consequently, members of the Order."

Rover closed his seawater eyes. "And the last generation to inherit that gene is dead."

Sol, determined to purge the doom from my expression, cushioned Rover's statement with a soft, "As far as we know."

The four of us ruminated on humanity's unfavorable predicament for a while, and then Claus said something about inventory, and the conversation turned to vanadium concerns and weaponry advancements. But as the trio exchanged fresh ideas and witty insults, my thoughts lingered on the Seventh Order and the genetic mutations they claimed to possess—claims we'd once categorized as impossible and absurd—and I couldn't help thinking about a little old woman in the woods.

***

I ambled along the tree line, tossing Richard pinecones every few hundred feet so he could mimic fetching behavior, get distracted, and forget to retrieve the cones altogether.

The mutt was living his best life here at Camp Ptarmigan. The men all spoiled him silly—Beckett and Grismond, namely—and he was never without company, or *scraps*.

But as happy as I was to have him here, and as thrilled as he was to be the Interior Company's honorary pet, his presence also kept the whereabouts of Belgatian citizens top of mind. And achingly fresh.

Richard had successfully fled the unrest in Belgate, which meant someone had opened the Gates for him to do so. Someone had, intentionally or not, let him *out*.

Will thought the Pans were responsible. Said they had no need for containing survivors and left it—morbidly—at that. But my waning optimism told me a fellow band of refugees had escaped, and Richard had expertly sniffed out their exit path.

"Then where are they?" Mason had countered at lunch today, the distress over his own family bleeding through. "Where have thousands of residents fled?"

And, considering that everything west of Belgate was now demon territory, there were only two logical answers to that: they fled east like us, only to be cut down by Stretch and crew, or they hiked south as my father intended. But according to Rover, the Southern Ridge no longer promised safe passage, and according to Beckett, its rivers ran dry this time of year. A thirsty landscape wasn't exactly sustainable for an exodus of that size. Not for much longer, anyway.

Tom had sent scouts into the Range weeks ago, but the woods were quiet. His men hadn't found a single survivor on their excursions—not even a *corpse*. And I didn't want to think about what that meant for our families, neighbors, and elders.

Quiet laughter jolted me out of my thoughts, and I halted in place, straining to listen. That delightful sound was unmistakable, but so was the cool, monotone voice that followed, and I didn't know what to make of the coupling.

I wandered into the golden aspen grove on my left and approached a gentle-sloping river, fascinated by the babble of voices.

I spotted Fudge first. He crouched at the river's edge, washing his clothes and training gear in a swimming hole and then tossing them into a wicker basket. Will sat on a boulder several feet away, picking at the scab on his shoulder. He'd removed his stitches last week—as I'd shrewishly implored—and I was pleased to see his wound healing up.

It did surprise me to see him so casually shirtless, but I supposed he'd had to adapt to the lack of privacy the barracks offered. I just hoped no one had teased him too much about his scars—mostly for the harasser's sake. He'd likely kill anyone who so much as looked at his torso the wrong way.

"Will, do you think you could teach me to fight, like you've been teaching Alex?"

Will stiffened, and he turned to glare at his freckled companion.

"I mean, I know we were in the same training cohort, but I've never really taken the whole thing seriously until now. I want to jump ahead in physical training, and you seem to know what you're doing. So ..."

Will scowled, and he didn't answer for a while as he dunked his wrist brace in the brook. Then he tossed the garment into his meager pile of belongings and snatched his shirt off the rock. "Do you even want to fight?"

The Ellsian stared back at him like he wasn't sure he should answer honestly. "No. But I have to."

"Why?"

"Same reason as you. I can't just stand by and watch everything burn."

The prince gave a shallow nod of understanding, but Fudge wasn't fooled; the Rhean's reluctance was obvious.

"You don't want to teach me, do you? Is it because I'm not strong enough? Like Alex?"

Will huffed. "Strength has nothing to do with it. Alex is just belligerent."

I gaped at him, and it was like he could sense my indignation because he tried again.

"She's a fighter. Even if she doesn't know how to take an enemy down, she'll try anyway. It's in her blood." He cocked his head at his fellow trainee, and I was shocked by the overt sympathy swimming in his eyes. "But you're different. You *can* fight. I'm just not sure you were meant to."

Fudge bit his cheek and lowered his gaze to the water.

"It's not a bad thing, Fudge. If there were more people like you, there wouldn't be a war in the first place." Will tugged his shirt over his head. "Besides. There are other avenues available to you, different ways you can contribute to this cause. You don't have to wield a weapon to win a war."

Fudge sighed as he snatched up his laundry basket. "It's okay. I'll just wait for boot camp. Thanks anyway." He began walking down the riverbank, and I could see the conflict on Will's face, the irritable hesitation, the unwelcome concern.

"I'll help you," Will conceded, and Fudge glanced back at him in surprise. "But you need to recognize that you're not going to survive out there—not as a swordsman."

The boy's face fell, and gritz, it felt like he'd just struck me in the sternum with a *polearm*. But Will's unconcealed wince assured me I wasn't the only one.

"What I mean is, everyone has a different skill set. We need to find a martial discipline that suits you first. Maybe something with less brute force." The Rhean wet his lips, then squinted at the yellow canopy above him. "Archery takes significant upper body strength. But a hand crossbow or a sling could work."

"I've never used a projectile weapon before," Fudge admitted.

Will gathered his things and joined him at the fork in the river. "Let's see what Sol has up for grabs." He gripped Fudge's shoulder and steered the directionally challenged boy back toward camp. "Even without vanadium ammunition, you could still inflict injuries that give your comrades the upper hand. I've read that slingers were essential to ancient civilizations. Sometimes they were even more effective than bowmen ..."

Fudge beamed at Will's atypical monologue—as did I—and I pressed myself against a tree trunk to avoid detection as they ambled back toward camp.

A month ago, Will would have offered Fudge a clipped rejection or completely ignored his request. But things had changed, and I could see the big brother in him now.

"Are you stalking your boyfriends?"

I jumped.

Tom stood behind me, smiling evilly, and Richard sat next to him with two different pinecones protruding from his mouth.

"I'm not—they're not—what do you *want*?"

He raised an eyebrow. "Sol's finished. It's ready."

***

"And school?" Tom asked.

"What about it?"

"Have you been going?"

"Of course I've been going! I'm not a dropout."

"It was just a question."

"*Patrons*, Tom. Stop tormenting me."

He tsked at my impatience and then reappeared at the armory door, balancing a newly forged weapon on his fingertips.

Its presence—and vanadium properties—flipped my stomach, but I couldn't deny its beauty. A unique, mountainous hamon embellished the silver spine. Black leather encased the grip, and a polished, disc-shaped pommel sealed off the hilt.

"It's gorgeous," I whispered, gingerly taking the weapon in my hands. It was thin, well-balanced, and perfectly weighted for a soldier my size. It would flex enough to absorb the shock of a bigger opponent, but it was the furthest thing from flimsy.

And despite the loud, visceral distrust emanating from my co-spirit, I felt at ease holding the instrument capable of damaging—and potentially dislodging—my long-term passenger. Clasping the sword felt like a satisfying checkmate . . . against myself.

I'd have to thank Sol tonight for both empowering me and gifting me a work of art. I could see the dedication in the fine detail. I could feel the meticulous labor in that glassy, flawless surface. It wasn't just a survival tool; it was a sculpture, and I finally understood why the Ancients named their weapons.

I caught a glimpse of my reflection in the art piece—curious hazel eyes, parted lips, and a narrow face curtained by a mop of tangled hair. My smile slipped at the young girl staring back, just a fraction. But Tom was too perceptive for his own good.

"What is it?"

My gaze flicked to his, then back to the tool he'd invested in. "I still think the Pans are using living humans as vehicles, and the thought of murdering our own soldiers sickens me," I confessed. "I know what's expected of me, but this beautiful, custom sword feels so ... heavy. And that's not how I wanted to feel when I finally earned a weapon of my own."

Tom nodded as if he'd predicted my response. "That's indicative of something called *honor*, Al. And it normally takes years for these boots to shed their bloodlust. Sometimes decades." He traced the design along the hardened edge of the blade. "Serving in the military gives you license to kill, but that doesn't mean you should kill needlessly."

"Isn't that the point?" I murmured. "Leaving the battlefield with the highest body count?"

He tilted the sword vertically between us, and my fingers instinctively curled around the hilt. My insides coiled at the way it complemented my grip so perfectly.

"The point is to end this war, and that means sustaining an army long enough to do so. So the only *expectations* I have of you are prioritizing your safety and the safety of civilians—even if it requires lethal force—and doing so without endangering your comrades or the mission. That, and consulting me before you reveal anything else to the Command. Alright?"

"You forgot *minding orders*."

"It's a lost cause."

I snorted, lowering the blade to my side and admiring my laudable brother instead. He'd done so much for me these past few weeks. With his reputation on the line, he'd handed me my dream, and now he'd given me a *choice*.

He wouldn't respect me any less if I opposed military protocol. He wouldn't love me any less if I stood my ground—even if my position lacked evidence and sound alternatives. And I wasn't sure I could ever repay him for that.

"You need a weapon of war, Al. But use it as you see fit, okay?" He flashed a crooked grin. "If you want to avoid kill blows, shin-chops are underrated, and you can bench a Pan if you lop off his nondominant hand. Knees are also—"

A watery laugh burst from my lips as I crashed against his chest. "Thank you," I whispered into his shirt, wrapping my free arm around his back. "Thanks for being here. Thanks for believing in me."

He cradled my head with his right hand, just like our father used to do, and the tight embrace activated emotions I hadn't experienced in years.

He sighed into my hair. "Man. Do you have to be a soldier? Can't you just be a field nurse? Or like, a teacher?"

"Can't *you*?"

His chest rumbled with quiet laughter—a postpubertal man's laugher—and I closed my eyes, committing the deeper, scratchier sound to memory.

"Sir!"

Tom and I pulled apart to acknowledge the soldier in the courtyard. His eyes were wide and haunted, his complexion flushed, and his expression planted a fresh crop of dread in my heart.

"The Pans were spotted six miles west of here," he said between oxygen-starved breaths. "They're headed straight for Holly."

44

Tom and I shared a tense look.

"No," he said immediately.

"Tom—"

"You aren't ready yet. You haven't been trained for comb—"

"Tom!" My grip tightened on the sword at my side. "If you go, I go."

His tortured expression almost made me reconsider, but I couldn't bear the thought of another wartime separation, and I refused to wait here all alone, begging the Fates to send him home in one piece. I couldn't do that again.

"Let me fight with you," I pleaded. "While there's still a point in doing so."

Lashes fluttered over honey eyes, batting the emotion away.

He looked up at the sky, and I had a feeling he wasn't asking my parents for help this time, but forgiveness. "Stay in the rear," he decided. "I'm trusting you not to make the same mistakes as last time."

I nodded, rejoicing at the opportunity to directly assist the nation's war efforts—and for once, with explicit permission. "And I'm trusting *you* to focus on the fight. Don't worry about me."

"Don't ask for the impossible, Al."

***

The trees thinned around us, and too soon, too quickly, we reached the Eastern Piedmont. A lowering storm brewed overhead, and across from us—at the summit of the grassy subpeak—the first row of demons appeared.

The first of an inestimable number.

I didn't need to read my officers' sober faces to understand how unfavorable this situation was. We were outnumbered and underprepared. We'd forfeited the high ground, and we lacked the fortifications and siege defenses characteristic of citadels.

This was the making of a massacre.

Fudge trembled beside me, his small form encased in steel and leather, and the sight of him in a warrior's getup made me sick to my stomach. I grabbed his shoulder pauldron to seize his attention. "Stay here," I instructed, choosing hypocrisy over a dead friend.

He stilled, lifting his helmet off his brow to look me in the eye. "What?"

"Stay in the trees. It's gonna be a bloodbath."

"But I—"

"Stay," I ordered, my voice cracking slightly, and he swallowed. But he dipped his chin in concession.

I moved along the tree line to stand between Will and Mason. No one breathed a word, but there was palpable unease in the air. We thought we'd decimated their numbers at Goddard Mine, thought we'd bought ourselves a few months of peace and recuperation. But the Pans were back and stronger in arms—a positive feedback loop we hadn't anticipated.

"They're from Belgate," Mason said thickly, staring up at the army with cold, pale eyes. "I recognize them."

By this, I assumed he meant these Pans had also gutted Belgate, but when I followed his gaze to our opponents, I realized his unsettling observation was, in fact, a sinister discovery.

Squinting, I could just make out the Pans' size, shape, hair color, and race—combinations that resembled our neighbors, our teachers, our smiths, and our merchants. Combinations that, even from afar, betrayed several identities.

Among them, I spotted classmates and fellow housewives-in-training who'd fallen victim to Godric's wrath. Distant cousins and relatives, professors and Council members. Even a few postpartum mothers. But the overwhelming majority? Boys of fighting age who'd lost their respective Tournaments—and young men who, until now, had escaped their role in a "poor man's fight."

My eyes hopped from figure to figure. *Are you somewhere in there, Dad? Were you recruited to kill me?*

"Where's your helmet?" Will hissed.

I spared him a distracted glance. "I gave it to Fudge."

Three seconds later, he was standing in front of me, blocking my view of the foothill. His angry gaze jolted me to my senses—anchoring me to the present moment—and as I scrambled for justification, he yanked his helmet off and shoved the metal can over my head, adjusting it so the visor sat perfectly over my eyes.

It smelled like *boy*, but I didn't dare speak as he tucked my hair into my leather gorget, scowling at my braid like it would be the thing to kill me.

I scoured my mind for a cheeky comment, a feeble joke, a *thank you*, but nothing came. I just held his gaze for as long as possible, hoping this silent, intimate encounter might last forever.

Hoping his steady, brazen eye contact might somehow delay the inevitable.

Charitably, Will granted my wish. He stared back at me through tousled bangs, his jaw wound taut with unvoiced concerns, and even though he didn't speak to me, I heard his warning loud and clear.

The world will be worse without you in it. Be careful.

Then reality struck.

Tom yelled something from the center of our configuration, and the demons poured over the hill like an ash flow—voices roaring, metal clanging. The violent collision of blood and smoke had my heart fleeing up my throat, and I watched the eruption unfold with fearful, rapt attention. Searching for weaknesses to exploit, players to target, and holes to patch.

Predictably, the Grismonds of the world dominated the field, trampling their opponents like bugs beneath their feet, skewering their enemies like wild boar. But skilled swordsmen and glaive-bearers prevailed as well, and seasoned federates sliced into demon joints while deflecting blows to their heads, necks, and limbs.

Still, the garrison's lightweight armor provided minimal protection in open field battle, and the Pans' stolen gear had seen better days. Under these conditions, even graceless thrusts could snuff out a soul: a laceration to a demon's ribcage had him bursting into ashes; a perforated abdomen had a man voiding his bowels on the grass. And where shoddy armor didn't fail, it permitted blunt force trauma. (Undergo enough contusions, broken ribs, and concussions, and a finishing blow would come soon enough.)

Given our strategic disadvantages, it didn't take long for the Pans to pierce our front line, and as they barreled for the heart of the company, I readied myself, widening my stance, unsheathing my virgin blade, and raising my scrappy, wooden shield to my chin.

This is what you signed up for, I told myself. *Now prove to them you can handle it.*

Prove to yourself you're fit for combat.

I glanced back at Fudge—his small form dwarfed by the towering pines, his sundown-blue eyes juxtaposed by a world of ash. He gazed back at me, pouring forth his confidence in me, his admiration, and I twirled back around with a stronger spine.

Screw preparing for impact. I can pierce back.

I took a rigid step forward, then another, and before my survival instincts could kick into gear, I joined the tempest.

I moved the way Will had taught me, swooping and spinning and dodging my way through a metal jungle. Knocking weapons loose from civilian hands. Redirecting swords and spears into the earth—or other Pans.

Tom's advice was fresh on the brain, so when I wasn't dancing with Death, I took the offensive, aiming for the demons' knees and shins and fingers. Doing everything I could to keep them from harming others and, temporarily, out of harm's way.

The wind howled, abusing my eardrums, and my pulse roared as I fought to protect the very things trying to kill me. When I finally distanced myself enough from the mayhem to catch my breath—and examine my powdery trail of violence—something struck me from behind.

Something heavy, hard, and kinetic.

The force sent me crashing into wild rye, and I shoved the human-shaped projectile off me, refusing to inspect the corpse any further, lest I find a familiar face. I rolled into a sitting position and glared at the Pan who'd kicked the body downwind.

She watched me from her rocky outcrop, wetting her lips. She was smaller than her male counterparts—short, petite, and underweight—but her skeletal appearance did nothing to boost my confidence. If anything, it made her possessor twice as dangerous, for a demon who kept a vulnerable host alive, mobile, and proficient in battle was leagues beyond a trainee of equivalent stature.

She smiled at me, exposing a lattice of black gums and crooked teeth, and I recoiled.

"Choose a cause, soldier. Abstention will not cleanse your soul," she taunted, lifting a glaive drenched in human blood. She cocked her head so far to the right it looked like she'd suffered a neck injury. "Do you wish to die a traitor or a weakling?"

My fingers curled into wet earth. She'd been watching me, then. She knew I wouldn't kill her, so she'd sought me out like a predator tracking the runt of the litter, happy to purge the field of a slippery fence-sitter.

An easy target, an easier kill.

Before she could send her weapon through my gullet, though, a sword tip penetrated her gut, spattering my shins and boots in black acid. And just as the Pan registered her demise—just as she realized she'd become prey to a bigger animal—she burst into a cloud of toxic dust. Banished to the netherworld from whence she came.

Her remains dispersed quickly in the wind, and seconds later, the ash cleared to reveal Grismond's soiled, angry face.

I expelled a shaky breath. *Bless you, Lady Fortuna.*

"Thank you," I said hoarsely, my gratitude lost to the howling storm. But as thankful as I was for the timely rescue, I couldn't help thinking about the growing volume of blood on my hands.

It seemed that even when I abstained from murder, carnage followed—my bootprints were filled with it.

That's war, my soul mourned. *That Pan was right; the degree to which you participate won't absolve you of your sins. Not in the eyes of history.*

But I wasn't ready to hear it.

Grismond yanked me to my feet in one swift motion. He clapped me on the shoulder, spinning me around to face the bulk of the army, and then he stomped off for more kills. Unfazed. Undeterred. Unburdened.

Follow suit, you welt.

I couldn't think about the bloodshed underway, couldn't think about the Ellsians enlisted by Godric Sterling—turned to monsters, reduced to cannon fodder. I couldn't dwell on the excruciating realization that we hadn't found any evacuees in the Range because there simply *were* none. And though I yearned to find Will, Rover, and Tom in this mess and confirm their autonomy, their survival, I couldn't repeat Goddard Mine. I

couldn't let my connections cloud my judgement, not when Pans continued to spill down the hillside.

*So for Patrons' sake, wipe the ash off your lips, fix your helmet, and keep
moving.*

I pushed and shoved my way up the hill, tripping enemies, assisting
federates, and avoiding direct engagement. But when I finally made it to the
ridge—the loftiest vantage point of the Eastern Piedmont—I stopped dead
in my tracks to observe the hellish basin beyond.

At first, darkness was all I could fathom. Darkness and madness and
yellow grass. Then my senses revealed to me a sea of living shadows, a cyclone of ghostly demons amidst the black, and at last, I retrieved a label for
the unsightly phenomenon.

Pots.

The demons swam through the air like a bed of freshwater eels, constantly changing shape and appearance, diving below to enter a new body,
a new host. There had to be thousands of them, these unstable wisps of ash
and smoke prowling the upper valley for new arrivals.

They emerged from a sky-reaching beam of shadows and crimson
lightning—a tornado-like vortex anchored to the ground—and there, at the
grassy base of the swirling funnel, was a gateway composed of brambles and
stones and human entrails. The design resembled an ancient calendar of
sorts, or perhaps an alchemist's circle, or . . .

Horror sank its teeth into my spine. Or Will's *scar.*

For some ungodly reason, the same symbol carved into the Rhean's
chest was also inscribed here in the space between mountains, ejecting Pots
into the atmosphere, injecting evil into the world. Polluting bloodstreams,
splintering families.

The Pans had erected a portal on Ellsian soil—a sister to the one in
Rhea's stronghold.

And we were at its mouth.

45

Sol stood a few paces ahead of me, staring into the portal as the battle raged around him.

An elderly Pan crept up behind him, hoping to catch the blacksmith unawares, but I intercepted the creature on his lethal downswing. I sliced through his hamstrings, generating a contrail of smoke as I kicked his screeching body back down the hill.

"Sol!" I yelled. "Snap out of it!"

He remained still and distrait, captive to a traumatic memory—lost to the Rim. I glanced helplessly at our neighboring federates, but they were either engrossed in combat or bewitched by the same evocation.

"The turnings!" Sol finally called back, still watching the sky. "Godric's recruiting us."

My gaze flitted over the men who'd daringly approached the portal, and the sight of their writhing bodies punched a hole in my sternum. Newcomers fell to the ground to join their screaming brethren, begging for salvation as the Pots remade them, crying for their sovereignty as demon raiders bleached their eyes.

Life had become a nightmare since the wasting of Belgate, but this far exceeded a night terror. This was beyond comprehension, beyond explanation, beyond lifting your eyelids and forgetting the details.

Fresh blood spattered my body, speckling my helmet and chest plate.

Demons perished in plumes of ash, detonating around me like shrieking land mines. Men wailed as shadows feasted on their souls. Blades grated bones.

I couldn't breathe. I couldn't *think*. It felt as if the grass were growing all around me, weaving itself between bootlaces, ingesting my shins. All I wanted to do was evaporate.

But just before I lost myself to the chaos, Tom's whistle sliced through the tumult—the same whistle Grismond had used in the adit. *Retreat.*

With no hesitation whatsoever, the company sprinted for the trees, eager to flee the field of hijackers, eager to pass their responsibilities back to their commanding officers. I was quick to follow, and I drew a breath of relief when I saw the helmetless, raven-haired boy do the same.

I only made it twenty strides or so before I realized Sol hadn't moved, and I halted at the summit's edge, lifting my arms. "Sol!"

But my shouting didn't rouse him. It summoned a different force altogether.

Like a cloud bleeding ironsand, the swarm of Pots fell from the sky as one giant, dangerous cascade. The demons dropped with haste, they flew with intention, and my chest clenched at their trajectory.

"*Sol!*"

If he heard me, the desperation in my voice wasn't convincing enough. The wave of Pots crashed upon the piedmont like an avalanche, and I watched—petrified—as the shadows consumed him whole.

Body, mind, and soul.

My boots fused to the rocks beneath me, and I did nothing as my superior, my *friend*, vanished into a cloud of black, ghoulish phantoms.

"Let's go, Kingsley!" Beckett shouted from below.

Weak-kneed, I staggered down the hill, my vociferous heartbeat drowning out the eerie screech of body thieves, my spirit commanding me to save myself.

Nova said the Pans were born of human sin, but according to Sol, we'd each been sinning since our first greedy gulp of air. So how—on this battered, lightless earth—did we fight an army with unlimited reinforcements? How did we defeat an enemy bolstered by the very war we waged?

The demon barrage bit at my heels now, and I shed the restraint in my knees and ankles, trading control for gravity-induced speed. Outrunning my comrades. Outrunning possession.

I was one arena lap from the woods when I tripped over a corpse—or what I'd mistaken for a corpse, anyway. The obstacle was, upon closer inspection, an injured demon vacillating between a live and powder state.

Failing to leash my velocity, I stumbled over its mangled form, momentarily bear-crawling on all fours as I attempted to wield my momentum. But my tactic proved useless; I hadn't merely collided with the Pan—he'd seized my leg—and as I regained bipedalism, his grip slipped to my ankle, cinching around my boot.

Gritz.

The cessation of motion sent me sprawling to the ground again, launching me straight into a puddle of blood, mud, and demon gore. Rapidly, the cold enveloped me, strengthened by the wind chill, and it turned the adrenaline that should have saved me into a numbing toxin.

Snatching my second ankle, the crippled Pan yanked me toward him, dragging my resistant body through the hazard. Panicking, I plunged my fingers into the mud to stop myself, only to curse at the ten shallow lines I harrowed.

The monster shoved me onto my back, hovering over me with his sunken cheeks and wilting flesh. He peered at me like a vulture about to devour its carrion, and I recognized him as the demon I'd wounded moments ago in my efforts to save Sol's life.

As I stared up at his angry, ghoulish face, however, I realized our history didn't end there.

No. I'd pestered this man on a weekly basis for years. I'd inhabited his workspace so frequently that he'd come to see me as an insufferable coworker. He was no stranger to knowledge-seekers like myself—nor information-censors like the Council. And those censors had condemned him.

They'd condemned us all.

Mr. Wick reached for my neck with red, bony fingers, and I gazed up at the moon-eyed librarian, seemingly paralyzed. His features sent a shockwave through my system, knocking my brain loose from my body and leaving me dazed and motionless—just like Sol—and I feared if I didn't pull it together in the next five seconds, I'd likely follow the blacksmith into oblivion.

My sword beckoned me, its hilt burrowing into my hipbone.

This Pan was half-dead already; it would take nothing more than an upward thrust to end him, one good strike to escape this entanglement. But my heart didn't accept this logic.

Because this wasn't "just a Pan." This was a *person*—someone I'd known. And he was still in there somewhere, chained to the vile creature trying to kill me.

Frozen with indecision, I watched the wave of darkness crest above us—dense, daunting, and deleterious. Targeting the laggards and the injured, the Pots soared for the valley floor like an oil spill, and my entire skeleton went limp, as if it had already accepted a new, more competent host.

This was it.

I was demon dinner.

Mr. Wick's fingers curled around my throat, holding me in place for my demonic inauguration, and I crushed my eyes close, braving my end.

The temperature plummeted, and the dark of my eyelids turned an unearthly shade of black. Then someone shouted my name, and the weight pinning me to the ground disappeared.

I tasted ash and opened my eyes.

Tom sliced through the demonic storm around me, warding off the sea of Pots, the incoming Pans—forcefully carving an eye in a mystic hurricane. It was ludicrous to fight against the incorporeal, but I'd never seen anything more heroic.

"Get up, Al!"

His voice sent an electric current through me, reviving my motor system and kicking me into survival mode. I scrambled out of the mud, leaving behind a pile of empty, ashy armor as I tore for the trees.

Tom made to follow me, taking one last swing at the venomous powder cloud. But right as he turned away, just as he lowered his shield, a demon broke away from the hive.

Eye on the prize, the Pot dove straight for my brother's shoulder blades, and before I could voice a warning—before I could even *think* to do so—the demon sailed through his cuirass and entered his chest.

46

Tom pitched forward with gritted teeth, and my heart stopped.

No...

His sword dipped to the ground, and he swayed unsteadily from side to side, closing his eyes to the orbiting storm of shadows. My brain screamed in protest, but only his name—like a dead man's prayer—traversed my lips. "Tom..."

He stood in place with his head stooped, unmoving, unchanging, and for the briefest moment, I thought the captain might reject the demon in his bloodstream altogether—that his soul might prove too resilient, too stubborn, to relinquish control.

He shifted his weight, and my lungs denied me another breath as he uncurled his spine, lifted his chin, and ... smiled.

His grin, boyish and lopsided, still resembled the one I cherished, even with confusion and delirium weighing upon his lips. But when a milky fluid began flooding his eyes, clouding his pupils and drowning his honey irises, his lips stretched into something evil, something wicked. His manic grin expanded too far, too wide. It began distorting his face and ripping at cheek flesh.

"Tommy—"

He roared in pain—smiling all the while—and time twisted itself into minutes, hours, decades as my brother eroded before my very eyes.

The demon blanched Tom's olivewood skin, stripping away his vibrant undertones and replacing his *mestizo* heritage with a palette of decay. Tiny blood vessels spiderwebbed beneath his cheeks and forehead, and black arteries bulged from his neck, his hands.

In the interval of one broken, stupefied exhale, the left half of his face became just as unrecognizable as the right, and his agonized cries devolved into hysterical laughter.

The sounds perforated my denial, and I raced forward to stop his transformation, to do *something*, but iron hands snatched me back. Rover probably. I didn't dare glance away from Tom; I just kept kicking, thrashing, and pleading for release.

Not my brother. Not again.

From the eye of the storm, Tom regarded us with a disinterest that bruised, observing our retreating forces and the new puppets Godric had acquired on the battlefield. Then, with an expression of utter boredom, he turned away from us—as if he had somewhere else to go, somewhere else to build a life.

"Tom!" I wailed.

Wrenching myself free, I sprinted after him, tears spilling from my eyes and blurring the treacherous landscape. I didn't care about the demons afoot or aloft. I didn't cower at the threat of bodily possession. Even the shadowy squall between us didn't frighten me right now—Tom never being Tom again did.

"Stop!" I ripped off my helmet so he could see my face, my tears. "*Please.*"

The soldier locked eyes with me across the demon cyclone, a pair of glowing moons in charcoal sockets, and then he did the last thing I ever expected of him in that moment—the last thing I'd ever expect from Tom.

He sneered.

He sneered at me like I was a pathetic pest on the streets of Belgate, a stranger begging for skits. He sneered at my emotions, my attachment, as if my love for my brother was something to scoff at.

The mockery left painful, irreparable gashes between my rib bones—not because my heartbreak was met with scorn, but because there was no better way to signal my brother's departure. No better way to demonstrate his absence.

This soldier, this *Pan* … was not Tom.

Not anymore.

As if he hadn't just bludgeoned my heart into submission, he proceeded to walk up the slick, bloodstained hill and vanish into a wall of black gossamer. Leaving his title, his mission, and his life's ambition behind. Leaving *all* of us behind.

My knees gave out, and I crumpled to the muddy earth—sobbing uncontrollably, gasping for breath. *This isn't happening*, my denial roared. *This can't be happening!*

I didn't just lose my brother to Godric.

I didn't.

I—

But I wasn't allocated time to grieve. As soon as my hands crushed the grass beneath me, an onslaught of sensations rained upon me, unfettered and unwelcome.

Gritz. This shouldn't have happened, not with my gloves in pristine condition. Patrons, I even wore fingerless gauntlets today—with those barriers in place, no images should have penetrated my mind, let alone the deluge of memories that besieged me now.

But the instant my palms hit the ground, I knew its history was too heavy, too saturated, for my mind to process and retain. The magnitude of this robbery made the experiments I'd conducted with Nova and the federates feel like effortless party tricks. It made Titan's destruction feel facile and insignificant.

Even in a state of equanimity, this larceny would have fractured my psyche. And I was the furthest thing from equanimous right now.

But I couldn't peel my hands away fast enough, and I couldn't dam the river, either. I could only brace myself for impact.

Dozens of raw emotions surged through me at once, and I witnessed everything that had connected with the terrain since its prehistoric inception: ocean water, wildfire, flora and fauna, footprints and bootprints of hunters and countrymen, and the warriors who stood upon it now. My power bled onto the grass, leaching into soil horizons and filling the pores of the earth. Like a virus, that famished energy traveled by root systems and mycorrhizal networks, eventually scaling the wild rye to infect the bodies stirring in the valley.

And then, in one enormous batch of pain and carnage, I siphoned their human memories.

I ingested their emotions unwittingly, my hands unwieldy as cannon shots. I involuntarily consumed their secrets, their wrongdoings, their inner turmoil. And in the span of a few seconds, I absorbed a thousand life experiences and the traumas that accompanied them—a sequence of images too bright and horrific to separate into interpretable pieces, and a trench too shallow to reveal anything but widespread tragedy.

When I spotted Tom in the deck of face cards, I reached for him with no fingers. I lunged for him with no legs.

There he is.

Tom and his crooked smile.

Tom's pout and muffled snickering.

Tom punching the bully who made fun of my gloves. Tom placing illegal bets during the Tournament. Tom hugging me at the water tower.

Tom. Tom. *Tom.*

Crippled by the memory bank, I released a dolorous groan and collapsed onto my forearms. A broken heap. A broken soldier.

Rain descended, but I didn't move. Not until warm hands pulled me upright and tossed me over sturdy shoulders.

It occurred to me then that I was leaving the battlefield in the state of a waterlogged hay bale, but I was too exhausted to care—too dazed and drained and devastated to comprehend the scene I was leaving behind.

And as we scurried into the Range like shepherdless sheep, I spotted my brother once again. Only this time, his weary possessor glared after me on his hands and knees, surrounded by dead grass—and an army of sleeping demons.

47

Rover finally set me down, convinced I wouldn't bolt, and as we reassembled beneath the canopy, I honed in on the hallway of towering trees. The collage of fissured bark, drooping branches, and pine straw fostered a safe space for my mind—an endless wallpaper to assist my dissociation.

"Well?" Rover demanded.

His question wasn't directed at me, but at the two men on horseback he'd ordered to stay behind.

The bearded one carried a wounded comrade with him, and Grismond rushed forward to pull him from the saddle. "The Pans woke up a few minutes after we retreated," he said. "They shut down the portal before moving north. Cap was with them, along with our Turned."

Rover masked any emotions the report might have provoked. "Any insight on what put them to sleep?"

The second federate cleared his throat, eyeing me nervously. "Kingsley did something. Didn't you sense it?" He rubbed at his breastplate. "I felt this cold, hollow feeling in my chest, like the ground was tugging on my soul. She must have channeled her power through the soil and into the enemy somehow."

The army regarded me with wonder and fear—the defeated aching for hope, the powerless digging for seeds of redemption—but I answered them with silence. I couldn't even speak if I wanted to; Tom's name comprised half of my entire vocabulary right now. *Tom*, and *failure*.

Rover ran a hand over his grime-speckled face, clearing the powder from his eyes. I could barely tell he was blond beneath all the ash and blood. "You two, send word to Holly immediately. Warn them of the Pans' trajectory and imminent ambush. Mention that portals are no longer bound to the Rim." He assessed his shattered company, the injured, the traumatized. "Inform the Command we'll be trailing enemy forces by twelve hours. We need to regroup first."

The riders sped off again, and the rest of us walked soundlessly toward camp, our infantry forming a much shorter line than our pre-battle march. Less than a hundred of us remained; more than half had perished or succumbed to Godric's will.

I shuddered at the macabre imagery staining my eyelids, the grisly moments chiseled into the meat of my brain. The turnings had unlocked a new tier of horror for me today—a new degree of futility—and I wasn't sure how to cope with it yet, so I just simmered in the backwash.

My ankle throbbed with each step, and I began limping more and more intensely, falling behind. I was fairly certain I'd fractured something in my tussle with Mr. Wick, but we didn't have time to treat frivolous injuries. Not when a quarter of our company required immediate medical aid.

After stumbling over forest debris for the third time, though, I fetched a long, sturdy tree branch from the litter layer. I figured it would help keep the weight off my ankle—and any traitorous pinecones out of my vicinity—and I used Tom's knife to strip the crutch of extraneous stems and twigs.

The weapon weighed a million pounds in my fist, and I shoved it back in its scabbard before it triggered another meltdown.

Will and Fudge took notice of my painful hobbling, but they didn't try to speak to me in this state, and they didn't dare touch me. Instead, they shortened their strides to walk beside me, silently announcing that they were here to provide me company, and should I need it, emotional support.

It took another mile to reach camp, but when we arrived at the sandbag wall, it was not the refuge we'd sought.

My new home smoldered in crimson.

***

In our absence, the camp had been ravaged by demons and razed by flame, and the urban destruction awakened cruel memories of the city I'd abandoned.

Buildings, tents, and wagons blackened under red fire, windborne embers soaring through the air like frenzied insects fleeing the heat. Fragments of Will's carpentry projects littered the gravel, joining glass, armory debris, and human remains. And to top off the roaring, hellish landscape, smoke and rain-generated steam produced an eerie, blinding haze that made the burn area damn near impossible to navigate.

But even this suffocating mist couldn't hide my scent from Richard.

His barking cut through the fire's unsettling howl, and he scampered toward me from the riverbank, his tail wagging ecstatically.

My knees almost gave out for the second time that evening.

Thank the skies.

He joined me at the border of camp, licking my exposed fingers over and over, as if he were thanking me for coming back for him. As if he'd thought I'd deserted him.

With a choked sigh, I crouched to hold him.

"Jay," Rover breathed. He slid his injured comrade into Claus's arms and darted for the pub, its broken windows spitting angry flames.

I buried my nose in Richard's fur and closed my eyes. While we'd been fending off the Pans of Belgate, a second unit of demons had ransacked our base and torched our community, just as they'd evaded the Rim soldiers.

They'd wounded us from every feasible angle, just as they'd done at Belgate and Goddard Mine.

Looking back now, the ruse felt obvious. Their line formation, their portal preparation—they'd been waiting patiently for our mortal egos to doom us. And we'd swallowed the bait whole, overlooking the fact that their leaders had stolen memories of battle tactics and briefings and outpost coordinates. Ignoring that our enemies now possessed the knowledge of an entire Ellsian populace.

These Pans were as "human-minded" as the souls they'd conquered, and they were as vile as the worst among us. We had to stop thinking of them as some foreign species.

Federates searched the camp for survivors, some sprinting for the patients in the hospital wing, others checking on the corpses in the courtyard, but I knew anyone who'd stayed behind had died by flame or steel. An ambush like this didn't allow for evacuation, and these Pans were viciously thorough.

Meanwhile, Fudge and Will raced to save the chickens, only to return from the coop empty-handed—and, in Fudge's case, visibly distraught. I didn't have the heart to ask him if the birds had been slaughtered for food or if they'd expired in the blaze. Neither answer would do us any good.

Realizing that the most productive thing we could do right now was keep the fire from spreading across the valley, we worked to douse the flames in river water and clear combustible materials from the area. As a team, we managed to create an effective fuel break around the inferno, and we paused to watch the fire consume our beds, our amenities, and our possessions.

Rover emerged from Jaden's pub then, and the building instantly collapsed behind him, as if the entire structure had been waiting on their getaway—like its foundation had held out for as long as possible, trying its damnedest to spare its favorite residents.

Rover carried Jaden's limp body in his arms, and his rigid steps had me fearing the worst. But with one glance at his tense expression, I could tell she hadn't left us yet.

He joined me at the watering trough, coughing up ashes, and I stared at the pub owner's bloody clothes, her frighteningly pale skin. She was alive, but her breathing was too shallow for either of us to expel a sigh of relief.

"We need to keep moving," he said to me, hesitantly, as if he wasn't sure that was the right call, as if he wasn't sure of anything anymore. When I realized he was waiting for confirmation of some kind, I managed a small, lifeless nod, and his jaw ticked. "Do you mind giving the signal?"

I dropped my empty bucket and whistled loudly. Two men echoed me from the mist.

Rover commended the company's quick thinking as his soldiers trickled back to the tree line, their faces covered in soot, their spirits battered. "It's up to the rain now, boys. Let's move out."

We followed our lieutenant—and, as of nightfall, our *captain*—into the trees once more, trading hellfire for a lightless terrain.

***

The plan was to head for Holly.

Again.

Rover knew it was a bad idea. He knew the Command would have shut the city's curtain wall and barricaded the entrance. We'd find no aid there, no rest, no hospitality. Only war. But we marched on anyway, clinging to a destination and an inconsequential goal. At least this way, we could pretend we hadn't failed our loved ones yet—as long as we kept moving, kept marching, we couldn't ruminate.

And so, like livestock shuffling to the slaughterhouse, we moved as a broken unit, armor clinging to our bodies like dead skin.

About thirty minutes into a dismal, sorrowful silence, a sharp hissing noise zipped past my ear. My foot slammed into the underbrush mid-step, throwing me out of stride, and I stabbed my crutch into the earth to keep myself upright.

I scowled at my defiant boot. An arrow had wedged itself between the leather outsole and the ground, locking me in place. *The hell?*

I tried to dislodge the projectile, but the steel arrowhead had pierced the rocky substrate beneath me, effectively pinning me to the ground.

"What was *that*?" Mason yapped, unleashing his rapier from its sheath.

Probably the first of many, I thought, just as arrows began raining upon us with disturbing abundance, tacking men to trees and granite and hardy manzanita bushes. A few soldiers cried out, startled and alarmed by the archers' precision. Others yanked the arrows out of their armor and snarled into the dark.

Fudge, eager to assist, retrieved my flashlight from his belt, fumbling for the button, but when he aimed the tool at the foliage, nothing happened. The battery had finally died on us.

Richard growled at my side, undaunted, and I raised my sword, glaring at the shadowy spaces between tree trunks and the human shapes that filled them.

It appeared we'd been ambushed—just not by demons.

"Show yourselves," Rover demanded, clutching tight to Jaden, whom he now carried on his back. "You're obstructing an emergency response."

I wasn't sure his command would evoke a desirable outcome, and as an anxious hush fell over the woods, I suspected we were all about to die. But then ten figures in red cloaks materialized from the shadows like bloody gashes in the earth. They dropped down from the branches and poured out of the understory, armed with bows and arrows and throwing knives. Faces hooded, intentions unclear.

With undeniable poise, a cowled man jumped to the ground in front of me, barely making a sound with his impact. He held a nocked arrow at my face, holding me hostage with the strength of his fingertips alone, and I stared at the arrowhead blankly, unable to generate even a twitch of apprehension.

I'd just lost my brother, and Sol, and countless comrades. Jaden was dying, and a demon army was about to decimate the meager scraps of mankind. A tree gang was the least of my worries.

The shaft moved to Will, who'd taken a defensive stance behind me. The weapon lingered on him, the bow curving deeper with tension, and then it dropped to the man's side. His hood fell back, and suddenly the man was no longer a man, but a striking young woman.

Raven hair curtained phosphor bronze skin, and her brow shimmered with animal blood. Her vibrant war paint bordered two deep, prudent brown eyes—eyes that narrowed on us like a bird of prey pinpointing supper.

"Liam," she said, addressing Will for some inexplicable reason. "You're taller."

The Rhean prince bowed his head. "Siren."

48

Mason's mouth hung agape. "There's no way in *hell*—"

Siren's gaze swung to his, and his jaw snapped shut so fast I heard his teeth clack.

"What are you doing here?" she demanded. She wasn't asking Mason, but the Interior Company as a whole—as if she owned these woods, and we were trespassing on rebel territory.

She glanced at me, her eyes skirting over my armor, my sword. Then she scrutinized our haggard army and pinned Rover with an aggravated look. "I thought you had company in Yellow Valley."

"We did, but we didn't expect them to bring a portal," he replied coolly. His tone suggested he'd either met Siren before, or he knew her work—and he respected her enough to offer clipped transparency in a time of crisis.

The revelation piqued her interest, and her eyes flicked to the bleeding woman on his back. "Enemy forces passed through these woods hours ago. A separate unit?"

"So it seems," he muttered. "They burned our base to the ground."

She studied us closely, taking in our injuries, our dead eyes, our smoky stench, and as she did so, I took the opportunity to study *her*. She was, after all, an enigma—and apparently Will's acquaintance, which I planned to revisit once I had the mental capacity to do so.

A living legend from the Battle of Exeter, she wore a thin set of leather armor beneath her cloak, choosing to travel light despite the prowling Pans in her domain. And though it was hard to pin her exact age in the dark, she looked just shy of thirty—even if she displayed the comportment of a venerable matriarch.

She was still approaching her third decade on this planet, and she was already commanding a deadly forest guild. As a *woman*.

As shocking as it was to see a female archer in a leadership role, though, I was honestly more surprised that Mason's head hadn't shot off his body yet—and that upon meeting someone whose existence contradicted every belief he subscribed to, his brain hadn't blasted through his skull like the cap of a fermented product.

"You're headed to Holly in this condition?" Siren confirmed.

Rover nodded. "The sentries there aren't trained in combat. They need us, and our injured need medical attention." He hitched Jaden higher on his spine. "Please . . . lend us a hand or let us pass."

Her expression was grave, but she did not budge. "Holly's bolting every door shut as we speak. If the Pans engineer another portal to penetrate her walls, your trek will end in tragedy."

Rover's voice cracked as he admitted, "We have nowhere else to go."

They stared at one another, and I watched her fierce, unemotional expression yield to something softer—not exactly sympathy, but certainly a higher degree of understanding.

"Siren," Will cut in with the kind of impertinence only familiarity could cultivate. Her gaze crawled back to his, a flicker of irritation present. "Are you going to help us or not?"

Fudge gaped at his gall, but I was grateful for it. My ankle was growing stiff.

Siren looked us over, blood dripping down her cheekbone, and she grimaced. "I don't have much of a choice, do I?"

***

A quarter mile later, we reached the densest patch of forest I'd encountered yet—a stretch of woods unsplit by roads or trails or bridleways. With effortless grace, Siren and her crew guided us through the maze of underbrush and hazardous low-hanging branches, and in a matter of minutes, the clustered trees completely blotted out the sky.

In the distance, the rush of river rapids pierced the quiet, and the sound grew louder the further we ventured, providing the only sense of direction I could cling to. I hobbled along with my walking stick, the pain ebbing as my bones healed themselves.

Eventually, we reached a level clearing—a pocket of reprieve beneath the steepest slopes of the Eastern Range. Across the glen, log buildings and teepee dwellings glowed a pleasant auburn, and a rocky cliff bordered the far side of the encampment, spewing river water into a lake. Along the perimeter, candlelight illuminated wooden bridges, staircases, and ladders that interknit the pine trees, where even smaller cabins hugged the trunks and massive branches. It was too dark to discern how far the fort extended, but I could tell the base was immense, complex, and brilliantly camouflaged.

One of Siren's followers—another young woman in red—ran up to us from a sea of candlelight. "More refugees?"

Refugees.

I blinked, and the drought in my eyes told me I hadn't done so in a while.

Mason was the first to gather his senses. "Whom all have you taken in?"

The woman glanced at Siren, waiting for her nod of approval, then back at us. "Are you lot from Belgate?"

The world rocked beneath my feet.

"The four of us are," Fudge answered. He swallowed, then asked,

"Were there any survivors? Are they here?"

The woman nodded, opening her mouth to respond, but someone came sprinting toward us before she could get a sentence out.

The refugee wore plain clothes and a weathered robe, her left arm cradled in a sling. Her blond hair rippled behind her, unmade and tangled and frizzy. In the state she was in, I almost didn't recognize her, but Mason had no trouble.

"*Mom*?" he gasped. He raced forward to meet her, and they collided in a tearful embrace of astonished exclamations and heavenly praises. They pulled away to look at each other, taking in the changes, the strain in their features, then hugged again.

The three of us stood still as gravestones, watching their reunion, waiting for answers.

"Is Dad ... ?" Mason choked out, and she squeezed him tightly, shaking her head.

No. He wasn't.

"But your brothers are here," she assured him, her voice quivering. She burrowed into his armor, holding him upright so the news wouldn't send him to his knees. "They're safe."

After the longest minute of my life, they withdrew from each other, communicating silently through grieving, glistening eyes. And then Ellen Price took in the three teens before her, realizing she'd become the very messenger a housewife dreaded most.

Like a queen stripped of her title, stripped of everything, she barely resembled the model citizen who'd once sat at my dining room table to discuss her son's future. And yet, even in a state of mourning and vagrancy, it was clear she'd retained a sense of dignity and feminine poise, and it was that practiced composure that gave her the strength to apprise us of our families' whereabouts.

"Will, your father is here," she said, and the Rhean raised his head, his expression as neutral as ever. His posture shifted ever so slightly, though, and I could tell the relationship—however misleading—meant a great deal to him. "And Nikki, I believe your family made it to the southern border. I can't be sure; our paths forked. But I know they made it out of Belgate."

Fudge immediately began to cry, as if Ellen's words had just punctured a safe of bottled emotions inside him—emotions he hadn't permitted himself to explore or wallow in until now, lest they cripple him.

The group's attention swiveled to me, and Ellen hesitantly met my gaze. Her eyes held a river, and her mouth hung limp, unsure where to begin or how to relay the information.

"Alex . . . I'm *sorry*."

I stared at her for a few seconds, watching her tears slip down her face, watching her chin tremble. I closed my eyes, allowing the confirmation to sink into my bones, into my heart, before taking my first sip of paralyzing sorrow—and spitting it out.

I backed away from her, away from Fudge's devastation and Will's worried gaze, and then I took off after Rover before she could say anything else.

I couldn't process these ill tidings right now, not so soon after Tom.

I couldn't break in half just yet.

Accompanied by Beckett, I climbed the rickety stairs looping around a grove of ponderosas, ditching my makeshift crutch in favor of the wooden railing. The steps led me to a huddle of people standing outside a cabin, and I joined them in the doorway, waiting for a tragedy to unfold.

A treehouse, some distant, youthful part of me marveled. *You're in a treehouse.*

Inside, Rover knelt at the edge of Jaden's cot, his back stained red with blood. Glass punctured the bartender's stomach, the wound deep and grotesque and, considering the clotting time, far too tacky.

Evidently, sights like this no longer fazed me, and I mourned the ghost who would have glanced away to spare her stomach.

Rover took Jaden's hand in his and brushed the sticky hair from her face with the other. Her brown eyes fluttered open, rising to meet twin tide pools. "... Rove?"

"I'm here."

Her gaze swept the unfamiliar room, the unfamiliar faces tending to her injury, before landing on the man she'd followed to war. "I saw you in the fire, and I kept hearing your voice, but I thought I was dreaming." Her eyes watered. "You came back for me."

Rover released a guilt-ridden breath and shook his head. "I'm sorry I took so long. I wish I'd never left."

She picked up on his anger immediately, her smile fading. "Why did you return to Ptarmigan so quickly? Did you see smoke?"

"No. We were outnumbered." He hesitated, uncertain if he should burden her with anything else, then admitted, "They've taken Tommy and Sol ... and most of our company. We lost, Jay."

She glanced at me, tears spilling over her cheeks into her pillow, and the attention burned. "I don't understand. They still have soldiers pouring in from the Rim?"

"They used Belgate citizens this time," he seethed. "And while we slaughtered our own people, they set fire to our home." He leaned forward, his voice losing its edge. "I never wanted you to experience anything like that. I'm sorry I wasn't there."

She squeezed his hand, wincing as the medics applied pressure to her wound. "They burned everything, Rove. The horses ... the horses were trapped in the stables. I could hear them screaming, and I couldn't get to them ... I couldn't get to *anyone*."

He cupped her face, wiping her tears away with his thumb. "I know how that feels, Bug. I really do. But ... I might never have seen you again if you'd had the opportunity to be a hero."

A doctor pushed his way into the room. He peered down at Jaden, stopping just short of her cot, and his comprehension spoke a thousand condolences.

Still, he crouched next to Rover and examined her wound. His fingers hovered over the glass, and when he tugged on a protruding sliver, Jaden jerked upright, howling in pain. Blood gushed from her stomach, and he quickly placed a fresh rag over the wound, apologizing.

He urged her to lie back down, and then he squinted at Rover and shook his head. *No use*, the action said. *We're going to lose her.*

Beckett swore next to me, and I tasted sorrow again—felt it dripping down my throat and leaving rashes.

With great difficulty, the captain dragged his anguished gaze back to his oldest friend, holding her hand like it was the last thing mooring him to this earth.

Her eyes fixed on him, pupils enwreathing lantern light like a hearth losing its flame, and from that single exchange, she seemed to understand that nothing could be done to save her.

It was over for her, and over for *them*.

I couldn't swallow the expanding lump in my throat—I could barely even stand.

Rover's eyes brimmed with tears, but he tried his best to hold it together, unwilling to spend their final moments tending to his own grief. With a shaky exhale, he placed his other hand on top of hers and brought it to his lips.

"Stay with me," she whispered, "when I go."

"I'm not going anywhere," he assured her.

They were both crying now. A mess of slow, resigned tears.

I couldn't breathe.

"Hey ... Rove ..."

"Yeah?"

"D'you remember the cherry trees? The ones we climbed as kids?" Her feeble grin might have been the saddest thing I'd ever seen. "How we would ... fight the birds ... over them?"

Rover huffed a splintered laugh. "I fell and broke my wrist trying to pick more berries than you."

"You were always ... so competitive."

"I just wanted to be your knight in shining armor," he teased, taking her in like an overseas lover about to weigh anchor. "But we both know you never needed one."

"Not a knight," she agreed. "But ... I always needed *you*."

He cracked. "You always *had* me."

Another minute passed, all of us watching—painfully engrossed, morbidly transfixed. Friends and strangers, all witnessing the end of a timeless story.

"If I focus real hard, I can see them now ... the cherry trees. And the birds," Jaden said, closing her eyes, squeezing the water out. "And there's the sun," she sighed, "*Patrons*, I missed it."

"Jay." A plea, a resistant goodbye.

She took three small, gentle breaths, and then the world went very still.

Rover hung his head, still clutching her limp hand. His shoulders began to quake, and I couldn't bear looking at his face, hearing his broken sobs.

The walls were closing in on me from every direction now. They were no longer inching closer, taunting me with their increments, but soaring inward—too quickly, too synchronously—and I had to get out, out, *out*.

I ran.

I darted across the hanging bridges, through the city of trees, past the chain of cabins surrounding the lake. Seeking a place to hide, to implode, I rushed for the main lodge, hobbling through the halls to find the nearest washroom.

A skylight bathed the public lavatory in frigid grays—the color of vanadium steel, the color of war. It splashed against the paneling, the stone, the sinks, my muddied clothes and skin. It tainted everything.

The mirror showed me a bloody face begrimed with ashen remains. It showed me a fire-fleeing transient, her red eyes banded with unshed tears, her skin coated in soot. And her hair, having unraveled from its braid ages ago, clung to her filthy neck and forehead like swirling tattoos. The mass of knots framing her face would never untangle. The blood weighing on her curls would never really wash away, and neither would the pain.

Who was this monster staring back at me?

What had she *done*?

I fumbled with the faucet, pumping the handle and splashing cold water on my face, but it wasn't enough to erase my mistakes—or the person I'd become.

And I couldn't *be* the girl who'd ruined everything. I couldn't stomach the sight of the naive Alex Kingsley any longer.

I shed my armor and staggered for the showers, shaking with grief and panic as I twisted the spigot. Lake water spewed from the pipe, and I scrubbed at my skin and clothes hysterically, watching the blood and ash run off my body and drain through the slots in the floor.

I wanted to wash myself away, scrub myself to ruins.

Vanish down the drain.

I slid to the ground, every inch of me stinging and burning and aching, and the fact that I was falling apart made me cry even harder. It screamed *weakness*.

Tom was right all along; I was young and inexperienced, and I had no idea what I was doing. I wasn't a federate soldier, and I wasn't ready to be one, either. I was just some kid who was in way over her head, and now my entire family had been snatched away from me.

Of course, it wasn't just *losing* them that stung—I'd been through that before. It was that the world had given them back to me, had teased me with a brief reunion, a brief moment to rekindle that stashed and buried love, only to rip it fiercely and completely from my possession. Life had provided a snapshot of what I could have, then battered the image to ruins, leaving me with nothing but the shards of a broken dream.

And for the first time since the crows descended, I was truly terrified of this war—not because I feared dying, but because I feared living another day.

I couldn't watch another comrade vanish into the dark like Sol. I couldn't let another loved one sacrifice himself like Tom and Dad and Styx. I couldn't survive another friend losing her life to our enemies' moral bankruptcy.

I was terrified to see what this life had in store for me—and what it would do to me if I dared to love again.

My wooden stall groaned open, and I sensed two arms approaching me from the darkness, two open palms, hesitant and unsure. I leaned into the figure tentatively, and then all at once—crashing against a solid chest and the warmth it promised.

The shadow pulled me in, wrapping itself around me, and the icy water rained over both of us now, pooling where we sat and bleeding us of color.

I sat against him, crying, drowning, eroding until my racking sobs turned to shuddering breaths. A calloused hand stroked the wet hair from my face, the other reaching upward to shut off the valve. But the shadow didn't leave my side, even after the residual water finished dripping from the showerhead. Even after the stone floor began to bite and bruise our bodies.

Will held me until my tears ran dry, and he never said a word.

49

I found myself sitting on a low, narrow bed, wearing a pair of clean sweats and a soft black shirt. I wasn't sure whose clothing it was or whose cabin we'd been assigned for the night. Then again, I wasn't sure of anything except the pressure behind my eyes and sinuses—a constant reminder of my breakdown, and an omen of an impending reoccurrence.

Will knelt on the floor across from me, wrapping my swollen ankle. We both knew I'd heal up soon enough, so I wasn't sure why he bothered.

Still, I found comfort in his silence.

He didn't look at me like I was one bad thought away from shattering. He didn't breathe with caution or discomfort. He only worked meticulously, silently, *gently*—the way you handle something that's already broken.

He finished the bandage and rose to his feet, looking me over for other wounds to patch, and I swore there was something different about his pensive expression tonight. I could see it in his jaw muscles, in the slope of his lips.

Perhaps it was anger that had boiled over, intended only for his father and the grief he'd enkindled. Perhaps the weight of his secrets had finally become unbearable, and he simply dreaded their inevitable exposure. Or maybe it was just the look of someone who'd experienced his own set of tragedies—incidents he wouldn't wish upon any living person, Ellsian or otherwise.

It was a gamble, of course; he wore so few emotions on his face, I didn't have enough practice distinguishing one from the other.

But there was definitely something there.

Something *new*.

***

I lay on my side, staring at the cabin walls and sniffling periodically.

Richard checked in on me every few minutes, gifting me a nervous lick or nose-nudge, and I reassured him with a gentle squeeze. He didn't understand why I was in pain, and he didn't deserve to be shut out, so despite my emotional paralysis, I resurfaced for him each time he asked.

I didn't want to move or think or be. I just wanted a good story to curl up with, a fictional universe to replace the real world—the world in which my parents were dead, and my brother and his friends were all indisposed turncoats.

Will emerged from the cabin's tiny washroom, pulling his hair back in a loose knot. His bangs were just short enough to slip free, and they fell back over his forehead to mask, ironically, the very mutation that evolved to enhance emotional expression. He'd changed as well, replacing soiled navy and black with, predictably, more navy and black.

As he drifted out of sight, I heard him open the door to leave.

"Wait," I blurted, panicking.

The floor creaked.

The request under my tongue felt selfish and pathetic. He'd already stayed with me for hours now—I couldn't deny him a reunion with the other refugees. But I still yearned for human contact, for comfort, for a friend, even if he didn't know what to say to me right now. Even if he said *nothing*.

"Could you ... ?" But the word wouldn't leave my lips. It was stuck to my prideful tongue, and the plea died with Will's patience.

The door shut close with a hasty click.

I wasn't sure why I expected anything else, really. This was Will, the unfeeling robot. He wasn't Fudge. He wasn't Tom or Rover or Jaden. I couldn't expect him to take on a mourning mess of a girl when he had his own glut of issues to sort out, and I couldn't ask him to meet my every arising need just because my support system had collapsed. That wasn't fair.

But then the bed squeaked, and a warm body landed beside me—shoeless.

Smothering a flutter of a smile, I rolled over to face him.

"Yeah," he said, linking his hands beneath his head and glaring at the ceiling. "I can."

***

It was almost daybreak, and the colorless sky drowned the world in eerie silver.

I wished Fudge or Rover were here to fill the silence—I'd even settle for Mason. Instead, I was left with the company of my own imagination, and my brain doodled all the potentially malignant creatures lurking in the shadows of the lake's circumference.

There was something indescribably creepy about reservoirs before dawn. There were things that stirred in the depths that shouldn't be stirring, things that I couldn't see, but I could sense.

I was about to loop back to camp when I heard it.

"*Alex.*"

My whole body flooded with ice water, and I forced myself to turn around, knowing very well that the whisper hadn't belonged to rustling leaves or nature's bed-breath.

A sopping wet soldier stood, hunched and motionless, in the littoral, as if he'd just emerged from the deep like a human Excalibur.

I would have steered clear of the disturbed man if I hadn't recognized his badge and battle scars—if I hadn't spent every day at Camp Ptarmigan memorizing his features, afraid the king of the underworld might reclaim him.

"...Tom?"

Abandoning my reservations, I rushed into the lake, sloshing loudly to meet him in thigh-deep water. Why was he here? Where the hell had he come from?

My brother stared at the ripples bouncing between us, pensive and inert, and for a moment, I just watched the Phoenix Commander with agonizing incertitude.

Tom was possessed; I'd seen it happen. His presence didn't make any sense, and this whole encounter reeked of trickery. But I was entranced by his return, intrigued by his submissive posture, and I couldn't convince my body to retreat just yet.

His shoulders trembled like those of a weeping human, and he had this childish aura about him—the deportment of someone young and vulnerable and frightened.

Did I dare approach him? Did I call for help?

"Tom?" I tried again.

His head lifted, eyes of white opal springing to my face, and the sight of his wide, unnatural grin snapped me out of my stupor.

No, not Tom.

This was a demon with Tom's face, and it was obvious now that he hadn't been crying at all—he'd been laughing.

As I turned to flee, his hand shot out and seized my wrist, halting me in place. A numbing terror washed over me, and the Pan let out a mad, piping cackle. I squirmed in his grip, trying to escape, but as slippery as his hand was, it also proved incredibly strong and unyielding.

"Let me go," I rasped.

"Let you go? After what you've done?" His voice dripped down his chin like poison. "You refused to kill them, so they killed *us*."

He released me then, and with a startled yelp, I toppled into the water like a heap of discarded bycatch: crashing, sinking, decelerating. I squinted into the depths, expecting the same open, unobstructed liquid I'd waded through minutes prior, but as I plummeted to the lakebed, I also arrived at the horrible conclusion that I was not alone in this lake.

There were objects all around me—lifeless creatures floating just under the surface, butting against my limbs, brushing my skin. Bleached and supersaturated.

Bodies, I realized, and my stomach lurched. I was swimming among corpses, their pale, bloated appendages a stark contrast to the green, subaquatic gradient. Some of them rotted in armor, others in civilian clothes, and the women's long, wispy hair tickled my legs like a dreadful mat of muskgrass.

I'd fallen into a mass grave.

Aghast, I sprang to my feet and ran for shore, but I didn't get far—my leg was caught in a tangle of reeds and algae. I cursed and shook my foot, but it wouldn't budge, and when I peered into the stringy depths of the reservoir, I realized why.

A bony hand grasped my ankle.

A hand that belonged to Mr. Wick and his white, maggot-infested eyes.

Not just bodies, then. *Revenants.*

Mangled Ellsians swarmed me, rising up out of the water, their decomposing flesh as shiny and blubbery as larvae hatchlings. I tried to wrench away, but Mr. Wick's hand became a manacle around my boot, holding me captive in his lacustrine cemetery.

Immobile, the undead overpowered me. Wet hands pawed at my armor and tugged at my waist, and the demons' flesh stuck to my clothing, peeling away like glue or rotten cheese.

"It's your fault," one croaked. It had the face of Jaden, but not any of the traits that made her human. "It's always your fault."

I gasped stupidly. Out of air. Out of words.

"Alex ... *Alex* ..." They chanted my name over and over again, repeating it like a hex—like a curse.

Not-Tom waded closer. "You're the worst kind of killer, Al. You give your emotions the reins, and you end up killing uselessly, selfishly, and naively." Another step. "Our own mother—slain by your folly. The soldiers of Goddard Mine—buried alive or slaughtered because of your untimely interference. And all those federates at Yellow Valley—dead or turned because of your mighty moral compass." His pale eyes fell to the lake-dwelling librarian. "If you hadn't embraced pacifism, that Pan would be dead, and I'd still be here."

In my struggle to escape, I clawed a civilian in the face, and my fingers sank knuckle-deep into his flesh. I screamed and thrashed my arm about, desperate to detach myself from the gummy contents of his cheeks.

When I'd successfully freed my fingers, my brother reached out to balance me, steadying my flailing body. "One day soon, Al, you'll get what's coming to you. I can promise you that," he said, and with a hateful grin, he shoved me back under the water.

I jerked my arms inwards as I submerged, trying to shield myself from the flurry of bodies, but they were too strong for me, and they pulled me down, down, *down*.

Bubbles blinded me as putrefying hands curled around my wrists. Uncut fingernails scraped my skin, and rotting teeth sank into my shoulders. My lungs contracted painfully, and *gritz*—how could they burn in water of all things?

A long, black snake appeared, rising from the lake's murky underbelly and moving through the water like calligraphy. Evading my weightless kicks, it slithered into my open, screaming mouth, and I was suddenly gagging, choking, seizing.

I—I was *dying*!

"Alex!"

The nightmare evaporated.

Will hovered above me, pinning me to the bed. He was breathing hard, gripping my wrists tightly above my head, almost like I'd tried to claw at him or strangle him or—

Oh.

I panted, glancing frantically about the room as I tried to orient myself. Walls with planks of pinewood. A window with shutters. A closet across from the bed. A small sink in the back.

Safe.

I'm safe.

A single candle dyed the room a lovely shade of marmalade, and Richard's front paws rested on the horsehair mattress beneath me. He sniffed my face, his eyes blown wide with fear.

"It was a nightmare, Alex. Breathe."

I did, but my whole body shuddered on the exhale, and my eyes snapped close, trying to scrape away the stain of my dream.

Gritz, I was going to be sick. I was going to retch right here, face-up, and choke chaotically on my own stream of vomit. I'd never be able to look Will in the eye again—

"*Breathe.*"

I looked up at him again, anchoring myself to the crescent catchlights shimmering in his pupils—a pair of warm lanterns in the forest—and as I held his gaze, my chest began to rise and fall in time with his. Slowly adopting its rhythm, eventually matching its tempo. Rough at first, then smooth.

The nausea died, and so did the fear.

I nodded at him, swallowing the bile. *I'm okay.*

Will collapsed onto the mattress beside me, and I sat up to wipe the tears and sweat from my hairline. He was still here—long after I'd fallen asleep—dutifully fending off the night terrors and keeping me safe from my own mind. And I'd returned the favor by sleep-jumping him.

"I'm sorry," I whispered. My breath hitched. "I'm *sorry.*"

I felt it building up within me, the tower of horrible thoughts and feelings I'd repressed for days, for weeks, for years. I wasn't strong enough to hold it inside anymore, and I knew Will didn't want to hear it, but I was too enervated to stop the cascade from spilling over my lips.

"I just feel so…*guilty*, Will," I gasped, my chest tight enough to rupture. "My mom…she died both times because of me. I killed her. I killed my father's soulmate."

"That's—"

"The last real conversation I had with my dad, I broke his heart. His only kid—the last member of his entire family—told him she wanted to join the military. She pledged to abandon him and the land he tended to all his life! Patrons, I was basically signing a death wish and telling him I didn't care, even after he'd lost his only son." I bit my lip to keep the sob in. "Then I publicly humiliated him and ruined my future—the one thing he promised my mother he'd secure. And Tom! Tom was only turned because I screwed up. I finally have permission to wield a sword, and I can't help *anyone* with it. I just keep failing, over and—"

"Alex," Will interrupted, angling his head at me from the pillow. "You've been through a lot today, and your emotions are heightened. We can talk it through tomorrow, but right now, you need to rest."

Rest?

"I just did! And my brain tried to kill me."

His mouth twitched. "Try again."

"But I'm scared."

"Who isn't?"

I blinked at him, surprised by the admission. That wasn't like Will, acknowledging his own humanity, exposing his expertly masked fear—even in jest. But I supposed he was right. I'd seen my comrades' faces today, the darkness in their eyes, and there was no questioning it: they were all scared. All broken. All chipped and cracked and bruising.

Even Will.

"Look," he said, less brusque this time. "We all make mistakes. We all fail sometimes. And if we don't die young, we lose people we love." His brow lifted. "Heroes are no exception."

It took me a moment to understand what he was saying.

"Hero," I repeated, voice wobbly. "*Me.*"

He blew a puff of air between his lips. "You risked your life to help a bunch of idiots win their right to serve. You ran into a bomb-rigged mine to save trained and practiced soldiers. And you rescued your peers when they were abducted by demons you couldn't even kill." He lowered his knees, sprawling out over the length of the bed. "You can't reflect on your past and ignore all the good you've done."

I stared at him, astonished by his speech. That *was* Will, right?

The half-dead jester in me considered poking him in the ribs just to prove he wasn't some kind of hypnagogic hallucination.

"Nightmares will find you, conscious or not. But only one option leaves you better off come morning," he whispered, passing me a feeble grin. "That's what my mother used to say."

His mother probably knew a thing or two about nightmares, considering the family she'd married into, and her logic was sound. My eyes ached from crying, my brain had tortured itself into fatigue, and I felt like I'd been dragged behind a wagon all afternoon; if I wanted to be useful in any capacity tomorrow, I needed to sleep.

I fell back against a bed of thorns and landed adjacent to the Rhean prince—close enough that our elbows overlapped, close enough that our hips kissed.

Accepting this proximity was bold; I knew that. But it was warm there, lying shoulder to shoulder, rib to rib.

It was *safe* there.

I turned my head slightly, eyeing his collarbone, his chin, and finally, his charcoal-brown irises. His expression was wary, reflecting my own uncertainty, but it lacked its typical dissatisfaction. In its place was leashed surprise—and maybe a hint of curiosity.

Scrounging for any shattered bits of bravery, I rolled onto my side and, after a moment's pause, rested my head against Will's chest. My hand quavered as I placed it, palm-down, over his heart, and I curled my fingers around the ribbed neckline of his sweater, wondering if he was as afraid of me as I was.

It was the first time I'd deliberately touched him since the bonfire, back when I'd knocked him flat and nearly devoured his memories, and just several hours ago, he'd witnessed my loss of control—a slip up that sent an entire army to dreamland and rendered my gloves kaput. *Not exactly a confidence booster.*

His muscles tensed under me, and I expected him to launch me off the bed at any given moment. But despite the danger I posed to him, and despite his aversion to intimacy, he didn't shove me off, and he didn't shy away.

With a quiet sigh, he extracted the arm pinned between us so he could drape it over my back and clasp my shoulder. His other hand snatched a fistful of linen and yanked the quilted blankets over our entangled bodies to trap the heat in.

And then, beneath the covers, his fingers found the arm spanning his breast and gently enveloped my wrist, keeping me close to him—like a shield.

We didn't dare look at each other or attempt to break the silence; the entire situation was too mortifying. We just savored each other's company and closed our eyes to the madness.

In a world like this, it was all we could do.

50

I sat in the mess hall with Fudge, scowling at the desaturated food on my plate—then at Will, who'd ordered me to eat a serving of unripe fruit after I'd turned down a bowl of clumpy oatmeal.

I couldn't stand to eat at a time like this. I was sick to my stomach, sick of death and failure and flavorless plums. Even Richard wouldn't accept my unappetizing table scraps.

Dissatisfied, my gaze swept the dining area and the hapless Ellsians who'd aggregated at rock bottom. Most of our soldiers ate in silence, but distraction-seeking federates pursued conversation with willing refugees, several of whom I recognized: Chinger and two other trainees; Leith, my music teacher; Mia, a classmate of mine; and a big handful of weeds.

All people my father died for.

Siren's rebel group must have fetched refugees from the Southern Ridge and sheltered them here while the invasion persisted. I'd have to thank her for that—for saving my people when I'd been too busy playing soldier.

I spotted Rover and Beckett near the fireplace, exhausted and despondent. It looked like Rover hadn't slept a wink, and judging by the mud on his shoes and the dirt on his hands, I suspected he'd spent the early morning burying Jaden.

Bright, fierce, and loving Jaden—planted in the earth, so far from her ceiling.

Beckett's eyes gleamed, red and swollen. He might not have said it aloud, but he'd considered Jaden a goddaughter of sorts. He'd watched out for her all these years, threatening the creeps who defied Rover's warnings, correcting grunts who questioned her place among them, crushing sexists' arguments beneath his boot. He'd enjoyed her company, her luminosity, her kindness, and her death had blackened the forest in his eyes.

Wordlessly, he offered Rover his flask—the only real condolence he could provide to a man who'd lost his three best friends in one day.

The captain stared at the liquor for a moment, acknowledging the absurd time of day and the lack of food in his stomach. Eying his subordinates in the room, he seemed to weigh the consequences of setting a bad example. Then he accepted the drink with a tired, grateful nod.

I wanted to race over there and hug him, but I knew if I did, I'd reduce us both to broken, bursting spigots—and we had more pressing items to attend to.

As the two men mourned my favorite roommate, Mason approached our table with a scrutinizing look on his face. He stopped directly behind me, and I swiveled on the bench to squint at him.

"What?" I muttered, annoyed by his silent command for attention.

He scoffed at my tone and presented a book to me with one outstretched, rigid arm. "Here."

"What is this?"

"It's a book."

"I see that, Brains. What's it for?"

He pursed his lips, glancing at his brothers a table over. Kenny was the youngest of the Prices—eleven, bossy, and a hyperactive menace. The eldest, Brenden, was the spitting image of their father. He'd been training to take over as treasurer one day, and in Belgate, he was widely recognized as a brilliant, charismatic young man.

Whatever Mason saw in them made him stash his insults away, and his maturity disappointed me. I could've used a heated argument right now, maybe a good excuse to slap someone upside the head.

"Most people purchase books to *read* them," he responded tartly. "But you'll probably just lug it around in your pack all day since you seem to enjoy unnecessary physical labor."

My glare didn't falter.

"Look, I bought it for you when we were in Holly last ... since, you know, I burned your other ones." He jiggled the book at me, urging me to take it. "Cost me all my backgammon winnings for two weeks straight."

Bewildered, I accepted the gift and observed its cover with renewed interest. It was an older copy, soft and yellow and weathered. Its corners were cracked and discolored—the title blackened and illegible—and as difficult as it was to imagine, the scorch marks implied that Mason had salvaged the book from yesterday's blaze. He'd valued this gift enough to battle crimson flames for it.

That, or he just refused to waste his hard-earned money.

I gingerly flipped it open, half-expecting a misogynistic think piece, but it appeared to be a real novel—and most significantly, one I hadn't read before.

I passed him an incredulous look.

"Fudge helped me pick," he explained, gray eyes dipping away in discomfort. "He knew what we had in stock back at Belgate. Plus, the shop owner said the story has a hot-headed lead with an affinity for chaos. Thought you could relate."

The joke barely registered; I was too stunned by his thoughtfulness. "But ... why?"

Why would he do this? What did this gesture symbolize?

An apology? A truce? A bid for connection?

He blinked down at me for a beat, utterly lost, and then his face twisted up like a braided doughnut. "What? What do you mean *why?*" Pink blotches appeared on his cheeks like he was allergic to the very prospect of female companionship. "Patrons, just say thank you!"

I raised my brow, but his red, flustered expression managed to pull a weary chuckle from me. "You're right. It doesn't matter." I clutched the book to my chest. "Thank you, Mason."

He huffed, his lips twitching with exasperation, and the reaction thawed something hard and brittle inside me, something I never imagined could defrost.

We'd both lost our fathers to war—we'd both been dealt that blow. And as we stared at each other now, I could see in Mason the same feelings warring inside me: the grief, the guilt, the pride. We both understood the sentiments we couldn't bear to say, and for the first time in my life, it felt like we were fighting on the same side.

I smiled at him, embracing the sudden shift between us, welcoming the aftershocks, and he cautiously returned it.

"Alexandria?" came a woman's shaky voice, and Mason's gaze swerved to my left. "Can I speak with you?"

No.

Not now. Not ever.

Grudgingly, I turned my head, and all feelings of warmth and kinship drained back into the gaping hole in my chest.

Ellen Price stood at the head of the table, cradling her arm in its sling. Her appearance was less haggard this morning, her skin clear of dirt, her blond hair pinned back above each temple. It was like we'd traded mental states overnight, and I fought the impulse to run away from her a second time.

I was *not* prepared to face a world without him, to face the permanence of his death. I didn't want to—I couldn't. But my mother's early departure had taught me that if I ever hoped to survive this suffocating sadness, closure was inevitable.

Stiffly, I rose from the bench, and Ellen's damp eyes punctured my heart like vanadium bullets. "Your father saved us," she began, and when I didn't respond, she kept going—quickly, like I might bolt away. "The enemy had followed us, and Max told a large group of us to run ahead. He stayed behind with my husband to ensure our party's safe evacuation. But when I reached the summit, I was told they'd both been killed protecting the trailhead."

Everything hurt. My breathing, my gravity, my existence.

"I've never seen such bravery, such leadership. Your father remained calm and fearless in the face of calamity." She pressed her hands to her chest. "I saw the soldier in him that day."

I bristled at the description, and her eyes widened a sliver.

"You didn't know?" My lost expression unknotted her lips, and she squashed a smile. "Your father won the Tournament when he was your age. He outperformed every trainee in his cohort."

I must've looked like I was about to pass out, because she was suddenly standing in front of me, grasping my shoulder. Her hand, though firm, was notably feminine—soft and dainty and beautiful, even with her chipped and dirty nails.

"He was a fighter at heart, your father. But just before boot camp, your grandfather died, and Max chose to stay behind and tend to the ranch." Her crow's feet creased with amusement. "It also helped that Max had fallen in love with your mother. If there was any incentive to stay in Belgate, she was it."

Her explanations left my mind reeling. My father had almost gone to war? He'd had aspirations beyond Belgate? Beyond parenthood?

Why had he never said anything?

"He saved so many of us, dear. Know that."

I nodded awkwardly and excused myself, the revelation slamming around in my skull and leaving fat, sensitive bruises.

My father had once trained for the same war that would later take his son. He hadn't always been the rancher down Bellevue Road—he'd been willing to die for his people. He'd been gallant and honorable, and perhaps even rash and ardent like his daughter. But then he'd fallen in love. He'd given his life to his children and their futures.

And we'd turned our backs on him.

I stepped onto the raised deck outside, glad to possess a fully functional ankle again (a limp would have been downright pitiful at this point). My hands curled around the balustrade, the splintered wood digging into my gloves and pricking my fingertips, and I sucked in a lungful of fresh air, holding it hostage long enough to cool my burning heart.

Looking out over camp, I watched the different factions fraternizing, cooperating, and grieving. Siren's rebels, distinguishable by their vibrant red cloaks, tended to wounds, conducted chores and personal assignments, and relayed news to refugees. Meanwhile, soldiers wandered about camp searching for something to do or someone to aid.

A few minutes later, Will appeared beside me like a loyal shadow, far enough away to grant me grieving space, but close enough to extend comfort. He glanced at me sideways, asking his silent question, and I shot him a watery smile in return. *I'm okay.*

For a while, he just stood with me in companionable silence, and I wasn't sure how to convey my immense gratitude for his attuned, soothing company over the past twelve hours. I'd happily reciprocate such attentiveness, should he ever seek comfort in my presence, but knowing him, he'd probably favor solitude.

So what could I offer him now that wouldn't double as a selfish need? What could I buy him with no money? What gift would illustrate my appreciation for—

"Stop," he murmured, and I blinked.

"Stop what?"

"Overthinking." He moved toward me, but his gaze lingered on the settlement below. "Sticking close doesn't feel like an obligation, Alex. This is where I want to be. You don't owe me anything for that."

I pouted my lower lip at his mind-reading capabilities, but his response granted me the confidence to inch a little closer. "You're acting suspiciously ... charming, William."

Dark eyes swung to mine. "Just trying to dull the ache. The pain can be loud."

A sassy riposte didn't surface after that, so I just leaned into him and closed my eyes. The pain *was* loud, but so was the glacial, imposing energy of a royal heir—like a roaring blizzard that dulled my audition. In fact, Will's silence was the loudest of all, and in a little over a month, I'd come to crave his frequency.

Someone cleared his throat behind us, killing our peaceful intermission and kicking the clock forward once again. I buried my vexation and spun around to address the older man in the doorway.

Something about his gray beard and lengthy sideburns was oddly familiar, and I was still trying to pair his face with a fuzzy memory when Will swore and jerked sideways—as if to fly away. In a speedy blur, the man shot forward and slapped the Rhean prince across the face with the back of his hand.

I stared at the duo with my jaw on the decking, too flabbergasted to process what I'd just seen.

"Asa, I must be losing my mind. I very clearly remember drafting a plan to rendezvous in Averly should the army invade. Did I hallucinate that agreement?"

Will raised his hands in defense. "Harmon—"

"No. *No*, I didn't. But instead of meeting me like we agreed, you joined the *federates*! The Ellsian military! Enlighten me, Your Highness. How did you expect me to fulfill my duties fifty miles away, you insolent, inconsiderate brat?"

"I didn't—"

Incensed, the man seized Will by the sweater and slammed his spine against the deck railing. But I was too stunned—too intrigued—to draw my knife.

"I'm never leaving your side again, boy. Not when you sleep. Not when you piss." He had an accent I hadn't heard before, like the tip of his tongue was stuck to the back of his throat. "Your judgement clearly can't be trusted."

I looked between them, taking in Will's annoyed countenance and the bearded man's furious concern. And then it finally hit me—this lunatic was Will's fake father from Belgate, the Rhean immigrant Will had referred to as a *trusted guard*.

The man registered my appalled expression and bowed his head at me. "Harmon, the princes' humble servant."

"He's *not* a servant. We don't even have that status in Rhea. And for the millionth time, Harmon, don't call me that," Will scolded, rubbing the red mark on his cheek. "How did you even find me?"

"I figured you'd left on your own, like the naive clown you are, and that you'd eventually fall back on Siren, so I sought her out first. Too predictable, running back to your woodland clan."

"Okay, I get it. I should have contacted you when my plans changed. Now release me," Will muttered, and his guard reluctantly obeyed.

"From now on, you will never again leave my sight," Harmon declared.

"Never," Will repeated. "Seems a bit extreme."

"I swore to your mother I would watch over you," the man reasoned, not the least bit apologetic for slapping the heir across the face.

"I don't think she meant it in a literal sense."

"With all these spirits walking about, I'd rather be safe than sorry."

51

Inside a spacious council chamber, Siren and Rover briefed our forces on the latest developments in the Rhean invasion: namely, Holly's status; the sister portals; the undead army's newest recruits; and of course, my exceptional power to incapacitate the enemy.

When my abilities were finally addressed—and hesitantly explained—the strangers standing within a two-foot radius of me discretely widened our gap. And admittedly, I would have welcomed that kind of people-repelling property back in Belgate, but present-day Alex just felt like a disease in shoes.

Fudge bumped me with his shoulder. "Relax," he whispered. "It's just new to them. New things are scary."

"I'm not scary."

A disbelieving smile crinkled the skin of his forehead. "Alex, you cried, and an entire battalion dropped unconscious. You're *terrifying*."

I snickered and bumped him back, happy to see his humor resurface. He'd been in shambles all morning, wrestling with his grief, his anxieties, and a rough case of survivor's guilt. And though my battle ban may have saved his life, he'd had to watch the horror unfold from the sidelines, forced to witness our disastrous loss as a bystander.

At breakfast, he'd apologized profusely for not jumping in to save me before my brother did—for not having the courage to try. I'd smothered his speech with a tearful embrace and forbade him from taking any responsibility whatsoever.

"I've received word that Holly's curtain is compromised. The Pans have broken into the city," Siren announced, standing tall at the front of the room. The chamber fell quiet, so much so that we could hear the woodpeckers hammering away outside. "Sentries are currently holding enemy forces at Commercial Row, but civilians remain trapped in the West District. As we feared, a portal has been erected next to the Central Command Center."

Her update yanked the last shred of hope from my chest like a precarious split nail, and I wanted to scream. They'd opened another possessing machine around civilians—not to intimidate the Command, not to secure the city, but to reproduce the turnings in Belgate with a sample size six times as large. And, if their experiment proved successful, they were about to see their forces increase tenfold.

The boost in numbers would make their conquest of the Interior an easy feat, and it was becoming increasingly clear to me that this was no longer a war, but a ruthless massacre—and an undisguised genocide.

"You'll help, won't you?" asked Claus. He'd been uncharacteristically quiet since losing Sol, and his voice lacked its usual gruffness.

Siren nodded, but her eyes hardened with uneasiness. "Despite my grievances with the military, I would never turn my back on our youngest citizens, and as your allies, we'll offer you our resources, our manpower, and our home as we work together to purge the enemy from the homeland."

Rover appeared unfazed by her declaration, which told me this alliance had already been formalized behind closed doors, and the infantry was, as usual, the last to know.

"That being said, I will not send my people blindly into a war zone with a team of injured soldiers. Instead, we'll take the day to plan a liberation effort, rest, and enjoy a proper feast, and then we'll leave for Holly at first light. In return, my crew will be contractually protected by the Interior Company, should the Command attempt to seize this land or arrest us on the grounds of violating the Gender Clause. Those are my terms."

Her followers nodded in solidarity, not a stutter of hesitation present, and I marveled at their formidable cohesion. Will had mentioned to me that her crew consisted of runaways, castaways, and trained warriors who'd traded oligopoly and social mandates for community—a community that would fight and die for a brighter future. And these men, women, and genderless outcasts had all collected here beneath the canopy like orphaned wildlife, congregating at the boundary of modern civilization.

But this tribe did not reflect the homogenous makeup of a platoon, and these heroes did not undergo public trials to prove their utility. They'd earned their places in this pack, and they'd rallied behind a leader and a cause they believed in—a people united under one mission, one future, one heart.

This was an army.

Tom's men didn't share this opinion, however. They were skeptical of Siren's team, trading dubious looks when female members posed questions or voiced concerns, distrusting their intel, denying their participation record. They couldn't wrap their heads around a woman leading a brigade of all genders, and they failed to reconceptualize their famous male idol with fatty breasts and a uterus.

Sure, they'd accepted that women could fight—superhuman women, at least. But lead? Bark orders? Conduct game-changing operations throughout the Rim? That was something else entirely, and I wanted to witness the moment their paradigms imploded.

After an extensive debrief, the army divided into working groups, some tasked with pre-combat provisioning, others with evacuation logistics. The infantry committee, responsible for refining the battle plan, moved to a giant felled log with an Ellsian map carved into its upper half, and over the next three hours, we discussed how to retake the city.

Rover's men suggested more traditional, tried-and-true tactics, while Siren's crew, having relied on guerrilla warfare for years, presented their creative and unconventional strategies. And while each approach held merit, no one could deny that a small team of archers had immobilized the Interior Company in roughly thirty seconds, and it was this raw, humbling defeat that enabled an honest consideration of the unorthodox.

Desiring a visual aid, Rover began moving markers and stones across the war table, only for Siren to shake her head and move them elsewhere. And just like that, a dynamic was born.

Throughout the meeting, Siren struck down each of his suggestions, then candidly explain his faulty logic. But his ideas, while unrefined and mostly implausible, never stopped coming, and they prompted her to raise new questions and pose fresh hypotheticals to the group—situations and unintended consequences that never would have crossed my mind.

It was obvious that Rover didn't know what to make of the woman, but he seemed to respect her intelligence, her experience, and her straightforward answers, and their communication styles mated well enough to birth a half-decent plan.

When the meeting adjourned for lunch, I intercepted the officers in the open doorway. "So, where do I come in?"

The captain threw a monitory look my way. "You are not going *anywhere* until we figure out exactly what you're capable of. If you lose control again—"

"I was emotionally distraught yesterday," I protested.

"All the more reason for you to stay behind." He lowered his voice. "What if you encounter your brother again? How will his presence affect your discernment?"

"I can handle Tom," I insisted, but as soon as the promise left my lips, I knew it was a bald-faced lie. There was no telling what would happen if I saw that demon again, wearing my brother's skin like armor, abusing his body like a tank.

"We can't risk it," Rover said. "Like it or not, Fuse, you've become a critical asset overnight. You're connected to everything that's happening, even if we don't fully understand it yet. And I won't lose you to poor judgement." His eyes softened. "I can't."

I wilted under his sincerity.

"It's noble of you, Captain," Siren interjected, "but something tells me she'll fight regardless of your approval." She smiled at me with her eyes. "Compliance isn't a common trait among women in armor."

Fudge, who waited for me just outside the chamber, snorted loudly.

"But he's right in that your connection to the supernatural may very well hold the key to our triumph against Rhea," she acknowledged, "and we'll need you to sharpen this weapon of yours—study it, hone it, and train with it extensively—before you test it in an urban environment." Her gaze leapt from my hands to my face. "Having said that, you can't cage a falcon and ask it to fly."

I quirked an eyebrow at the woman, repressing a million questions about her extraordinary military journey so I could ask a clarifying, "Are you saying I can come if I promise to keep my hands to myself?"

"It's up to your superior officers. But we'll need every soldier we have, and a fighter with passion is twice as potent." She gave Rover a meaningful look on her way out the door, and he glared after her, angrily licking his molars.

"Rover," I soothed, stepping closer to block his view of the archer. "I just want to be there with you and support the company in any way that I can. I won't charge into battle, okay? I don't want to kill anyone, not when I know they're still human."

Witnessing Tom's transformation had only hardened my resolve. These Pans harbored helpless victims beneath their skin, and I knew now that possession had not erased their consciousness but *imprisoned* it. I'd felt them there in that memory bank at Yellow Valley, in Titan's mind at the river. These people were still alive, still fighting, and I wouldn't murder another innocent Ellsian.

I refused to murder someone's Tom.

"That's what worries me," Rover admitted. "You're trying to save everyone. That's just not possible in war."

I touched his arm, and he didn't shy away from it. Knowing Rover, I wasn't sure why I thought he would. "At least let me carry out part of the plan. The last thing I want to feel right now is useless." An image flitted across my mind of Rover, Will, and Fudge marching to their deaths without me, and I swallowed the dread in my throat. "Please don't leave me behind."

He considered my request, my plea, and after several agonizing seconds, he deflated like an empty waterskin. "You're just as stubborn as your brother, you know that?"

"Supposedly, we get it from our mom."

He cracked a smile, but it was a bit broken, a little chipped, and nothing like it had been before. His eyes glided over camp, and I watched that bright, glistening sea grow choppy again—its green waves darkening, its crests forming whitecaps. It was the gaze of a man now responsible for a country's welfare, and he couldn't afford to let attachment bar him from success. "Alright. I want you to come up with a way to destroy that portal in a timely manner."

Elation and gratitude filled the empty pools in my chest. Leave it to Rover to put his trust in my mental fortitude, of all things. "Nothing extravagant, I take it?"

He chuckled. "You kidding? This is your assignment for a reason, Fuse."

52

Now that I wasn't seeing red—or hysterically scrubbing the color from my armor—I could properly pore over Siren's settlement.

From above, cabin walls and staircases blended seamlessly into tree trunks, and sod roofs vanished into coniferous foliage. From a worm's-eye view, an intricate wooden city bloomed to life, its housing perched between natural stilts, its mud-spattered tents flanked by shrubs and boulders.

Enemies who scaled adjacent peaks would spy a small, unassuming encampment and likely dismiss the fort altogether. The High Court, meanwhile, would refuse to venture this far from the walls, and should they send the Command to extinguish Siren's base for them—or to dispel any fantastical rumors of her existence—unaccompanied officers would surely struggle to locate the village in a forest so dense.

Perhaps it was this strategic placement that explained the camp's longevity, or maybe General Iver had uncovered the village years ago and decided its founder wasn't worth aggravating. He didn't strike me as a brainless weed, after all.

My gaze settled on the picnic tables where Siren's members had gathered for lunch, and as they began clearing the tabletops of aspen leaves, I realized at least half of her task force were women.

Women who did not bear much, if any, resemblance to my peers back home.

The fair ladies of Belgate, well-groomed and willowy and presentable, had exchanged their autonomy and individualism for adulation, and come next year, their households would vote to maintain that lofty pedestal. In matching shoes and uniforms, they'd shrug their shoulders at the despotic laws of tiny men, play elegant instruments to muffle the sound of bloody gavels, and shield their eyes with pricey, wide-brimmed hats. They didn't seem to care what liberties their male counterparts stole from them, or whom they endangered, so long as their sisters and daughters received purses, praises, and preservation.

And preserved they were—buried alive with their own potential after mistaking shovels for wedding gifts.

But Siren's crew had abandoned the broken system and boldly claimed their individuality. They were scarred and misshapen, crass and uninhibited. They were slouchers, leg-uncrossers, and messy eaters, and they wore a variety of pant styles, including trouser choices that had never found their way to Belgatian markets.

Several archers bore visible tattoos, while others had chopped their hair short or shaved their heads entirely—all taboos for the unmarried, and all traits I revered. But as diverse as these women appeared, they also carried an identical strain of confidence in their postures, the same dose of assertiveness in their gazes, like they knew they could fold the average man into quarters and eat him for breakfast.

Peeking behind the curtain of this strange world was like jumping into another mountain river—even more shocking and refreshing than the last—and I couldn't help thinking that Jaden would have loved it here.

Tears stabbed at my eyes, and I blinked them away as an archer jogged over to Will and me. She looked to be a year or two older than us, and her skin, a lovely shade of russet brown, was as smooth and unblemished as pottery clay.

But it wasn't just her beauty that set her apart from the crowd. Unlike the bowmen who favored pixie cuts and ponytails, she'd twisted her black hair around the crown of her head like girdling roots. She'd even woven bird feathers into the braid—feathers that matched the pretty arrow fletchings in her quiver.

I also noticed that her crimson cloak barely reached her knees, and I wondered if she'd been here long enough to outgrow it or if she'd inherited a fallen soldier's uniform. Either way, she'd managed to style it well.

When she was just a few yards away, her face brightened, and she gasped, throwing herself into Will's outstretched arms.

My mind capsized into glacial water, and for a split second, I feared I'd never truly awakened from my nightmare.

Because in what reality would this robot welcome a hug like that? When would Will *ever* touch someone so unreservedly? I had to be hallucinating.

Will set her back down, and she pawed at his sweater. "Liam! I missed you."

The corners of his mouth sloped upward—high enough to make me bite my own tongue. "It's been a long time."

"Look at your hair!" she exclaimed, swatting at the small ponytail brushing his nape. He leaned back, gently seizing her hands to keep them away from his head, and she laughed like a wind chime.

My brain pulled itself out of the sea.

Will knew this girl. He knew this *place*.

I hadn't mulled over it much; I'd simply added Siren's dwelling to the mysterious plot of Asa Sterling, pledging to address the bizarre association after tomorrow. But now that I saw Will here, smiling in the company of an old acquaintance, all of my suspended inquiries bubbled to the surface.

When had he been here last? Who was he to these people? How did he know Siren so well he could request her assistance so brazenly?

And why did I feel so ... deceived? *Again?*

Will noticed me gawking at him and beckoned me over. "Val." He said her name sweetly, *familiarly*, like he'd said it a million times in the past four years. "Valerie, this is—"

"Oh, I know who she is!" She dropped his hands and turned to me with a smile so genuine, so benevolent, that it wrenched me from my train of thought. "This is the famous Alex Kingsley!"

My attention snagged on the flattering adjective, and I suddenly forgot how to speak.

"The federates filled me in last night," she explained. "They told me all about your journey to warn the Interior, how you disguised yourself as a man just so you could fight! Incredible!" She flexed her fingers like little rays of sunshine. "Then you partake in a full-blown military operation and challenge the Command head-on like that?" Another grin. "Siren's gonna *love* you."

In her expression I could read her admiration, but also her deepest sympathies. If the company had shared my story, she'd no doubt heard Tom's, and she was sparing me the condolences I didn't want to hear. She'd also chosen to highlight my mortal achievements, not my "gifted" ones. And while a male cadet might have overlooked that decision, it told me her emotional intelligence far exceeded the bubbly persona she'd adopted.

It also explained why she'd managed to break through Will's concrete defenses; her empathic accuracy was a piercing arrow in its own right.

After failing to deliver a coherent response, I tried to match her dazzling smile instead. Unfortunately, I felt like a dungeon troll with my unbrushed hair and blood-shot eyes, and I feared my grin reflected that.

"I'm the best tour guide in the village, by the way," she went on, and if my expression was as disturbing as it felt, she didn't comment on it. "If we live through tomorrow, I'll show you around camp and fill you in on the whole communal ecosystem thing. And if you ever need anything at all, or if you just feel like dropping by for a chat, you can find me in Cabin 12. I'm way better company than this gloomy sack of grain." She elbowed Will, whose scowl implied dissent. "You know it's true."

"Thank you, Valerie," I managed, and her smile sweetened.

She pecked Will on the cheek—a speedy, benign gesture, but one I'd nevertheless consider a death sentence. "See you at dinner!"

She dashed away in a blur of red, and I stared at the Rhean prince in utter disbelief.

He lifted his shoulder, trying to brush off the affectionate reunion. "She was here when I was a kid. We were close."

"I think that's the wrong verb tense."

"She's like that with everyone," he dismissed, rejecting my insinuation. "She has no concept of personal space or privacy or social etiquette. You two should get along great."

The jab pulled a grin out of me. "Whatever you say, *Liam*."

He winced at the name, his embarrassed gaze bouncing off the ground and back. "I was distrustful of everyone back then, even the people trying to help me. They didn't learn my real name until after Liam was cemented in their brains. But that trail of false identities . . . it's not something I'm proud of."

I knew transparency didn't come easy to him, and even though his mumbled context set off sparks in me, I tempered my excitement. "You're gonna run out of nicknames soon."

He breathed a weary sigh, smiling a little. "I know." He jerked his head at the lake. "Come on. Before Harmon puts me on house arrest."

***

Will led me up the rocky face of the waterfall, holding tight to my wrist after I almost slipped on the moss and fell to my untimely death. His palm was hot and dry against my skin, and it brought to mind our balmy early-morning encounter—just as the once-glistening sun would irritate my sun-burns to reinforce a lesson in negligence.

I'd found myself half-asleep just before dawn, tangled in his limbs and melded to his ribcage—his face too close, his skin too warm. He'd smelled heavenly, like river water and campfire smoke and the butterscotch resin of a ponderosa pine.

When Richard nudged us awake, I'd almost had a stroke. And, based on the way he'd catapulted himself off the mattress, so had Will.

Patrons. As if my breakdown last night wasn't embarrassing enough, my vulnerability had now manifested itself as physical dependence and in-appropriate clinginess—two things my Rhean bedmate sorely despised. And honestly, after attacking the royal in his sleep, then locking him in an embrace all night, it was a miracle he hadn't stabbed me yet.

Repressing a groan, I glared at his tatted knuckles and followed him up the invisible rock trail intended for hydro line maintenance. Just the thought of our entanglement set my face aflame, and I was tempted to jump off this boulder right now and drown myself at once.

The truth was, I'd enjoyed sharing Will's bed last night. His embrace had soothed me immediately, and in those hazy, torpid moments before awareness struck, he'd been so warm, so *soft*, like the pleasant heat radiating from a cup of tea.

That gooey feeling had melted my lofty walls within minutes, and without my ramparts, I felt naked and defenseless and raw.

Come to think of it though, Will had always been—in the most literal sense—hot-blooded. Be it at nighttime on a mountain slope, inside a mine shaft, or under a bucket of lake water, it didn't matter; he seemed to emit thermal energy anywhere and everywhere.

Perhaps he'd absorbed the sun, and that was why it was nowhere to be found. Or maybe my skin was just *that* cold.

We climbed up and up and up, and the mist grew thick and dense around me, dampening my skin, my knotted hair, my rumpled clothes. I placed my feet exactly where Will's had been, trusting only in the slippery route he'd memorized and nothing else. When we'd made it halfway to the top, he pulled me around the side of the plunging river and handed me a front-row seat to a stunning natural wonder.

The waterfall was enormous. It spewed a mountain's worth of alpine water into the glassy lake below—raging, gushing, rumbling. I found it mesmerizing, the way it collapsed in on itself over and over again, like someone had dumped a billion silver minnows over the lip of the cliff.

Releasing me, Will approached the edge of our outcrop and held out his hand. The vertical river hammered against his fingertips, and water droplets speckled his wrist and forearm where he'd pulled up his sleeve. I leaned forward to do the same, clutching the descending penstock responsibly, and I pretended not to see Will's eyebrow tick with amusement.

As the waterfall pounded against my glove, I marveled at its quantity, girth, and speed, having only seen such phenomenon depicted in illustrations before. Given Belgate's featureless valley and gentle-sloping mountains, I'd never witnessed a cataract in real life.

I'd never seen this much water in one place, period.

The Water Wars had made surviving reservoirs, natural or otherwise, more valuable than gold—a circumstance that had launched a pilgrimage to the fertile foothills of the Eastern Rim. Her summits wrung the clouds dry every winter, and water flowed down her crevices for capture and consumption each spring, placing her valleys at the top of our Patrons' wishlist. And while Ells had claimed these water bodies centuries ago, few citizens had come to witness their wild origins.

Even the river in Belgate, while natural, had been tamed and redirected, and Holly stored most of its available drinking water in massive tanks or towers. The rest of our national supply, I assumed, had been similarly caged or domesticated.

But this waterfall? It was wild. It was *free*, save for the hydropower tax it paid to Siren's community. And it roared like it knew nothing could stop it.

I glanced at the Rhean prince, hoping to catch him lost in thought or as equally enchanted by the spectacle as I was. But his gaze was fixed on me instead, and his mouth was drawn in a thin, contemplative line.

He eyed the settlement to our right, scanning its empty bank for on-lookers, and then he retrieved my wrist and pulled me toward the falling water. I frowned, questioning his sanity a bit, but he just kept tugging me along until we shimmied past the edge of the descending stream and stepped onto hard, flat sandstone on the other side.

Behind the misty barrier was a small alcove invisible to the rest of the world. It stored a blanket and a pile of dusty books, and a few trinkets had blown to the back of the rocky niche, including a toy boat I suspected Will had launched off this very ledge at one point or another.

I turned to him for an explanation, and of course, got nothing. He just sat down on the blanket, staring vacantly into the waterfall, and I silently padded over to join him.

Unsure how to channel my swelling curiosity, I examined the novels beside me, but I was surprised to find journal entries instead. I passed Will a timid glance. "Was this your place? Where you went to get away when you lived with Siren?"

It was a question full of smaller questions.

He nodded. "The noise blocks everything out. It helps me think ... or not think, depending on my mood."

Interesting. This was his way of slitting open his complicated past for me—not with words, but with a physical location. I'd let him see my inse-curities, and this was his best attempt at reciprocation.

I appreciated the gesture, but it only jumbled up my interpretation of him, and it left me feeling even more confused. Too many questions still pestered my brain, like why the portal design matched the scar on Will's chest. Or why, when I saw a glimpse of his memories, there was so much blood.

Did I dare ask him?

The waterfall blurred out the entire world, paring it down to a single windowpane of shimmering whites and grays and greens. We were secluded here, and so were our thoughts. They were free to find their footing without judgement, without expectation. It didn't matter if they lacked eloquence or precision, not here.

"I still don't know much about you," I admitted, my words barely audible over the sound of rushing water.

"No one really does."

I peered through the wall of water, its engine roaring and raging and drumming all around us. It fueled their electricity here, this waterfall; people relied on its strength and persistence for survival. But behind that powerful presentation was a lonely, hollow pocket of the past.

"It must be hard keeping everything to yourself," I told him. I'd had my father, Tom, and Nova to confide in about my curse, my history, and now I had an entire army. But Will was all alone in his grief.

"Bearing it alone has always been easier than letting people in," he said, and my gaze latched onto his profile and the muted light that flickered across his skin. "Until now."

I fidgeted, forcing myself not to respond too quickly. "What's changed?"

He glanced at me, and it was both accusatory and fond.

Ah.

I could sympathize with him on this particular dilemma; just a few weeks ago, I hadn't wanted to tell anyone about my mother and the curse pulsing beneath my gloves. I'd been reluctant to show Will that ugly piece of me—terrified of his reaction, and ultimately, his rejection. But I'd also yearned for true friendship and companionship, and my secrets were inherently incompatible with that need, so I'd come clean all at once like an insane person.

Thankfully, no one I'd truly wanted in my circle had come to see my demons as unforgivable or unacceptable, and if anything, the revelations had sealed and reinforced my inner ring of support.

I knew the same would prove true for Will if he'd ever crack himself open.

"Tell me something no one else knows about you," I requested, settling more comfortably onto his blanket and folding my arms over my knees. Predictably, he shot me that reserved, suspicious look of his, and I rolled my eyes. "It doesn't have to be anything serious. If you're capable of anything else, that is."

He huffed in mock annoyance, but his small grin faded as he reflected on his massive list of unexpressed interests and experiences. He thumbed the Rhean crests on his knuckles while he pondered my question, and I waited patiently for him to speak.

"Even though Godric is our enemy, and even though he can never be forgiven, I think . . ." A short, frustrated exhale split his lips. "I think I still love him." He pinched his eyebrows together like he couldn't understand it, like he wished he could deny it, and I realized he'd just selected the *most* serious topic of all time. "He was my king. He raised me. And I can't help thinking that somewhere deep in his bones, he's still the man my mother married. That somehow, just like his army, a crumb of humanity remains, and maybe, if I can find a way to access that part of him, he's still capable of being saved."

He locked eyes with me, setting his jaw.

"But if I could trade my father's life for yours—if cutting Godric down right now would bring Max back—I'd do it, Alex. Without question."

A startled breath whooshed out of me. "Will—"

"I need you to understand that," he pushed on. "I need you to know where my loyalty lies."

My throat tightened. "I haven't questioned your loyalty to Ells—"

"Not to Ells," he cut in. His eyes burrowed into mine, pleading, steadfast, and painfully sincere. "Ells doesn't have my loyalty. *You* do."

I could feel my heart beating in my throat, and I swallowed, hoping my esophagus might shove the pulsing organ back in place. It did not, but Will was waiting for me to acknowledge his vow, so I nodded, which seemed to assuage him a bit.

I wanted to do more, *say* more, but the waterfall would have drowned out the splintered reply anyway. Instead, I reached for his hand—an impulse, a thoughtless need—only to hesitate.

Ten years had passed since I'd last held someone's hand.

Ten years since I'd *wanted* to.

My fingers hovered awkwardly above ink-inscribed knuckles, uncertainty pinning the desire in place. My teary, fearful gaze returned to Will's, and he held it steady, just as he'd done last night when he'd brought me back from the depths of my nightmare and saved me from myself.

It finally struck me then, the best way to describe his eye color: *mollisol*. The color of dark, fertile soil. The color of macronutrients and arable land.

The color of home before the sky fell.

He silently turned his palm up, encouraging me to take the leap, and I boldly covered his hand with my own. His calloused fingers wrapped around mine, their warmth bleeding through my glove, and I felt a teary smile unfurl at the achievement.

Ten years behind me.

53

As the sky darkened to a shade of wet basalt, we stuffed ourselves with live-stock meat, trout, and Siren's garden greens—and the meal was so good, Will didn't have to force a single chicken wing down my throat.

Our variegated army drank the cellaret dry, its members greasing tongues, numbing wounds, and swapping stories they couldn't afford to leave untold—though Tom's men spent most of the night weeding fables from fact (only to discover very few inflated accomplishments).

It turns out Siren had indeed infiltrated the military, first by cross-dressing as a trainee at Ptarmigan, and then by serving as a bowman of the Rim for three years. She'd bonded closely with her unit at the Gorge, and when her charade inevitably failed, her comrades vowed to protect her and the value she brought to their team. But every fruitful harvest ends in frost, as my father would say, and Siren's secret eventually reached the dogmatists back at headquarters.

Almost six years ago to the day, the High Court sentenced her to death for her unlawful service. However, the weeds famously and disastrously un-derestimated their prisoner, and on the morning of her execution, Siren es-caped her holding cell and fled into the woods unpursued—the only spotty stretch of her timeline as far as I could tell, having spent my whole life scru-tinizing historical discrepancies.

Upon deserting the military, the convict established a base here at Fort

Leavick—close enough to Holly to taunt the Command but far enough to evade persecution. Easier for the government to suppress her story than lend it any credibility, her subordinates reasoned. And, having met the lazy, thickheaded officers myself, I was inclined to agree.

From there, she began recruiting her band of runaway brides, widows, and misfits by smuggling flyers into fortified cities and waiting for their bravest inhabitants to descend the curtain walls before dawn—slowly and artfully building her army in unmonitored forest corridors. Then, once she'd assembled a small team, she returned to the Rim to wreak havoc on Rhean forces, and it was here that she'd achieved a number of astonishing things, including her famous victory at the Battle of Exeter.

But Siren wasn't the only one here with an eccentric personality and a memorable story; her followers were just as bold and colorful and strange as she was.

Koji, for example, had joined me at the far end of the dining table. He wore thick charcoal eyeliner and spent most of the evening cleaning his teeth with a jagged blade. Three piercings adorned his face like a button-up mask—one silver bead at the philtrum and two flanking his lower lip. He told me he'd spent most of his adolescence in an insane asylum, and after one brief encounter with the man, it didn't take much convincing.

His friend, a broad-shouldered woman named Jo, had devoured the fish head on her plate with zero hesitation and proudly presented its eyeball on her tongue like an oyster pearl. Fuzzy blond hair covered her scalp, and to my utter delight, she spoke almost exclusively in curse words.

In fact, her size, stature, and severity reminded me a lot of Grismond—except she *actually* intimidated me.

And then there were crew members like Valerie who excelled at social engagement and hospitality. The young archer flirted with every soldier in sight, laughing at the unfunny and touching any deltoid muscle she could get her hands on. I was impressed by her self-confidence, but more so by her ability to steal every treat, pastry, and pudding cup from distracted, heavy-lidded fools.

Their origins were all so fascinating—as were the many skills and talents they possessed—but for some reason, they were more interested in *my* history and the lethal, supernatural properties of my covered hands.

Unfortunately for them, recounting seventeen years' worth of failure was the last thing I wanted to do before bed, so Fudge offered to quench their rabid curiosity on my behalf. He shared my journey from the lens of a keen onlooker, countering claims that I was a demigod or a medium, confirming that I did in fact place in Belgate's enlistment tournament, and gleefully informing his audience that I'd sentenced a group of demon scouts to a field of carnivorous grasshoppers.

That one *really* drew a crowd.

By the time he'd reached the fiasco of Goddard Mine, I was itching to shed my skin. There were too many eyes on me. Too much unearned respect in their gazes. Too much hope and admiration.

It was nothing like the Interior Company's first impression of me, and yet I might have preferred their cold, sexist disregard to the dread cooking in my belly tonight.

I felt like a phony, hearing my accomplishments laid out before my peers, before these actual war heroes who'd served their country—accomplishments scrubbed of murder, naivety, and luck. And as much as I adored Fudge for his positivity bias, his rosy perspective made me feel even worse.

Nauseated, I excused myself and wandered away from the fire pit, seeking the calming whir of a thriving forest. But when the croaking frogs and chirping crickets didn't bring me any comfort, I was forced to admit that what I *really* sought was a boy who could help slow things down in a world of abrupt and sudden change.

In a matter of hours, I'd lost my brother and his crew to Godric, I'd watched a friend pass away, and I'd learned of my father's heroic death and history. In one day, the power in my palms—a power I'd only recently begun to accept as a tool, not a death sentence—had made me a military asset and a shaky pillar of hope for our troops. Meanwhile, sentries were dying, civs were transforming into demons, and the only soldiers within a hundred-mile radius of Holly were sitting here feasting like kings as their people perished.

Guilt, sadness, gratitude, validation—I was drowning in a sea of conflicting emotions, and worst of all, I'd come to rely on Will of all people to keep me afloat.

There was no denying it after today: I needed Asa William Sterling in my life. I needed his dark, knowing gaze and tender silence. I needed his reluctant smiles and fitful intimacy, his strength and trauma resilience, and that flagrant dependency was as foreign to me as it was repulsive.

As I neared the fringe of Fort Leavick, I spotted movement—two shadowy figures haloed in the orange glow of a boundary beacon. I tensed at the silhouettes, my hand flying to Tom's knife at my belt, but then I noticed a tiny, shaggy ponytail and a shimmering veil of raven hair.

Will. And *Siren*.

My moral compass stood no chance.

Surrendering to temptation, I slipped behind a conveniently placed teepee, close enough to hear their exasperated voices but far enough away to avoid setting off Will's animal-like detection sensors.

"Passive aggressive. As usual," Siren murmured.

"You're one to talk."

"Enough skirting around the topic, Liam. Just spit it out already."

He folded his arms over his chest and glared at the woman who matched him perfectly in height and temperament. "You're pregnant."

She scoffed, and I waited for her to laugh at the preposterous, unfounded claim or angrily refute his assumption. But she didn't say a word; she just looked away with a scowl on her face.

I squinted at the warrior and her slim, muscular torso as if I'd be able to detect a baby bump from here. But the only excess weight on her body was the impressive set of knives at her hip, so either Will's detective work was remarkable, or a certain brown-eyed archer was prone to blabbing.

Back in Belgate, pregnancy wasn't news; it was an expected update, and morning sickness was considered the natural consequence of marriage. But Siren's pregnancy appeared to be an unexpected development—and presumably confidential, if Will had to pull her away from camp to confront her about it.

"You're keeping it," he guessed, and he said it so candidly, so nonchalantly, that it stunned me into breathless silence.

The mere concept of a woman's choice was criminalized in Ells. Abortion promised a death sentence, and any failed attempts to terminate a pregnancy would have a woman birthing and surrendering that child behind bars. Nowhere in this country did women speak about "keeping" the fetuses we were legally bound to carry, so hearing him address the action so bluntly, as if the decision itself was an inherent liberty, was perhaps the most attractive thing I'd ever heard a boy say.

"I'm as surprised by the decision as you are," Siren replied, confirming both the pregnancy and her acquiescence. "I suppose it just ... feels right."

"How does the father feel?" Will asked, but his wary tone suggested he already knew the answer.

"No idea. Haven't seen him since July."

The prince practically blew steam at that. "Don't tell me you still plan on fighting tomorrow."

Her gaze snapped to his like a deadly lightning strike. "I'm fully capable of leading this liberation effort."

"It's not about capability," he hissed. "It's your *duty*. You've committed to bringing human life into this world. Personal safety is now your self-inflicted responsibility—at least until that kid is born."

"Well, you'd know plenty about responsibility, wouldn't you, Liam?" she rejoined. "You want to lecture me about duty? Why don't you lead by example?"

Will stared at her like she'd just slapped him across the face, and I had no idea the Rhean emigrant could look so *wounded*. Without another word, he stalked off toward the fire pit—toward my teepee—his eyes ablaze, his brow drawn tight.

I quickly pressed myself to the animal hide as he stormed past, holding my breath until he was safely out of earshot. *Jeez.*

I'd found their relationship perplexing enough before this confrontation, and now I wasn't sure what to make of their dynamic. Siren had clearly taken Will in after he'd fled Rhea, but they didn't speak to each other like a crew member and his superior officer, so what did their private history make them? Foster siblings with an age gap? An adoptive mother and her nomadic son? Or did Will just consider her his deranged aunt who lived in the woods?

The archer sighed deeply. "Did you know as well?"

Panic sprouted in the pit of my stomach, and I looked to the shielded moon in defeat. Should've known I couldn't fool the Reaper of the Canopy, the Crimson King, the Red-Rim Raptor—or any other odd titles she'd earned for herself.

But before I could apologize for eavesdropping, someone chuckled from the trees, and the raspy, mischievous sound was a dead giveaway. "I had my suspicions."

"You two have been here one day, and you've already found me out," Siren complained. "How?"

"Because we know you," Beckett answered. "And we care about you."

A beat passed.

"You also haven't touched the rum," he explained. "Very few scenarios would explain such … restraint."

Siren said nothing to that, and I peeked around the corner of the teepee again, watching her toe the tree roots underfoot. Beckett stood at ease beside her, taking an airy swig from his flask like he'd spent many long nights conversing with the woman.

"The girl. She's Kingsley's sister, isn't she?" Siren deduced, and my surname kicked my heart to the back of my ribcage.

"Yes. They're twins in the face of legal hurdles and disobliging authorities—quite a force to be reckoned with. But she also reminds me of you. She's got the same stubborn glint in her eye that blinds her to consequence," he teased.

I tried to justify the news, to find the connection in a root ball of bizarre revelations, the clarity in a mess of chaotic, intersecting lines. If Beckett knew Siren so intimately, did that mean he'd fought beside her when she'd served as a federate? Had Tom completed that trio?

Did everyone just know everyone around here? Or were they all members of some secret rule-bending club?

"You know, the Sterling boy has a point," Beckett said, his humor hardening, and Siren sucked on her teeth. "There's nothing more to prove, Blake. You don't have to ride this war horse to the grave."

The archer murmured something I couldn't quite make out, and she snatched the flask out of his hand—as if to steal a few gulps for herself— only to recall her sobriety as the rim grazed her lips. She shoved the liquor into Beckett's chest with a vicious growl, and he tucked his chin to his collar and laughed.

**

After his argument with Siren, I wasn't sure I should approach Will at all. He'd spent the remainder of the night scowling at the lake, and his mood indicated that if he had deadly, poisonous quills to erect, he *would*.

So, when the crowd began to disperse, and the prince still hadn't budged—or blinked—I thought I better ask Fudge about sleeping arrangements. Preferably, I'd borrow a blanket and crash outside someone's tent or cabin. Hopefully, I'd avoid another sleep-induced physical assault that way.

But just as I tapped him on the knee, Will stood from his log and stretched his elbow behind his head. The movement hiked his sweater up over his belt loops, exposing a waistline of smooth, pale skin, and I waited awkwardly for a goodnight nod or a dismissive *sleep well*.

Instead, he peered down at me, his expression soft and borderline affectionate, and he asked a quiet, casual, "Ready?"

My mouth parted in disbelief. I felt the others watching us with raised eyebrows, trading sly looks or gaping at one another, and to my right, Fudge and Valerie's playful grins invaded my periphery. But their insinuations didn't embarrass me like I expected, and I didn't feel compelled to jump in and correct any misunderstandings. In that moment, all I felt was relief.

I nodded gratefully, and Will offered me his hand.

I stared at it for a moment, the cursive writing on his wrist, the rough skin of his palm, and something shifted inside my chest.

Maybe depending on someone like Will wasn't as criminal as I'd made it out to be. Placing my trust in a Rhean-born swordsman had proved to be one of the best decisions I'd ever made for my physical health and mental wellbeing, and perhaps this foreign feeling of attachment—this gravitational pull toward a male nonrelative—was also a direct result of his emotional caretaking.

Maybe *dependence* wasn't so bad when the bad habit was Will.

With a smile dancing on my lips, I clasped the Rhean's hand, and he pulled me to my feet.

54

My unit stepped through the bombarded gateway with our eyes peeled and our blades unsheathed, careful not to disrupt the quiet lull of urban vacancy.

The stench of smoke, spoiled food, and coppery blood bit at my nostrils, and I was immensely grateful for Siren's pungent, pitchy under-nose salve, even if it felt like I'd inhaled a fascicle of pine needles.

We moved quickly and steadily through the wreckage, but as eager as I was to halt Rhea's barbaric ingress, I was also nervous to see the city's viscera after two long nights under siege. We may have arrived too late to end the carnage, and there was a very real possibility that Holly and its unequipped populace were forever changed and irrecoverable.

Still, if even one life could be spared today—if we could reunite just one gallant father and his evacuated children—I'd bravely endure the horrific sights that accompanied a fallen city.

In the residential district, debris smoldered in hellish, ruby flame, and wagons and food carts lay strewn about the streets. Shattered windowpanes created a hazardous footpath, and blood-spattered windowsills and doorways wove a grim narrative of civilians being dragged ruthlessly from their homes.

As we traveled east, human shrieking echoed down empty city blocks, and excluding the family pets and alley rats roaming about, that vocalized terror was the only sign of life in this quadrant.

Everyone else was missing, dead, or evacuated, and I steered my gaze away from the bodies in uniform—sentries we'd left to fend for themselves.

Sentries we'd failed.

We pushed forward, creeping through backstreets to avoid demon soldiers or loud, inconsolable residents, and about twenty minutes later, our team arrived at Commercial Row.

As expected, a beam of shadows spewed from the town square like a magnificent volcanic plume, and as much as I'd wanted this assignment—and a victory that justified my peers' admiration—I was devastated to see that Siren's intel was unerring.

A sister portal indeed. Smack dab in the middle of town.

At the base of the demon entryway, human corpses formed the same geometric pattern as the entrails at Yellow Valley, their limp bodies positioned unnaturally on cobblestone, their empty blood vessels pulsing neon red and flashing in time with the portal's lightning strikes.

But most harrowing of all was the carbon-black vortex that emerged from the design itself—a vortex comprising thousands of evil, ghostly creatures chasing corporeality.

My trepid gaze climbed the column of shadows to the roiling thunderclouds it pierced overhead, and I was pleased to see far fewer Pots today. Unlike the plague of the Eastern Piedmont, these arrivals more closely resembled a flock of hungry, bodiless vultures. They languidly circled the portal, waiting to claim a suitable host.

Like fish in a pond, Sol had said, and I hated that his nightmare had sprouted here in the heart of our country. I could only hope that he'd been spared this knowledge wherever the Fates had taken him.

And whomever he might be.

A demon platoon stood guard, but safeguarding this portal was only half the task; they had also corralled at least two hundred civilians into the courtyard. The residents knelt on the ground like animals awaiting slaughter, their hands locked behind their heads, their faces caked in soot. A few of them wept, surrendering to their grief and terror, while others glared at the Pots like they were silently daring the demons to seize their bodies and endure a fatal autoimmune disease.

Peering around a food stall of expired dairy products, I spotted a balding, sinewy Pan dragging a resident behind him and tossing her to the cobblestone with the others. The woman's dress was torn and muddied in a way that suggested she'd been hustling through narrow spaces, climbing fences, and stumbling over garbage, and black blood sullied her hands and cheeks like she'd fought off her assailant.

My stomach sank, and I looked over the civilians again.

These weren't merely internees. These were people who'd outlasted armed sentries and their less fortunate neighbors, people who'd managed to evade demon forces for over 24 hours. They were *survivors*. And while that tenacity had spared them from certain death, it had also distinguished them as the strongest and most desirable candidates for Godric's army.

"Good thinking, Alex," Claus whispered, pulling me back to the operation at hand. We ducked behind the water tower, and he crouched to remove the pipe bombs from his pack. "I love a straightforward demolition project."

Mason shot me a dubious look over his shoulder. "This was *your* idea?"

Claus held up a stretch of tape for me, lengthy and taut, and I used my knife to quietly saw through it. "Yeah, and it's an *executable* one because Fudge, Claus, and Koji helped me tackle the chemistry and engineering aspects. Why does it matter?"

He made a face. "In case you haven't noticed, you have a knack for getting yourself into horrible situations."

"And in case *you* haven't noticed, I'm still kicking."

Claus quickly and effortlessly attached the bombs to the third leg of the water tower, his chubby fingers shockingly dexterous, his attention uncommonly anchored. Rover hadn't been kidding when he called the man a specialist—Claus was a professional in the world of incendiary munition. He thrived at this sport.

"You sure this will work?" Mason grumbled.

"I'm about 60-40 at the moment," I admitted, nodding at Claus for the all-clear.

"Is that 60 percent sure? Or 60 percent doubtful?"

"I'm 100 percent sure you're annoying me. Does that help?"

"Yee of little faith," Claus admonished, lighting a match. "Sit at the feet of wisdom, greenies."

The instant the wicks ignited, our trio raced to the adjacent shoe factory and scaled its metal dumpster so we could watch the spectacle unfold from a distance. Claus then raised his three plumpest fingers and counted down, and even though he was off by four whole seconds, the bomb detonated successfully.

The explosion rattled the pavement, startling a whole rooftop of crows into flight like gargoyles liberating themselves from the gutters. Every being in the courtyard—human and demon and alley rat alike—then paused to watch the tower groan and sway above them.

If the structure fell to the right, it would crash onto the factory roof and flood the complex, not the street, which would simultaneously give our position away, condemn our souls, and disastrously impede our rescue effort.

"Come on," I begged the tank. "*Come on …*"

The tower teetered to the left, twisting on its broken leg, and wicked triumph tugged at my lips.

Like a felled tree, the reservoir came crashing to the ground, the impact bursting its storage tank open and sending 170,000 gallons of water flowing onto cobblestone.

The resulting tsunami obliterated the polygram of human corpses, instantly shutting the portal off, sending its wispy vultures into a panic, and enraging its keepers. But before the Pans could punish us for our intervention, the flood knocked them down like flimsy shooting targets. It washed their platoon away with the tower debris, slamming them against buildings and streetlamps and metal benches. The civilians, meanwhile, were sent flailing in all directions, helpless passengers to the torrent.

The backflow smacked against the dumpster beneath us, and Claus tipped his head back and released a celebratory whoop as we rocked back and forth.

Jubilant—and tentatively optimistic about this liberation effort—I slapped Mason's floppy hand after he'd failed to offer me a high-five, and his lips twisted into a knot of begrudging commendation.

The portal was down. We'd leveled the playing field.

Now a fair fight could commence.

As the floodwaters dispersed throughout the business district and drained into the sewer system, the newborn river settled to a traversable, ankle-deep pond. This shift allowed the battered Pans to stagger to their feet again, and their sodden forces were incensed, to say the least.

The bomb and its ensuing flash flood had also alerted every enemy on patrol—as well as any Pans combatting the East District's dwindling line of defense—effectively summoning all demon reinforcements to Commercial Row.

Just as we'd been banking on.

The moment their backup arrived, so did ours, and like tears of forgotten gods, hundreds of vanadium arrows rained upon the courtyard, expertly impaling demon soldiers and polluting the shallow lake with their ashes. A dozen archers appeared on the surrounding rooftops, and Siren single-handedly killed eight Pans in the time it took to slide down the shingles.

If I hadn't ached for the human lives she'd just expunged, I might have applauded.

Her followers moved lithely across burning buildings—huntresses of the skyline. Several women leapt to the ground with their bows in hand, their ruby cloaks rippling like flags, their unmade hair streaming behind them, and I almost cried at the visually arresting image. Something like that demanded to be captured in a lasting medium, and if I had any artistic bones in my body, I'd paint the scene on every confining wall in Ells.

As Mason and Claus hopped off the dumpster to join the fight, I rushed for the civilians cowering in the shadows. They stood under the rafters, staring at the archers in confusion or watching severed body parts float by with haunted eyes.

I approached them, and though my clear, hazel irises seemed to bring them some relief, their wariness didn't falter.

"My name's Alex," I told them gently, and my voice seemed to speed up their comprehension a bit. They still didn't know what to make of a female soldier, though—their prejudice was as insuperable as their distress. And, if my ego was fragile enough, that inveterate bigotry might have cost them salvation.

Don't want my help? Fine.

Perish for all I care.

That was how the old me would've handled this, anyway.

But if they couldn't see a leader in me when they needed rescuing, then I'd have to fool them; I wouldn't fail the people of Holly the way I'd failed the people of Belgate—regardless of their prehistoric doctrines.

So I loosened the tension in my throat, straightened my spine, and channeled, to the best of my ability, Tom's charisma, confidence, and obnoxious sense of authority.

Cracking a smile, I sheathed my sword and said, "Sorry about the bath."

55

"What's the holdup?" I complained, stomping across the roof of the Central Command Center after bringing the civilians straight to its barricaded entrance. "I've got hundreds of people waiting for their emergency shelter down there." And, as evidenced by their outraged whisper-shouting and beseeching body language, they did *not* approve of me scaling the military's fire escape.

Skittish little welts.

"Change of plans," said Fudge. Like me, he wore a borrowed set of women's armor, and the leather suited him much better than the steel shell he'd donned at Yellow Valley. Next to his sword, a braided sling hung from his belt, and I wondered if Will had managed to construct one in time, or if Fudge had struck gold at the bottom of the weapons bin. "Turns out the Command needs some help evacuating."

My gaze dropped to the concrete rooftop. "You mean they're still in there?"

Two days later?

Jo scoffed. "Locked themselves in like children."

"*Like?*" Valerie drawled, keeping an arrow nocked and aimed at the streets below, and my eyes jumped from her bow to her perfectly symmetrical face, then the rosy tint of her cheeks. The color almost looked artificial, and now that I thought about it, her lips were oddly vibrant today. Even that silvery sheen on her eyelids didn't glisten like sweat …

My mind snagged on the obvious.

Was this woman wearing makeup? To *battle*?

I opened my mouth to comment on the absurd practice, but my displeasure was fleeting. The contrast between her vigilant demeanor and her sweet, elegant aesthetic left me more baffled and amused than anything.

Fudge sighed with disapproval. "The demons bombed an emergency exit on the east side of the building, and after failing to lure the Command out of their bunker, they've decided to smoke them out." He gestured to the dark fumes billowing out of the ventilation system. "We counted eleven Pans on the second floor. You think you and Jo can handle it?"

Jo beamed at me, cracking her neck in response, and I gave a reluctant nod. Handle it? *Sure.* Murdering a dozen people to spare the officers who believed they were better off dead? *Less easy.*

Fudge smiled, and his encouraging sapphire eyes almost cured my sour mood. "Great. In the meantime, Valerie and I will lead your group to the grade school on Murphy Lane. We've been directing civilians there, so the Command can meet up with us when they're ready. I suspect they'll want food—and coddling." He paused, suddenly aware of how assertive he'd become—and how he'd never once issued directives before today. "I … does that … work?"

Bashfulness pinkened his face, and I huffed a laugh. "It does." For the most part. As much as I could use Valerie's assistance right now—and her ability to shoot without indecision—I knew Fudge needed her more. "Lead on, Private."

Gratitude swam in his eyes, and he reached out to squeeze my forearm. "Try not to shatter their minds, okay?"

I mirrored his grin. "No promises."

Returning to the fire escape, I descended two stories and assessed the exterior wall. Deciding my best point of entry was the window to my right,

I stretched my hand as far as I could from the ladder rung—without plummeting to distant cobblestone—and clasped the upper edge of the cornice band. With a solid grip on the molding, I transferred the rest of my body onto the building face, balancing my weight on the belt course below the window trim.

Palms tingling with anxiety, I pulled my body up until I had both feet planted firmly against the windowpane. Then I pushed off the surface as hard as I could and swung back down through the glass—rolling into a corridor amidst demon soldiers, smoke, and window shards.

I instantly flipped the electrical switch, and the Pans groaned and stumbled into the walls like panicked goats, shielding their eyes from the yellow hues that pierced the haze. But I didn't waste any time admiring the effects. I headed for the large steel door at the end of the hall, taking out obstacles by the knees, shins, and hamstrings. Slicing my way through their jumbled unit and leaving a trail of crippled soldiers behind me.

"Save some for me, welt!" Jo snapped as she sailed through the window.

Reluctantly, I spared a few Pans for her taking and hurried past the writhing creatures before my empathy clawed me to pieces. When I finally reached the bunker door, I banged my fist against its singed, dented surface. "Open up! This is a rescue mission, you weeds! Out!"

Behind me, Jo finished off the Pans I'd wounded, and though I tried my best to block out the sound of skewered flesh and clanking armor, I couldn't ignore the black smoke pooling in from the east end of the corridor—nor the orange glow creeping up the stairwell.

Had they really left a fire unattended, assuming the Command would have called it quits by now? Or was someone downstairs feeding the flames?

To my left, a demon started knocking out ceiling lights, dimming the space with each furious stroke, and I found myself racing a setting sun. "Quickly!" I yelled, pounding on the door again.

When the arguing inside the chamber reached its crescendo, a heavy scraping sound cut through the clamor, followed by rapid unbolting.

"Six o'clock, Kingsley!" Jo hissed.

I pivoted. An injured Pan had escaped her, barreling for me like a train off its tracks—a train with an *axe*.

I reacted instinctually, unfaltering, unthinking, just as Will had instructed.

With a curse on my lips, I dropped to a crouch as the demon swung for my head, and I drove my sword up through his exposed armpit on my ascent. Straight into a soft spot. Angled right at the meat of his chest.

The door slid open just as the Pan burst into ashes around me, and I gasped out a guilty, broken, "No!"

I didn't mean—I hadn't meant—

"Patrons! Watch where you swing that thing!"

Pained, I tore my gaze from the Pan's shabby boots and armor to the open doorway.

Colonel Burroughs—or Long-Nose, as I would indefinitely describe him—stood in front of me with a deathly pallor and a twitching jaw muscle. Behind him, thirty other men and their wives watched on with disbelieving gazes, a somber General Iver among them.

"We've cleared a path for you. Grab any wounded," I ordered, my voice strained but dominating. "The smoke is getting worse."

I had to admit that I savored those astonished, fearful gazes, even if I didn't feel like much of a hero right now.

Wiping the ash from my face, I signaled for Jo to take the rear, and then I led the group of injured, coughing weeds toward the western stairwell, deciding it was easier to traverse the first floor than a potential structure fire. To my relief, there were no questions asked, no protests pitched, and no attempts to reclaim authority. In fact, the entire evacuation went much smoother than expected, with little to no resistance from Pan and veteran alike.

Which was … odd.

These officers were the kings of war and bloodshed. Chiefs of conquest, weathered warriors, and resource robbers. They were Godric's greatest enemies, so why on earth would he only send eleven Pans to retrieve them?

Had he really bet the farm on a half-baked plan to starve the weeds of oxygen?

I halted at the final flight of stairs, and my dry, irritated eyes sank to the foyer below, then widened in horror.

A sea of dead sentries filled the chamber, transforming the workspace into a gruesome, bloody grave.

Black smoke and pine pitch had masked the smell of death thus far, but now that I could see the massacre and the chain of human entrails, the metallic stench walloped me across the face and turned my stomach.

So many bodies drenched in carmine.

So many lives destroyed.

They'd defended the Command until their final breaths. Even after their superiors had closed and sealed the bunker door. Even after they'd been left to fend for themselves—without leadership, without aid—their staunch allegiance met with nothing but cruel obliteration.

But this mausoleum was not left unattended.

Between my party and a barricade of debris and broken furniture stood a line of Pans, their bloodied swords as dry as rust.

56

The Pans had been skulking here in darkness since bombing the exit, waiting for the Command to emerge from their bunker like bugmen awaiting the exodus of a poisoned wasp nest—and we'd just rewarded them for their patience.

My leg bones burrowed into the stairwell as I frantically measured the strength of our opposition. *Twenty … thirty-five … forty-two … forty-eight …*

We had too many wounded among us, too many unarmed and unfit soldiers to execute a head-on assault. The collision would devolve into a death charge before blades even kissed, and judging by the Pans' cocky grins and dawdling behavior, they knew that.

"What's the hitch, Kingsley?" Jo called from above, blind to our demon occupants.

Every muscle in my body went taut, and my neck all but cinched my throat close. *Trap*, I failed to say, too aghast to communicate my alarm. *We've stumbled into a trap.*

Hell, we'd lured the Command out *for* them, fetching the weeds from their safe room and escorting them straight to the enemy's doorstep. Poor Fudge thought he'd gifted me a golden opportunity to impress the Command. The kid would combust if he knew he'd simply ushered me into the lion's den.

Think, Kingsley. What are your options?

Fighting as a group was asinine. The Pans had already demolished the ceiling lamps, so we couldn't lean on disorientation tricks, and even if we managed to break through their line, we'd still need to dismantle the barricade—or beat them to the demolition site on the other side of the building. And while bolting for the exit was a straightforward and appealing solution, the wounded would fall behind, and a good number of us would taste steel.

But if Jo and I could hold the Pans' attention long enough for our party to scatter in multiple directions—down the stairs and out the first-story windows, back to the perilous fire escape, through the sweltering stairwell and eastward—maybe then we'd stand a chance.

My bones corkscrewed out of the floor, and I retreated a step, Plan C quickly taking shape in my mind. But just as I spun on my heels, a sharp crashing sound erupted above us, succeeded by curses and startled shouting. Heads swiveled toward the commotion, and the Command buzzed with trepidation and indecision.

"Fire!" someone yelled from the upper half of the staircase, where the walls now glowed a hazardous scarlet. "They've set fire to the second floor!"

Gritz. They had bastards surveilling the perimeter?

Had they watched me enter the building?

Had they known I *would*?

This was like Belgate all over again—demon assailants launching bottles of death into windowpanes and doorways. Torching homes, burning memories, taking lives. Always ten steps ahead of us. Never lacking auxiliary weapons.

My veins thrummed with raging panic as I examined the Pans' lazy, smug smiles. They already considered themselves victors, and whether we surrendered now or joined the sentries on the floor, they would see Godric's vengeful dream to completion.

"Kingsley!" Jo pressed.

The coughing grew worse, as did the acrid smoke and irritating heat, and I could feel the distress swelling within our huddle like rising yeast. My elders' short, frightened breaths filled my ears, and the stench of blood and forfeit stained the back of my tongue.

These men recognized the dead-end ahead of us, and they knew I'd failed them. They knew I'd failed us all.

General Iver stood beside me, one hand on the hilt of his sword, the other clamped to the bloody gash at his side—a wound that told me he'd reluctantly joined his colleagues in that room after putting his life experience to good use.

A wound that almost made up for his rock-ribbed personality.

Almost.

He appeared to be the only one of us truly prepared for certain death, and his stern eyes narrowed to slits as he stared down the demon blockade. He glanced at me then—his thick mustache shading that grim, stubborn line of his mouth—and I knew he intended on dying with dignity today. Self-sacrifice was expected of every federate, and he was willing to lead by example.

After kissing his wife's tear-streaked face, he dropped down a stair, and my arm flew out to stop him.

"Private." His tone carried warning, but I was so taken aback by the military address, the word failed to register as a direct order from the top brass of the military.

Private.

Perhaps a slip of the tongue, but I would not remember it that way, and if I lived to tell the tale, neither would the federal army.

I pressed my hand to his chest and the wall of badges there. "If you want to live, General, stay off the ground."

He scowled at me, unsure and distrustful, but he stayed put as I descended the last of the staircase. Shedding my indecision, I stripped off my glove and shoved it into my left-hand pocket, and with my vanadium sword in my dominant hand, I slowly approached the Pans.

My veins pumped hot adrenaline down my wrists, and though my limbs would have trembled a month ago, I now understood what war promised—what it feasted on, what it stole—and my own survival was the least of my worries.

A demon smiled at me, then at the cluster of officers behind me. "First you hide in your metal box, and now you send a child to lay down her life for you? How shameful."

My gaze swept over the Pan's deteriorating armor and vacant, opal eyes. He'd once been a strong and healthy man, but Godric had turned him into a mountain of decaying flesh and hatred. Today, he'd slaughtered the men I now trudged past like deadwood. Ergo, today he was my enemy.

An enemy with the soul of an ally, my humanity whispered.

Grinding my molars, I kicked the unhelpful thought aside and muffled my heartache. If I didn't do everything in my power to stop Godric's army, I couldn't save *anyone*, just as Will had said. And that was the whole reason I was here, wasn't it? To save lives? To stop this war?

This pathway may have germinated as a personal rebellion, but it had since blossomed into my best attempt at protecting my people from a madman's punishment. It was the same reason Tom had joined the fight before me: to spare human life, to keep families intact, and ultimately, to end the violence.

Except I wasn't just fighting for the civilians in the streets; I was fighting for the new relationships I'd forged after a decade of seclusion. I was fighting for them, for the future of them, for me, and for us. For my parents, and Jaden, and Beau, and the young soldiers who'd given their lives before me. I was fighting for the human souls trapped in Godric's clutches—fighting for them when no one else would.

And for now, in order to prolong my species' survival, I had to bench my conscience.

"Shameful," I repeated, my gaze roaming over the floor of corpses. "That about sums it up, doesn't it?"

The demon's grin faltered, and I watched his mouth part into an "o" shape as I pushed off the balls of my feet and charged the platoon.

They hadn't expected a solitary attack. Most of them stood there in a line, dumbfounded and suspicious—until I turned the first two Pans into mounds of ash and armor.

That really seemed to get the blood flowing.

Three more Pans advanced, and I swung wide, clipping their blades with Sol's vanadium masterpiece. I reared back and lunged at them again, entertaining this wolf pack with my blatant delusion, and though my blade never struck home, it granted me the proximity I'd sought.

I smacked my bare hand to a demon's peeling face, and white fire roared behind my eyes, engulfing me in a blizzard of pain and terror. A second later, he crumpled to the ground in a lifeless heap of flesh, and I didn't get the chance to see his friend's reaction—I was already slicing his face in half and silencing his battle cry.

Black powder claimed my vision for a moment, and I blinked back the tears in my eyes, exhaling through my nose to clear the ash away, swallowing the penitence lodged in my throat.

When the ash settled, I was no longer a pawn to be taken lightly; I was now a threat to be dealt with.

The Pans surged toward me, and their broken line became a missile intent on blasting through my body and striking the staircase behind me. A condensed mob bombarding me all at once. An *opportunity*.

I waited until the demons were half a stride away before dropping to the ground and slapping my hand to the floor. The instant my palm struck stone, an invisible, concentrated force rippled out from my arm, hitting the demon horde like a radial shockwave.

It knocked the Pans to their knees and ravaged their souls.

In a shapeless dimension, animated obituaries bled through white ether like watercolor paintings. Toddlers taking their first steps, children riding bikes. Memories of women dancing under moonlight—real, undiluted moonlight. I saw families and pets and childhood friends and comrades. Hugs, and kisses, and burials. Intimate details of a soldier's home life, forgotten memoirs of swallowed souls.

Sweet laughter rang off the walls of whatever realm I'd invaded, but it cut out the moment I yanked my scorching palm from the stone.

I looked up.

An arc of Pans littered the foyer, their white eyes now as black and glossy as obsidian—I'd killed over forty of them in mere seconds, and I hadn't sacrificed a drop of blood.

The remaining Pans stood stock-still along the outer edge of the room, staring at me with awe and haunted realization. They'd never witnessed a human victory like this before, not without human loss. And for the first time on Ellsian soil, these immortal creatures had experienced a loud and brutal *checkmate*.

Behind me, the Command stiffly descended the smoky stairway, pissed and ready to redeem themselves, and they each passed me a glance of recognition and concession on their way to the barricade. A look that said, *point proven*.

On the cusp of oblivion, I'd cleared a path, and because of me, these men and their wives would leave this building alive. So, despite the guilt in my bones and the crescent burning through my palm, I took a moment to savor their silent acknowledgement.

Jo shoved her way through the line, swearing up a storm at their sluggish pace. She was already loading fresh arrows by the time she spotted me kneeling on the floor. "You left some scraps for me after all, huh kid?"

I pulled my bottom lip between my teeth. "All yours."

With tears in my eyes, I pushed to my feet—swaying a bit from a dizzying head rush. Then I fished my glove from my pocket and turned my back on the bloodshed.

***

With the assistance of Belgatian refugees, Fudge and Valerie rescued civilians across Holly and established a field hospital at the school. Meanwhile, our coed company blocked the demons' progression on the northeastern front, effectively cutting off the invasion at its head.

We were taking back the city a few blocks at a time, and Patrons, it was a memorable sight—runaways and industry scraps fighting side by side, men and women working to save the same weeds who sent them to die for democracy or who forbade them from doing so.

Quite picturesque, really, save for the black sludge that spattered everyone's clothes and skin.

Acidic demon slush, I realized, scowling at the ugly black water that covered the entire district. *Didn't consider that.*

My gaze lifted to the active courtyard, searching for familiar faces. To my profound relief, Mason and Will appeared unscathed—though I suspected Harmon, who currently hogged their demon adversaries, had something to do with that.

The two boys acknowledged my arrival with heavy sighs, and I'd like to think they were expelling anxious thoughts, not exasperated ones, but it was difficult to say.

On the north side of the street, Rover and Siren fought spine to spine—archer and swordsman barking orders at their troops, shielding one another from aerial assaults or demonic infantry, and alternating kills. I couldn't tell if they enjoyed collaborating, but they also coordinated their attacks so well, it was hard to believe this was their first time doing so.

Nearby, Grismond greeted new arrivals with swift expulsion from the mortal world. He'd suffered an injury on his right side, so he altered course by instead seizing his opponents' heads, arms, or shoulders and yanking their bodies into his sword like a shish kebab. He, like Jo, appeared to be having the time of his life, and I wasn't sure what to think about that.

At the corner of the block, Beckett wielded sister blades, and I was stunned by his agility and precise, energy-conserving tactics. He defeated a whole circle of Pans in one calculated spin, then scowled at the old tavern ablaze behind him as if he'd planned to patronize the establishment post battle.

As I trudged through the grimy pond, I tried not to reflect on all the innocent lives destroyed today. The Pans I'd allowed Jo to slaughter, the demons I'd killed with a single palm print. It was necessary, I knew—for now, they were necessary sacrifices. But that didn't make them any easier to grieve. It didn't make their human memories any easier to peel from the shrine in my brain.

Amidst the din of yelling and clanging metal, I heard a misplaced shriek—a cry of anger, not distress—and I watched, appalled, as a child tore into the intersection and made a beeline for a Pan.

Cursing, I chased after the boy and snatched him up before he could lose his head. He screamed and squirmed in my arms, determined to bring harm to his opponent with a measly kitchen knife.

"Lemme go!" he cried through a film of snot and tears. "He killed him! He killed him!"

I carried him across the street like an unruly calf and set him on his feet again before his thrashing got me stabbed. Kneeling across from him, I held him still and gently pried the knife out of his fist. "You can fight when you're big enough to wield a weapon of war," I told him, pushing him toward the same alley he'd emerged from. "For now, go find a soldier in red. They'll escort you to the school."

His bottom lip trembled as he took me in, and like the civilians of Commercial Row, he was bewildered by my eye-shape, my lengthy braid, and the pitch of my voice. "But … but you're a—"

"I'll take care of him," I promised, my gaze bouncing to the Pan and back. The boy's damp eyes glistened with terror and heartbreak, desperate for action and hungry for justice. "Hey, I've got superpowers, okay? Leave it to me."

That appeared to satisfy him, and he finally scrambled away from the source of his pain.

I only wish I could've done the same; the demon he was so bent on killing was Tom.

57

A gust of September wind tossed the loose hair around my face, and the smell of petrichor came with it, diluting the harsh odors of battle. Above us, the sky rumbled with deep, guttural thunder, and I afforded the brewing storm a wary glance.

That sound used to terrify me—it used to spark acute fear in my heart. But it was hard to fear anything more than the predicament I found myself in right now.

I turned to the demon with my brother's face, and I was instantly reminded of my blood-curdling nightmare. In the back of my head, I could still hear that horrible, haunted laughter and those hateful words dribbling out of his tarnished mouth.

You're the worst kind of killer, Al.

One day soon . . . you'll get what's coming to you.

Unlike Dream Tom, however, the real thing didn't waste time spitting insults. He threw his whole weight into his attack, and I scrambled to ground myself, focusing on my anger at the situation, at the demon, at the world. Anger was vitalizing, and it could be wielded like a scalding fire iron, but sorrow . . . sorrow was truly disabling. If I so much as *grazed* the topic of my unspent love for him—or worse, all the time I'd spent sparring with him, learning his technique, and memorizing his advice, only to weaponize his precious counsel against him—I'd disintegrate.

So, anger it was.

Our swords clashed under lightning strikes, and I stumbled through the fight the same way I'd survived Will's daily training sessions: crack-handedly. Just as my moody teacher had thoroughly reinforced, I remained light on my toes, condensed, and hyperaware of my surroundings. But the demon was much stronger than me, and he drove me backward with every swing and jab and slice, advancing too quickly for me to recuperate.

In seconds, my shoulder blades smacked the wall of a building, and before I knew it, a diamond-shaped foible was soaring straight for my frontal lobe.

I spun to the side just as his sword pierced my skull's shadow. The weapon sent chunks of brick flying, and I almost peed my pants as I sprang off the wall and scampered out of reach.

Having absorbed Tom's wealth of fighting experience, this demon soldier easily surpassed my unrefined capabilities. But I didn't have to match his skill class; I just had to be faster than him. Faster, smoother, and wiser.

So I bolted away from his riposte, and I made him chase me.

Demon-Tom growled as he swung for me again, grimacing as I dodged and parried and rolled out of range. The tactic was dicey—if he made contact, I'd be a bloodstain on the ground, but if he continued to miss and whiff and crash against my guard, he would tire. And then, like the mosquito who narrowly avoids a backhand slap, I could strike him in his exposed areas.

"Running from a fight?" he taunted, voice low and distant and unfamiliar.

I threw a loose brick at his face, and he dodged it with an irritated snarl. "Out of *shape*?"

His irritation began to ferment, and with frustration came messy footwork and a brash, predictable fighting style. I memorized his offensive pattern, and when he committed to yet another graceless, lethal blow, I slashed at his bicep, striking flesh for the first time.

His sword fell to the ground with a metallic splash, and as soon as I overcame my paralyzing astonishment, I hurriedly seized the blade from the water and tossed it in the dumpster behind me.

I'd … done it.

I'd outlasted my opponent in the most perilous Deadlock yet.

Disarmed and exhausted, Demon-Tom glared back at me as he nurtured his limp arm. Black smoke billowed from the cut, and I wondered if the laceration would keep leaking demon fumes for the rest of his life, or if it would close and heal like any mortal wound, given time.

"Tom," I whispered, but his blind gaze registered nothing, and my lashes fluttered shut to hold the water in.

My brother was still in there—perhaps deaf to my pleas, perhaps entirely unreachable—but I knew his soul hadn't expired yet, just as the "sentimental" Rim soldiers, whom the Command had ridiculed and ignored, knew their turned hadn't simply evanesced. What I'd seen today at headquarters confirmed it: Tom's soul was bewitched, not his corpse, and I would be horrendously remiss if I didn't test that theory.

Opening my eyes, I sucked in an anxious breath and sheathed my sword. As reckless as it was, I had to shock my brother into recognition—I had to strike a chord deep inside him—and this was the only way I knew how.

Demon-Tom tilted his head at me, perplexed by my surrender, and he wasn't the only one.

"Alex! What are you *doing*?" Will bellowed from the courtyard, sneaking glances at me between violent collisions with his enemies. For once, his face was incredibly easy to read: pure and livid astonishment.

I ignored him and stepped closer to Tom. He didn't retreat from me, but he did furrow his brow like he was considering the best way to kill me with his bare hands.

The dark veins around his temples and eyes had expanded over the last few days, and his skin was peeling and cracking like sunbaked clay, exposing patches of scaly black flesh across his face. If I'd met him deprived of any prologue, I might have described him as a goblin, a monster—a grotesque and foreign creature—and it gnawed at me to witness his degeneration.

Watching someone so dear to you become rotten and ill and perverted was a weapon in its own right, and I feared this harrowing psychological attack had played out exactly as intended. Godric wasn't interested in merely killing his enemy—he wanted to break us in the cruelest way possible. And regardless of this war's final outcome, he'd succeeded.

I plucked my knife from my belt and presented it to the demon soldier.

"Don't let—!" cried Will, but the sky cracked its whip and silenced him.

Not now.

My brother peered at the weathered knife, then at me, and though his enmity didn't melt at the sight of his weapon, he looked a lot less certain about strangling me now.

"You're still in there, Tom," I said. "Show me."

A slow, suspicious blink. "You're confused."

"No. I'm *not*." I pressed the knife into his open hand.

This launched Will into defense mode. He came sprinting toward us, sword drawn and shield abandoned. He was going to kill my brother—I could see it in his angry, panicked eyes. My chest constricted, and I threw my hand out, pleading for patience. "Wait!"

I was asking him to do the one thing no soldier should ever do on the battlefield.

Hesitate.

The Rhean halted twenty feet away, his chest heaving with stress and exertion, his sweaty bangs clinging to his forehead. He didn't question me, but he looked like he wanted to slap the stupid out of me.

My gaze swung back to Tom, who continued to stare intently at the knife, turning it over in his hands and frowning at the chip in the blade. Did he recognize me at all? The weapon? The bond between us? I wasn't sure, but I wanted to believe that I'd flagged a signal.

When Fudge had freed the lions, he'd insisted that the creatures' animalistic instincts prevailed—that their need for autonomy had overpowered Godric's war plans. So why wouldn't this law of nature apply to Homo sapiens as well? Why wouldn't our biological need for connection override any orders to eradicate the very source of our love?

For a brief moment, Tom's old, human expressions resurfaced as he inspected the knife he'd crafted so long ago. Something about it had jogged his memory, and the shift in him uncaged my hope.

"It's me, Tom. *Al*. Your baby sister." Hot water filled my eyes. "You and me, remember? That's what you said. You and me till the bloody, bitter end."

His blank gaze snapped to mine, and he sneered at my tears.

Then he used his knife to slit my throat.

58

There was so much blood. And pain.

But mostly blood. It was hot, and dark, and everywhere. And gritz, that couldn't all be *mine*, could it?

Someone screamed my name, and I watched Tom's sludge-speckled boots vanish from view. Gone again, like he'd always been a ghost.

Gray sky and wet cobblestone merged with strange, gritty images: black birds, a forest, a man, and a bullet wedged in my spine.

As the lights shut out, unwelcome emotions invaded my headspace. First came a barrage of guilt and shame and sorrow, followed by the agonizing sting of betrayal. And last but not least, icy, crippling despair as it dawned on me that I'd never reached the person calling my name—as it occurred to me that I never *would*.

Then I plunged into sweet nothingness.

59

Good news: I healed incredibly fast.

Bad news: I now bore a huge, disgusting scab across my entire neck, and *Patrons*, it itched.

According to the first responders, I was "circling the drain" by the time I'd reached the field hospital. Believing I was unsalvageable—even for a self-healing spirit kid—the doctors moved on to other patients in need. Understandably, their dismissal did not fly over well with the men who'd transported me there, so after a contentious exchange, they'd patched me up to the best of their ability and left the rest to Lady Fortuna.

I'd been out for two whole days, they said, but I'd sprung back faster than anticipated. (Frankly, it was a miracle I'd sprung back at all.) The entire medical team was flabbergasted, and their curiosity cost me a slew of uncomfortable tests, physicals, and interviews.

"Does this mean I can't die?" I asked from my cot, idly picking at the scab.

Nasir, the only surgeon in Siren's village, looked at me like I'd just asked if I could eat him. "Of course not! *Can't die*?" He slapped my hand away from the wound and plopped himself on a wooden stool. "I want you to listen very carefully, Alex. Your body heals at an unprecedented rate, but the energy responsible for that—spiritual or otherwise—differs from your enemies' athanasia. You can mend quickly, but you can't regenerate. That means you won't regrow limbs, organs, or *heads*. Do you understand? You are not immortal. Once your body fails you, that's it."

Disappointing update. But considering I'd witnessed a spirit's demise before, it wasn't all that surprising; my mother had sacrificed herself to spare my life, and I'd sensed the permanence of her expiration almost immediately. For reasons unknown, spirits could be destroyed without a vanadium weapon, and my co-host, however powerful, was no exception.

Nasir helped me into a sitting position. "In fact, if that boy hadn't held his hand to your neck for over an hour, you'd have gone into hemorrhagic shock. That's how close you came to buying the farm, as you border-burghs like to say."

I suspected this boy was Will, but I didn't ask.

As Nasir and his team conducted their discharge assessment, I rubbed my abdomen where the phantom bullet still throbbed. I'd suffered the same nightmare multiple times this month—twice now after near-death experiences. The events always took place in a moonlit forest, and I was always getting shot in the back, which told me this was either an ominous vision or an altercation that had, impossibly, already taken place.

Unless...

My stomach swooped.

Could it be that this was the spirit's memory? And every time I came close to biting it, I somehow triggered the spirit's own traumatic death? Or was the memory shared with intention, like some kind of warning?

I hadn't even considered that a channel of communication existed between us, but perhaps this spirit was trying to send a message.

There was still so much to learn about this power and the alien soul inside me. Though, after what I did to those Pans in Holly, it was hard to feel excited about my evolving capabilities.

When Nasir let my visitors in, Fudge tackled me to my cot and wouldn't release me until Mason physically pried him off. Apparently, he'd learned about the trap at headquarters soon after parting ways, and before he'd had the opportunity to apologize, I'd arrived at the school half-dead and drenched in blood. So much blood, in fact, that Valerie had kindly sacrificed her cloak to plug my throat up.

Will had initially used his shirt to slow the bleeding, but it was completely soaked through in minutes. Valerie had donated her iconic garment to the fissure in my neck while the doctors argued over my viability, and the cloth had saved my life.

"Washed out just fine," she assured me with a tender smile. "Lends itself to an amazing fable, too, doesn't it?" She spread her hands apart like a banner that read, "Stained with the blood of the indomitable Alex Kingsley. Beat *that*, Jo."

Nasir scoffed at this, but I found the whole thing pretty funny.

Rover was the next to arrive, and he smothered me in a bear hug that preceded lots and lots of motherly ranting. Despite the losses he'd endured this week—and my irresponsible brush with Death—his eyes shone a little brighter today, and he stood a little straighter than before.

Leadership suited him, I decided, even if he loathed it.

Siren interrupted his lengthy lecture with incisive praise, which honestly felt like a million skits, and then she filled me in on what happened after I'd . . . died.

We'd successfully driven the demons out of Holly before nightfall, sparing thousands of cornered civilians from Godric's influence. Siren estimated that a few hundred Pans had perished in battle, but she assured me Tom wasn't among them. Multiple reports indicated that he'd vanished into the Range with a troop of Pans, and she suspected they'd returned to Belgate to recalibrate.

As far as governance was concerned, the Command now faced the jarring reality that one woman had saved their lives and another had coordinated an effort to retake Holly with minimal losses. The weeds were dazed, to say the least. A little flummoxed and nonplussed. "Sounds like they need some time to process it all," Siren teased with a contagious smugness.

But it was impossible for them to deny our involvement in the liberation of Holly, and therefore, impossible for them to deny our merit, though I wouldn't put it past Colonel Long-Nose.

Siren's most shocking update, however, was the arrival of a few thousand Rim soldiers, atrociously and unforgivably late. But their numbers were strong, their warriors fierce and experienced and hungry for retribution, and if Godric were to strike again, it would take a legion to penetrate the Interior.

So, even though the sun was still missing from the sky, the world was rotating on its axis yet again. (Albeit with no plans to save or spare the possessed.) Rover and Siren had no intention of reevaluating our kill-on-sight policy, even after I'd detailed the human memories I absorbed at the Command Center, even after I'd revealed to them Tom's hesitations.

Rover tried to convince me that Tom I knew was gone. He'd tried to kill me—he'd left me for dead, bleeding out on the cobblestone. Even if his soul was still there, the essence of who he was had been destroyed.

And maybe he was right. Maybe the Tom I knew was gone, irrecoverable. Maybe his soul *was* still there, but it had been bent and twisted beyond repair. Maybe it was pointless to consider him anything but dead.

So, to ease the captain's mind, I set the subject aside. But deep in my heart, I knew this mindless, defeatist approach was exactly what Godric wanted from us—to exalt human cruelty and ruthless ignorance, to demonstrate Ellsians' lack of empathy and innovation. It was all a sick joke to the Rhean king, and I wouldn't play into his manipulative hands. I wouldn't quit on my neighbors, my friends, or my countrymen.

And I sure as hell wouldn't quit on Tom.

***

Hours later, I paid a visit to Will's private treehouse.

It was the same cabin we'd shared the first two nights at Fort Leavick—small, plain, and crammed between massive tree trunks, a good twenty feet off the ground. According to Valerie, Siren had built Will this residence soon after she'd established her base here, and though she'd offered the space to visitors, refugees, and flu-ridden villagers over the years, she'd never assigned the cabin to another soldier (allegedly, on the off chance he returned to Leavick).

I wondered now if she'd always predicted he would.

I found him hunched over the cabin's fogged window, wan and shirtless, clenching the old sill so tightly he was bound to contract splinterpaw. Thick locks of hair had sprung free from his ponytail, and his trousers hung low on his hips like he had no intention of wearing a belt today—or leaving this room.

"Will?"

He ducked his head at the sound of my voice, like it was everything he wanted to hear and simultaneously, the last thing he needed.

When he didn't budge from the sill, my fingertips brushed the smooth of his back, and he flinched at the contact, the temperature of my skin, my plea for reunion.

I waited for him to recover, to adjust to my presence, and after loosing another sigh, he leaned into my touch, granting me permission to spin him around.

He still wouldn't look at me—only his hands, as if he could still see my blood on them. As if I'd stained his skin forever.

"Hey." I tilted his chin up, relieved that touching his face no longer elicited a trauma response, but instead, a kind of resigned fondness. Eventually, he submitted to my gaze, and his mollisol eyes were so full of every emotion, every fear, that I nearly ambushed him in a tearful embrace. "Stop," I choked, restraining myself. "I'm fine."

He brought his hand to the slope of my neck, and his thumb feathered over my scab.

"See? Good as new."

The caressing ceased, and wet eyes veered to my face. "I watched you bleed out … I watched you *die*."

The pain in his voice cracked something small and fragile inside me, and it took everything in my power not to burst into tears. "I'm sorry, Will. I never meant to put you through that." His hand dropped back to his side, and I reached for his fingers, unwilling to break contact. "But thank you … for saving my life. *Again*."

He glanced away, an irritated puff of air cracking his lips. "You'll never have to thank me for that."

I squeezed his hand. "Then how should I express my gratitude?"

"Staying armed is a good start."

I was too exhausted to muster a laugh, but a sheepish nod seemed to pacify him, and we stared at each other for a few seconds, basking in each other's company and purging the living nightmares from our heads. My lonely right hand found his forehead, and I gently spread the worry lines apart, clearing the ripples in his brow, erasing any remnants of shock and fear and anger.

I grinned at his palpable bewilderment, and he reciprocated with a faint smile of his own. "Better?" he grumbled.

"Better."

The tension between us thawed, and my gaze skated across the amused arc of his mouth, then dropped to his naked collarbone and the symbol carved across his breast. I lowered my hand to his solar plexus, and when he didn't pull away, I softly traced the mark of a demon portal.

It was a ghastly scar. Layers of raised flesh, twisted and stretched. A spectrum of color, healed but unhealed. Such a deep, intricate wound would have posed serious health risks to any child, and considering how many years ago Will had received it—and how long he'd had to recover and heal from the incisions—I could only imagine how gruesome it was the day it happened.

I'd heard of scarification before, be it ancient tribal traditions or radical expressions of individualism. But this was no art form. This had not been done with a deliberate, loving hand. This cicatrix was rushed and cruel and—

My eyes narrowed on his right pectoral muscle. Two scar lines stopped just short of a vertex, and the tangency error left a noticeable gap of untouched, unmarred skin.

It was as if the design was ... incomplete.

"I have to leave," Will said abruptly, jerking me from my thoughts.

"Should I wait here?"

"No." His tone was guarded, and he withdrew from me like what he was about to say demanded physical and emotional distance. "I mean I have to leave this place. I have to return to Rhea."

My face must have said it all because he looked like he'd just pulled the pin out of a grenade and wasn't sure what to do with it.

"I need to end my father's reign of terror," he elaborated. "I think I might be the only one who can." I shook my head too many times, back and forth, and I felt his hands steady my shoulders. But the gesture only fed my panic. "I can put on an act, Alex. I can learn his secrets. And if I can't convince him to end this, then at least I can find a way to shut off the p—"

"No," I said.

"*No?*"

He'd pushed me off a precipice, and I was flailing against the lethal pull of gravity, destined to break upon impact. "That's stupid, Will. That's ... that's the stupidest thing you've ever said. Ever."

His grip tightened. "I can stop him."

"We won this battle together," I insisted. "*We* can stop him."

"How many more people have to die first?"

I stared at him, afraid of the resolve on his face and the contrition in his eyes. Afraid of losing him in a way I did not anticipate. So I stepped into his frame, looping my arms around his middle and ensnaring him like ivy.

I didn't know what else to do.

"We have an army now," I assured him. "We can win this, Will. Don't give up on us yet."

With a resigned nod, he held me back, wrapping his arms around me and resting his cheek on the crown of my head. But even then—heart to heart, soul to soul—I could feel him slipping away.

60

Richard's whining pulled me out of a deep, medicated slumber.

It was early morning. The sky was a gloomy, catbird gray, and the log cabin creaked and groaned on its lofty perch as howling wind roared through the trees. Branches rubbed against the walls, and a sleepless Richard whimpered at the earth's disruptive composition.

I soothed him with drowsy, indolent scritches, but my exposed arm had me shivering after thirty seconds. The temperature had dropped significantly overnight—a precursor to an early winter storm.

I tucked my appendage under the covers again and rolled over, searching for my local human furnace. But I was met instead with a heap of cold, empty sheets.

Intuition chased me out of bed, and I seized my new cloak from the closet and hustled down to the lodge, my dread revived and aggravated. "Have you seen Will?" I asked the early risers.

Koji and Beckett both stiffened, and Rover winced at the fireplace, refusing to meet my gaze.

I looked to Siren, my gut toppling into frigid waters. "When did he leave?"

***

I ran, weaving through the pines, leaping over the creek. Vacillating between panic and indignation. Did Will really think he could avoid this confrontation by running away before sunrise? Did he think I'd just shrug it off and move on with my life as if he'd never entered it? Did he think *any* of this through?

He'd set out just before me, so I located him on the shady trail around the half-mile mark, panting furiously. "Will!"

He stilled, twisting his head back, and my eyes flitted over his attire. He wore a stranger's winter coat, and he'd fastened his carving knife and vanadium sword to his belt. On his back, he carried a large traveling pack, a sleeping bag, and a massive canteen of water.

"You can't just *leave*!" I hissed. This was ridiculous; he was just one teenage boy, one *kid*, traveling through a dense, demon-infested forest to a home he'd forsaken. All on his own.

The federates would label his desertion a betrayal. They'd assume he'd left to deliver confidential information to the enemy, say he'd been a spy all along. All that trust he'd built and nourished would shatter the moment he returned to Godric.

"Alex, I have to go," he said calmly, impassively, apathetically. Like the two of us were still unacquainted tournament contestants, and I'd just imagined everything we'd been through this past month-and-a-half. "It's my family who's killing yours. It's my responsibility to end this ... or die knowing I did everything I could."

I shortened the distance between us, imploring him to turn around. "Let me come with you, then. I'll get my stuff. We can go togeth—"

"No!" he snapped, and I shrank back. I'd never heard him raise his voice like that, and he seemed to realize he'd alarmed me, dropping his shoulders and closing his eyes. As soon as he collected himself, he swiveled to face me fully. "Just ... stay here. *Please* stay here. I'll be back in two months. If not, then assume I'm dead, and don't come after me."

Two months?

"You can't expect me to do that, Will." There was still too much that needed to be said. Things I wasn't ready to say—things he wasn't ready to hear. "Don't say you're doing this to protect me. You know I hate that."

"I'm not doing it for you." He stared down at his fist, the crests on his knuckles. "I'm tired of doing nothing. I'm sick of waiting for them to up-heave my life every time I settle in. That's all I've ever done—*wait.*"

The wind picked up again, inhaling and exhaling through the pines like a mighty beast waiting to devour the wayward prince. Untamed hair billowed around our faces, and I was suddenly back in Belgate, speaking to my father for the very last time.

"What if something goes wrong?" I pressed. I could feel things spiral-ing out of my control, slipping through my fingers and leaving blisters. "What if you get hurt? What if you—" I swallowed my words and amended my question. "What if they convince you to stay?"

He didn't say anything to that—didn't lie to me about his safety, didn't reassure me that something like that would never happen—and I thought my chest might cave in on itself.

"You're just gonna leave Harmon behind, then? You'd abandon Siren after all she's done for us?" I knew he cared for them, even if he tried his damnedest to suppress it, but there was nothing in him that indicated re-luctance or remorse—just emptiness in those dark, emotionless eyes. It in-furiated me how easily he could dismiss his feelings, how he could walk away so effortlessly from everyone and everything without a proper good-bye. Just like Tom.

Neither of us spoke for a stretch of time, and each second of silence punched another divot in my heart. "Fine," I said thickly. "Just ... be safe."

I felt the tears coming, and I loathed how sensitive I'd become in his presence, how vulnerable. I knew this was a juvenile response to his depar-ture. There was a good chance Will might actually succeed, and infiltrating

Godric's circle could very well win us this war.

It was selfish, trying to keep him here for my benefit alone. Yet the pain persisted.

I turned for camp, refusing to cry in front of him, but he caught my wrist before I could slip away. "Alex …" His grip scalded the skin beneath his touch. "I'll talk to Godric, I'll figure out his plans. Then I'll come back."

"Don't make a promise you can't keep."

"I'm not."

I wasn't sure if he meant he wasn't making a promise, or if he wasn't planning on *breaking* it. But it didn't matter; he was still going somewhere I couldn't follow.

As his fingers loosened, my composure fractured. "Will, you just … you can't leave me too." I closed my eyes to block the torrent. "*Everybody* leaves."

Mom, Dad, Tom. Sol and Jaden.

They all left me behind for another place, either blank space or heaven or somewhere in between. Places I couldn't see, places I couldn't reach.

When I opened my eyes, Will stood a dagger's length away, shaking his head. "I'll never leave you," he said. "But I have to *go*."

A quiet huff escaped me, and the tears spilled down my face. "You sound like Nova, talking in riddles."

"It's not a riddle, Alex."

He leaned forward and pressed his lips to my cheek.

If I hadn't watched him do it, I might have mistaken the pressure on my skin for a shift in the weather—it was so delicate, so soft. He set his forehead against my temple, his cold, wind-blushed nose grazing mine like a silent plea for understanding.

Like a passionate storm gust, I could feel him all around me, his scent, his energy, his intensity. But most of all, I could sense when he disappeared, leaving the world abruptly still and silent in his absence.

61

For the rest of the day, I pouted behind the waterfall, preserving my scraps of dignity like a dragon defending her meaningless, ostentatious jewels.

I was fine.

I *was*.

And I wasn't about to muse, mourn, and mope over a *boy*.

I just needed to self-isolate for a day, maybe a week, so I could reflect on the poor decisions that led me here. Revisit, reassess, realign.

Was rumination productive? Maybe not, but I was still coping with my abandonment better than Harmon. Will had laced his drink with a powerful sedative, and by the time the guard awoke, the prince was long gone. Harmon hadn't reacted well to being drugged—or ditched, *again*—and I'd last seen him stalking off into the Range, fully armed, to kill the next animal that dared fidget in his presence.

A shadow suddenly appeared at the edge of the cascade, and I straightened, eyeing my sword on the other side of the alcove. Who could that even be? Another villager? A demon?

Certainly not Will.

"It's me," Siren announced, slipping through the mist, and I slumped against the cavern wall in relief.

"How did you find me?"

"What, you think I didn't know about Liam's little hiding place?" A snort. "Please. Every teenager I recruit craves a private hideout, and there are a whopping three places to choose from." She rolled her eyes. "They all think they're so clever."

She sat beside me and crossed her legs in front of her. She didn't try to make me feel better, or give me advice, or even really acknowledge my mood. She just sat with me in silence, listening to the river pummel the pond below—allowing Will's soothing white noise to fill the chamber around us.

It was refreshing, receiving attention without pity, awe, or suspicion. It made me feel at ease, and for the first time that day, I actually wanted to talk about the mangled feelings trapped in my chest.

I was debating the best way to approach the conversation when she extracted a knife from her cloak.

"I believe this is yours? Wright went searching for it last night, and before he left for Holly again, he asked me to return it to you—assuming I'd be able to find you, that is."

My fingers curled around the weapon that almost killed me, and just as I'd feared, the cherished object felt like a foreign instrument in my grip. It was too polished for a daily companion, too clean for a butchering device—courtesy of Rover, probably. The weight was wrong, the length too short and awkward. It felt like a tool and less like an heirloom.

Less like Tom's.

"Not every soldier's lucky enough to retrieve a scarskit," Siren said. She flashed the thick metal bangle on her wrist. "The blade that almost cost me my bow arm. I wear it now as a daily reminder of my foolishness—and my resilience."

Her attempt to bond with me pulled the plug on my broody cogitation, and just like that, my feelings spilled from my lips like hot bile. "I don't feel very strong right now," I confessed. "I think somehow, despite everything I've endured, I've grown weaker."

The archer chuckled, as if she'd been waiting patiently for the dam to break. "What makes you say that?"

I didn't know why it was so easy to open up to Siren of all people. Fudge was right there, steadily sweet and sympathetic and safe; Beckett always offered good advice and a witty salutation; and if I ever confided in Valerie, she'd probably throw a party to celebrate my debut as a bona fide girl friend.

Siren was very much a stranger to me still, and yet I felt this immediate, unjustified kinship between us. Perhaps it was because I missed Jaden so much, and Siren exuded the same competent and protective sororal qualities that I'd come to depend on.

Or maybe it was because, in a lot of ways, she reminded me of Will.

"All these experiences, they should've made me stronger, more confident, but they've just made me fearful." I shook my head at myself. "I'm constantly terrified of losing the people I care about."

I never used to let anyone close enough to leave a mark. Not after Tom, not with my curse. But Fudge and Will and Tom's company had all taken precious pieces of my heart—and I'd all but *handed* them the scalpel.

She scanned my face and smiled. "I see myself in you, Alex."

Skepticism bowed my lips. Siren was practically sculpted tungsten. Her sharp, hooked nose was strong and elegant—like the beak of a red-tailed hawk—and her high, prominent cheekbones and chiseled jawline gave her a staid, diamond-like face. Even her raven hair and bronze skin shone like armor, reflecting any prejudice back at her cynics, letting nothing penetrate.

She was invincible, inside and out.

How could she possibly see herself in *me*?

"In the few short days I've known you, I can see exactly where we run parallel. You're brave and virtuous, but you seek only credit, not glory. You think differently than your peers because your whole life, you've been forced to bend the rules, outthink your elders, and create self-serving loopholes. You're a pistol who's fiercely independent, stubborn, and recusant—for better or for worse," she said, and my skin warmed at her generous list of attributes. "But you've done something I've yet to accomplish, Alex. You've learned to open your heart in the belly of war. You've learned to bleed."

I thought she might have been insulting me at first, but the sincerity in her gaze told me otherwise.

"Opening myself up has just made me more vulnerable, though." Vulnerable to diseases like heartache, loneliness, and *pining*. "As a soldier, my concern for others is crippling, isn't it?" I glanced at my knife. "Isn't affection a weakness that my enemies could easily exploit?"

"That's just what the Command wants you to think," she dismissed. "They teach us that emotional attachment is detrimental, that we're all just cogs in a machine—easily sacrificed, easily replaced. They think that what binds us is our hatred for Rhea, our loyalty to Ells, not our interpersonal relationships. But it's solitude that makes us vulnerable, Alex."

We locked eyes, and I realized her irises were not a deep, uniform, and disarming brown like Jaden's, nor a warm, impish, honey color like Tom's. Instead, they reminded me of the deserts I'd seen while clutching artifacts—iron deserts so red, they looked like temples stained by human sacrifice.

"Your friendships are your first line of support," Siren continued. "They're your fiercest army, and an army built on love and fellowship is a rare and precious thing." She tapped her nail against the blade of my knife. "You may fear for their lives, but that fear adds weight to your purpose. It gives bite to your swing. And it is *far* more powerful than nationalism."

I couldn't deny that my friends had saved my life on multiple occasions, just as their emotional support had offered me crucial visibility in my darkest hours. And though it broke me to see them fall, it was also true that my desire to protect them had forced me to lead.

E. GALLEGOS

And by leading, I'd rescued countless others.

As I chewed on this counterpoint, Siren idly flipped through Will's journals. She chuckled, and I couldn't tell if it was what he'd jotted down that she found so amusing or if it was because he'd written it in perfectly neat, legible cursive—as any royal would.

"You know, Liam was a frightened, squirrely kid when we first crossed paths, and after what his family did to him, his mental state was ... fragile," she put. "I turned him into a soldier so he could survive the next chapter. I taught him discipline and humility so he wouldn't draw attention to himself, to fight so he could properly channel his pain, and to internalize his emotions so he could preserve his own heart." Her tongue probed at her cheek. "At the time, it seemed like the right thing to do, but now I regret my influence."

My brows jumped. "Why?"

Sure, she may have raised an actual robot, but without her, who knew where Will would've ended up or who he might've become? Considering Belgate's loathing for Rhea and the lies we'd been fed, her emotional anesthetizing had undoubtedly saved him.

"I might have prolonged his life by teaching him those things, but I also stripped him of his identity. By teaching him what I did, I taught him how to hide, how to conform. I taught him how to *run away*." She bent her head, and the shameful expression looked unnatural on her face. "Two years later, he'd grown tired of traveling and recruiting members for my cause. He didn't want to fight in this war—he didn't belong to either side— so I fashioned some permits, and he left with Harmon for Belgate, where, at least for a while, he could go to school, pretend to live a normal adolescence, forget his roots."

"And now he's back where he started," I murmured.

"No, Alex. That's just it—he's changed. He's realized who he is, where his place is. I think he's done running from his past." She tipped her head at me. "You've helped him achieve that."

I buried my eyes in the heels of my palms. "You mean I've sent him to his death."

A soft chuckle melted into the violent rush of the waterfall. "No. You inspired him to take action. You reminded him what it is to *feel*. You've brought about a change in him—as you've done for others, it seems."

I peeked at her between my fingers.

"I've learned a lot these past four years, and I've realized that shutting off our emotions, even in war, is not always the right answer. If you're strong enough, and you are, you have to embrace those feelings and use them to your advantage. Don't do what Liam and I did. Be stronger than that."

Stronger?

But ... they were the strongest people I knew.

"I don't know if I can," I admitted.

"You're bleeding now *because* you can," she said. "And when you heal, you'll look back on your scarskit and realize just how strong you are."

She watched the daylight fracture through the waterfall, scattering hypnotic bands of silver across the sandstone. Beads of shadows. Spectral flames of heaven.

She tore her gaze from the dancing caustics to grin at me. "Besides. If anyone can incite real change in this world, it's not another man devoid of empathy. I can tell you that."

For as long as I could remember, I'd wanted to change the world and a woman's role in it, and surely, I was off to a good start. But had I really accomplished anything? Women were still bottom feeders in this callous ocean—royal mummies locked in their tombs. Godric Sterling was still invading. Pans were still being slaughtered.

And Tom ... Tom was still gone.

"How do you know my brother?" I asked, forgoing any rational segue.

"Who, Kingsley?" She smiled crookedly as if his signature grin had instantly sprung to mind. "I met Tom at the Rim. It was his first year in the army, my last. He saved my life."

I gaped at her. Tom had saved *Siren*?

Why on earth had he never mentioned her to me?

"When I left the ranks, we became business partners, so to speak. He lent me a portion of his annual salary to feed and support my team, and from headquarters, he always requested an extra wagon's worth of perishables. In exchange, I'd keep him updated on Rhea's progression along the Rim, take credit for his unapproved projects—things like that. Per his request, I also searched for Belgatian survivors, and I was told to inform him immediately should I find a certain Max Kingsley."

My chest tightened with unexpended love.

I should've known Tom hadn't left such an important task to his own scouts. He probably hadn't told me because he was allergic to getting my hopes up—the same reason he never wrote me a damn letter.

Siren nudged me with her elbow. "The kid was always in over his head. Family trait?"

She had no idea.

"He was a good soldier," she reflected, staring out at the water again. "A good friend."

My suspicious gaze fell to her belly. Tom *couldn't* be . . .

Revulsion coursed through me, then concern.

Could he?

The archer rose to her feet, paying the alcove another fond glance. She turned to go, but my final question tumbled from my mouth before I could leash it. "You say you've closed yourself off emotionally, but I've seen you with Will and Beckett and your followers. You really do care about them, don't you?"

She paused, her lips moving without sound, and for a second, I thought she might tell me I asked too many questions. But then her mouth curved upward, and a short, breathy laugh burst from her lips. "Of course I do. But holding them at a distance, releasing myself from personal attachment—it's the only way I can do what I do. It's the only way I can send my people to die." She glanced at her stomach, and it stoked her waning smile. "But when this is all over, and the skies heal overhead, maybe then I can finally demolish the walls I've built." Her shoulders lifted. "Maybe we're *all* capable of change."

She left me there in the private alcove, and I stared at the door of white water for a few heartbeats, listening to the earth's forceful bloodstream.

I moved for damp stone, leaning forward with my palm open. The inner edge thrummed against my fingertips, my glove, and icy mountain water seeped into my skin, running down my arm in mesmerizing corkscrews.

I am the river, the river is me.
Dam me, confine me, and I will break free.

I felt an old, defiant grin tug at my lips, and I clenched my fist.

The river was fierce, unyielding, perpetual. It was forever flowing, raging, gushing. Eroding the stone confines around it. Breaking the mold it was given. Shaping the world it touched.

I push and I push my way back to the sea.
Oh, I am the river, the river is me.

—Bursting from its cage.

End of Book 1

Acknowledgements

Thank you to the Wattpad community—the readers who found *Breeder* before it was polished, before I was confident, and before I fully believed this story deserved to exist outside my own head.

The 2020 Watty Award didn't just validate the work. It convinced me that self-publishing was the right path, and I wouldn't have taken the leap without you.

This one's always been yours.

About the Author

Erica's writing journey began in 5th grade with her first illustrated book, *Running Rain*. Since then, she's won a Watty Award (*Breeder*, 2020), sat on a world-building panel at WattCon (Los Angeles, 2022), and published the first two books in *The Ephemeral* trilogy.

She gravitates toward fantasy—with slow-burning romantic subplots, of course—and she aims to write stories that are inclusive, bold, and at times, deliberately uncomfortable. If she's doing her job right, someone, somewhere, is calling her a "Nasty Woman."

When she's not building new worlds, Erica works to green the business sector and reduce greenhouse gas emissions in her home state. She also survives a chaotic semiannual road trip with her partner, Petr.

To stay up to date on *The Ephemeral* trilogy and her upcoming fantasy saga *GODSGIVEN*, subscribe to her newsletter, follow her on social media (@egalleguess), or join her Discord server (The Gritz).

egallegosbooks.com | @egalleguess | Discord: The Gritz

Ikelos (The Ephemeral: Book 2)

The prince is missing. Her souls are hungry.
And crossing the border may doom them both.

Two months after reclaiming the Interior, Alex Kingsley has become the army's most valuable asset—and its greatest liability. Her power is extraordinary. Her conscience is inconvenient. And the Command is counting on her to forget the difference.

To make matters worse, Will still hasn't returned from Rhea. With each passing week, hope feels harder to hold, and though her friends urge patience, waiting feels like a betrayal she can't survive. But she refuses to abandon the prince—or the only future worth fighting for—so she defies her commanding officers and crosses the Rim with a moral code no one else will honor.

In the bowels of a dying kingdom, surrounded by uneasy allies, she learns that mercy, like love, leaves no one unscathed. And when the mission begins to unravel, Alex must choose: save humanity...or save its soul.

Grab your copy today!

www.ingramcontent.com/pod-product-compliance
Lightning Source LLC
Chambersburg PA
CBHW020001120726
47903CB00004B/1089